TRINITY BLOOD

ILL
KIYO

HARACTER DESIGN
THORES
SHIBAMOTO

VOLUME FIVE

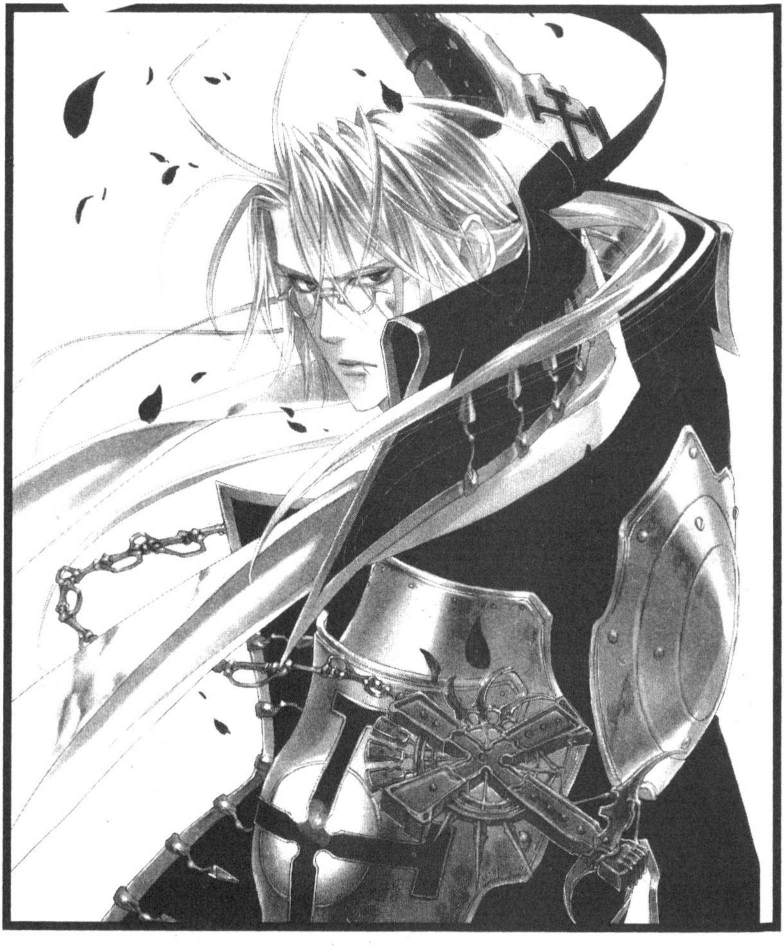

Trinity Blood Volume 5
Story By Sunao Yoshida
Art By Kiyo Kyujyo
Character Designs by Thores Shibamoto

Translation - Beni Axia Conrad
Associate Editor - Christine Boylan
Retouch and Lettering - Star Print Brokers
Production Artist - Bowen Park
Graphic Designer - James Lee

Editor - Lillian Diaz-Przybyl
Digital Imaging Manager - Chris Buford
Pre-Production Supervisor - Erika Terriquez
Production Manager - Elisabeth Brizzi
Managing Editor - Vy Nguyen
Creative Director - Anne Marie Horne
Editor-in-Chief - Rob Tokar
Publisher - Mike Kiley
President and C.O.O. - John Parker
C.E.O. and Chief Creative Officer - Stuart Levy

A  Manga

TOKYOPOP Inc.
5900 Wilshire Blvd. Suite 2000
Los Angeles, CA 90036

E-mail: info@TOKYOPOP.com
Come visit us online at www.TOKYOPOP.com

TRINITY BLOOD Volume 5 © Kiyo KYUJYO 2005
© Sunao YOSHIDA 2005 First published in Japan in 2005
by KADOKAWA SHOTEN PUBLISHING CO., LTD., Tokyo.
English translation rights arranged with KADOKAWA
SHOTEN PUBLISHING CO., LTD., Tokyo through TUTTLE–MORI
AGENCY, INC., Tokyo.
English text copyright © 2008 TOKYOPOP Inc.

ISBN: 978-1-4278-0014-5

First TOKYOPOP printing: February 2008
10 9 8 7 6 5 4 3 2 1
Printed in the USA

TRINITY BLOOD™

VOLUME 5

WRITTEN BY

SUNAO YOSHIDA

ILLUSTRATED BY

KIYO KYUJYO

TOKYOPOP®

HAMBURG // LONDON // LOS ANGELES // TOKYO

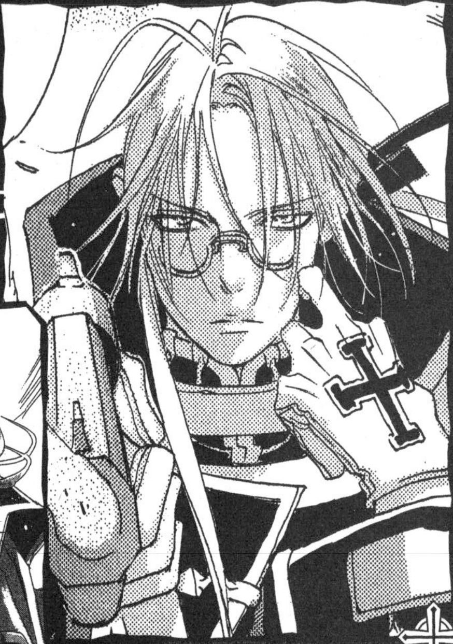

Abel Nightroad

An absentminded, destitute traveling priest from the Vatican's secret AX organization. His official title is AX enforcement officer. His job is to arrest law-breaking vampires. And he takes 13 spoonfuls of sugar in his tea.

Becomes

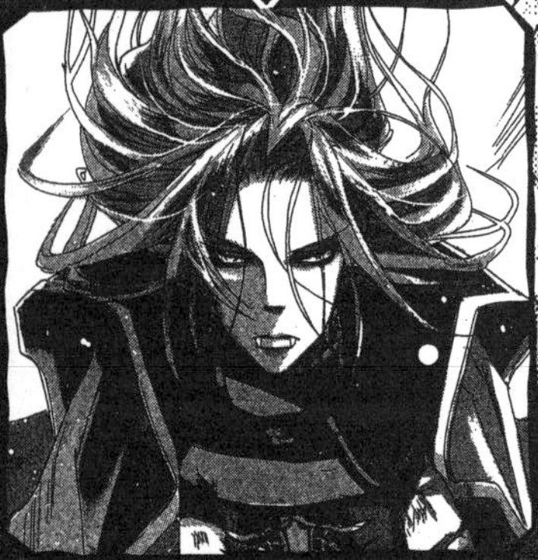

Crusnik

When Abel's threatened and left with no other means of escape, he transforms into a Crusnik, a mysterious vampire who drinks the blood of other vampires and possesses great power.

Story

Civilization has been destroyed by a catastrophe of epic proportions. Mankind is at war with vampires, an alien life form that appeared when the earth changed. The Empire and the Vatican attempt to negotiate peace, but they are stopped by two forces: the betrayal of Ion, one of the two messengers from the Empire, by his erstwhile best friend Radu, and by the martial intervention of the Inquisition. Meanwhile, Father Abel Nightroad is forced to activate the Crusnik, terrifying his companion, Sister Esther.

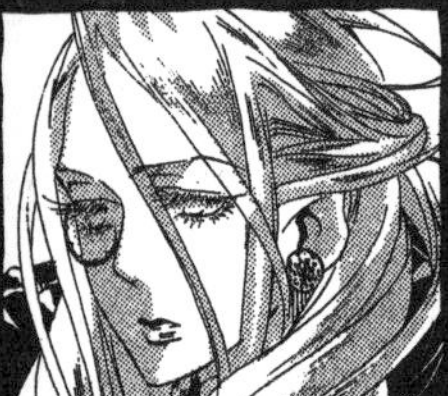

Caterina Sforza

She is Abel and Tres's superior, the director of the Vatican Special Services Annex.

Characters & Story

Tres Iqus

Like Abel, he is also an AX enforcement officer. His code name is "Gunslinger." He is more machine than human.

Esther Blanchett

A novice nun with a strong sense of justice. After she lost her church and friends in a battle with vampires, she chose action over despair and followed Abel when he said, "I am on your side."

Radu

He is Ion's best friend, the Baron of Luxor and an inspector from the Empire.

Ion

A messenger from the Empire, a Noble of Moldavia titled Earl of Memphis and one of the Tzara Methuselah.

Petros

The Director of the Department of Inquisition, also known as the strongest and most violent knight in the Vatican.

CONTENTS

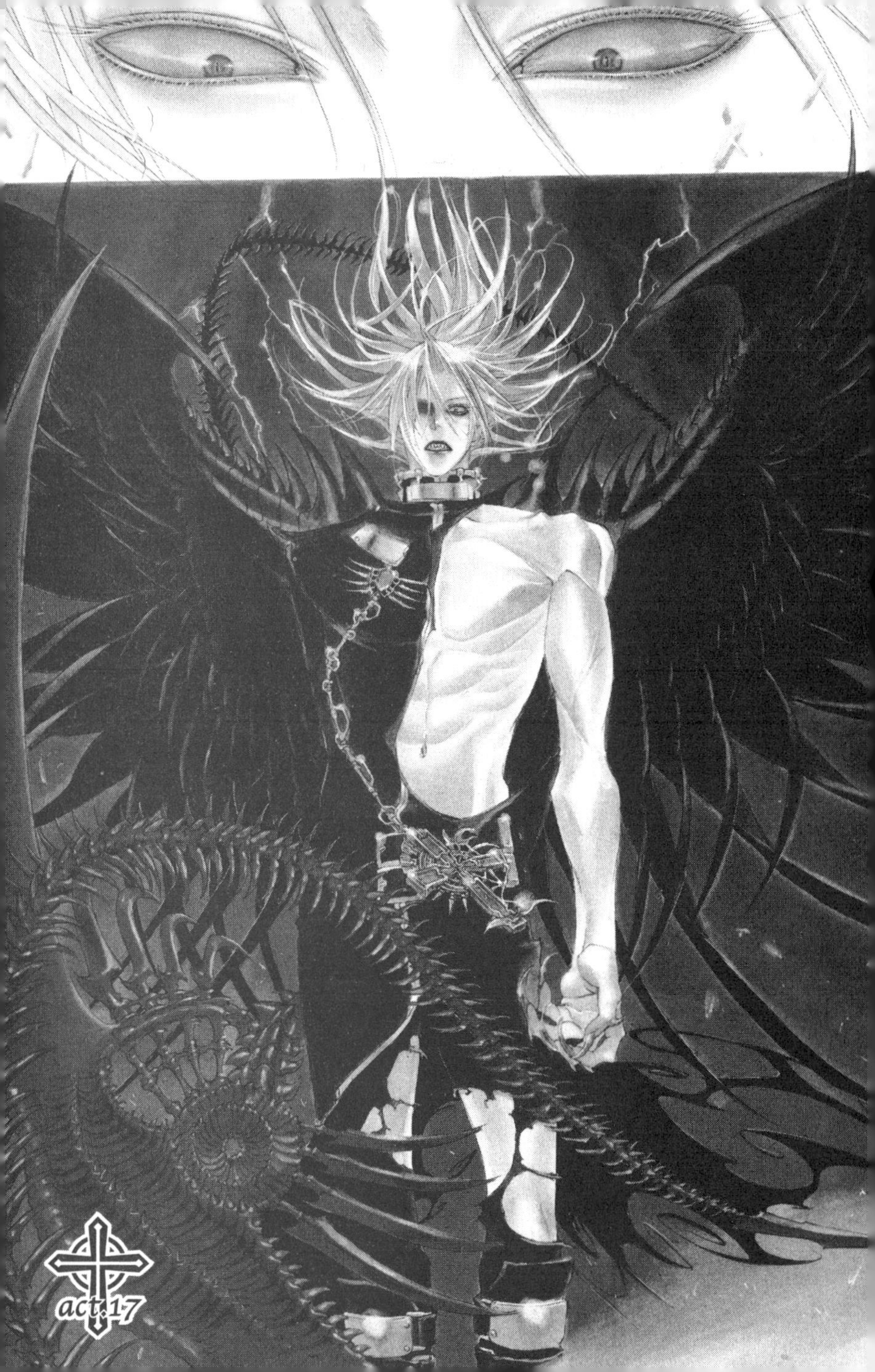
act.17

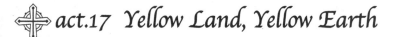

act.17 Yellow Land, Yellow Earth

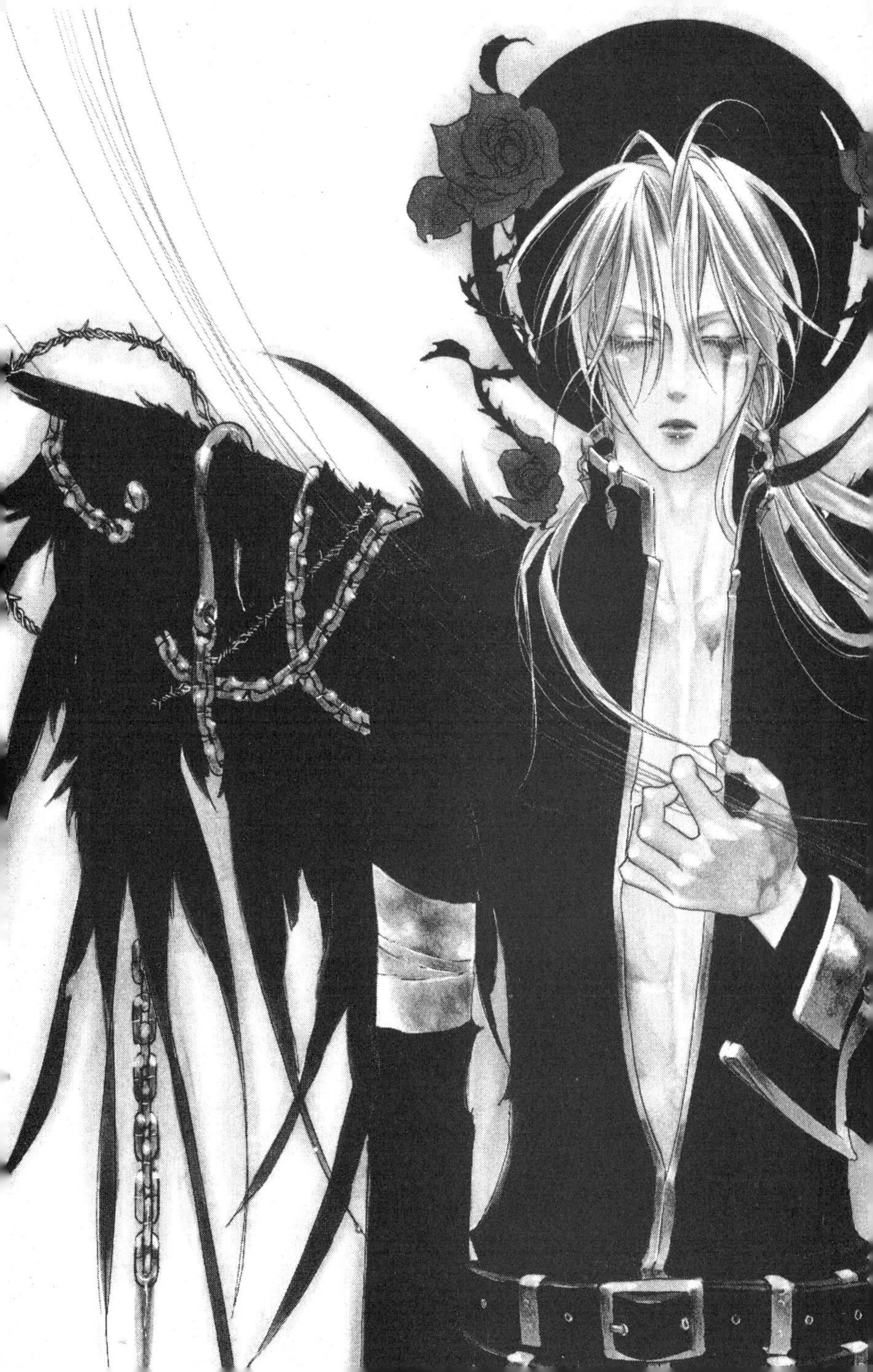

TRINITY BLOOD

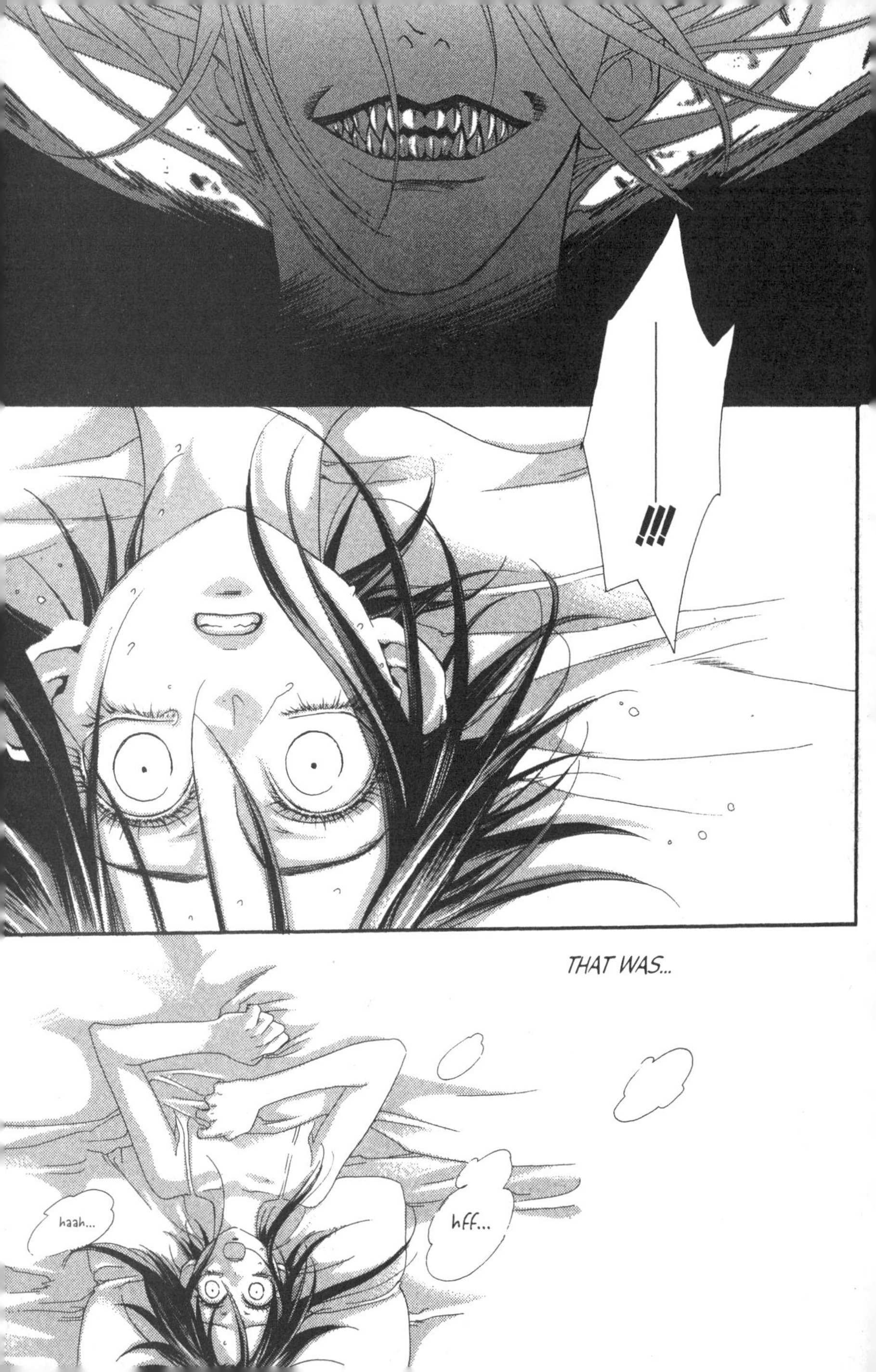
!!!
THAT WAS...
hff...
haah...

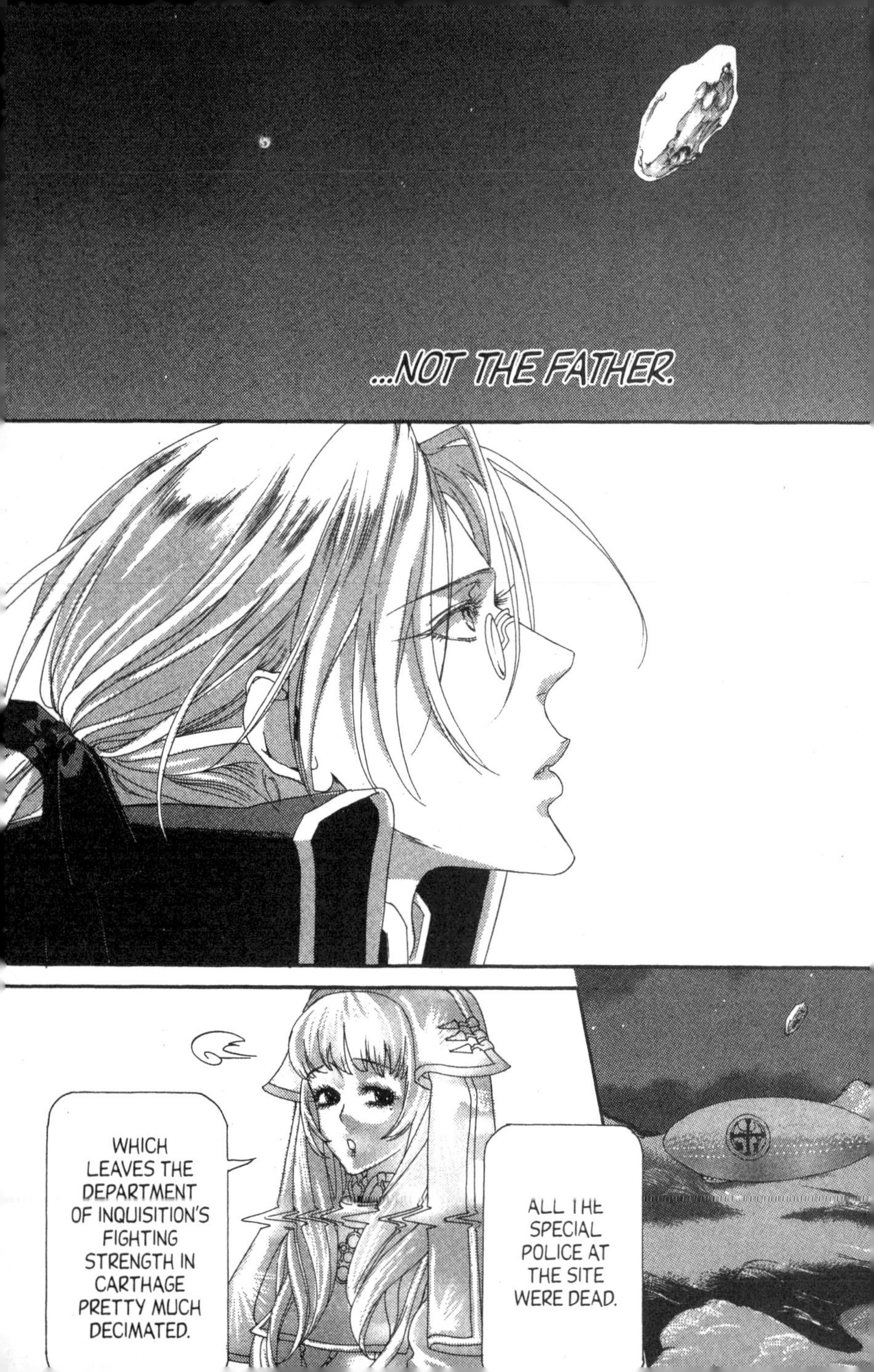
...NOT THE FATHER.
ALL THE SPECIAL POLICE AT THE SITE WERE DEAD.
WHICH LEAVES THE DEPARTMENT OF INQUISITION'S FIGHTING STRENGTH IN CARTHAGE PRETTY MUCH DECIMATED.

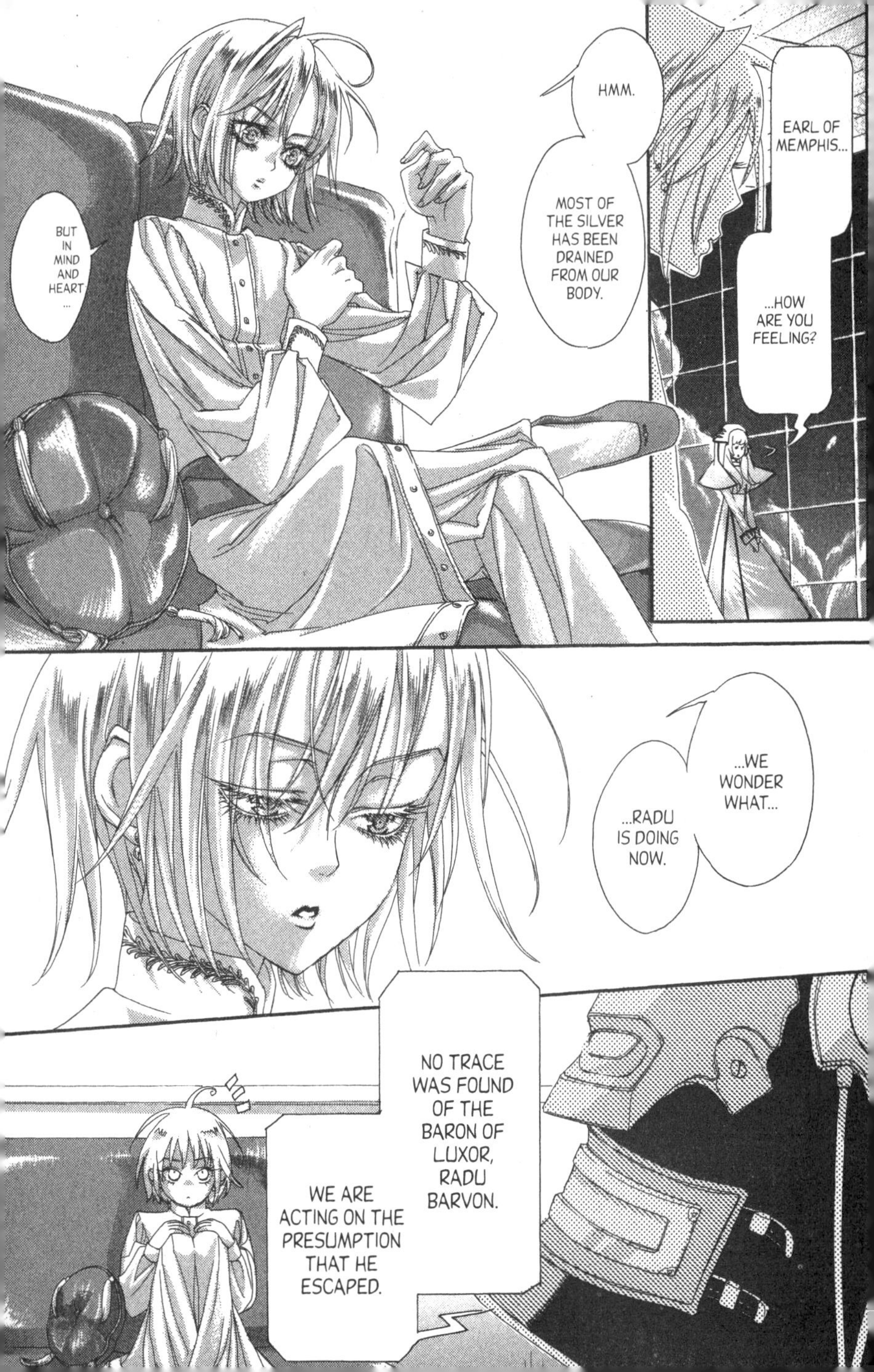
EARL OF MEMPHIS...
...HOW ARE YOU FEELING?
HMM.
MOST OF THE SILVER HAS BEEN DRAINED FROM OUR BODY.
BUT IN MIND AND HEART...
...WE WONDER WHAT...
...RADU IS DOING NOW.
NO TRACE WAS FOUND OF THE BARON OF LUXOR, RADU BARVON.
WE ARE ACTING ON THE PRESUMPTION THAT HE ESCAPED.

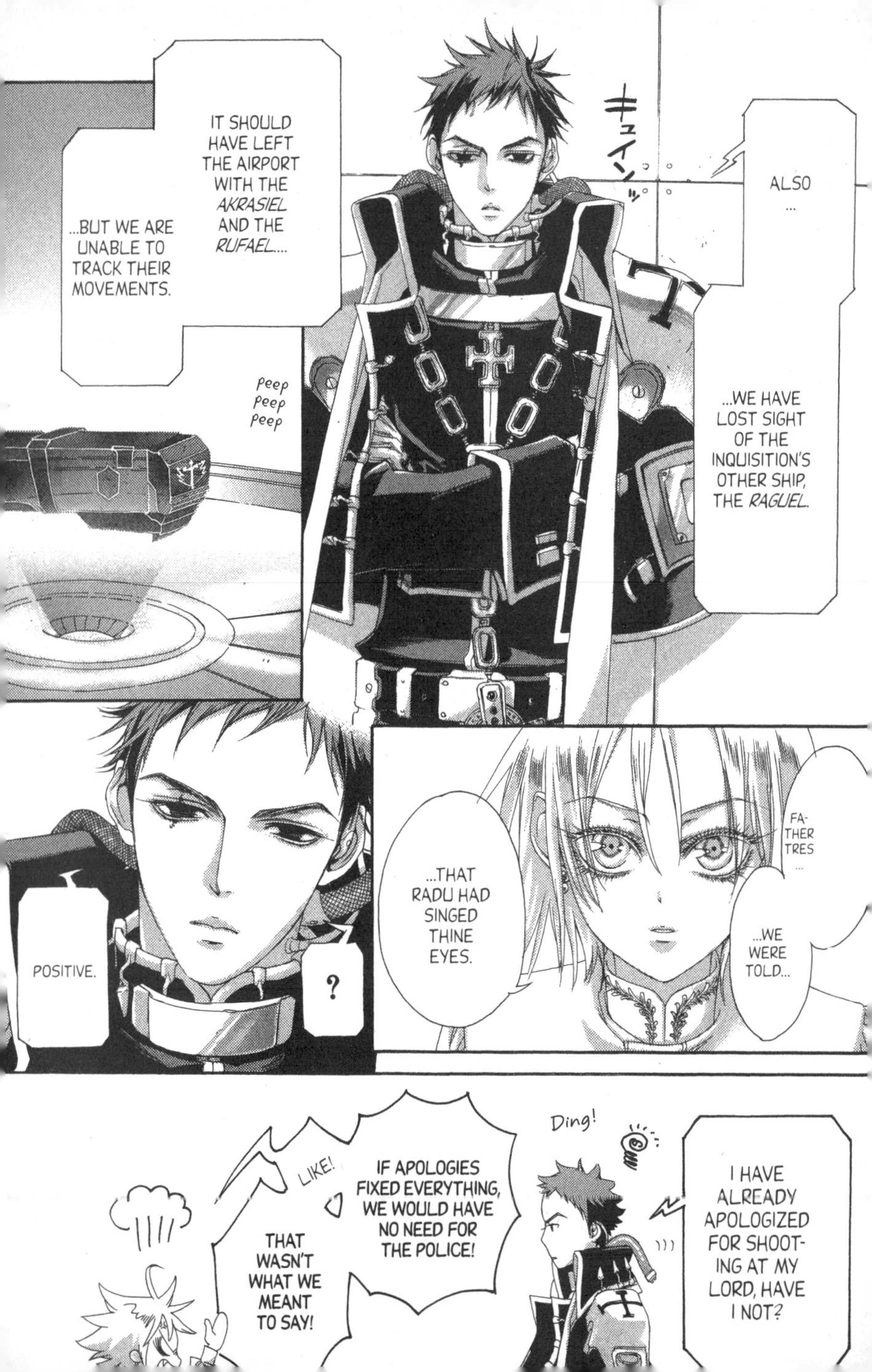
ALSO ...
キュインッ
...WE HAVE LOST SIGHT OF THE INQUISITION'S OTHER SHIP, THE *RAGUEL*.
IT SHOULD HAVE LEFT THE AIRPORT WITH THE *AKRASIEL* AND THE *RUFAEL*....
...BUT WE ARE UNABLE TO TRACK THEIR MOVEMENTS.
peep peep peep
FA-THER TRES ...
...WE WERE TOLD...
...THAT RADU HAD SINGED THINE EYES.
?
POSITIVE.
Ding!
I HAVE ALREADY APOLOGIZED FOR SHOOT-ING AT MY LORD, HAVE I NOT?
IF APOLOGIES FIXED EVERYTHING, WE WOULD HAVE NO NEED FOR THE POLICE!
LIKE!
THAT WASN'T WHAT WE MEANT TO SAY!

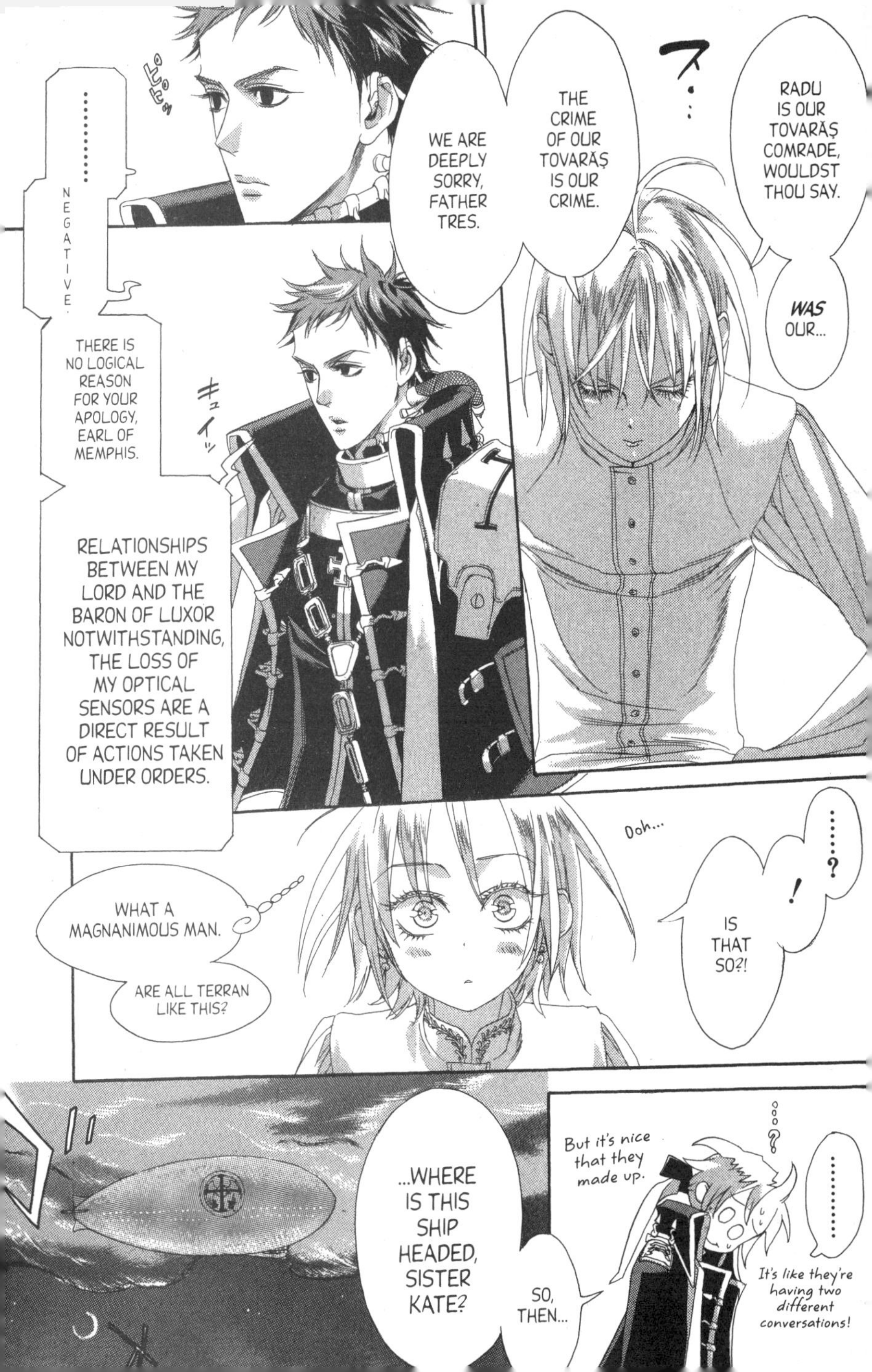

RADU IS OUR TOVARĂȘ COMRADE, WOULDST THOU SAY.
WAS OUR...
THE CRIME OF OUR TOVARĂȘ IS OUR CRIME.
WE ARE DEEPLY SORRY, FATHER TRES.
....
NEGATIVE.
THERE IS NO LOGICAL REASON FOR YOUR APOLOGY, EARL OF MEMPHIS.
RELATIONSHIPS BETWEEN MY LORD AND THE BARON OF LUXOR NOTWITHSTANDING, THE LOSS OF MY OPTICAL SENSORS ARE A DIRECT RESULT OF ACTIONS TAKEN UNDER ORDERS.
......?
!
IS THAT SO?!
Ooh...
WHAT A MAGNANIMOUS MAN.
ARE ALL TERRAN LIKE THIS?
....
But it's nice that they made up.
It's like they're having two different conversations!
SO, THEN...
...WHERE IS THIS SHIP HEADED, SISTER KATE?

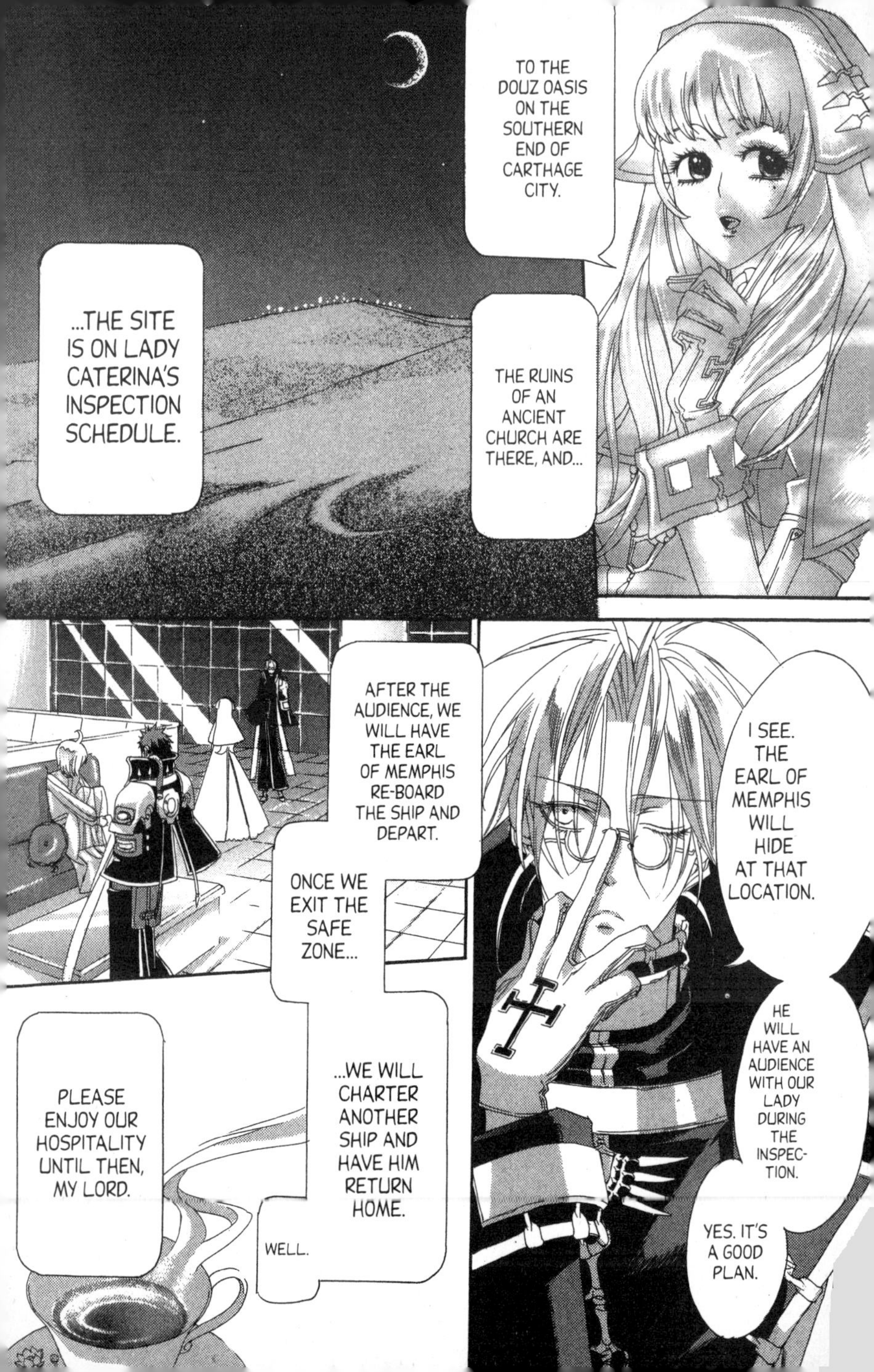
TO THE DOUZ OASIS ON THE SOUTHERN END OF CARTHAGE CITY.
THE RUINS OF AN ANCIENT CHURCH ARE THERE, AND...
...THE SITE IS ON LADY CATERINA'S INSPECTION SCHEDULE.
I SEE. THE EARL OF MEMPHIS WILL HIDE AT THAT LOCATION.
HE WILL HAVE AN AUDIENCE WITH OUR LADY DURING THE INSPEC-TION.
YES. IT'S A GOOD PLAN.
AFTER THE AUDIENCE, WE WILL HAVE THE EARL OF MEMPHIS RE-BOARD THE SHIP AND DEPART.
ONCE WE EXIT THE SAFE ZONE...
...WE WILL CHARTER ANOTHER SHIP AND HAVE HIM RETURN HOME.
WELL.
PLEASE ENJOY OUR HOSPITALITY UNTIL THEN, MY LORD.

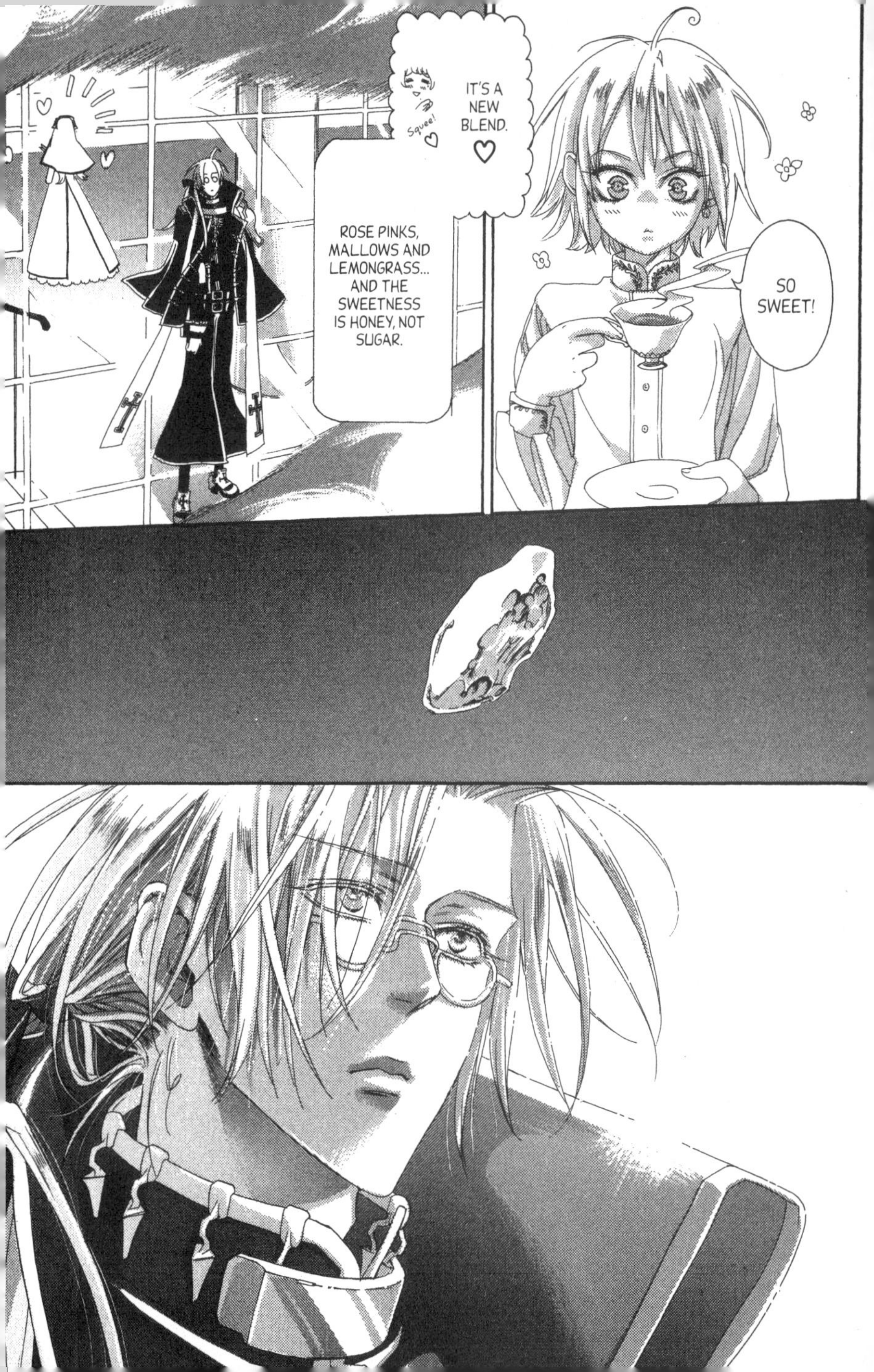
SO SWEET!
Squee!
IT'S A NEW BLEND. ♡
ROSE PINKS, MALLOWS AND LEMONGRASS... AND THE SWEETNESS IS HONEY, NOT SUGAR.

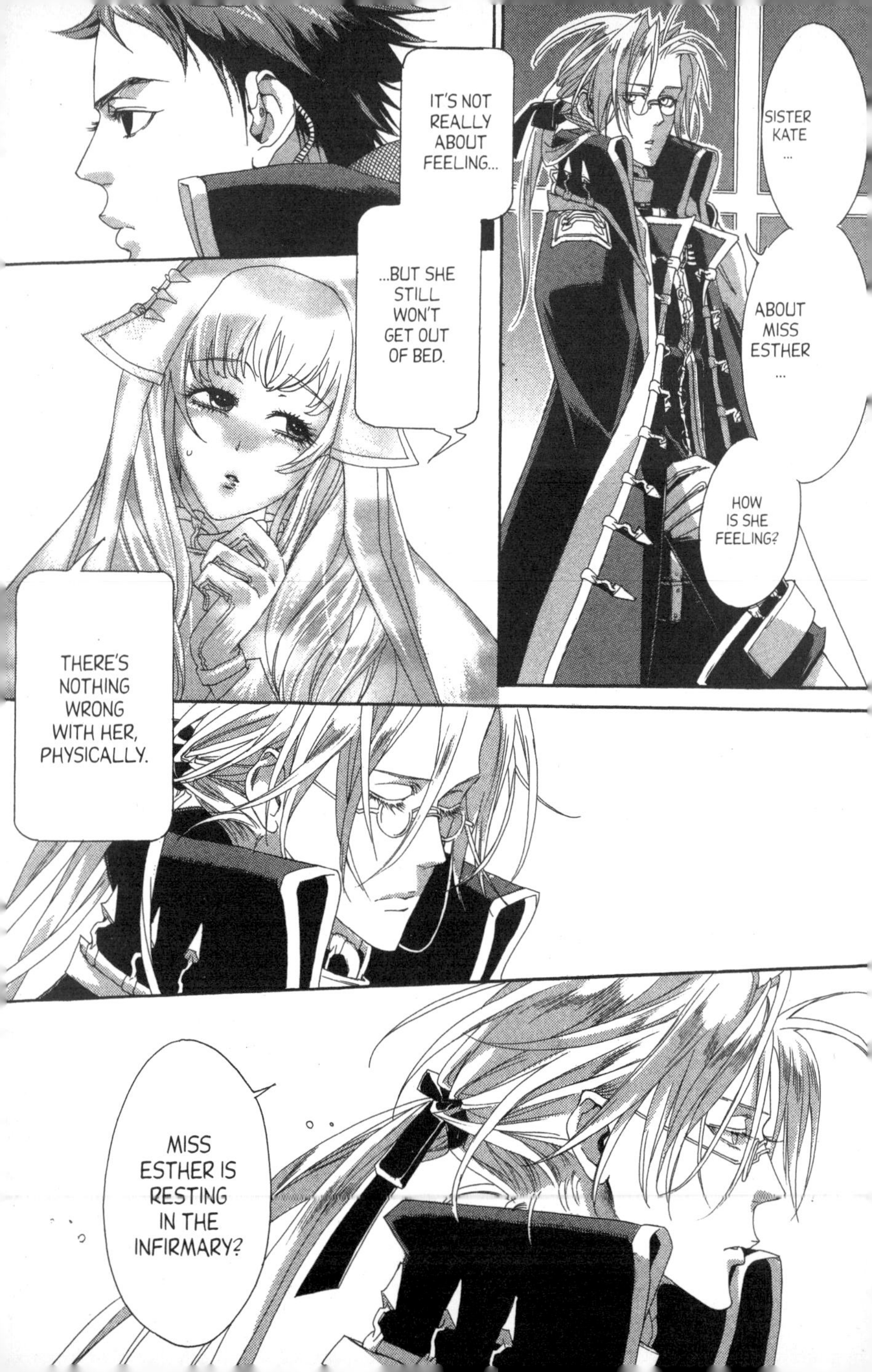
SISTER KATE ...
ABOUT MISS ESTHER ...
HOW IS SHE FEELING?
IT'S NOT REALLY ABOUT FEELING...
...BUT SHE STILL WON'T GET OUT OF BED.
THERE'S NOTHING WRONG WITH HER, PHYSICALLY.
MISS ESTHER IS RESTING IN THE INFIRMARY?

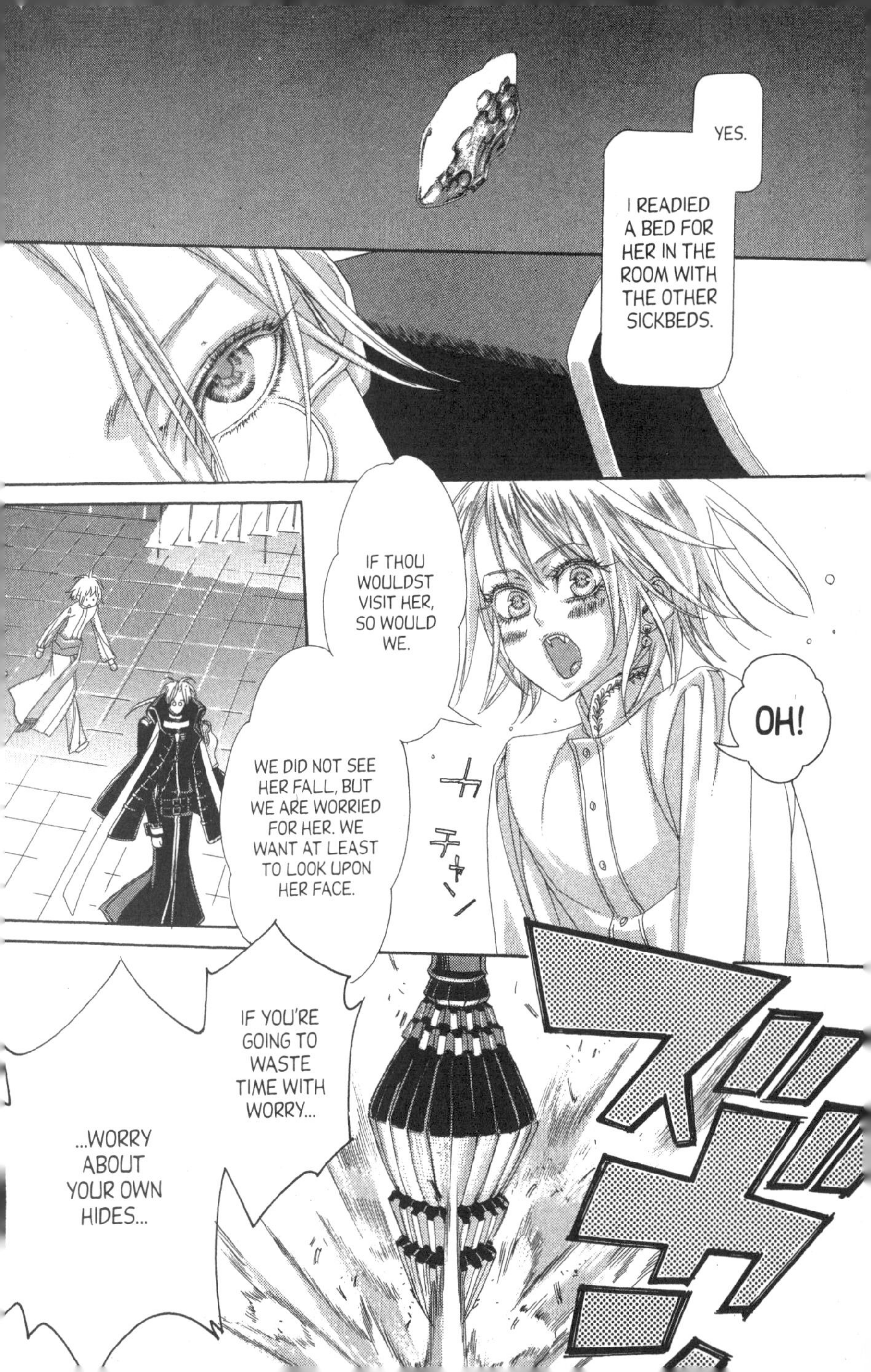
YES.
I READIED A BED FOR HER IN THE ROOM WITH THE OTHER SICKBEDS.
OH!
カチャン
IF THOU WOULDST VISIT HER, SO WOULD WE.
WE DID NOT SEE HER FALL, BUT WE ARE WORRIED FOR HER. WE WANT AT LEAST TO LOOK UPON HER FACE.
IF YOU'RE GOING TO WASTE TIME WITH WORRY...
...WORRY ABOUT YOUR OWN HIDES...

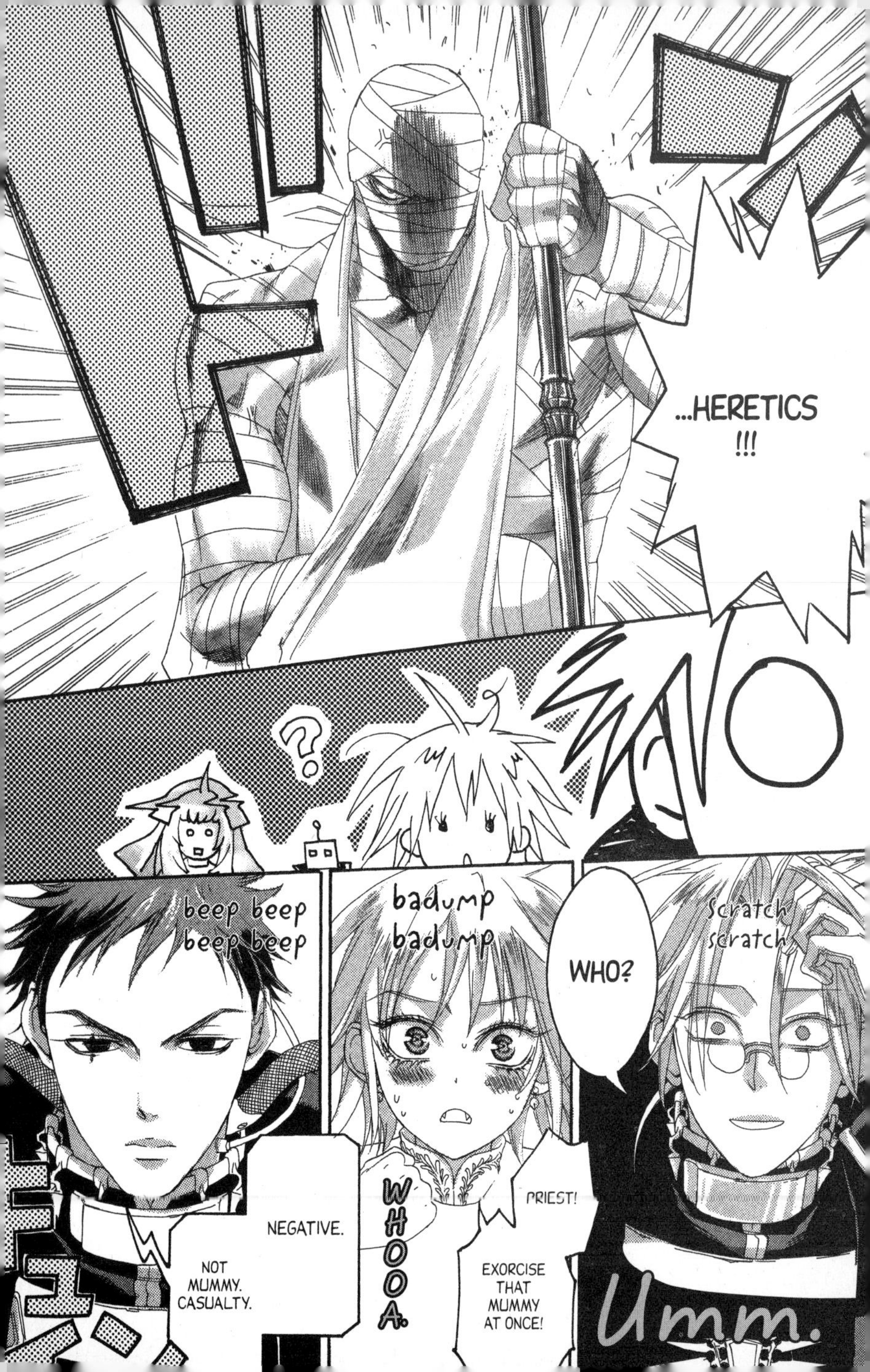
...HERETICS !!!
?
WHO?
Scratch scratch
Umm.
badump badump
PRIEST!
EXORCISE THAT MUMMY AT ONCE!
WHOOOA.
beep beep beep beep
NEGATIVE.
NOT MUMMY. CASUALTY.

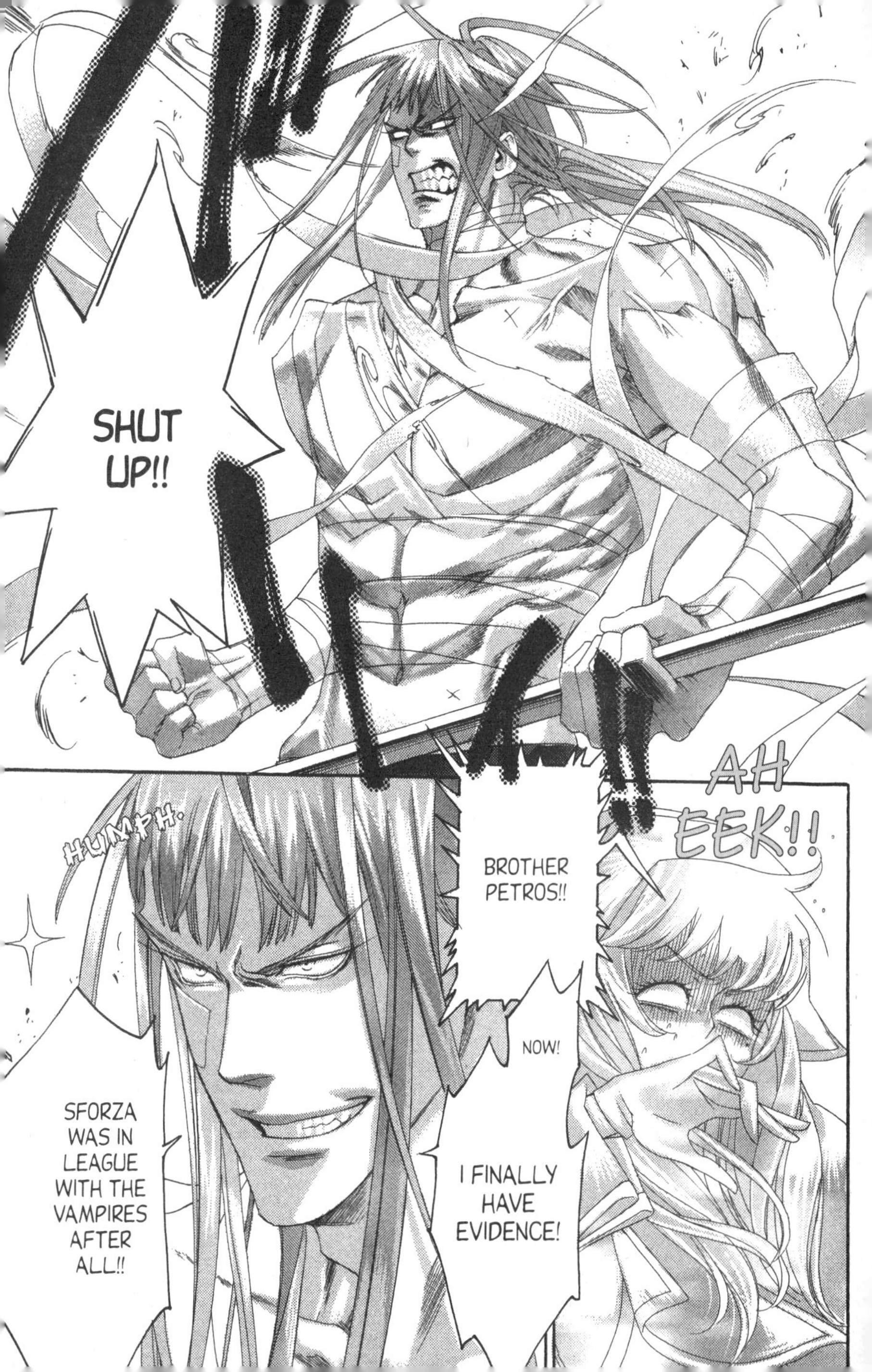
SHUT UP!!
AH EEK!!
BROTHER PETROS!!
HUMPH.
NOW!
I FINALLY HAVE EVIDENCE!
SFORZA WAS IN LEAGUE WITH THE VAMPIRES AFTER ALL!!

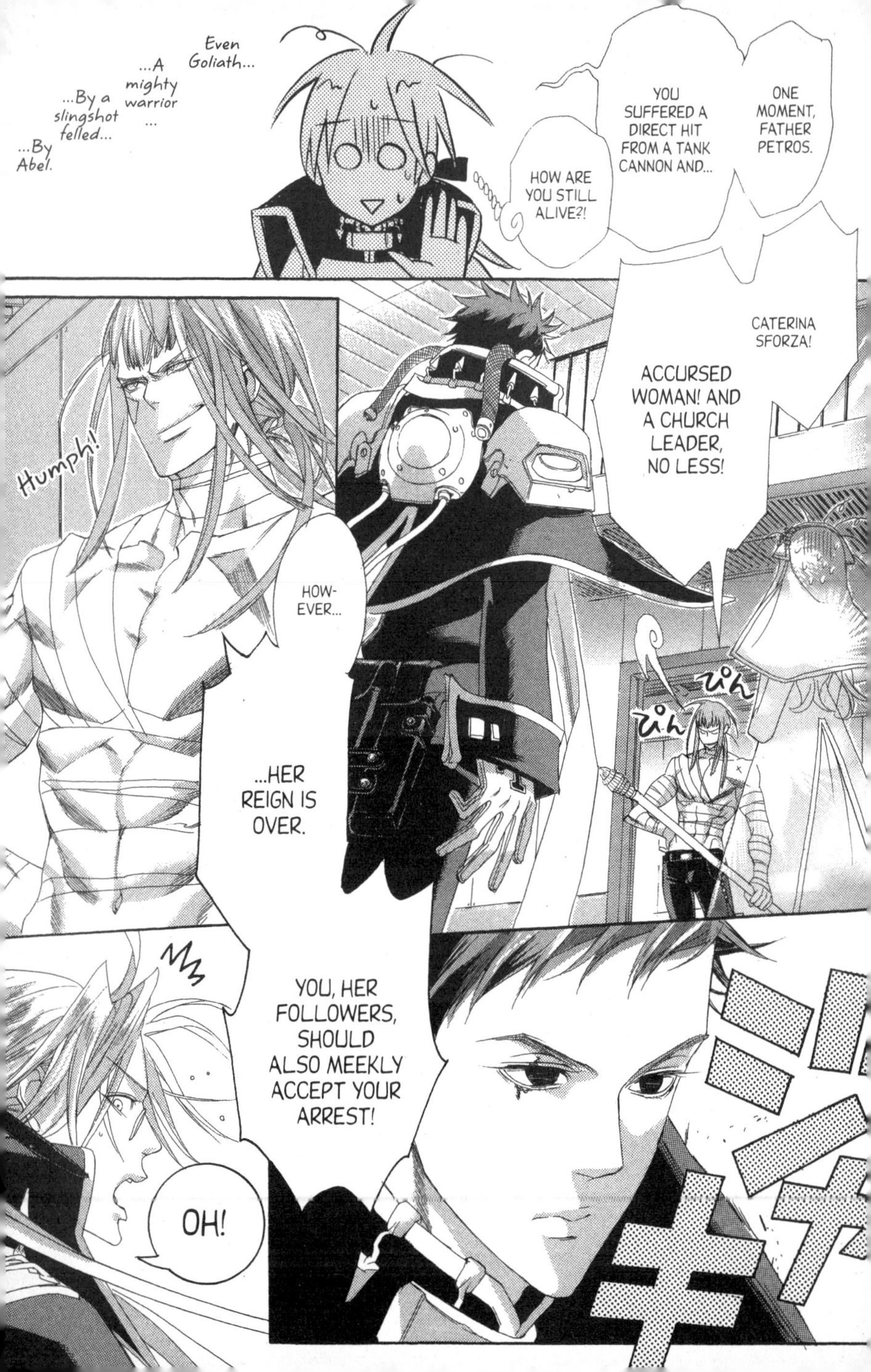
ONE MOMENT, FATHER PETROS.
YOU SUFFERED A DIRECT HIT FROM A TANK CANNON AND...
HOW ARE YOU STILL ALIVE?!
Even Goliath...
...A mighty warrior...
...By a slingshot felled...
...By Abel.
CATERINA SFORZA!
ACCURSED WOMAN! AND A CHURCH LEADER, NO LESS!
ぴん
ぴん
HOW-EVER...
Humph!
...HER REIGN IS OVER.
YOU, HER FOLLOWERS, SHOULD ALSO MEEKLY ACCEPT YOUR ARREST!
OH!

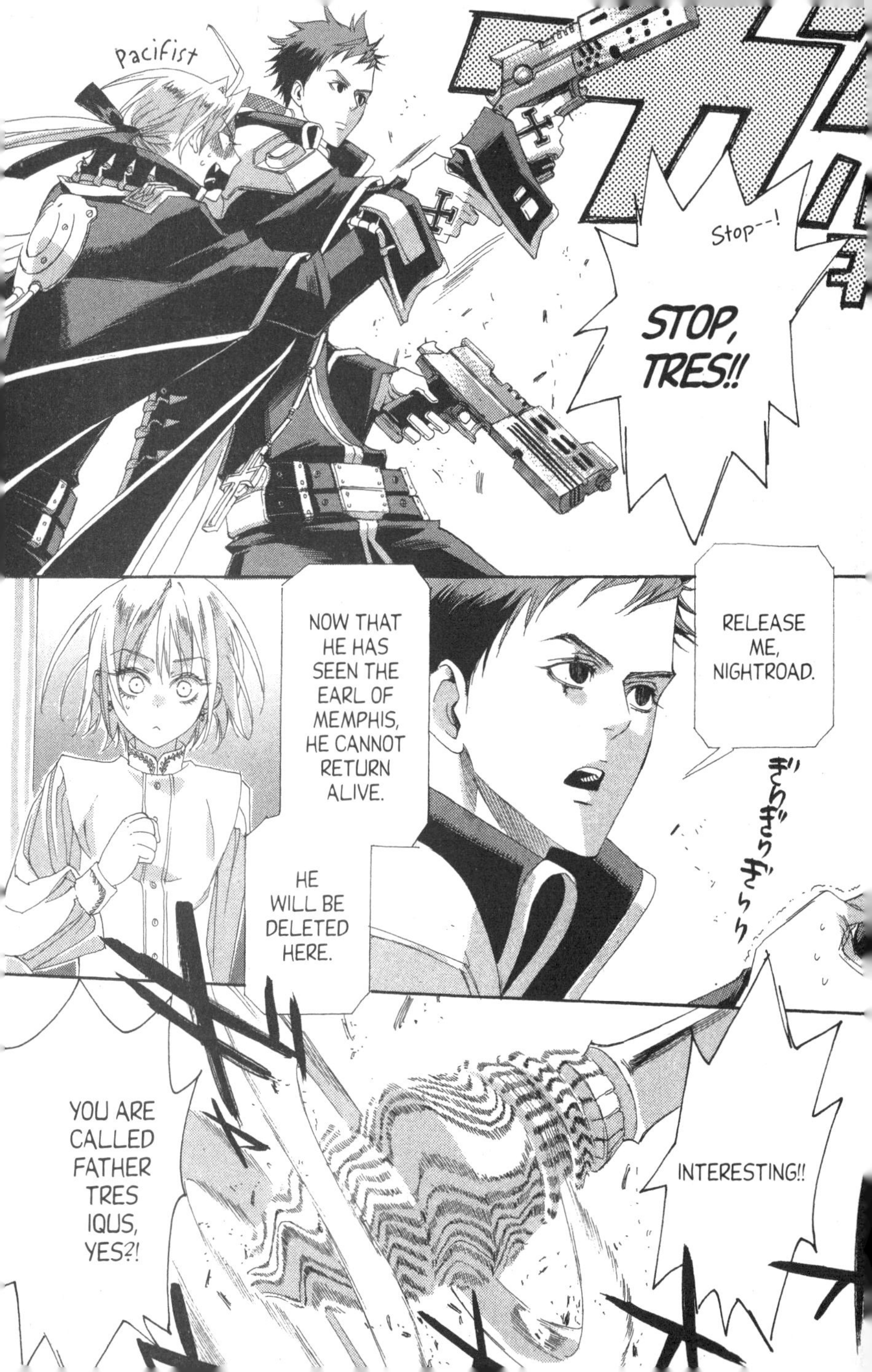
Stop--!
STOP, TRES!!
Pacifist
RELEASE ME, NIGHTROAD.
NOW THAT HE HAS SEEN THE EARL OF MEMPHIS, HE CANNOT RETURN ALIVE.
HE WILL BE DELETED HERE.
INTERESTING!!
YOU ARE CALLED FATHER TRES IQUS, YES?!

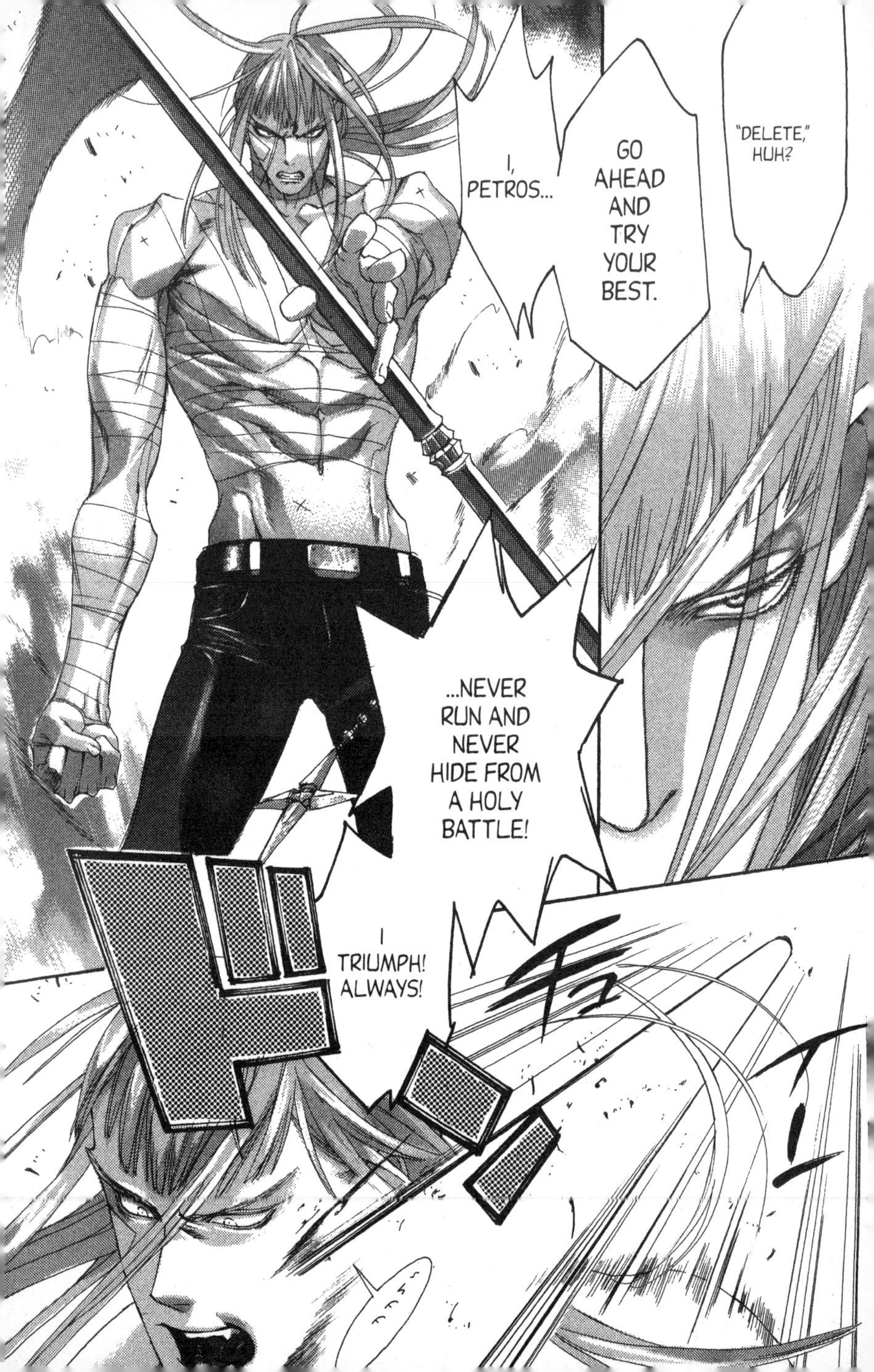
"DELETE," HUH?
GO AHEAD AND TRY YOUR BEST.
I, PETROS...
...NEVER RUN AND NEVER HIDE FROM A HOLY BATTLE!
I TRIUMPH! ALWAYS!

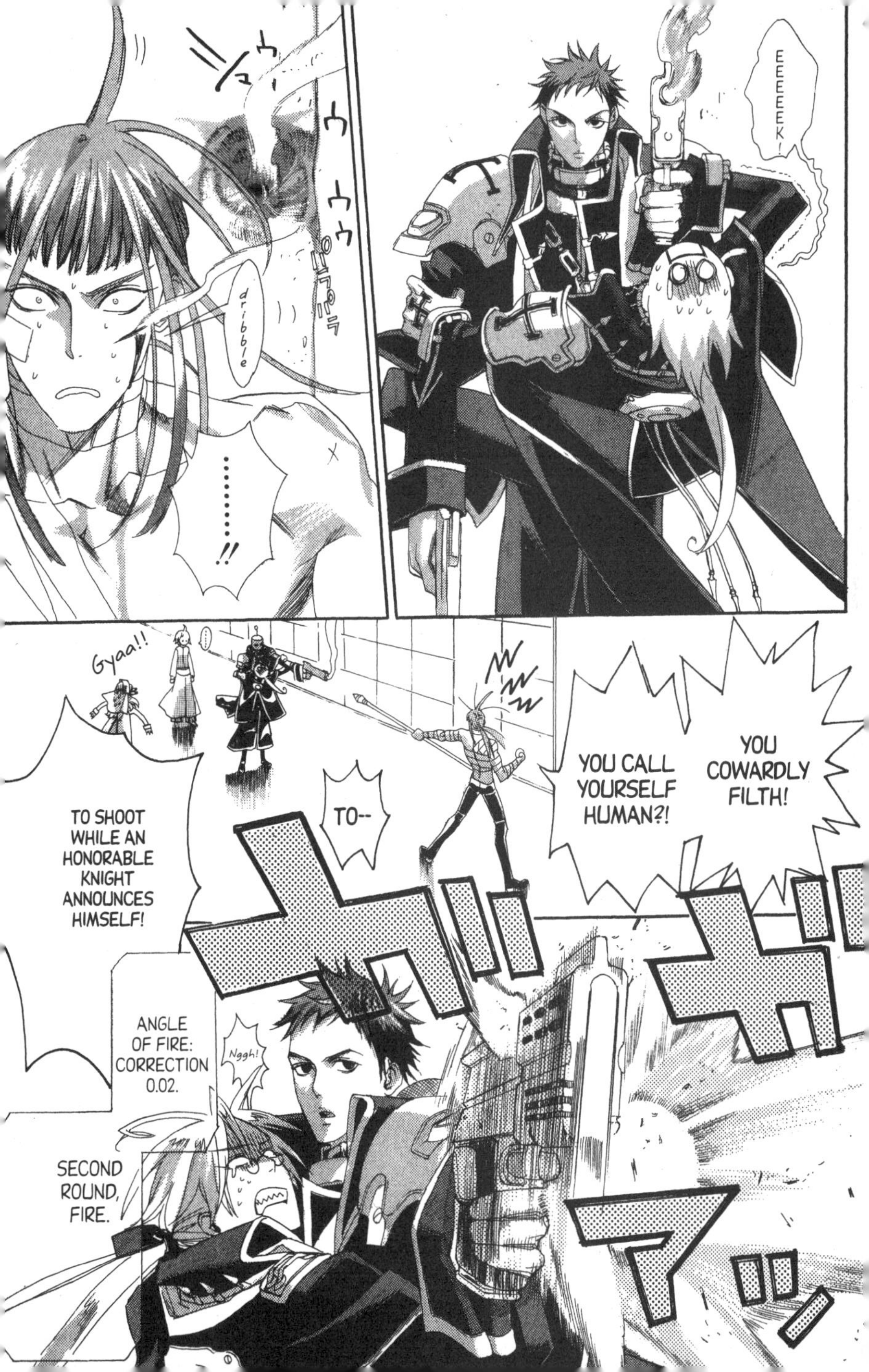
EEEEEK!
dribble
……!!
YOU COWARDLY FILTH!
YOU CALL YOURSELF HUMAN?!
TO--
Gyaa!!
TO SHOOT WHILE AN HONORABLE KNIGHT ANNOUNCES HIMSELF!
ANGLE OF FIRE: CORRECTION 0.02.
Nggh!
SECOND ROUND, FIRE.

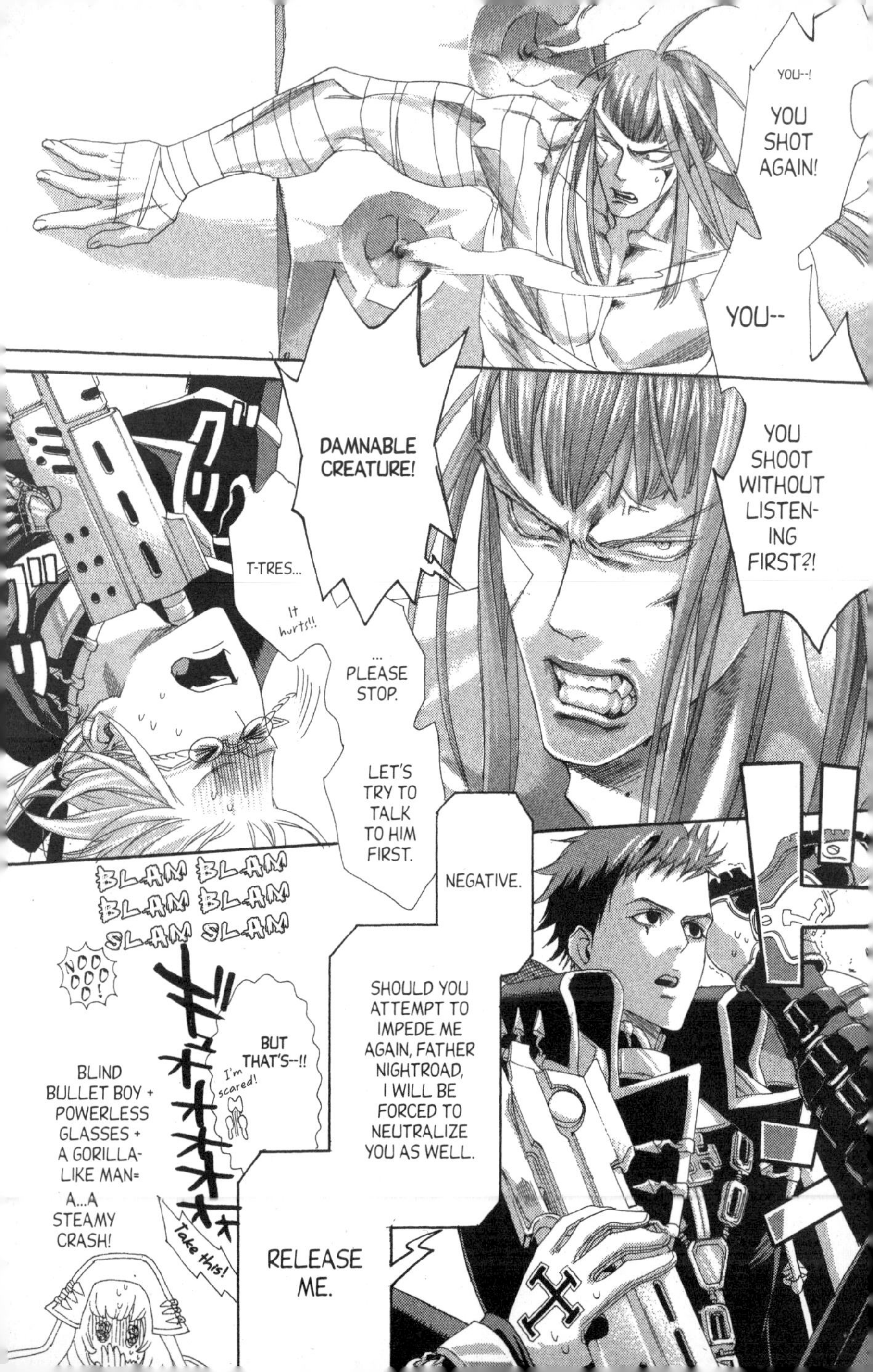
YOU--!
YOU SHOT AGAIN!
YOU--
YOU SHOOT WITHOUT LISTEN-ING FIRST?!
DAMNABLE CREATURE!
T-TRES...
It hurts!!
... PLEASE STOP.
LET'S TRY TO TALK TO HIM FIRST.
NEGATIVE.
SHOULD YOU ATTEMPT TO IMPEDE ME AGAIN, FATHER NIGHTROAD, I WILL BE FORCED TO NEUTRALIZE YOU AS WELL.
RELEASE ME.
BLAM BLAM BLAM BLAM SLAM SLAM
NOOOOOOO!
BUT THAT'S--!!
I'm scared!
Take this!
BLIND BULLET BOY + POWERLESS GLASSES + A GORILLA-LIKE MAN= A...A STEAMY CRASH!

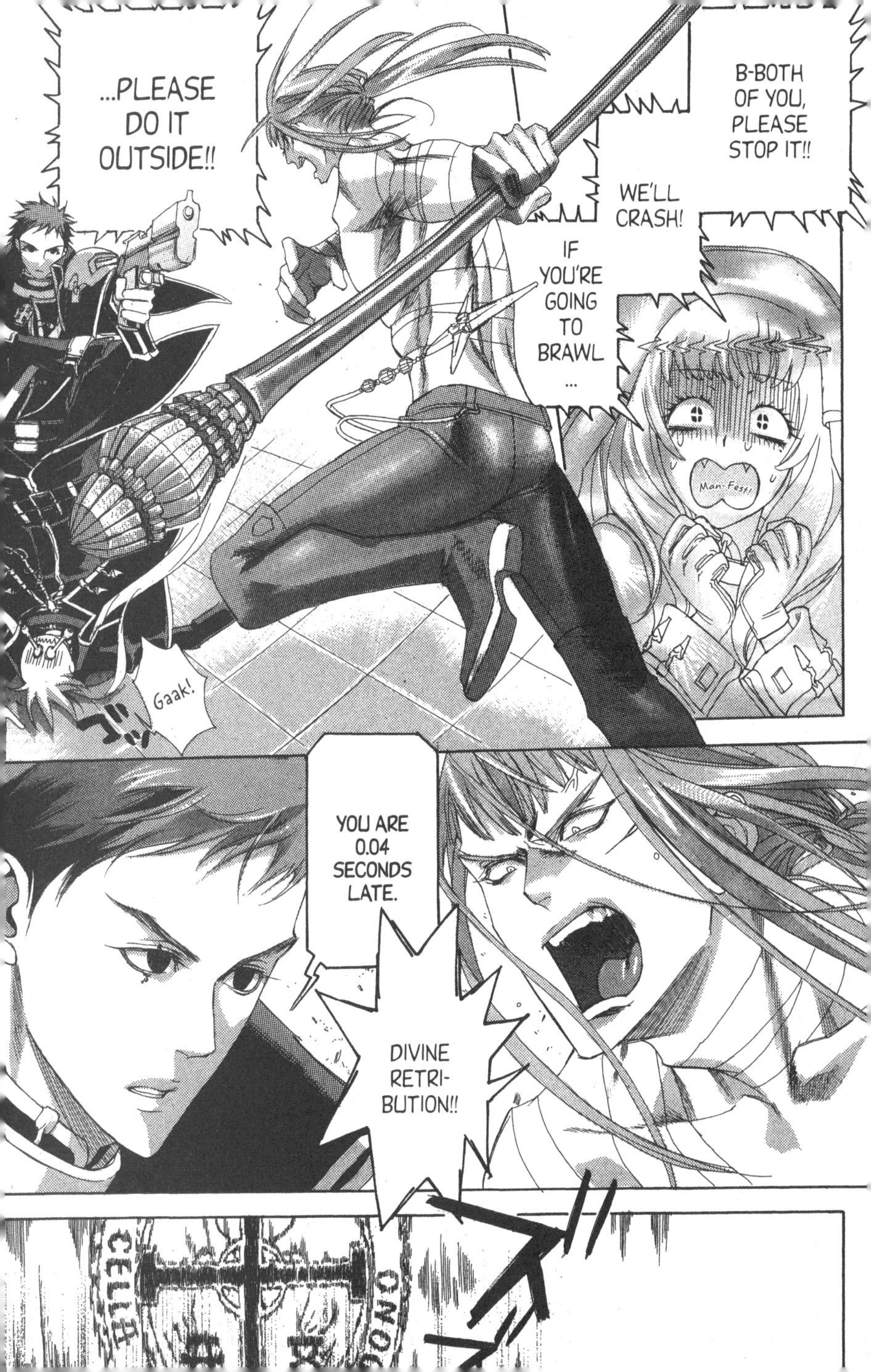
B-BOTH OF YOU, PLEASE STOP IT!!
WE'LL CRASH!
IF YOU'RE GOING TO BRAWL ...
...PLEASE DO IT OUTSIDE!!
Man-Fest!
Gaak!
DIVINE RETRI-BUTION!!
YOU ARE 0.04 SECONDS LATE.

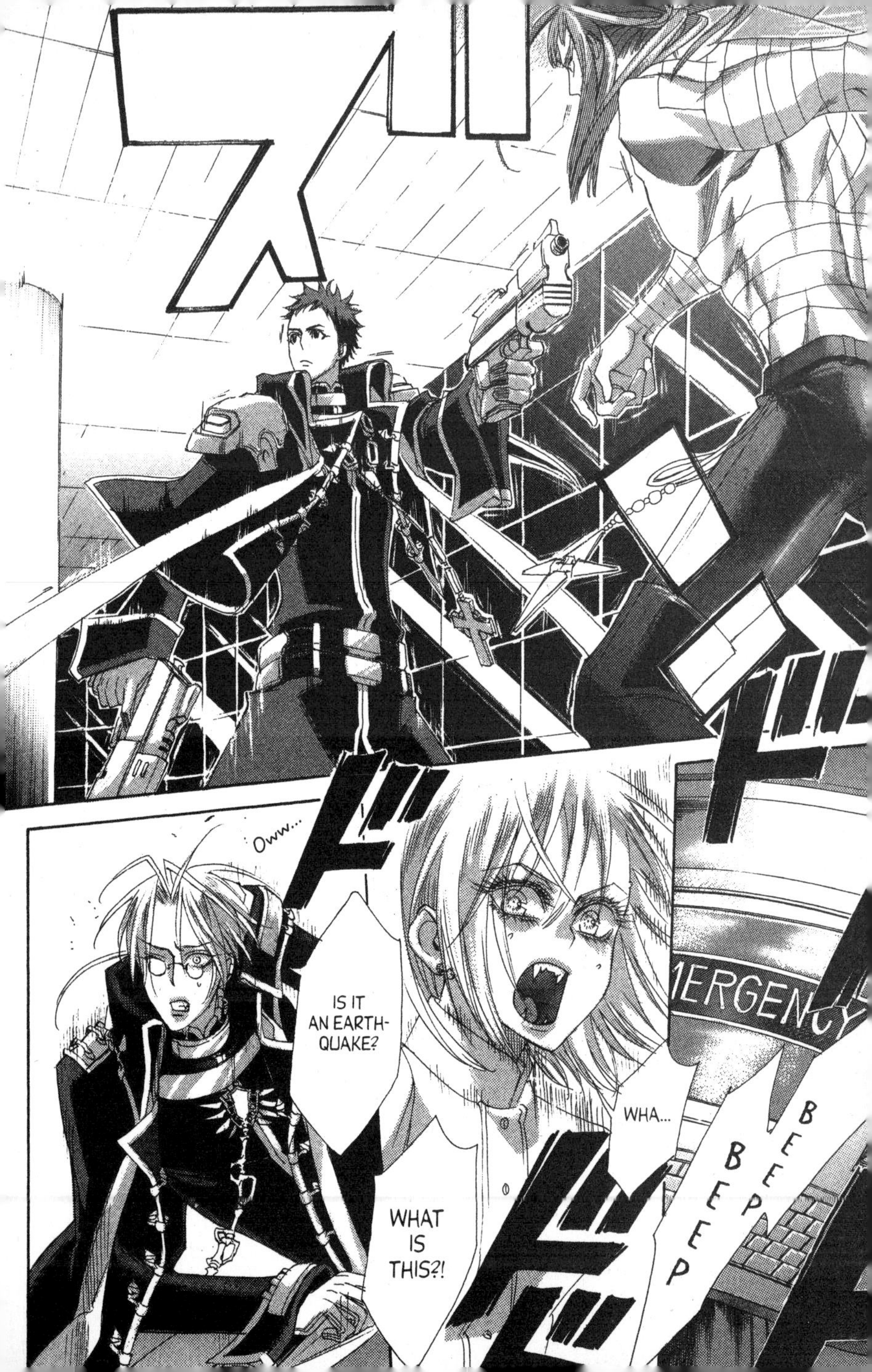
スッ
ドドド
ERGENC
BEEP BEEP
WHA...
WHAT IS THIS?!
Oww...
IS IT AN EARTH-QUAKE?

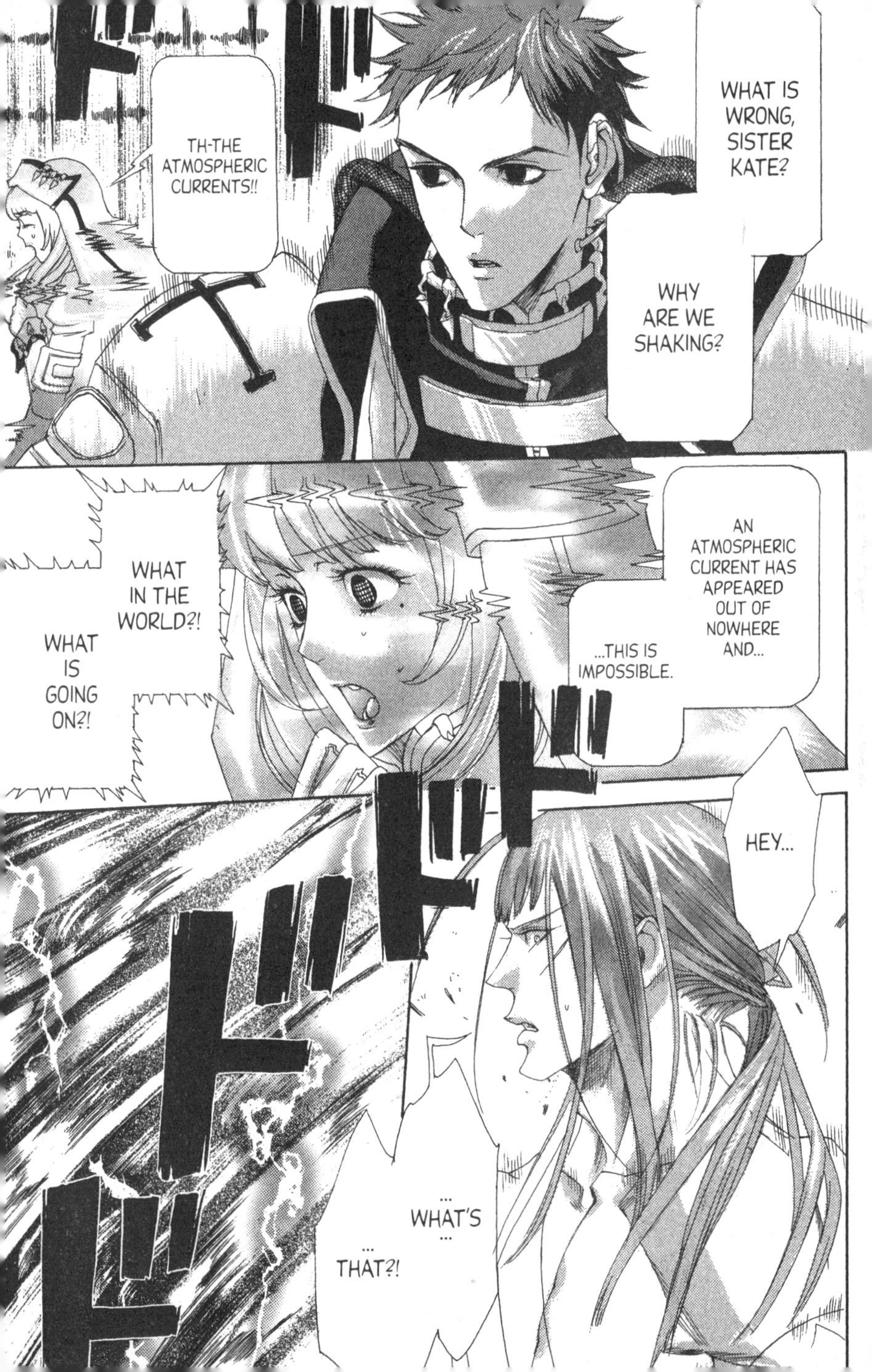
WHAT IS WRONG, SISTER KATE?
WHY ARE WE SHAKING?
TH-THE ATMOSPHERIC CURRENTS!!
ドド
AN ATMOSPHERIC CURRENT HAS APPEARED OUT OF NOWHERE AND...
...THIS IS IMPOSSIBLE.
WHAT IN THE WORLD?!
WHAT IS GOING ON?!
HEY...
ドドドド
...WHAT'S...
...THAT?!

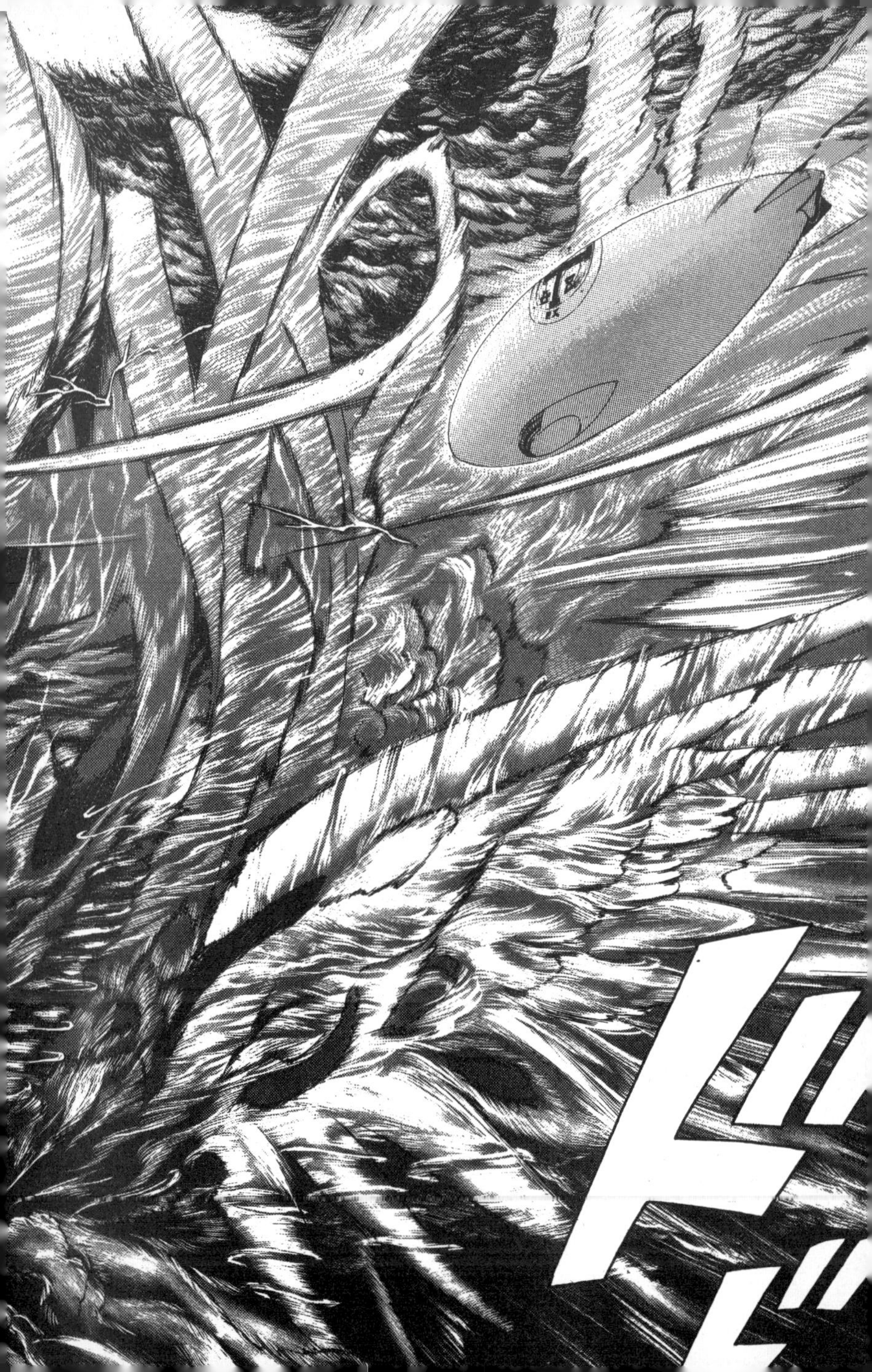

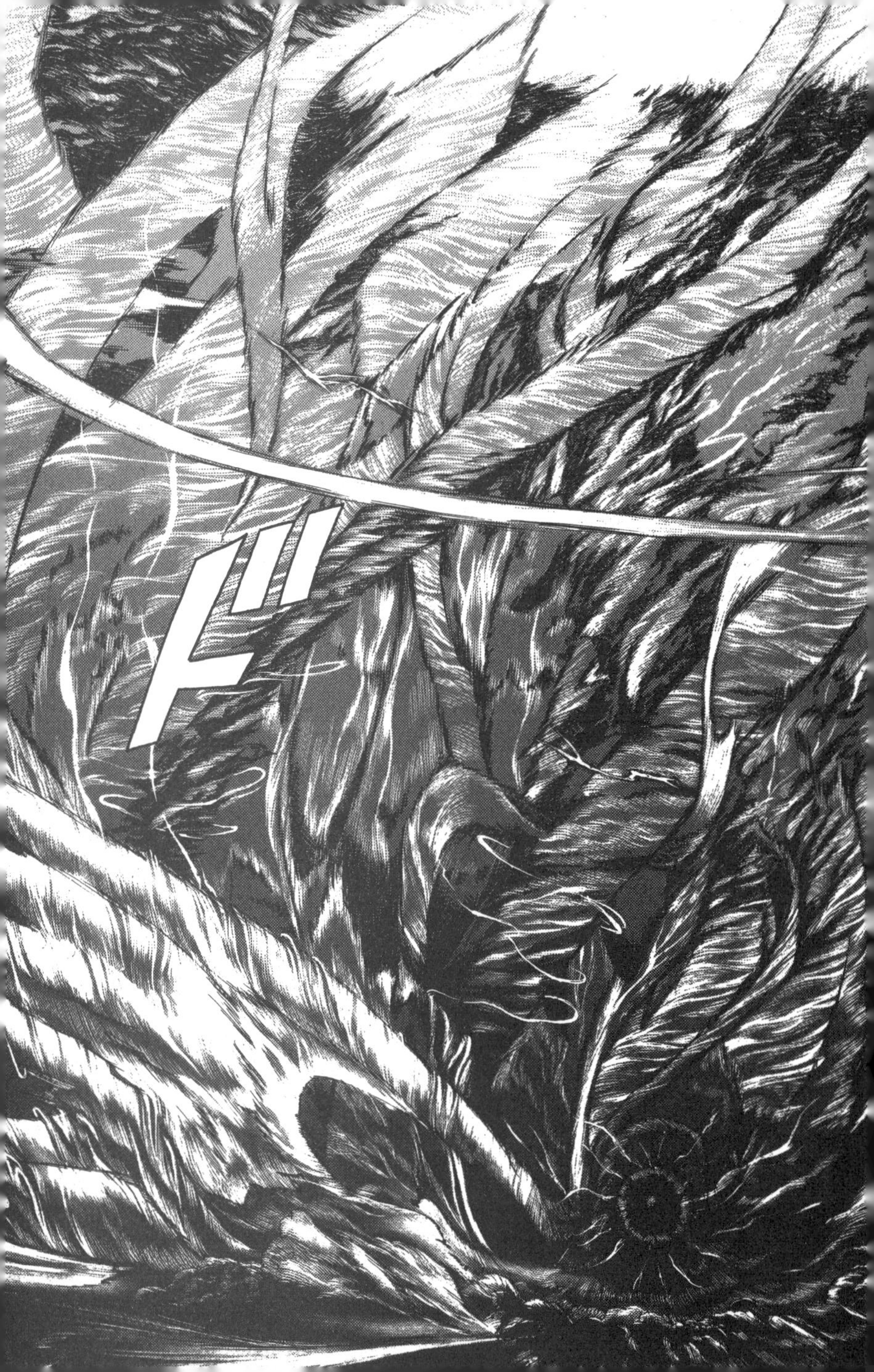
ドッ

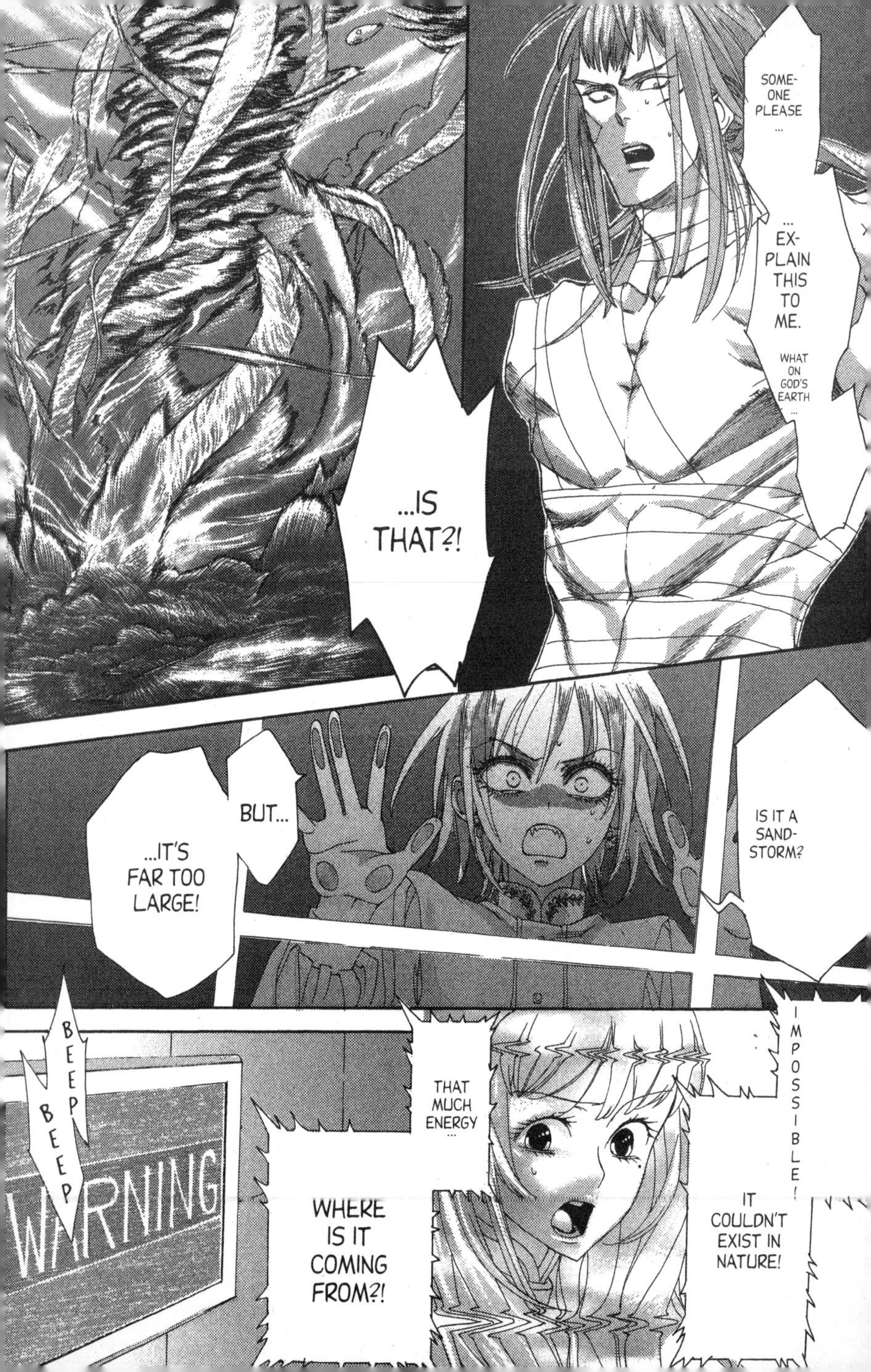
SOME-ONE PLEASE ...
... EX-PLAIN THIS TO ME.
WHAT ON GOD'S EARTH ...
...IS THAT?!
IS IT A SAND-STORM?
BUT...
...IT'S FAR TOO LARGE!
IMPOSSIBLE!
IT COULDN'T EXIST IN NATURE!
THAT MUCH ENERGY ...
WHERE IS IT COMING FROM?!
BEEP
BEEP
BEEP
WARNING

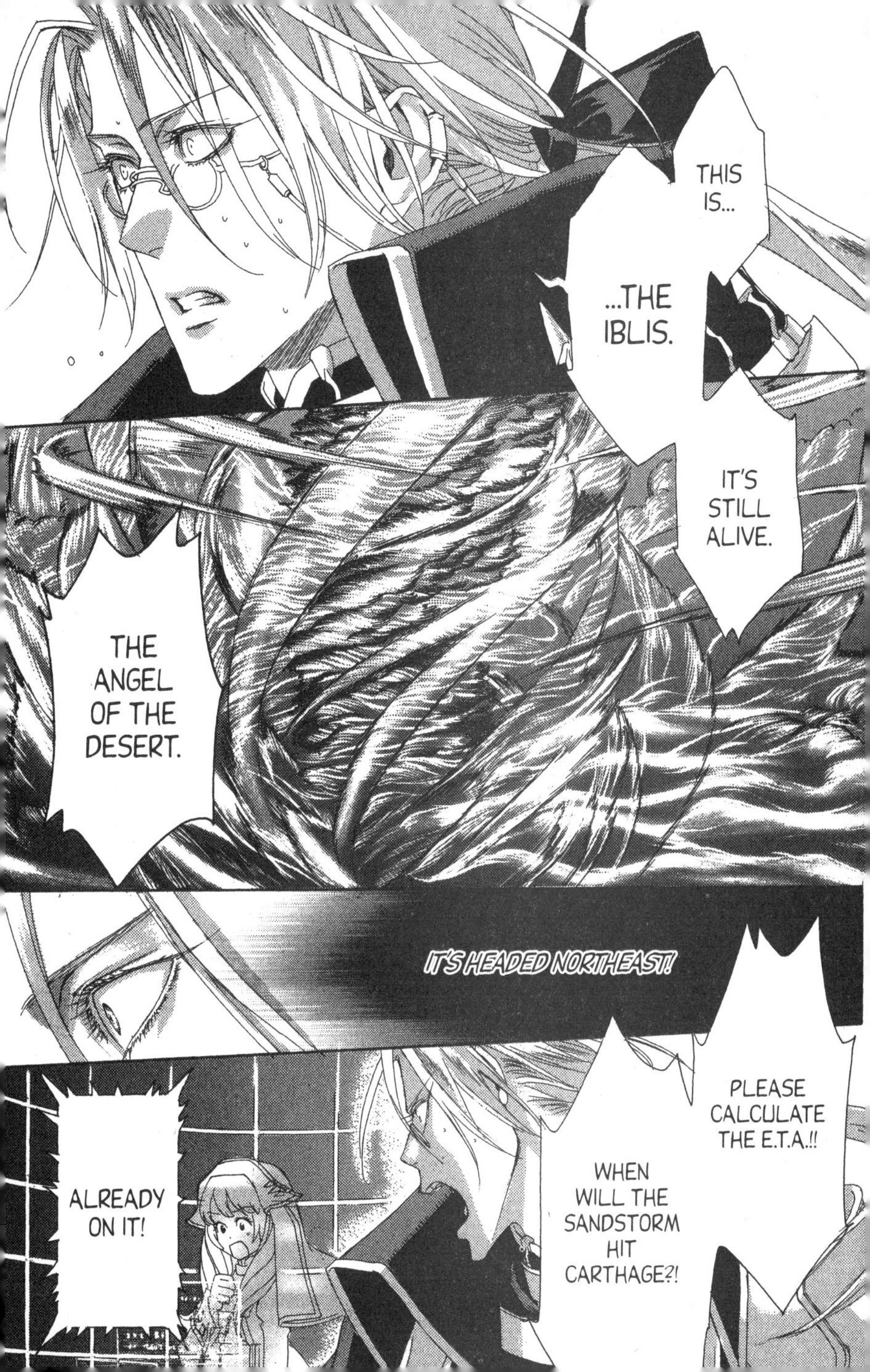
THIS IS...
...THE IBLIS.
IT'S STILL ALIVE.
THE ANGEL OF THE DESERT.
IT'S HEADED NORTHEAST!
PLEASE CALCULATE THE E.T.A.!!
WHEN WILL THE SANDSTORM HIT CARTHAGE?!
ALREADY ON IT!

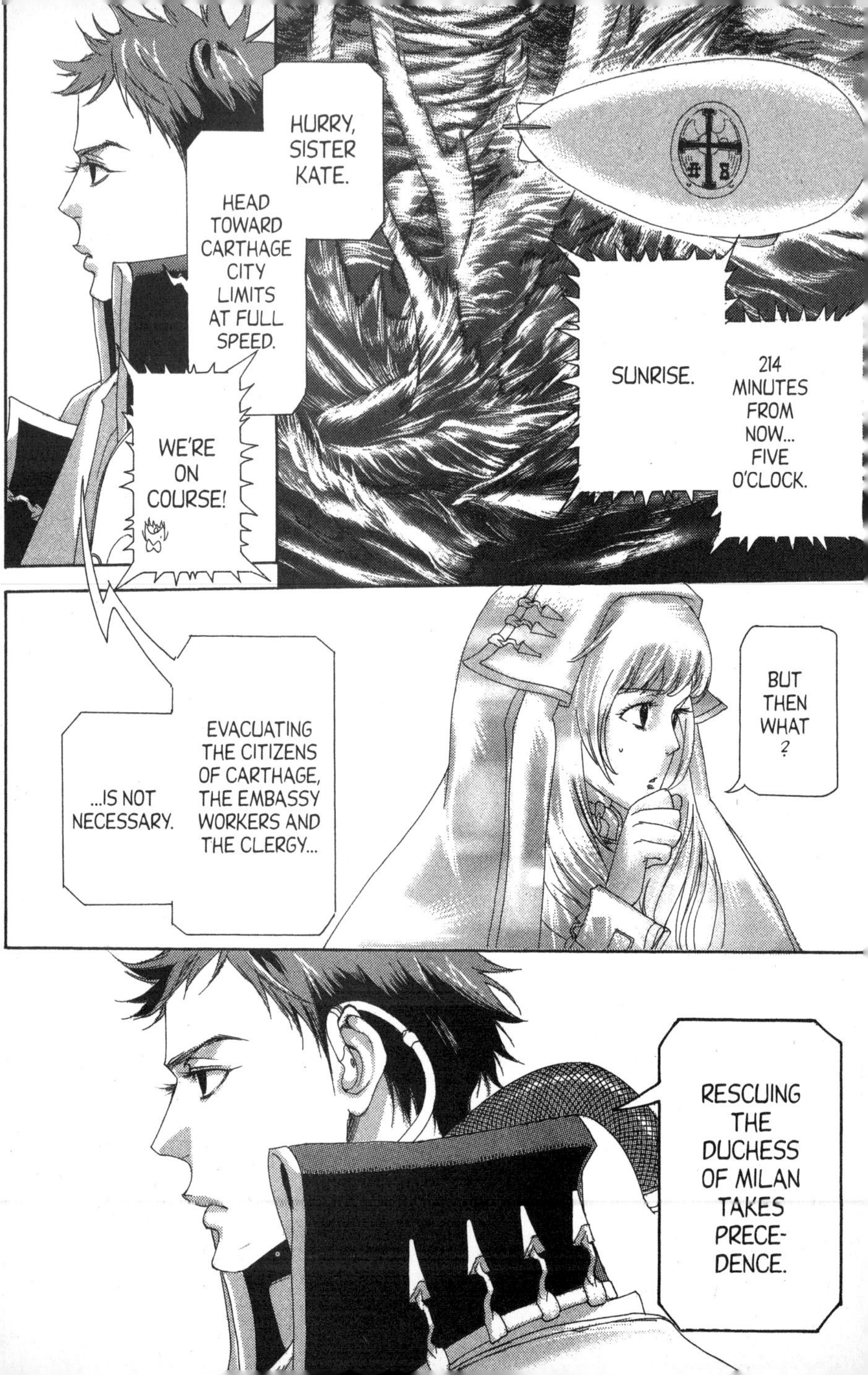
214 MINUTES FROM NOW... FIVE O'CLOCK.
SUNRISE.
HURRY, SISTER KATE.
HEAD TOWARD CARTHAGE CITY LIMITS AT FULL SPEED.
WE'RE ON COURSE!
BUT THEN WHAT?
EVACUATING THE CITIZENS OF CARTHAGE, THE EMBASSY WORKERS AND THE CLERGY...
...IS NOT NECESSARY.
RESCUING THE DUCHESS OF MILAN TAKES PRECE-DENCE.

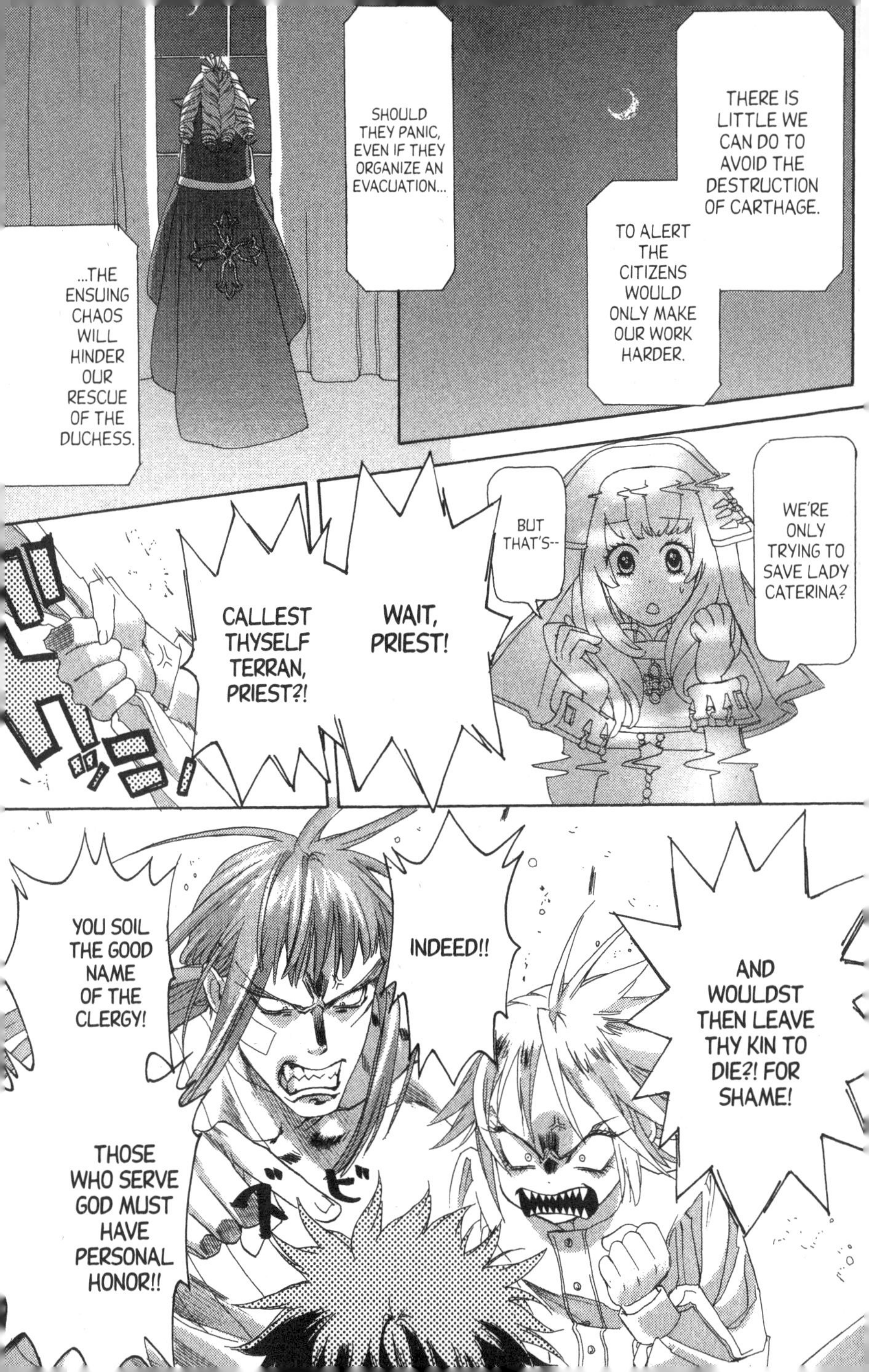
THERE IS LITTLE WE CAN DO TO AVOID THE DESTRUCTION OF CARTHAGE.
TO ALERT THE CITIZENS WOULD ONLY MAKE OUR WORK HARDER.
SHOULD THEY PANIC, EVEN IF THEY ORGANIZE AN EVACUATION...
...THE ENSUING CHAOS WILL HINDER OUR RESCUE OF THE DUCHESS.
WE'RE ONLY TRYING TO SAVE LADY CATERINA?
BUT THAT'S--
WAIT, PRIEST!
CALLEST THYSELF TERRAN, PRIEST?!
AND WOULDST THEN LEAVE THY KIN TO DIE?! FOR SHAME!
INDEED!!
YOU SOIL THE GOOD NAME OF THE CLERGY!
THOSE WHO SERVE GOD MUST HAVE PERSONAL HONOR!!

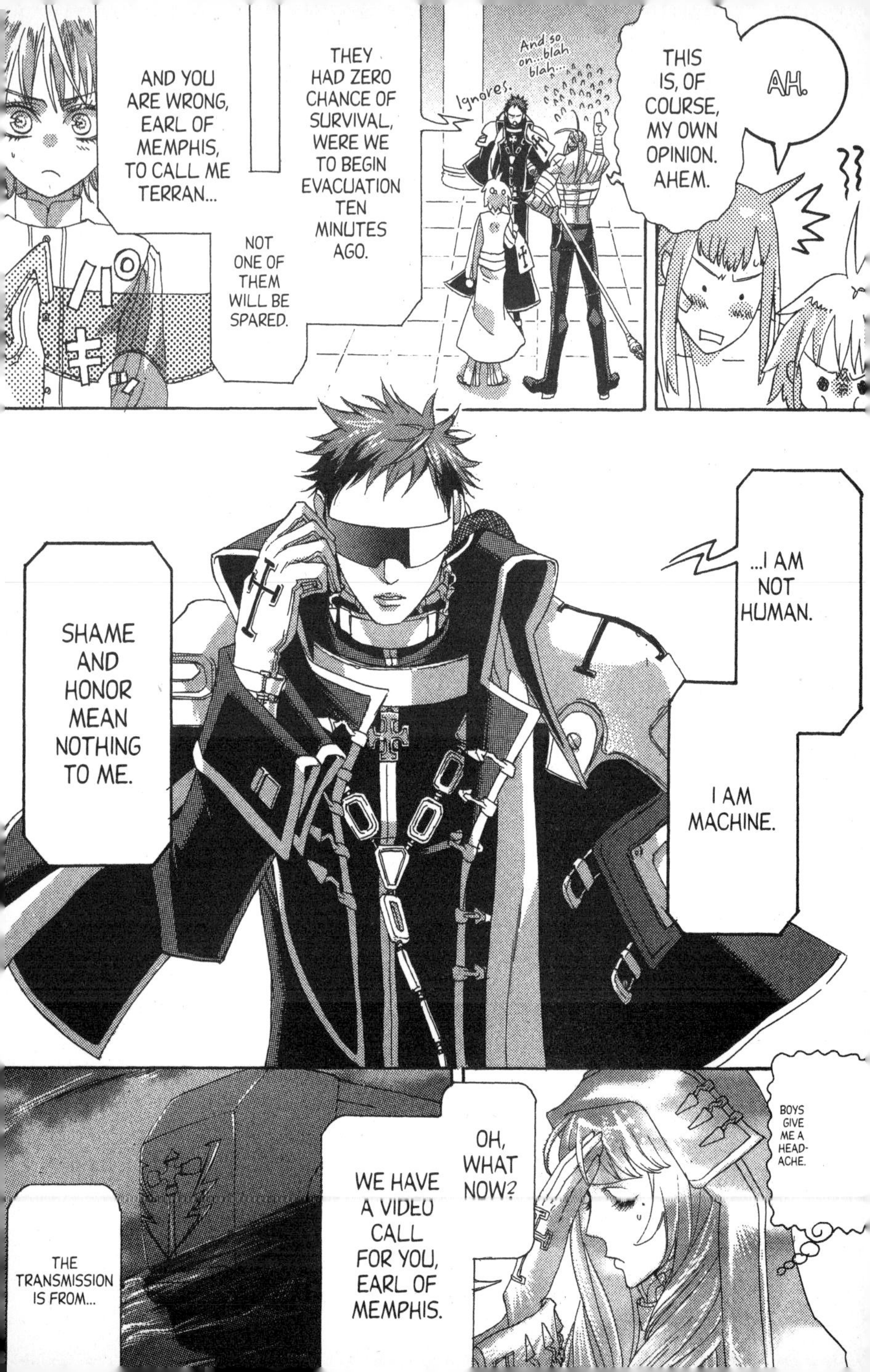
AH.
THIS IS, OF COURSE, MY OWN OPINION. AHEM.
And so on...blah blah...
Ignores.
THEY HAD ZERO CHANCE OF SURVIVAL, WERE WE TO BEGIN EVACUATION TEN MINUTES AGO.
NOT ONE OF THEM WILL BE SPARED.
AND YOU ARE WRONG, EARL OF MEMPHIS, TO CALL ME TERRAN...
...I AM NOT HUMAN.
I AM MACHINE.
SHAME AND HONOR MEAN NOTHING TO ME.
BOYS GIVE ME A HEAD-ACHE.
OH, WHAT NOW?
WE HAVE A VIDEO CALL FOR YOU, EARL OF MEMPHIS.
THE TRANSMISSION IS FROM...

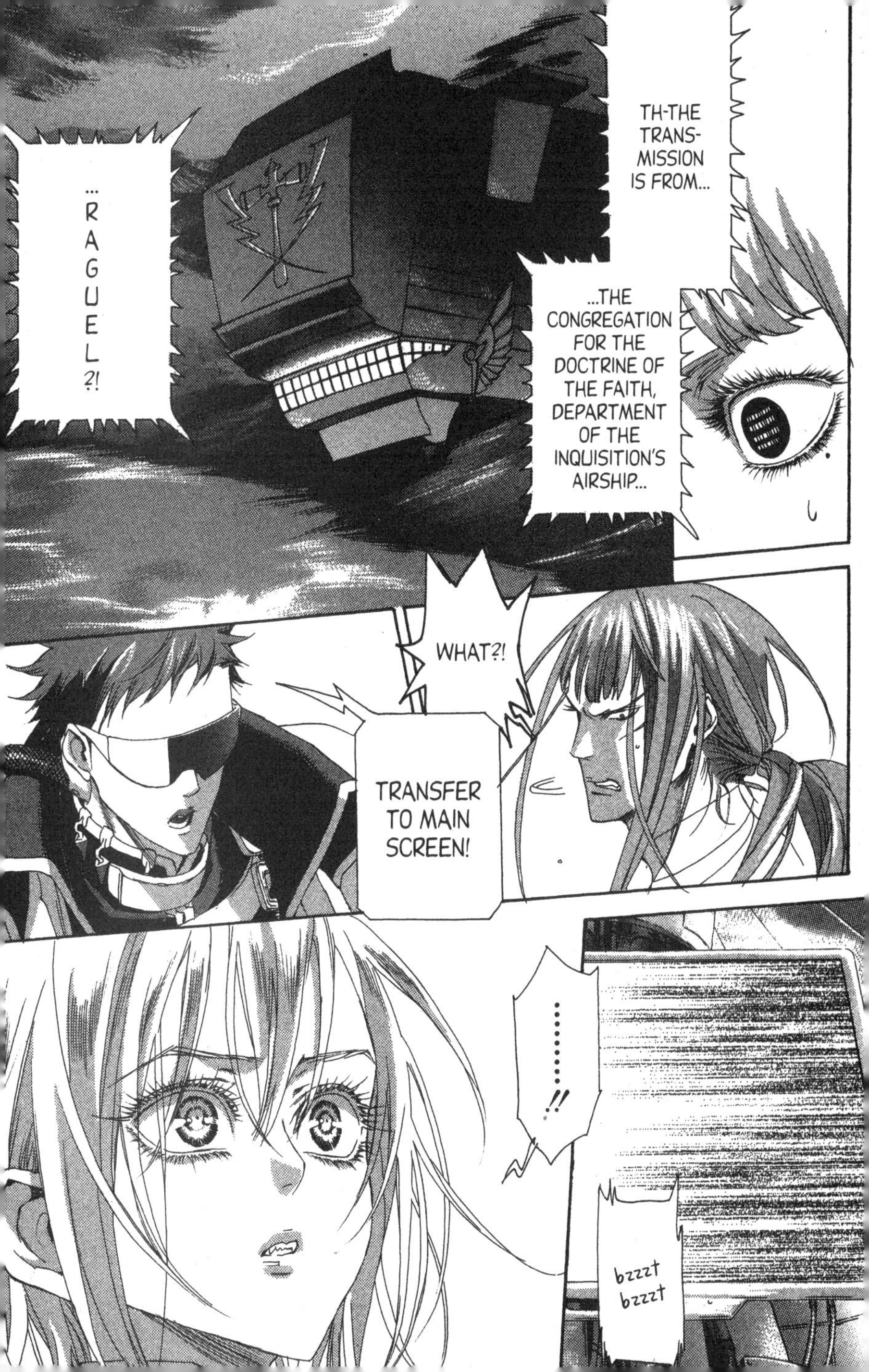
TH-THE TRANS-MISSION IS FROM...
...THE CONGREGATION FOR THE DOCTRINE OF THE FAITH, DEPARTMENT OF THE INQUISITION'S AIRSHIP...
...RAGUEL?!
WHAT?!
TRANSFER TO MAIN SCREEN!
.........!!
bzzzt bzzzt

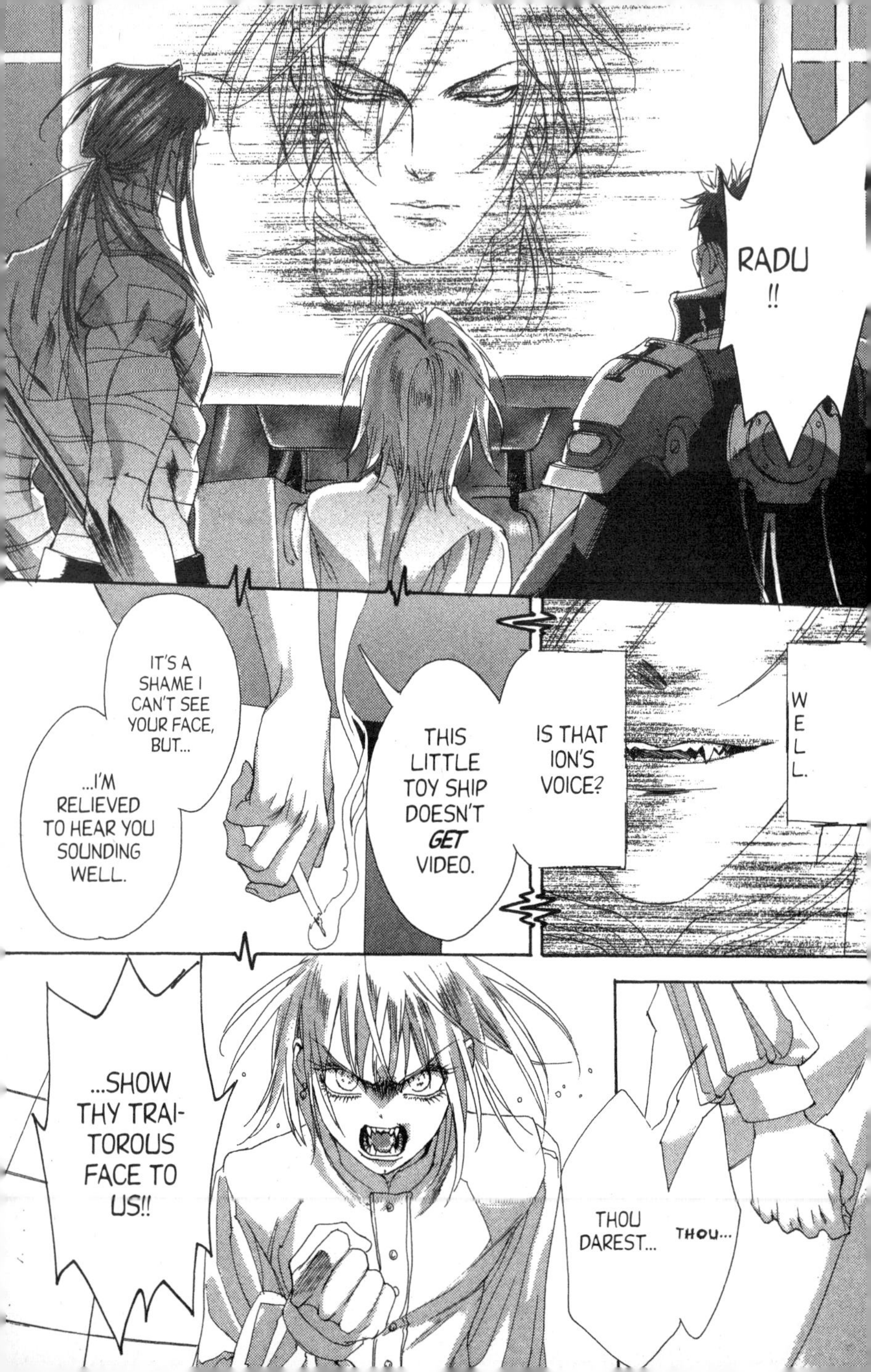
RADU !!
WELL.
IS THAT ION'S VOICE?
THIS LITTLE TOY SHIP DOESN'T GET VIDEO.
IT'S A SHAME I CAN'T SEE YOUR FACE, BUT...
...I'M RELIEVED TO HEAR YOU SOUNDING WELL.
THOU...
THOU DAREST...
...SHOW THY TRAI-TOROUS FACE TO US!!

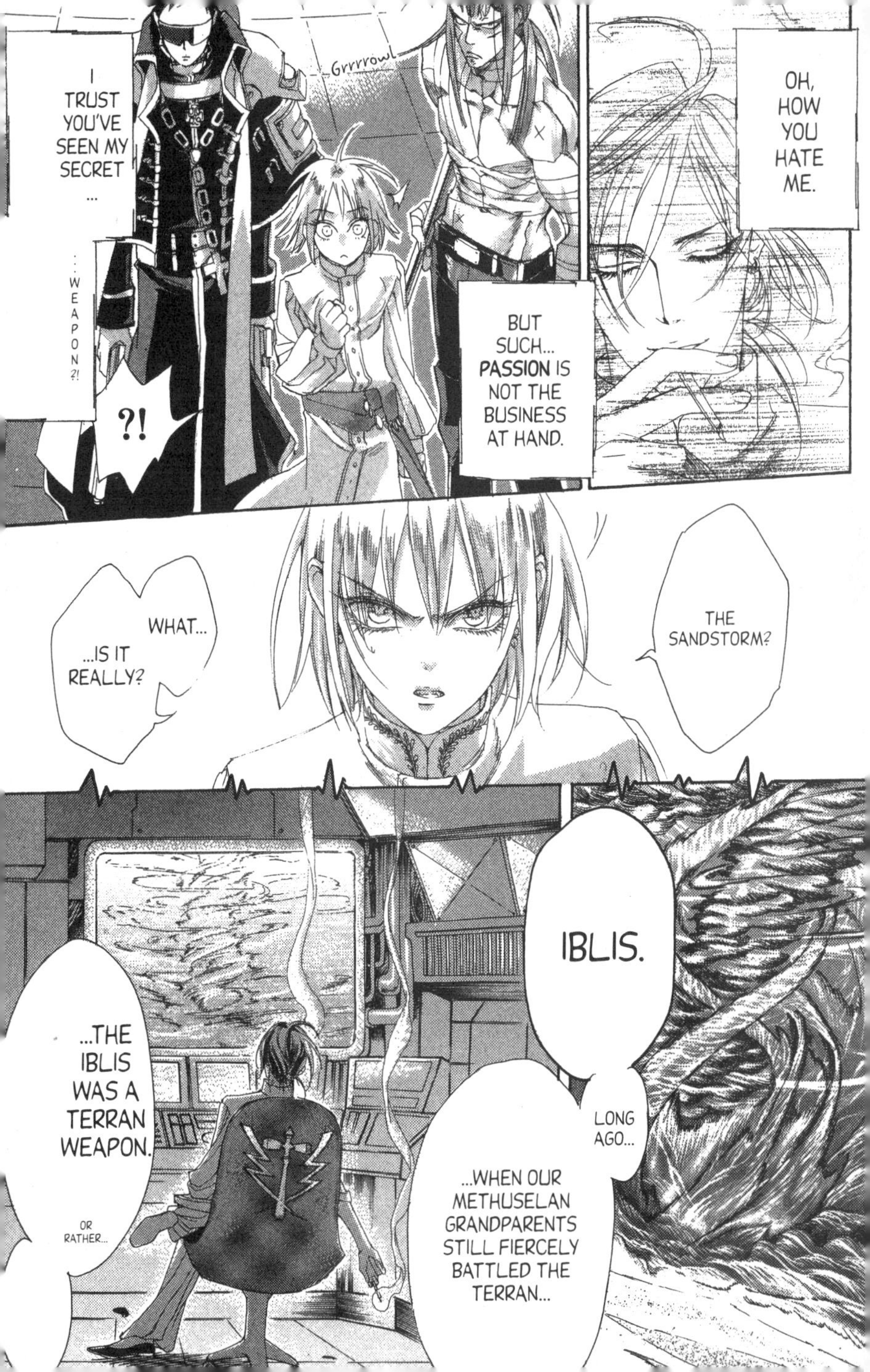
OH, HOW YOU HATE ME.
BUT SUCH... **PASSION** IS NOT THE BUSINESS AT HAND.
Grrrrowl
I TRUST YOU'VE SEEN MY SECRET ...
...WEAPON?!
?!
THE SANDSTORM?
WHAT... ...IS IT REALLY?
IBLIS.
LONG AGO...
...WHEN OUR METHUSELAN GRANDPARENTS STILL FIERCELY BATTLED THE TERRAN...
...THE IBLIS WAS A TERRAN WEAPON.
OR RATHER...

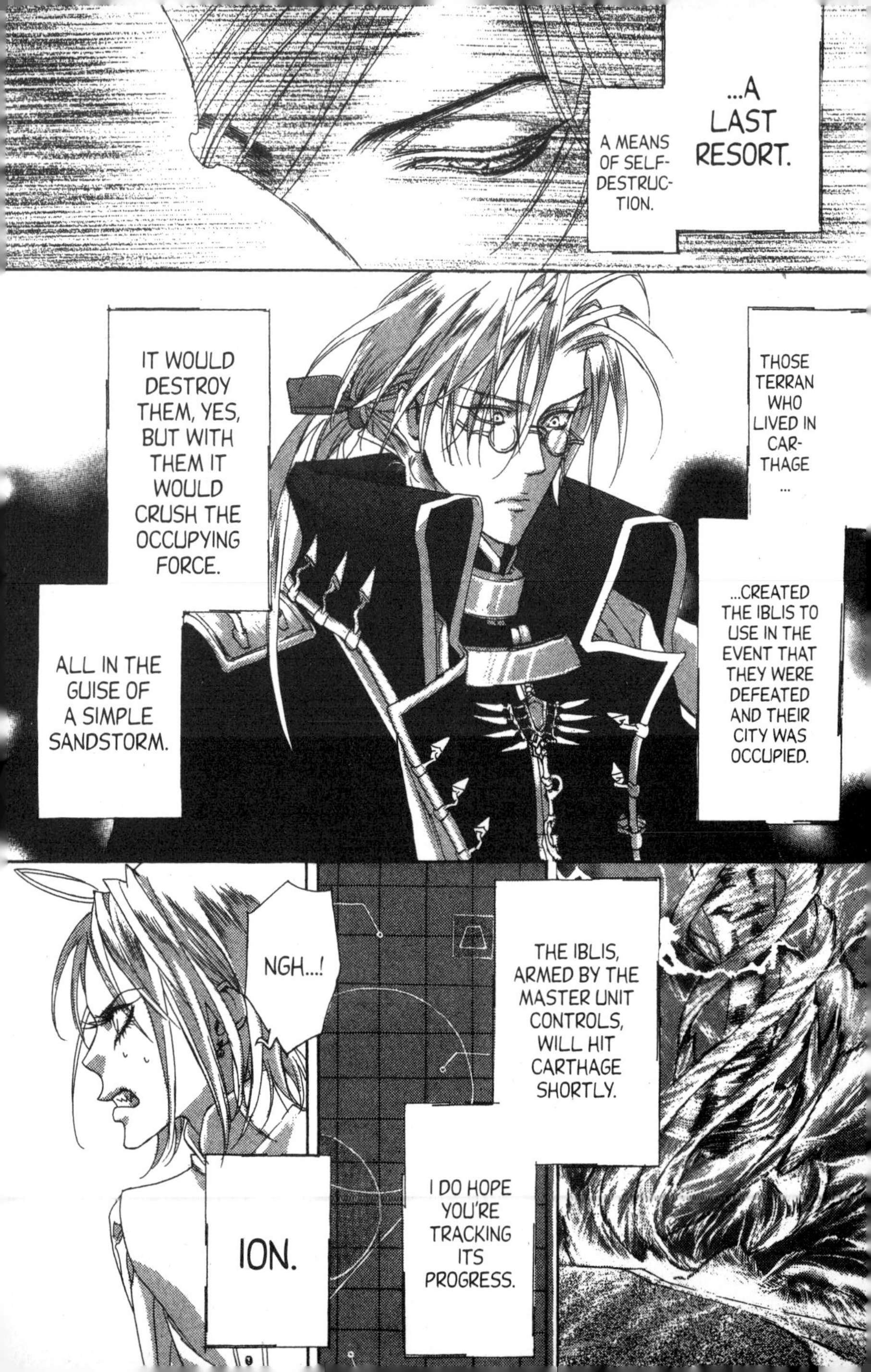
...A LAST RESORT.
A MEANS OF SELF-DESTRUCTION.
THOSE TERRAN WHO LIVED IN CARTHAGE ...
...CREATED THE IBLIS TO USE IN THE EVENT THAT THEY WERE DEFEATED AND THEIR CITY WAS OCCUPIED.
IT WOULD DESTROY THEM, YES, BUT WITH THEM IT WOULD CRUSH THE OCCUPYING FORCE.
ALL IN THE GUISE OF A SIMPLE SANDSTORM.
THE IBLIS, ARMED BY THE MASTER UNIT CONTROLS, WILL HIT CARTHAGE SHORTLY.
I DO HOPE YOU'RE TRACKING ITS PROGRESS.
NGH...!
ION.

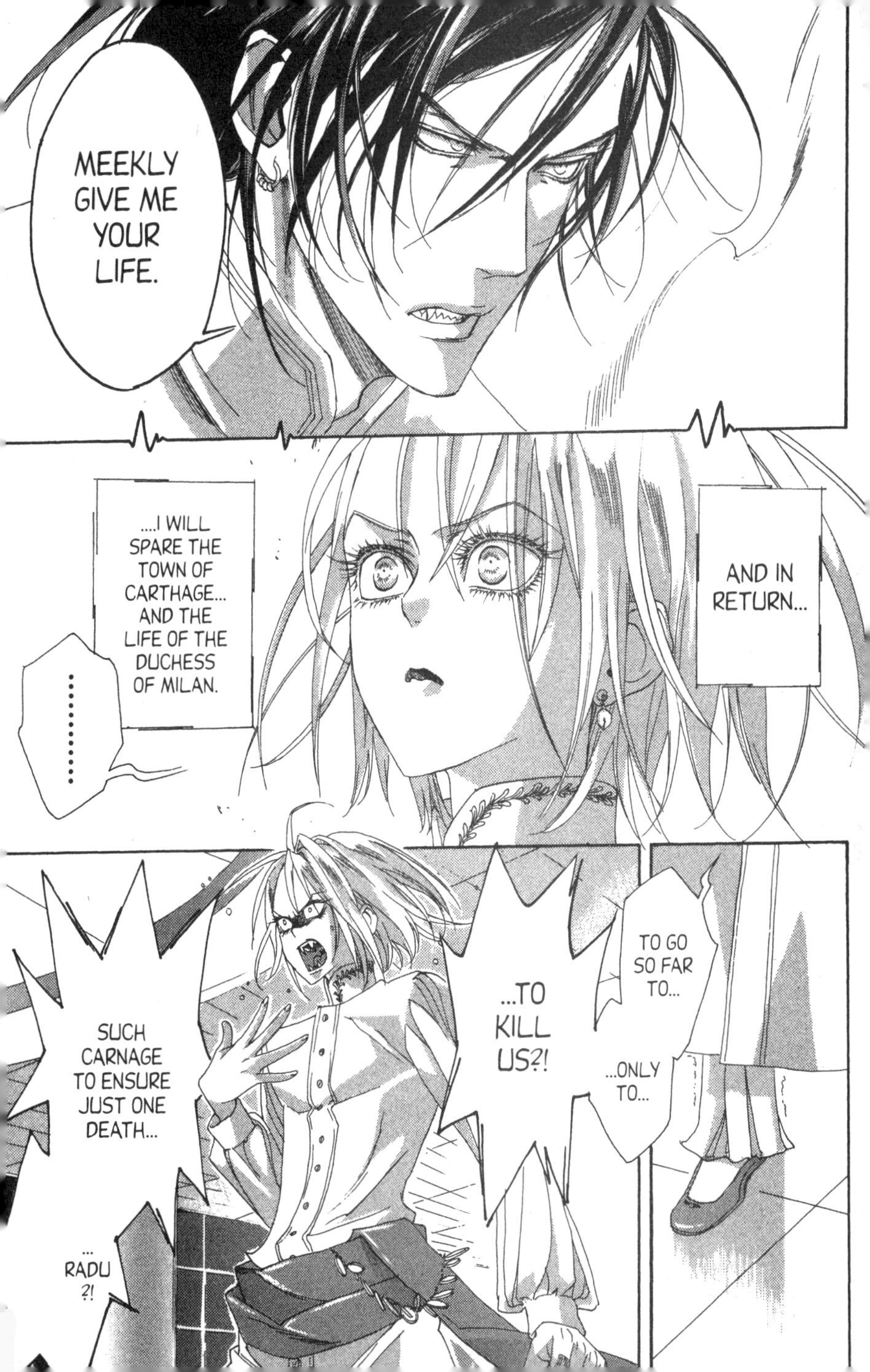
MEEKLY GIVE ME YOUR LIFE.
AND IN RETURN...
....I WILL SPARE THE TOWN OF CARTHAGE... AND THE LIFE OF THE DUCHESS OF MILAN.
....
TO GO SO FAR TO...
...ONLY TO...
...TO KILL US?!
SUCH CARNAGE TO ENSURE JUST ONE DEATH...
... RADU ?!

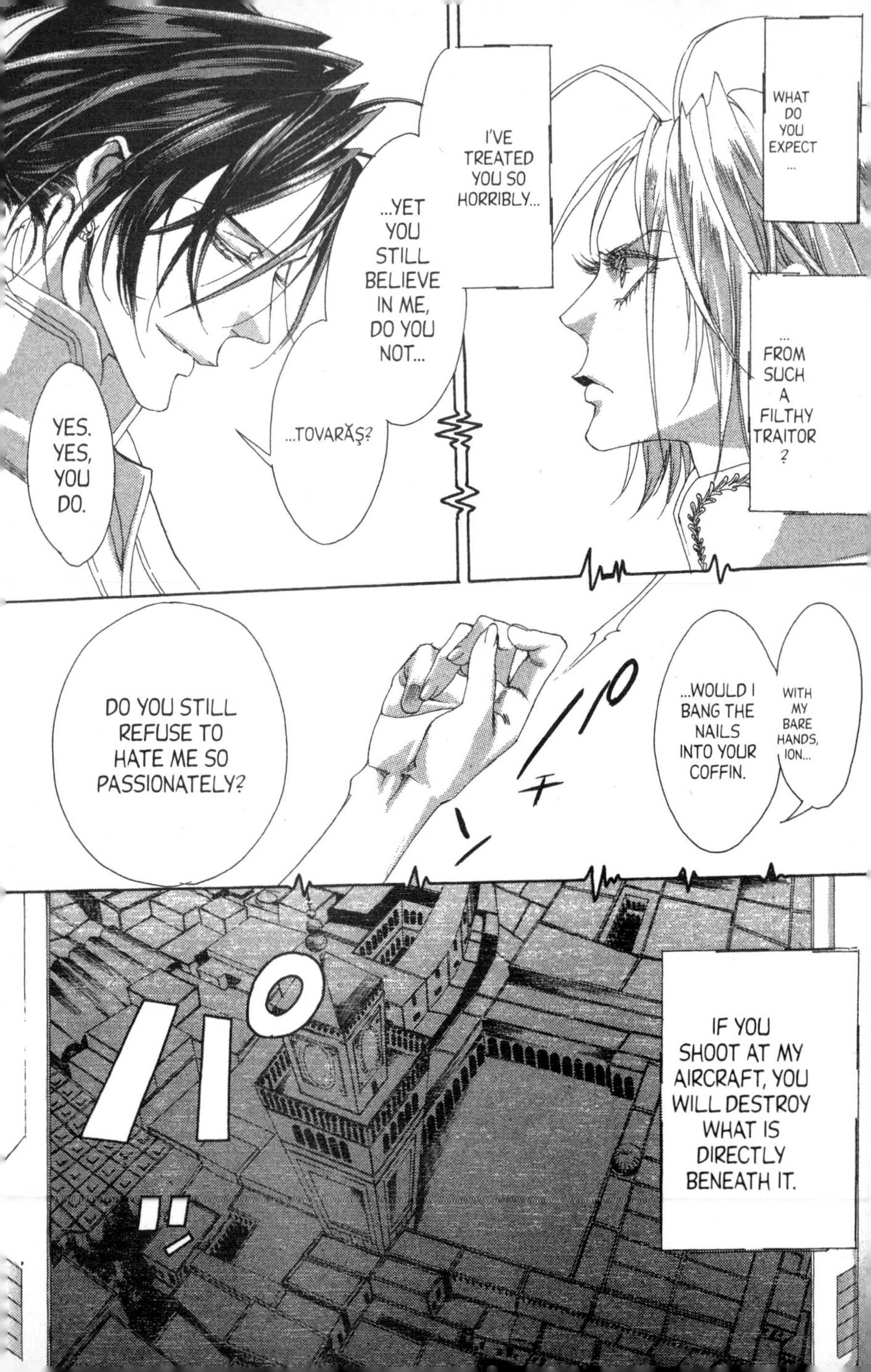
WHAT DO YOU EXPECT ...
... FROM SUCH A FILTHY TRAITOR?
I'VE TREATED YOU SO HORRIBLY...
...YET YOU STILL BELIEVE IN ME, DO YOU NOT...
...TOVARĂŞ?
YES. YES, YOU DO.
WITH MY BARE HANDS, ION...
...WOULD I BANG THE NAILS INTO YOUR COFFIN.
DO YOU STILL REFUSE TO HATE ME SO PASSIONATELY?
IF YOU SHOOT AT MY AIRCRAFT, YOU WILL DESTROY WHAT IS DIRECTLY BENEATH IT.

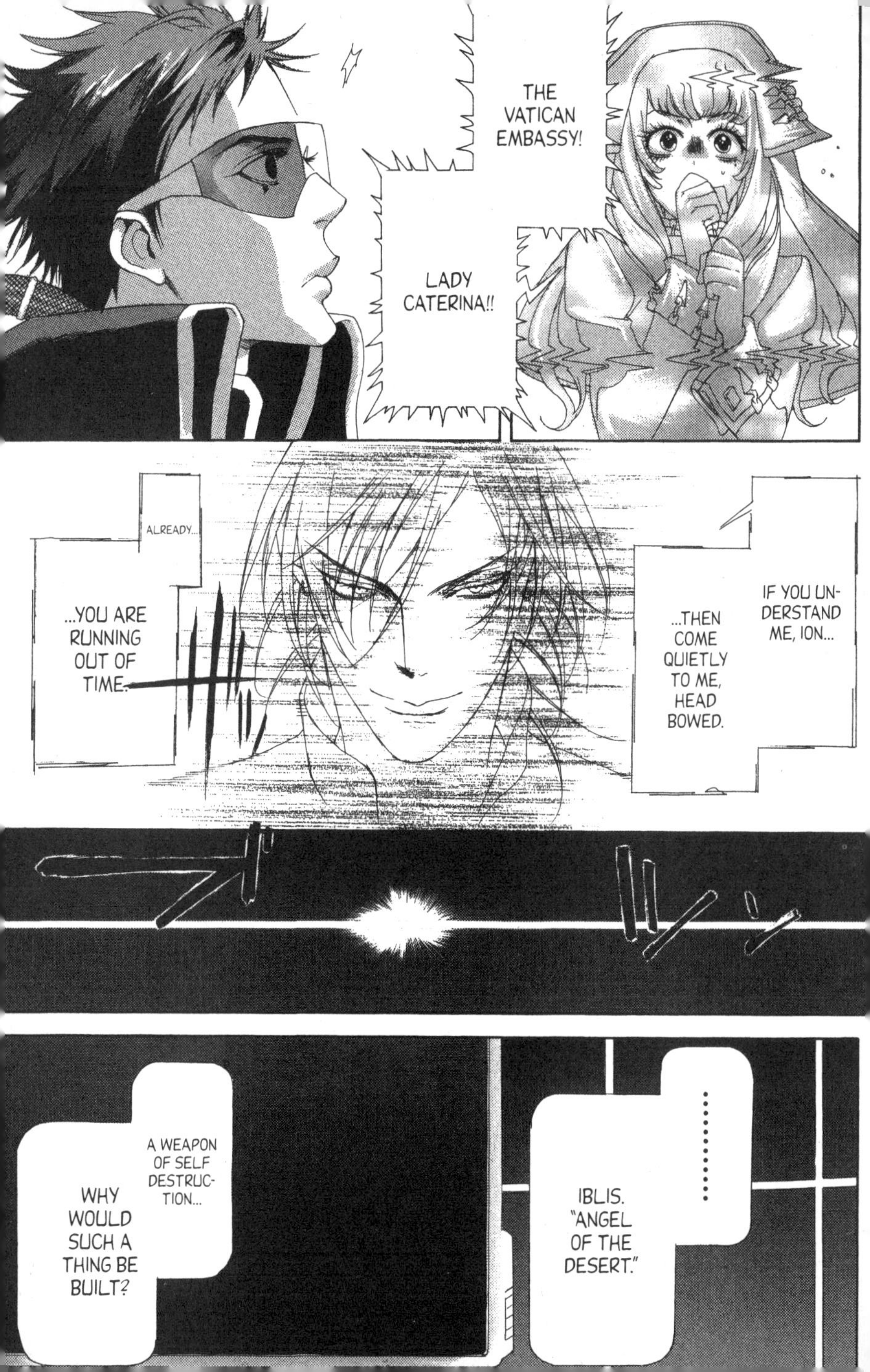
THE VATICAN EMBASSY!
LADY CATERINA!!
IF YOU UNDERSTAND ME, ION...
...THEN COME QUIETLY TO ME, HEAD BOWED.
ALREADY...
...YOU ARE RUNNING OUT OF TIME.
....
IBLIS. "ANGEL OF THE DESERT."
A WEAPON OF SELF DESTRUCTION...
WHY WOULD SUCH A THING BE BUILT?

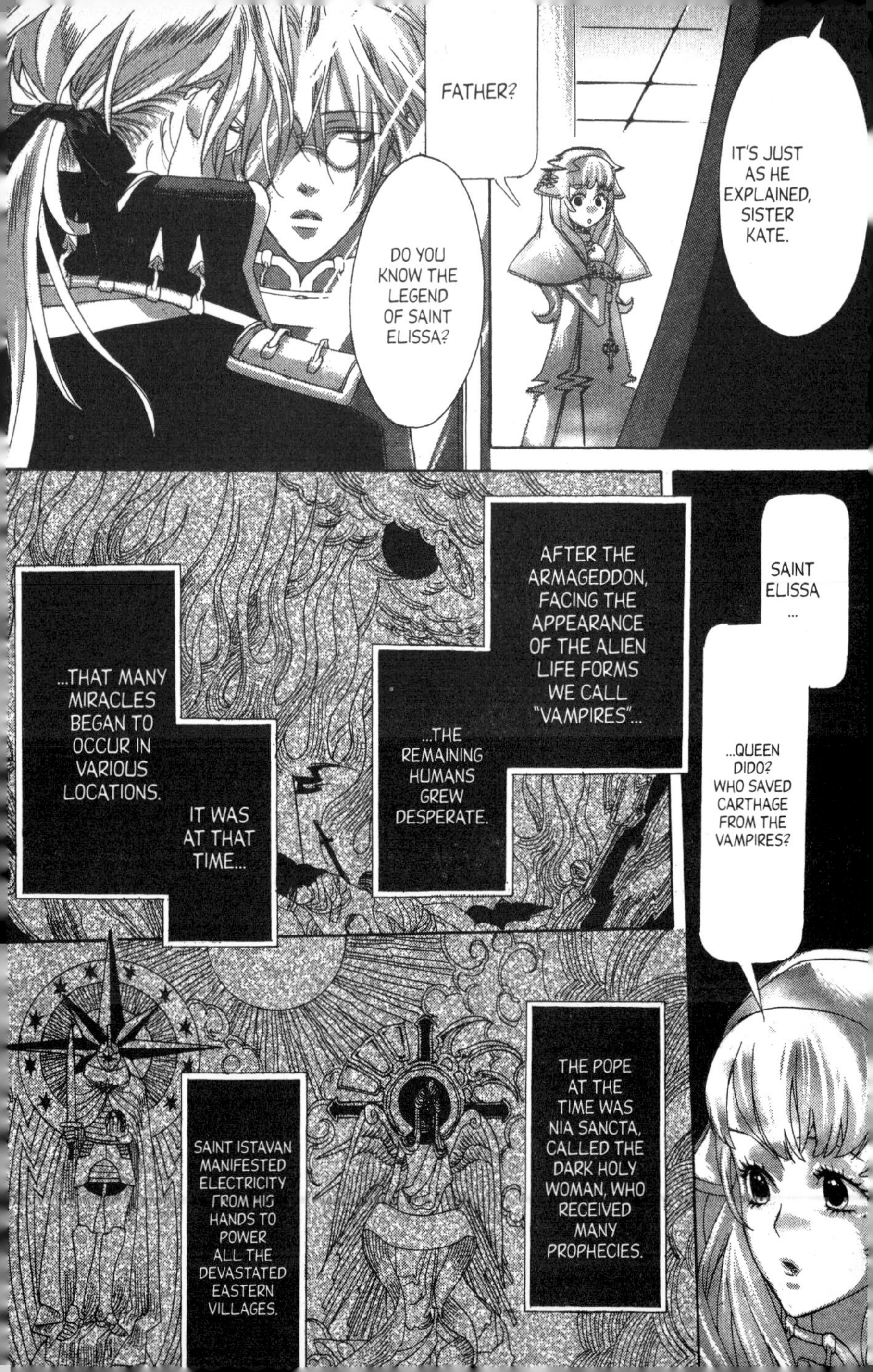
IT'S JUST AS HE EXPLAINED, SISTER KATE.
FATHER?
DO YOU KNOW THE LEGEND OF SAINT ELISSA?
SAINT ELISSA ...
...QUEEN DIDO? WHO SAVED CARTHAGE FROM THE VAMPIRES?
AFTER THE ARMAGEDDON, FACING THE APPEARANCE OF THE ALIEN LIFE FORMS WE CALL "VAMPIRES"...
...THE REMAINING HUMANS GREW DESPERATE.
IT WAS AT THAT TIME...
...THAT MANY MIRACLES BEGAN TO OCCUR IN VARIOUS LOCATIONS.
THE POPE AT THE TIME WAS NIA SANCTA, CALLED THE DARK HOLY WOMAN, WHO RECEIVED MANY PROPHECIES.
SAINT ISTAVAN MANIFESTED ELECTRICITY FROM HIS HANDS TO POWER ALL THE DEVASTATED EASTERN VILLAGES.

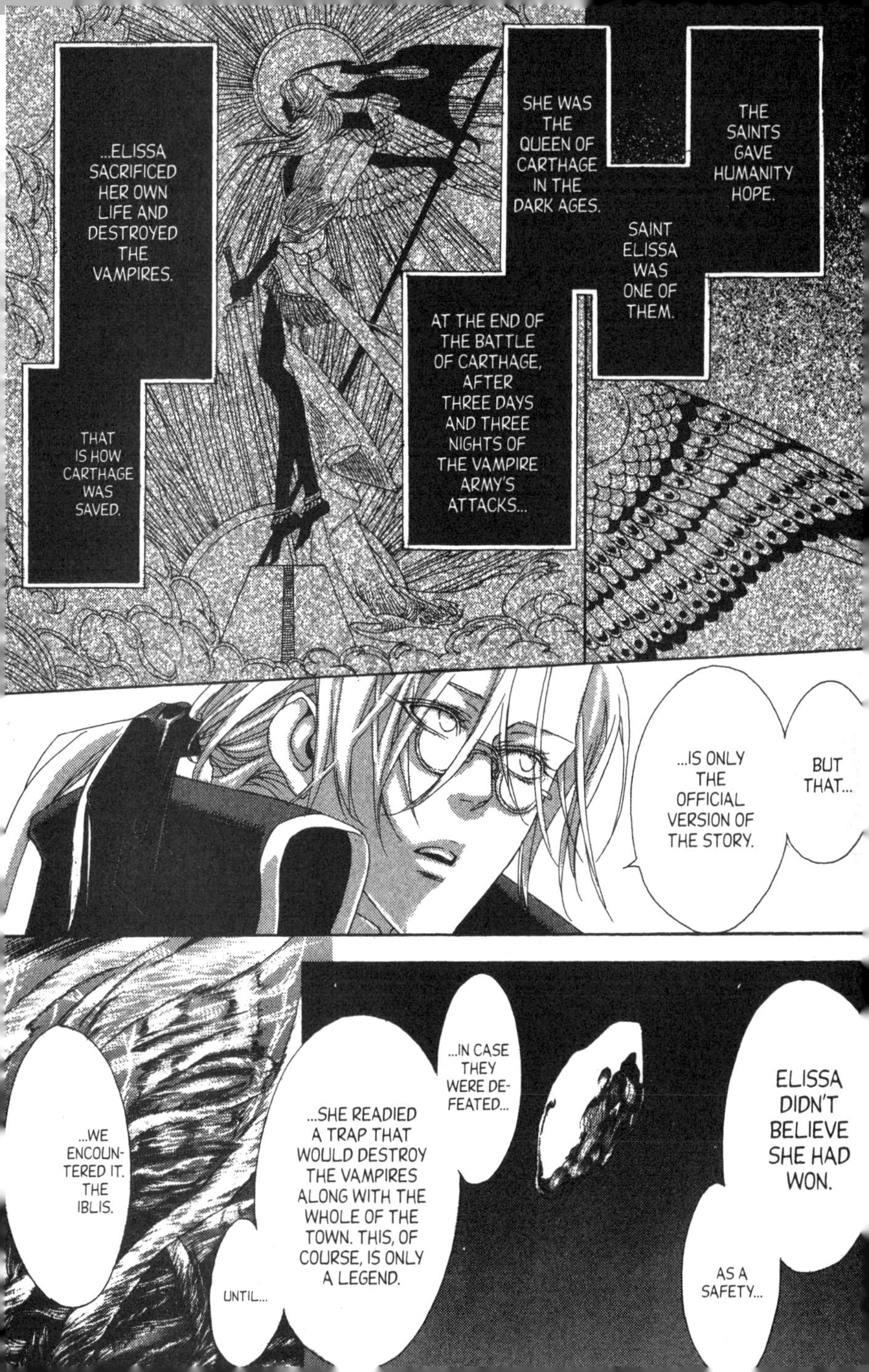
THE SAINTS GAVE HUMANITY HOPE.
SAINT ELISSA WAS ONE OF THEM.
SHE WAS THE QUEEN OF CARTHAGE IN THE DARK AGES.
AT THE END OF THE BATTLE OF CARTHAGE, AFTER THREE DAYS AND THREE NIGHTS OF THE VAMPIRE ARMY'S ATTACKS...
...ELISSA SACRIFICED HER OWN LIFE AND DESTROYED THE VAMPIRES.
THAT IS HOW CARTHAGE WAS SAVED.
BUT THAT...
...IS ONLY THE OFFICIAL VERSION OF THE STORY.
ELISSA DIDN'T BELIEVE SHE HAD WON.
AS A SAFETY...
...IN CASE THEY WERE DE-FEATED...
...SHE READIED A TRAP THAT WOULD DESTROY THE VAMPIRES ALONG WITH THE WHOLE OF THE TOWN. THIS, OF COURSE, IS ONLY A LEGEND.
UNTIL...
...WE ENCOUN-TERED IT. THE IBLIS.

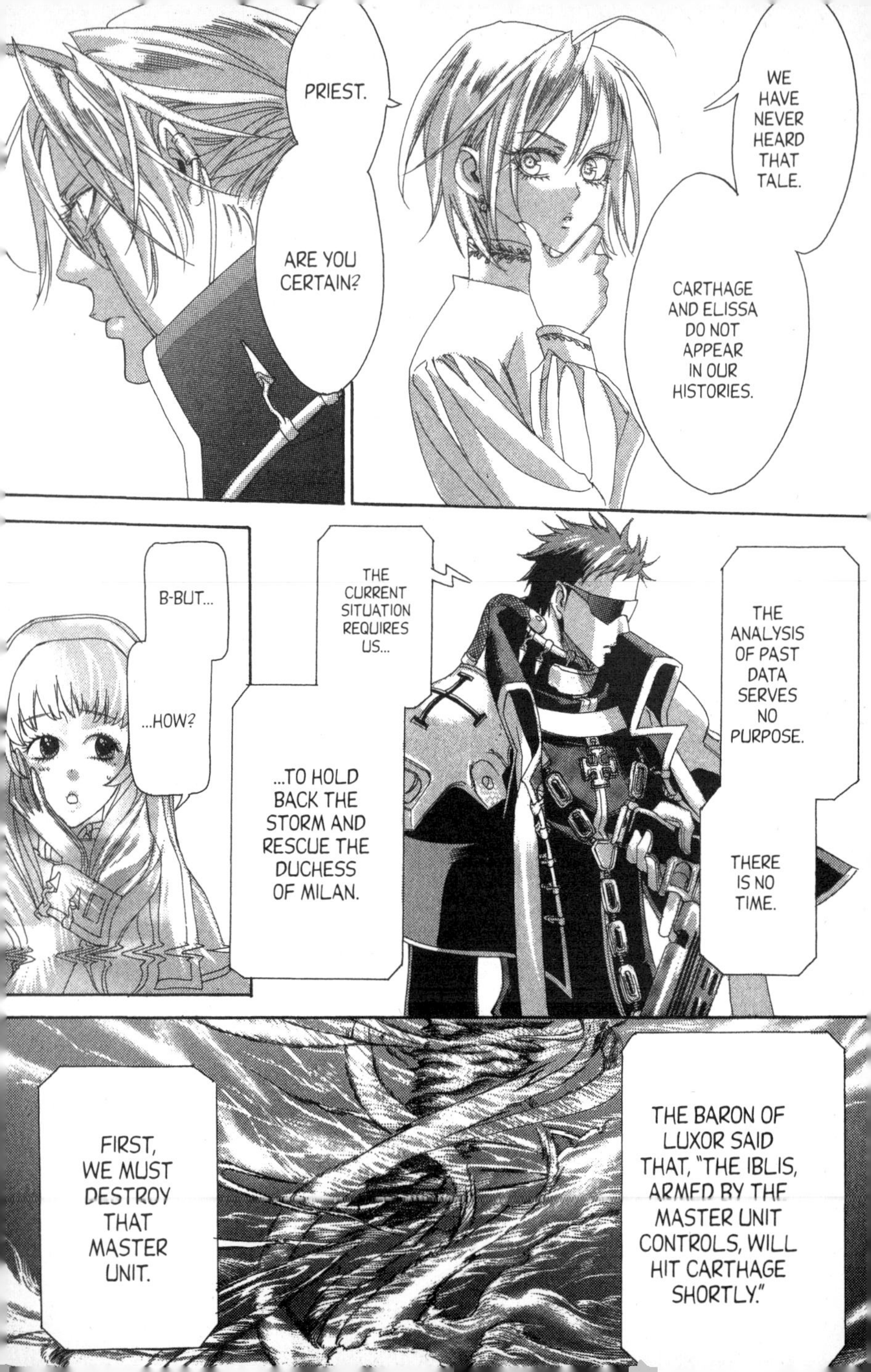
WE HAVE NEVER HEARD THAT TALE.
CARTHAGE AND ELISSA DO NOT APPEAR IN OUR HISTORIES.
PRIEST.
ARE YOU CERTAIN?
THE ANALYSIS OF PAST DATA SERVES NO PURPOSE.
THERE IS NO TIME.
THE CURRENT SITUATION REQUIRES US...
...TO HOLD BACK THE STORM AND RESCUE THE DUCHESS OF MILAN.
B-BUT...
...HOW?
THE BARON OF LUXOR SAID THAT, "THE IBLIS, ARMED BY THE MASTER UNIT CONTROLS, WILL HIT CARTHAGE SHORTLY."
FIRST, WE MUST DESTROY THAT MASTER UNIT.

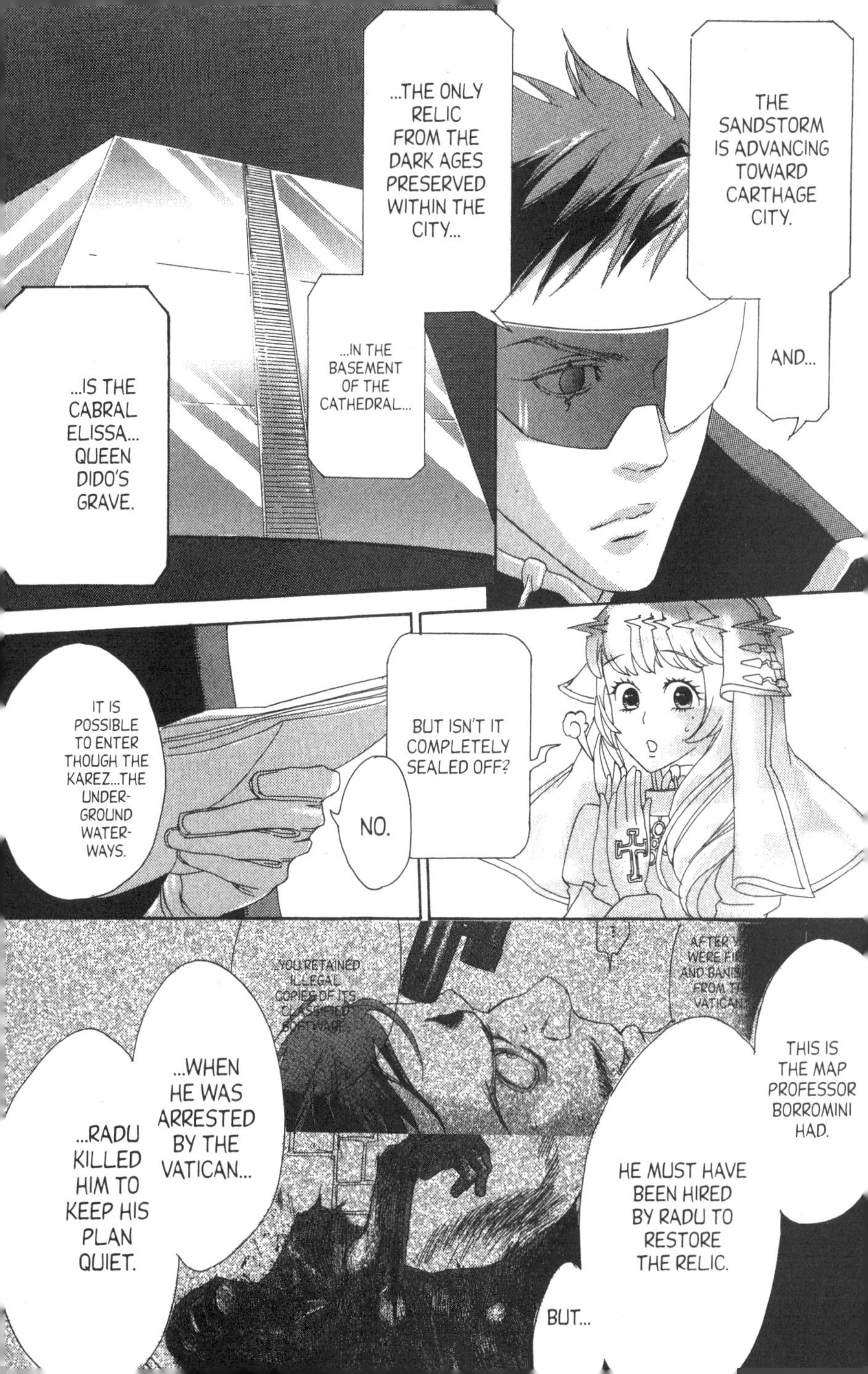
THE SANDSTORM IS ADVANCING TOWARD CARTHAGE CITY.
AND...
...THE ONLY RELIC FROM THE DARK AGES PRESERVED WITHIN THE CITY...
...IN THE BASEMENT OF THE CATHEDRAL...
...IS THE CABRAL ELISSA... QUEEN DIDO'S GRAVE.
BUT ISN'T IT COMPLETELY SEALED OFF?
NO.
IT IS POSSIBLE TO ENTER THOUGH THE KAREZ...THE UNDER-GROUND WATER-WAYS.
THIS IS THE MAP PROFESSOR BORROMINI HAD.
...YOU RETAINED ILLEGAL COPIES OF ITS CLASSIFIED SOFTWARE...
HE MUST HAVE BEEN HIRED BY RADU TO RESTORE THE RELIC.
BUT...
...WHEN HE WAS ARRESTED BY THE VATICAN...
...RADU KILLED HIM TO KEEP HIS PLAN QUIET.

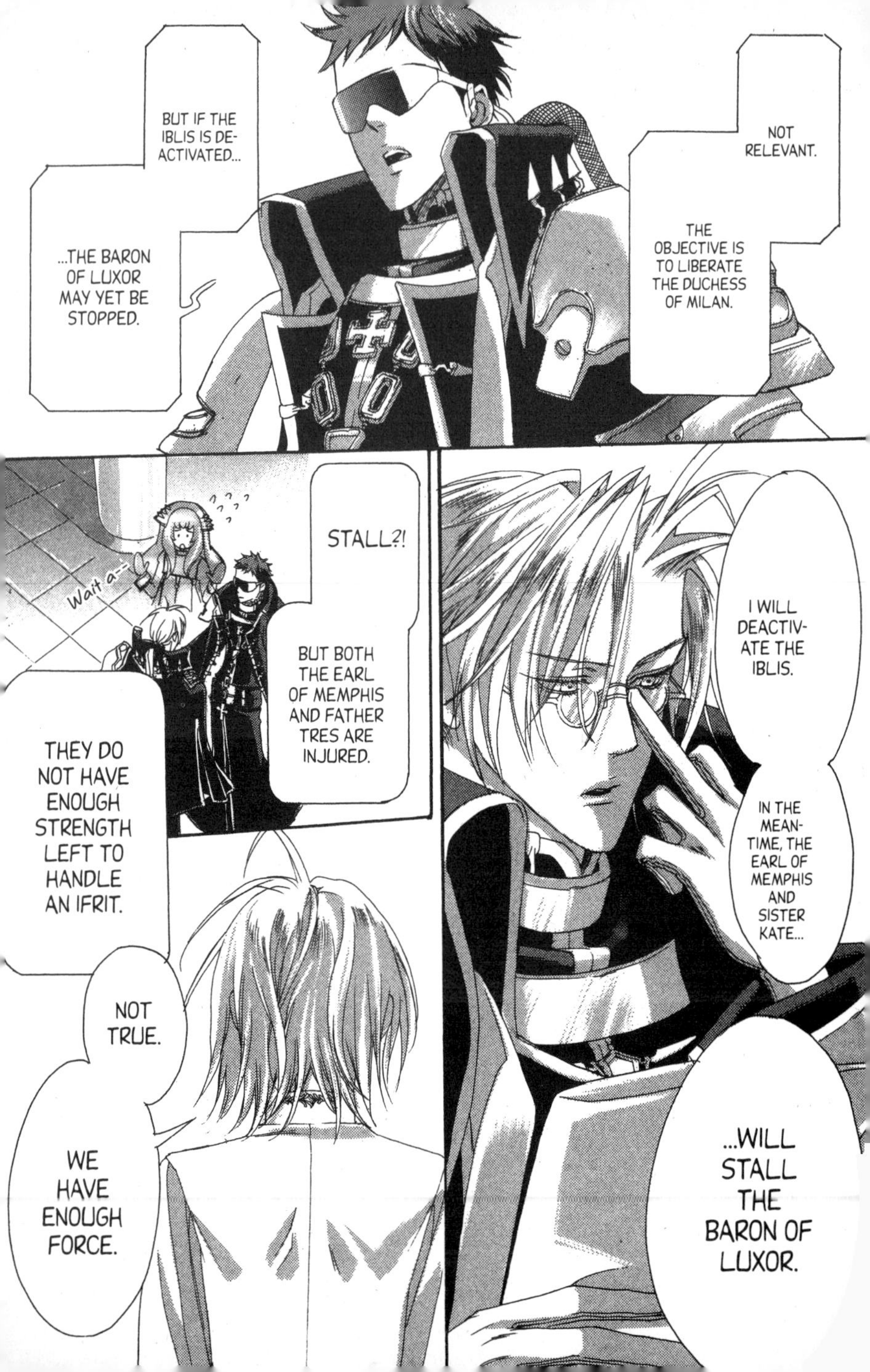
BUT IF THE IBLIS IS DE-ACTIVATED...
...THE BARON OF LUXOR MAY YET BE STOPPED.
NOT RELEVANT.
THE OBJECTIVE IS TO LIBERATE THE DUCHESS OF MILAN.
I WILL DEACTIV-ATE THE IBLIS.
IN THE MEAN-TIME, THE EARL OF MEMPHIS AND SISTER KATE...
...WILL STALL THE BARON OF LUXOR.
STALL?!
Wait a--
BUT BOTH THE EARL OF MEMPHIS AND FATHER TRES ARE INJURED.
THEY DO NOT HAVE ENOUGH STRENGTH LEFT TO HANDLE AN IFRIT.
NOT TRUE.
WE HAVE ENOUGH FORCE.

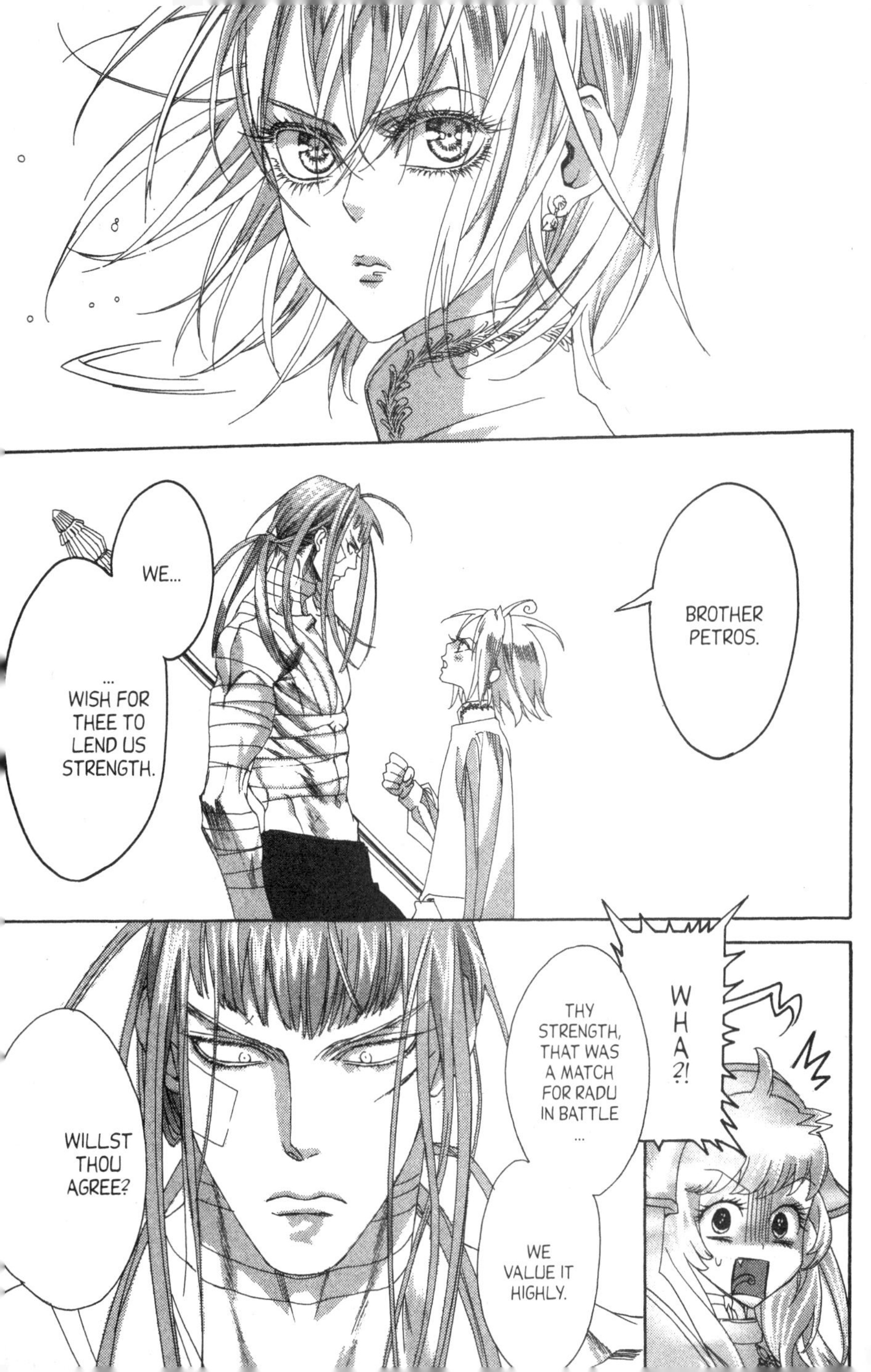
BROTHER PETROS.
WE...
... WISH FOR THEE TO LEND US STRENGTH.
THY STRENGTH, THAT WAS A MATCH FOR RADU IN BATTLE ...
WE VALUE IT HIGHLY.
WILLST THOU AGREE?
WHA?!

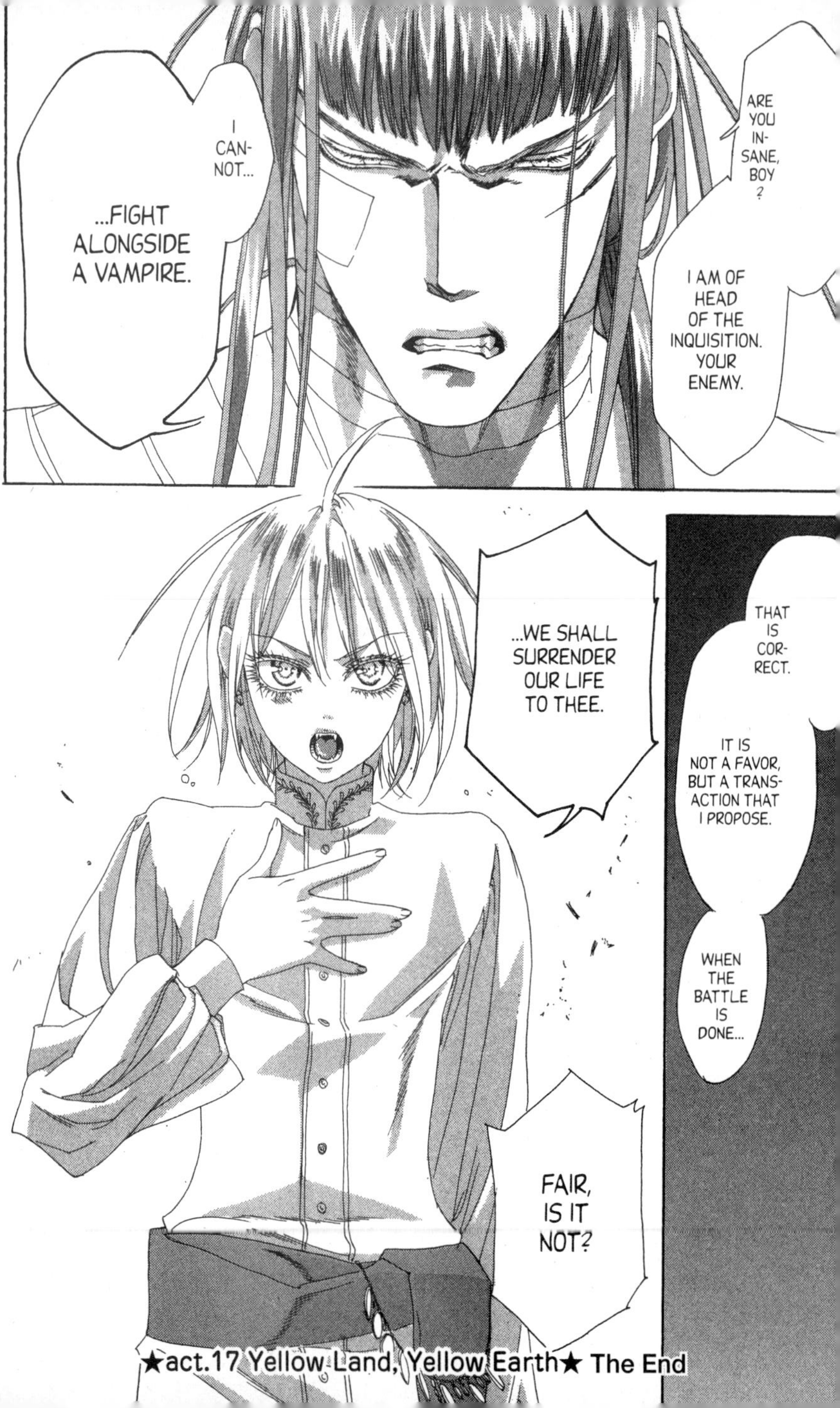
ARE YOU IN-SANE, BOY?
I AM OF HEAD OF THE INQUISITION. YOUR ENEMY.
I CAN-NOT...
...FIGHT ALONGSIDE A VAMPIRE.
THAT IS COR-RECT.
IT IS NOT A FAVOR, BUT A TRANS-ACTION THAT I PROPOSE.
WHEN THE BATTLE IS DONE...
...WE SHALL SURRENDER OUR LIFE TO THEE.
FAIR, IS IT NOT?

★act.17 Yellow Land, Yellow Earth★ The End

act.18 Santa Sangre

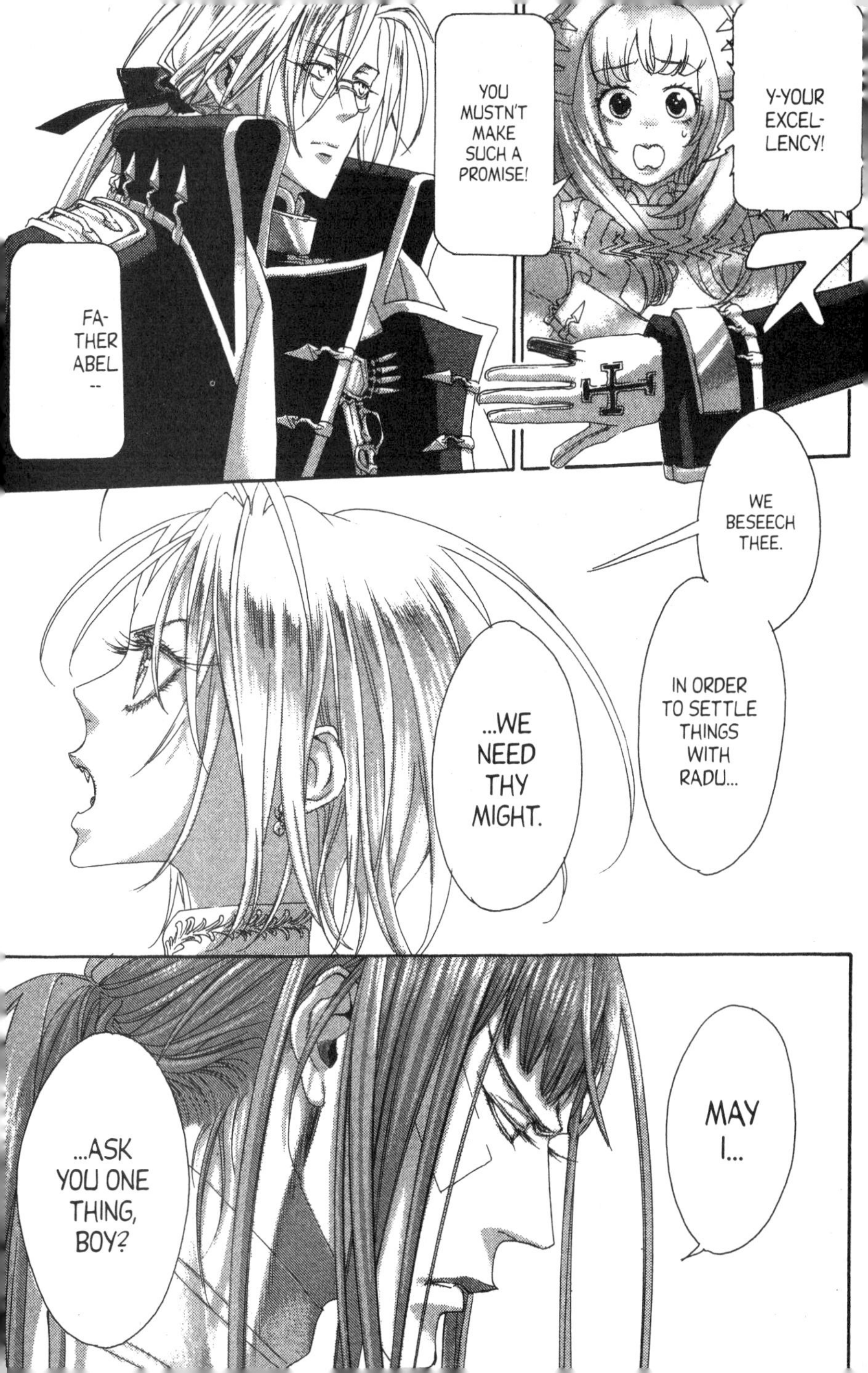
Y-YOUR EXCEL-LENCY!
YOU MUSTN'T MAKE SUCH A PROMISE!
FA-THER ABEL --
WE BESEECH THEE.
IN ORDER TO SETTLE THINGS WITH RADU...
...WE NEED THY MIGHT.
MAY I...
...ASK YOU ONE THING, BOY?

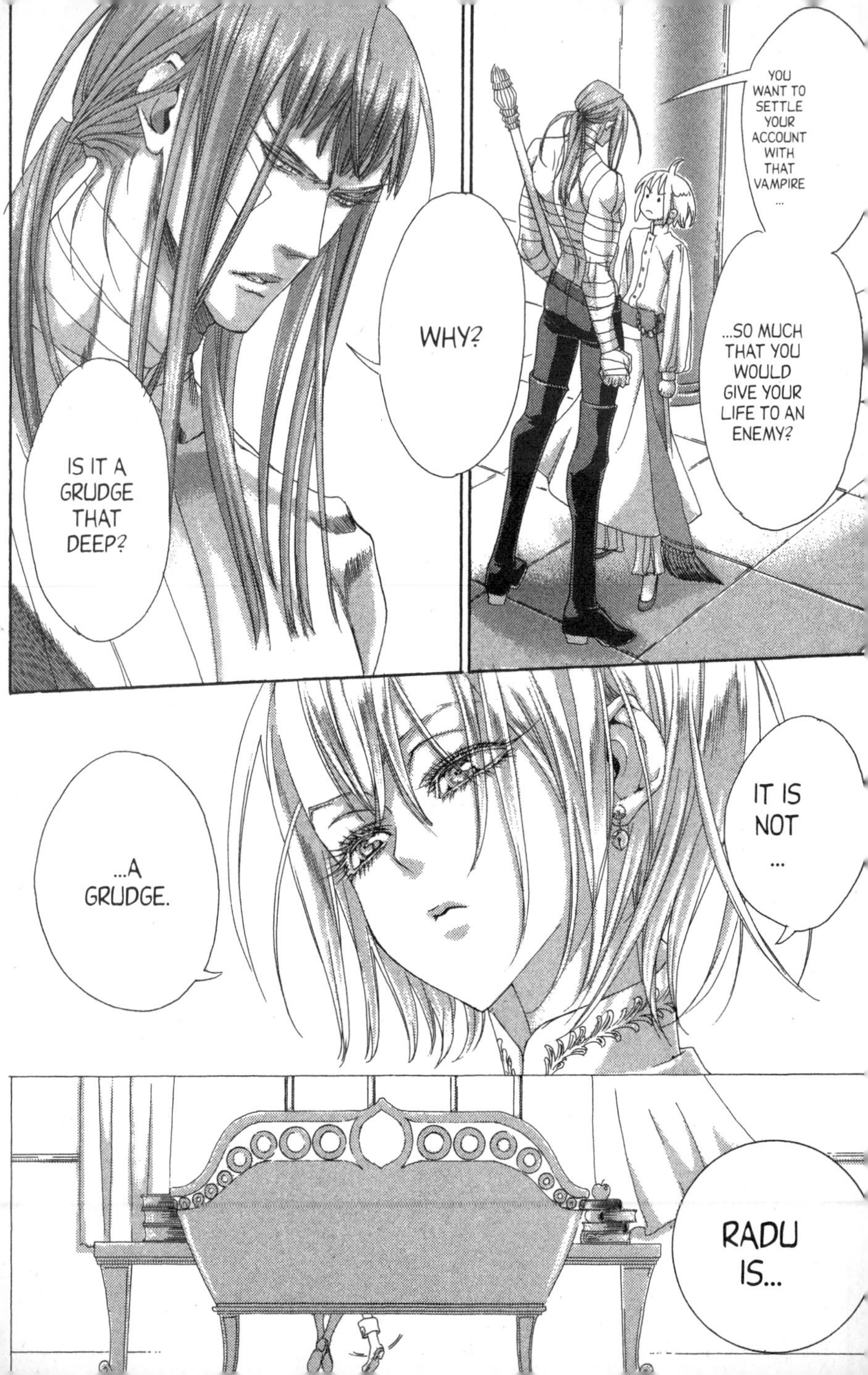
YOU WANT TO SETTLE YOUR ACCOUNT WITH THAT VAMPIRE ...
...SO MUCH THAT YOU WOULD GIVE YOUR LIFE TO AN ENEMY?
WHY?
IS IT A GRUDGE THAT DEEP?
IT IS NOT ...
...A GRUDGE.
RADU IS...

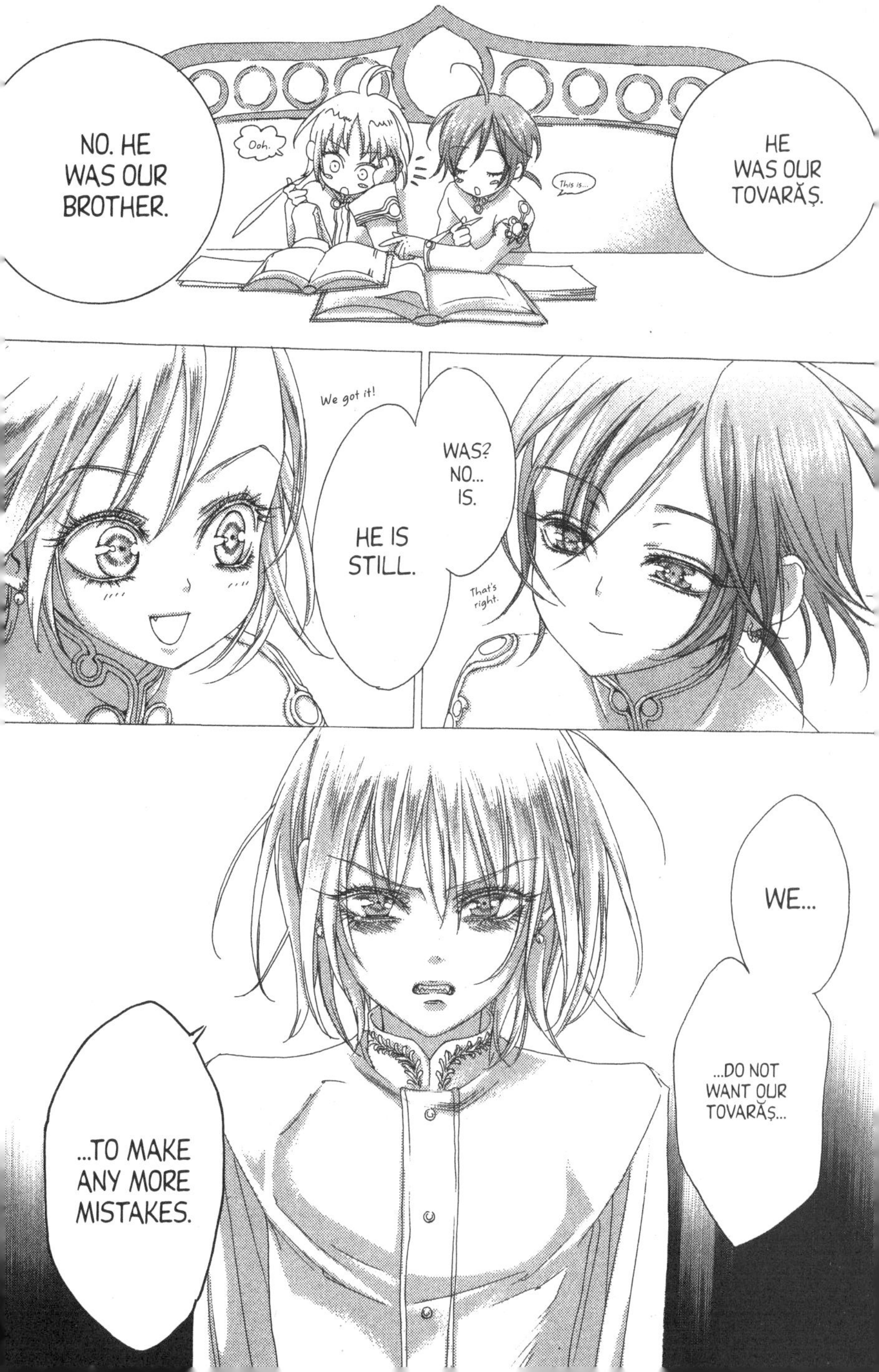
HE WAS OUR TOVARĂȘ.
This is...
Ooh.
NO. HE WAS OUR BROTHER.
WAS? NO... IS. HE IS STILL.
We got it!
That's right.
WE...
...DO NOT WANT OUR TOVARĂȘ...
...TO MAKE ANY MORE MISTAKES.

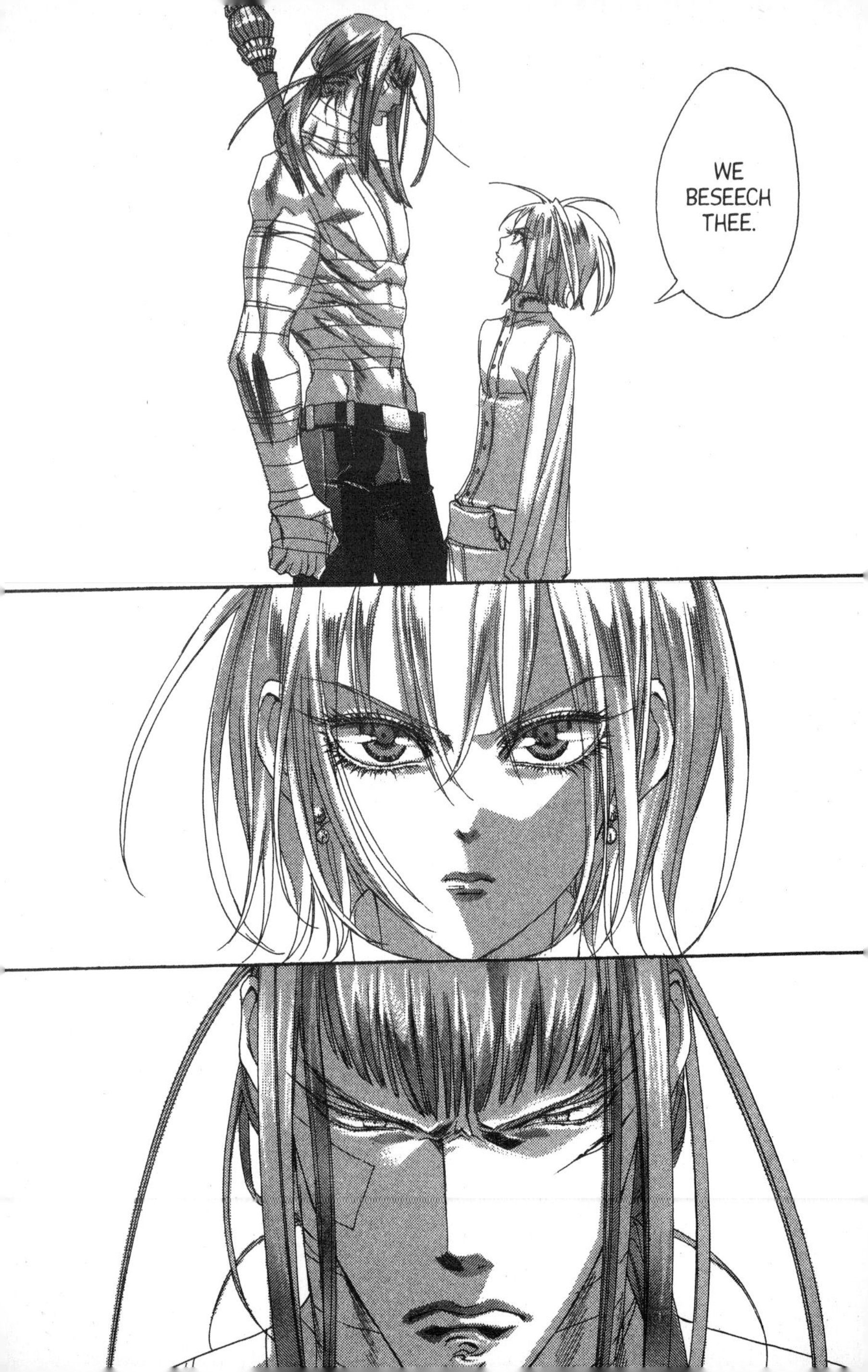
WE BESEECH THEE.

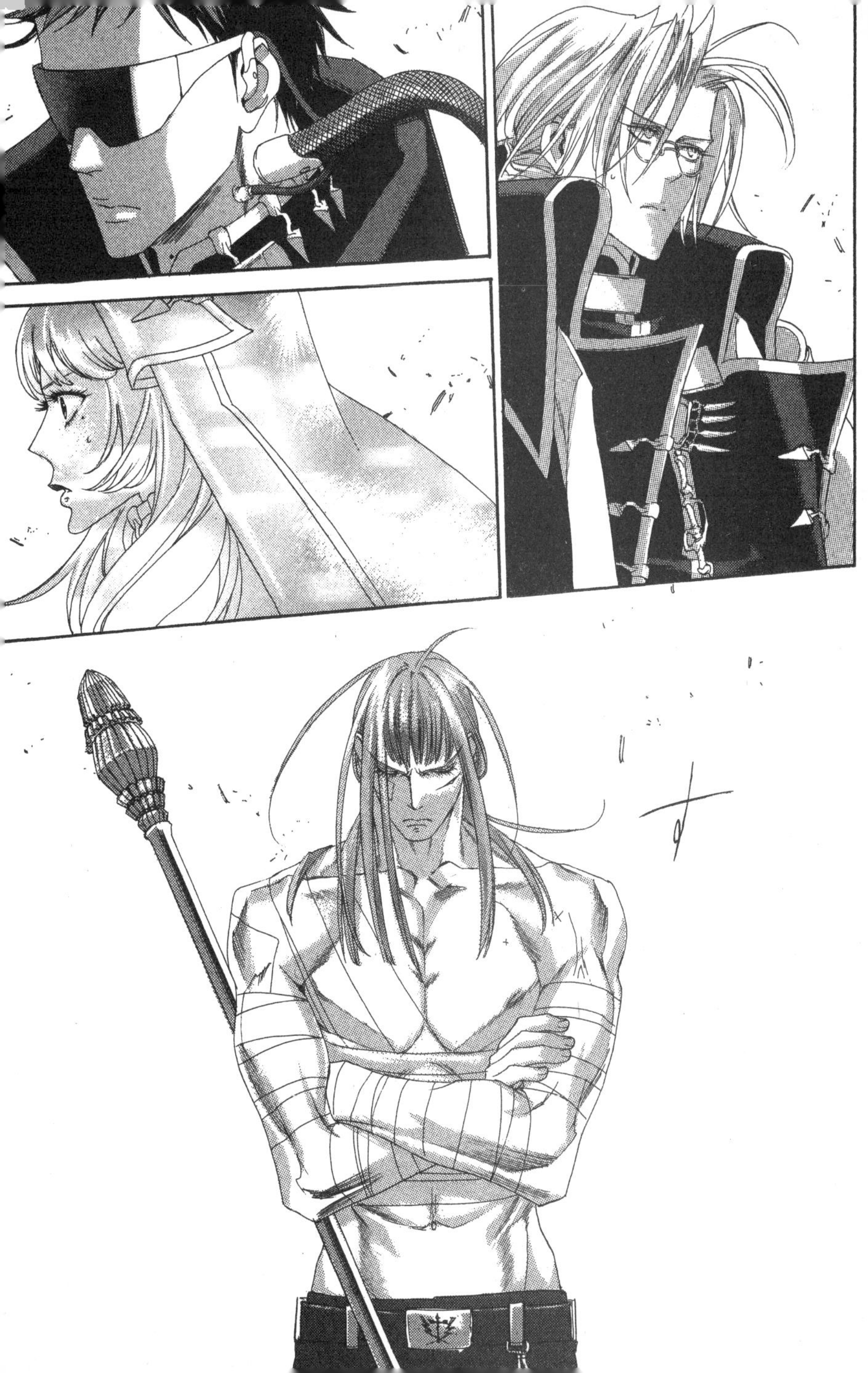

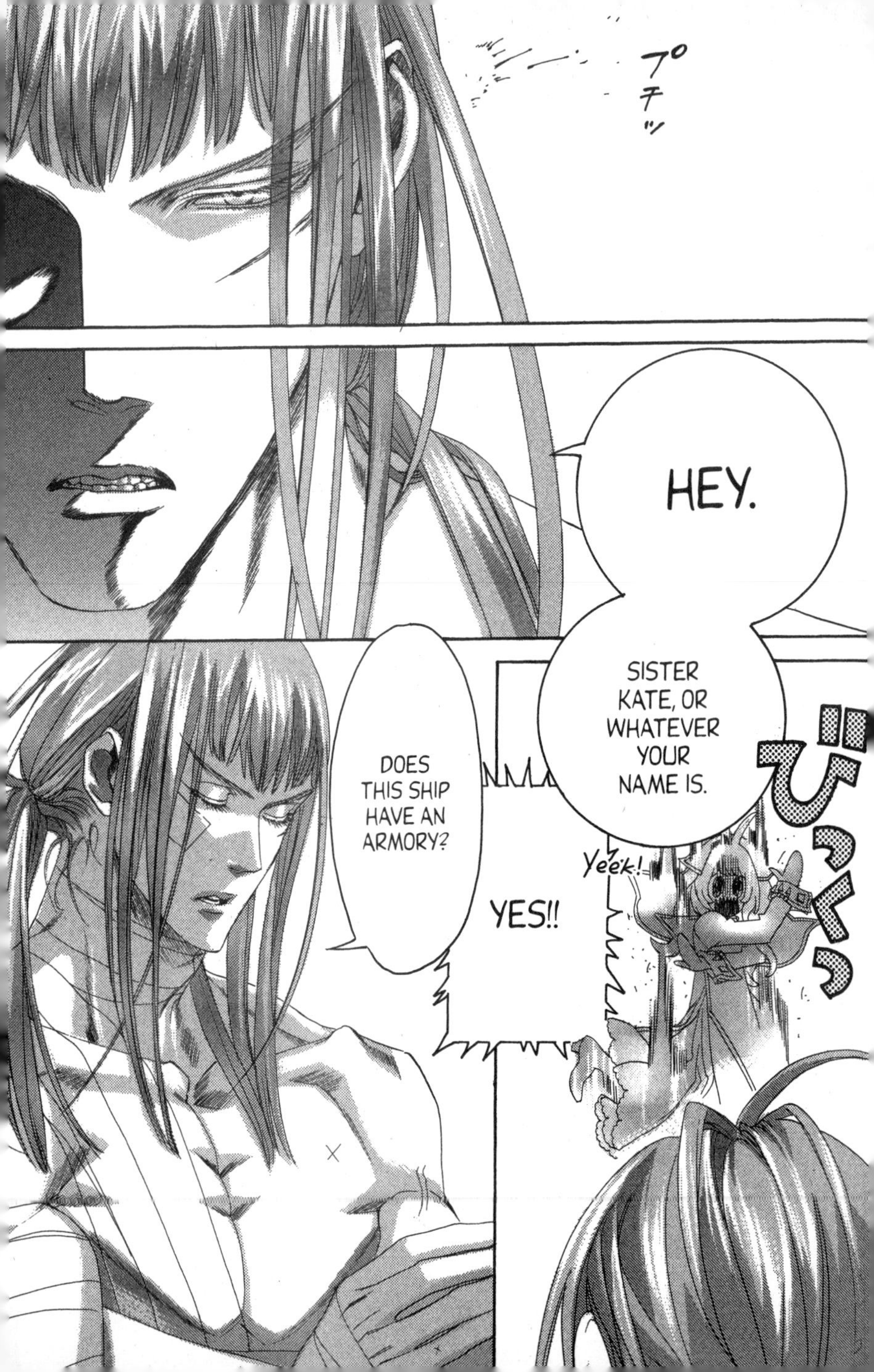
プチッ
HEY.
SISTER KATE, OR WHATEVER YOUR NAME IS.
Yeek!
YES!!
DOES THIS SHIP HAVE AN ARMORY?

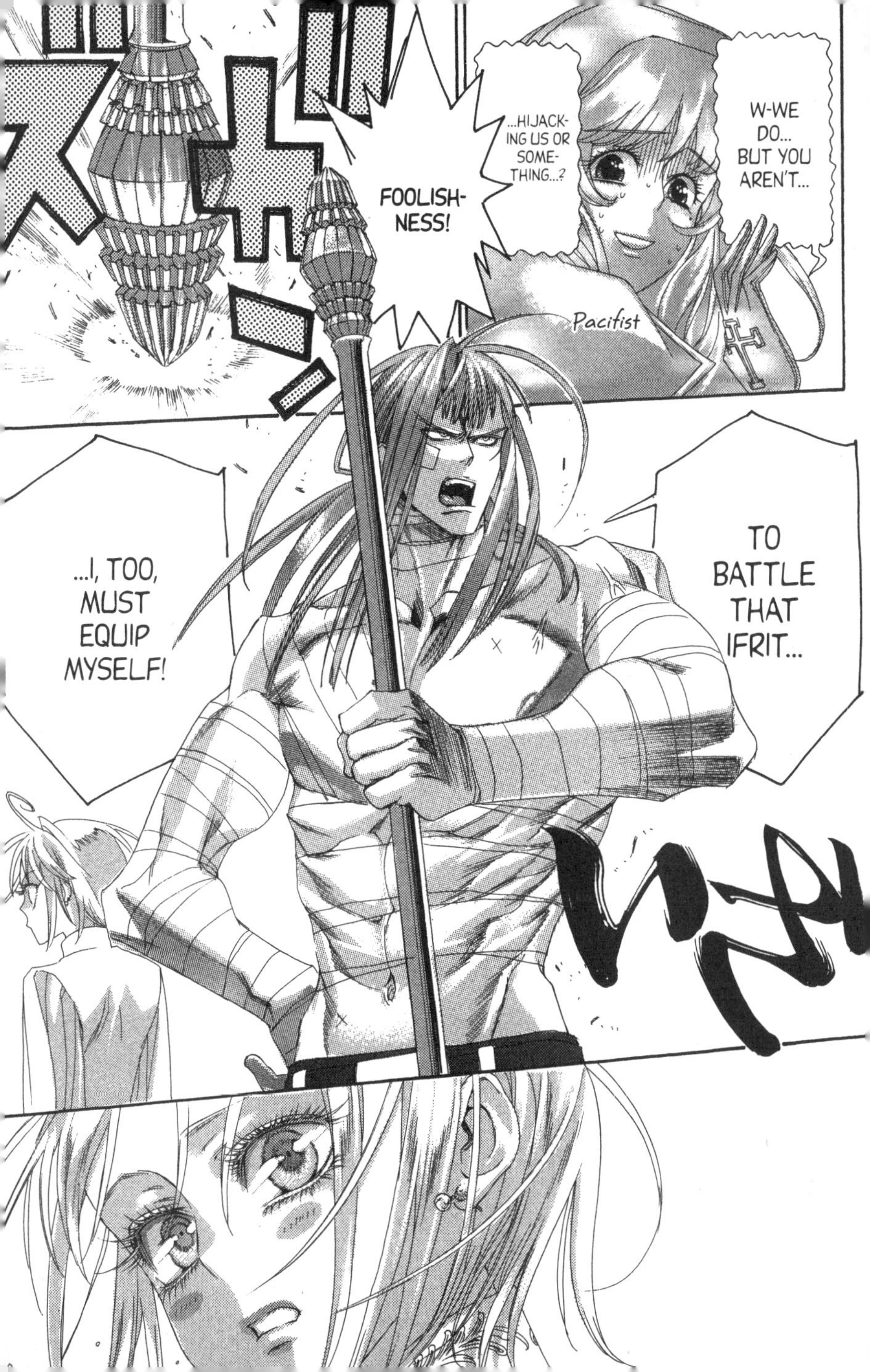
W-WE DO... BUT YOU AREN'T...
...HIJACKING US OR SOMETHING...?
Pacifist
FOOLISHNESS!
TO BATTLE THAT IFRIT...
...I, TOO, MUST EQUIP MYSELF!

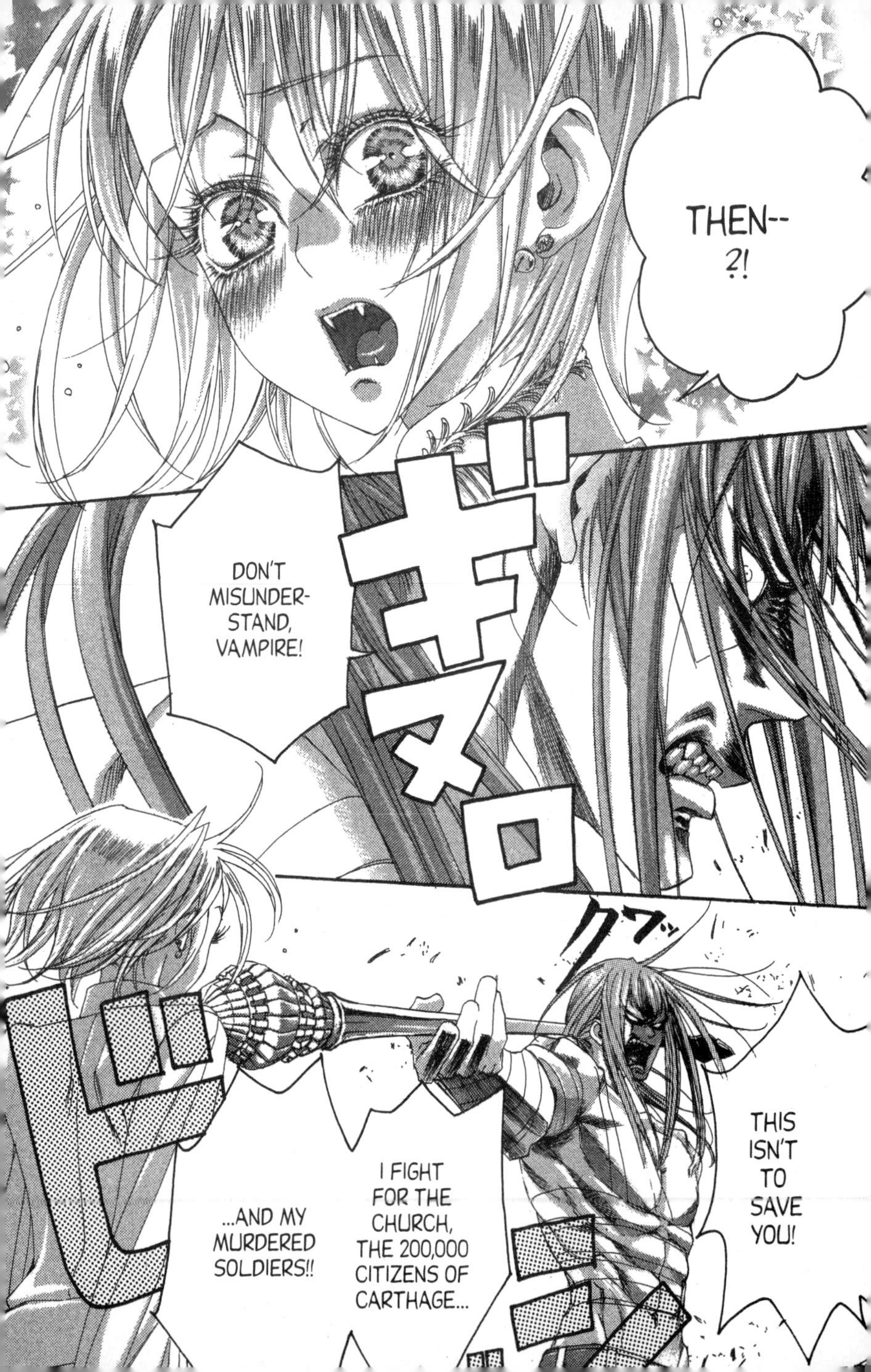
THEN-- ?!
ギロ
DON'T MISUNDERSTAND, VAMPIRE!
クワッ
THIS ISN'T TO SAVE YOU!
I FIGHT FOR THE CHURCH, THE 200,000 CITIZENS OF CARTHAGE...
...AND MY MURDERED SOLDIERS!!

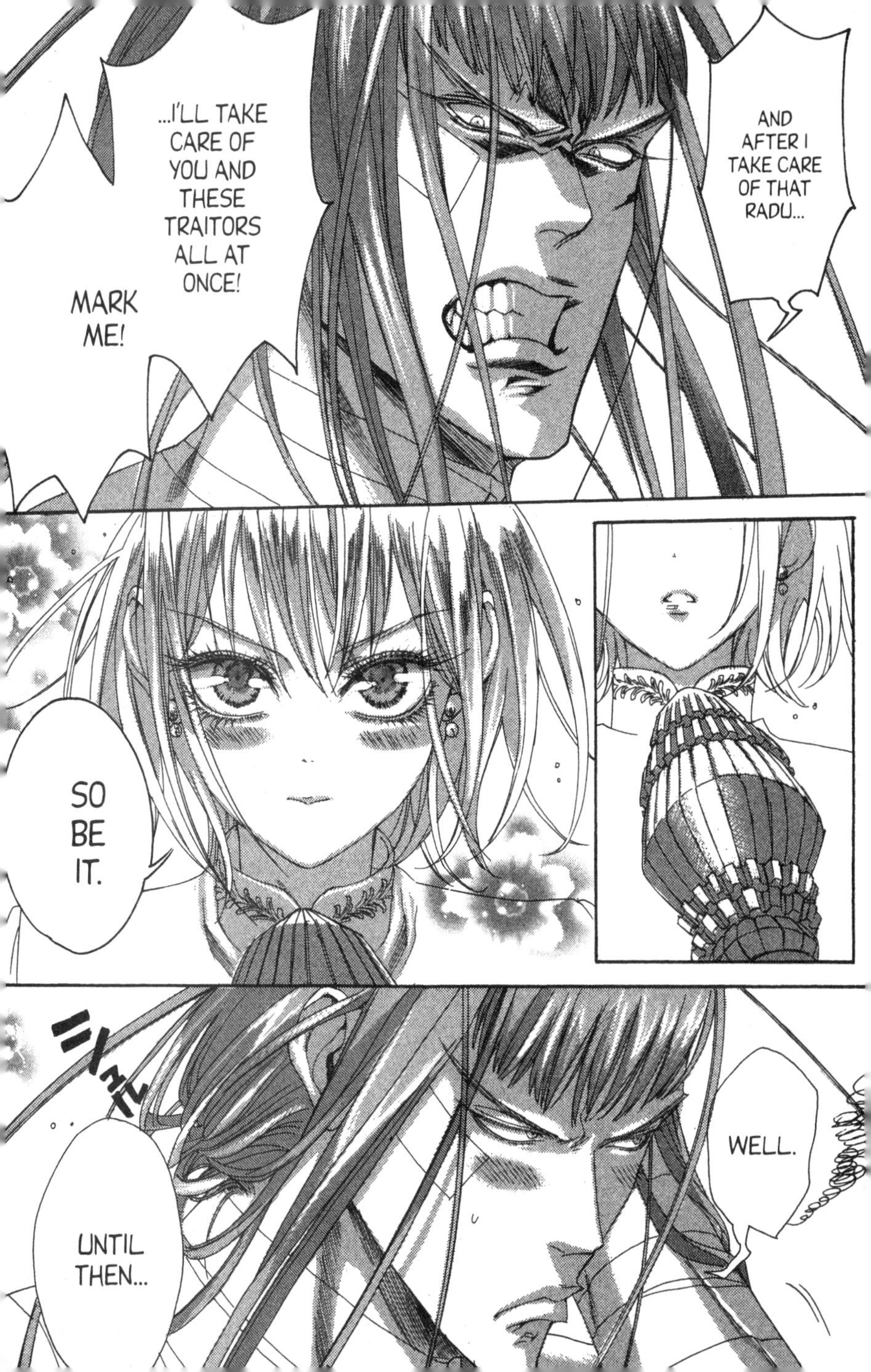
AND AFTER I TAKE CARE OF THAT RADU...
...I'LL TAKE CARE OF YOU AND THESE TRAITORS ALL AT ONCE!
MARK ME!
SO BE IT.
WELL.
UNTIL THEN...

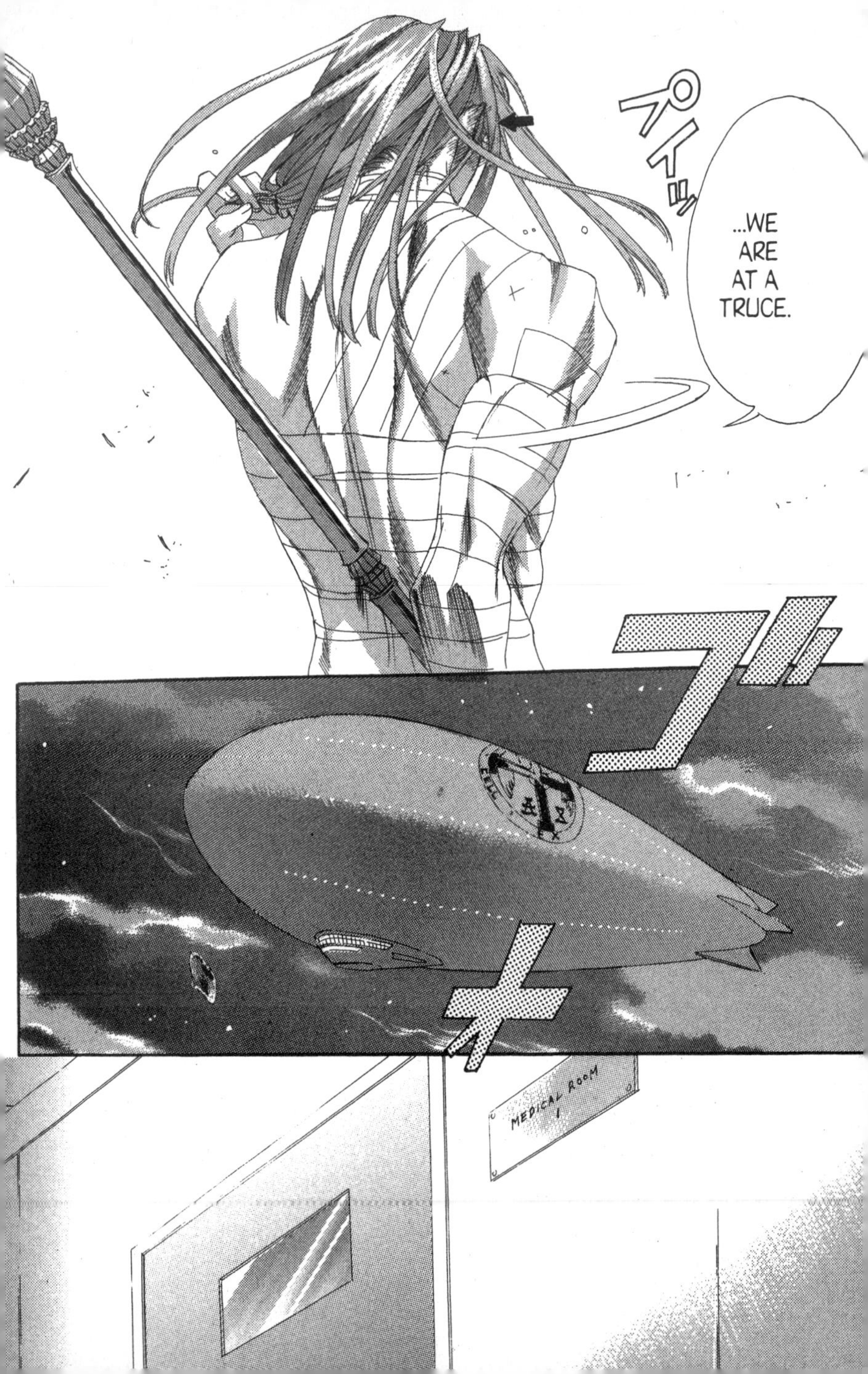
...WE ARE AT A TRUCE.
MEDICAL ROOM 1

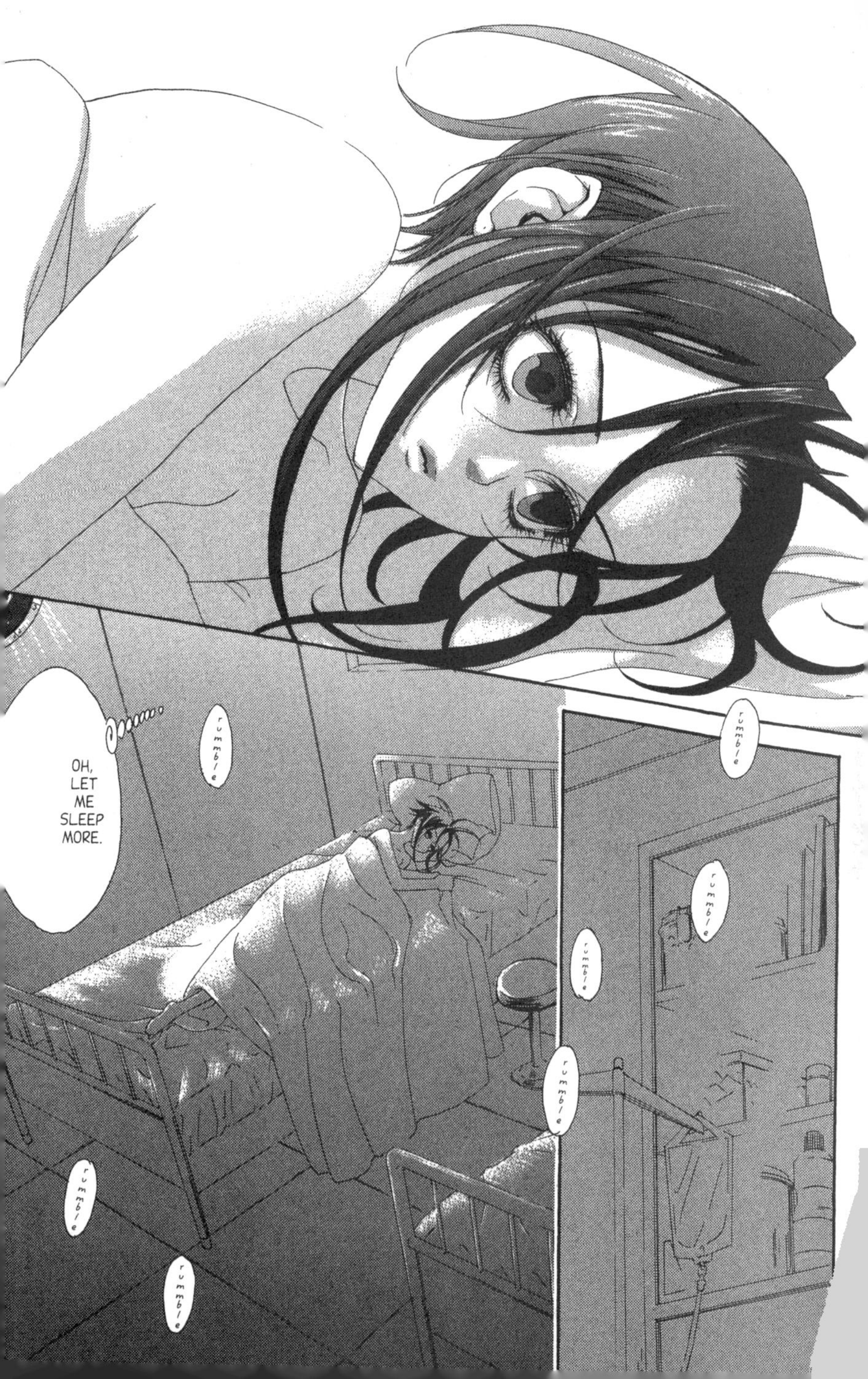
rumble
rumble
rumble
rumble
rumble
OH, LET ME SLEEP MORE.
rumble
rumble

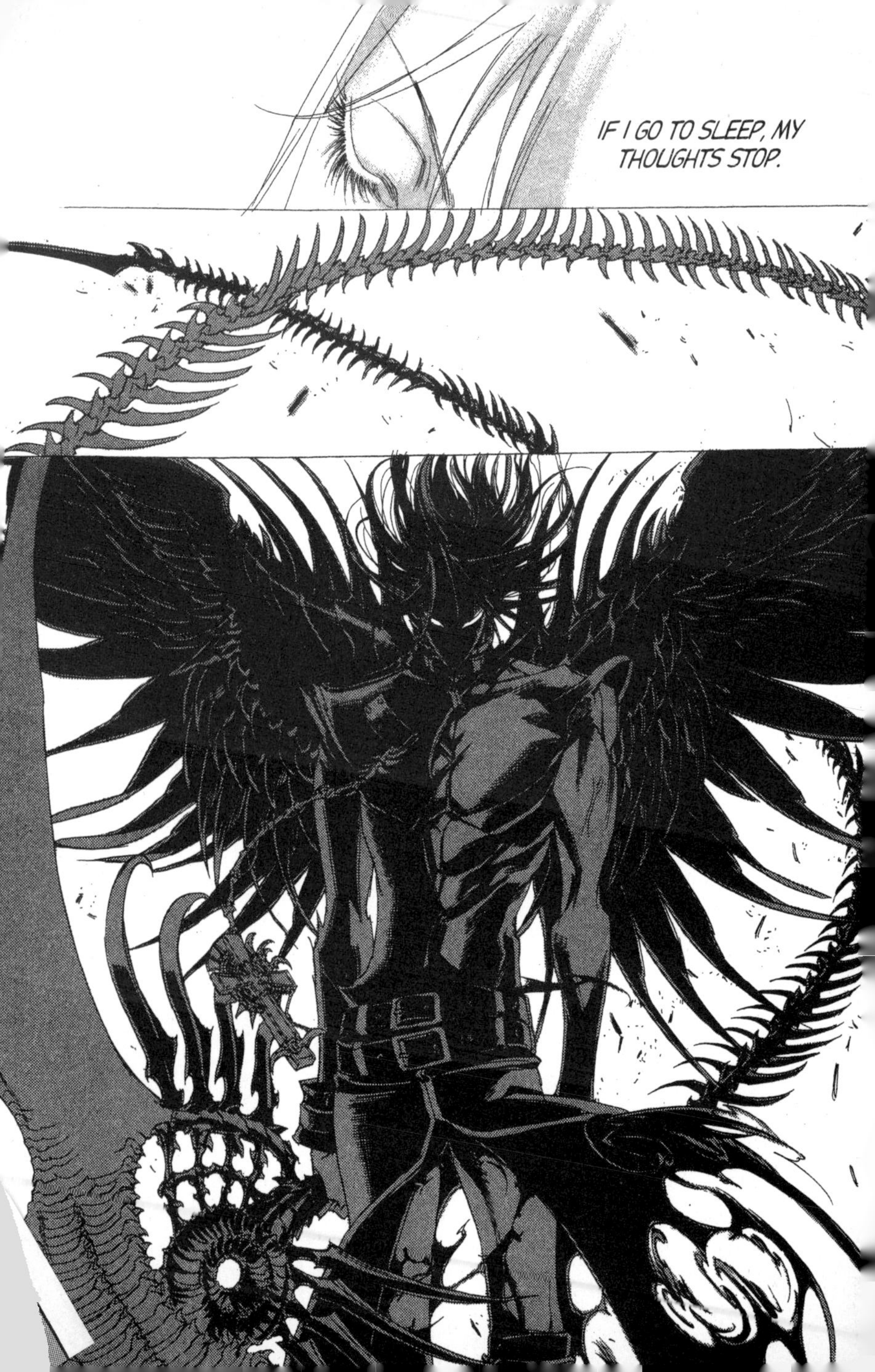
IF I GO TO SLEEP, MY THOUGHTS STOP.

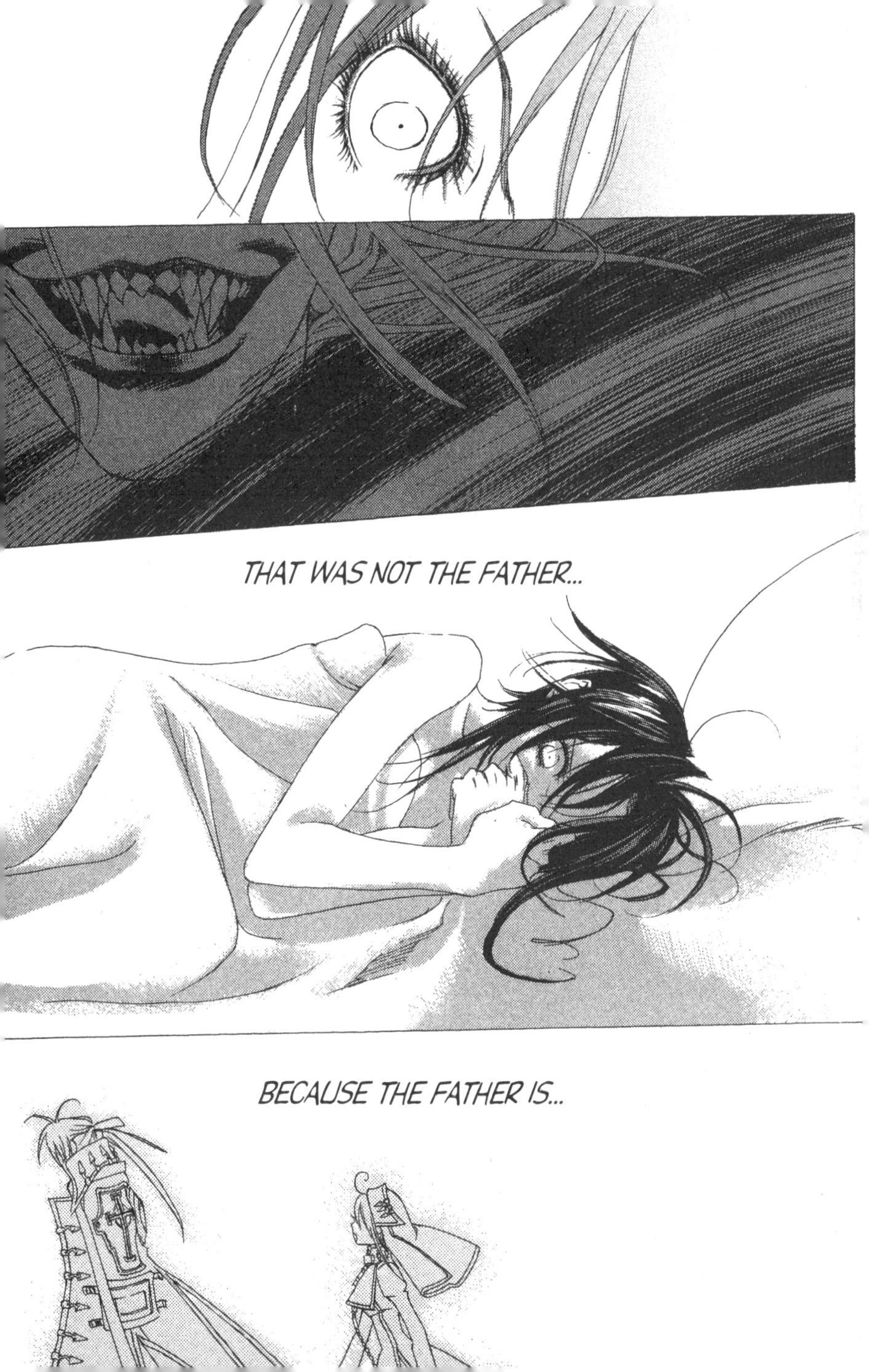
THAT WAS NOT THE FATHER...
BECAUSE THE FATHER IS...

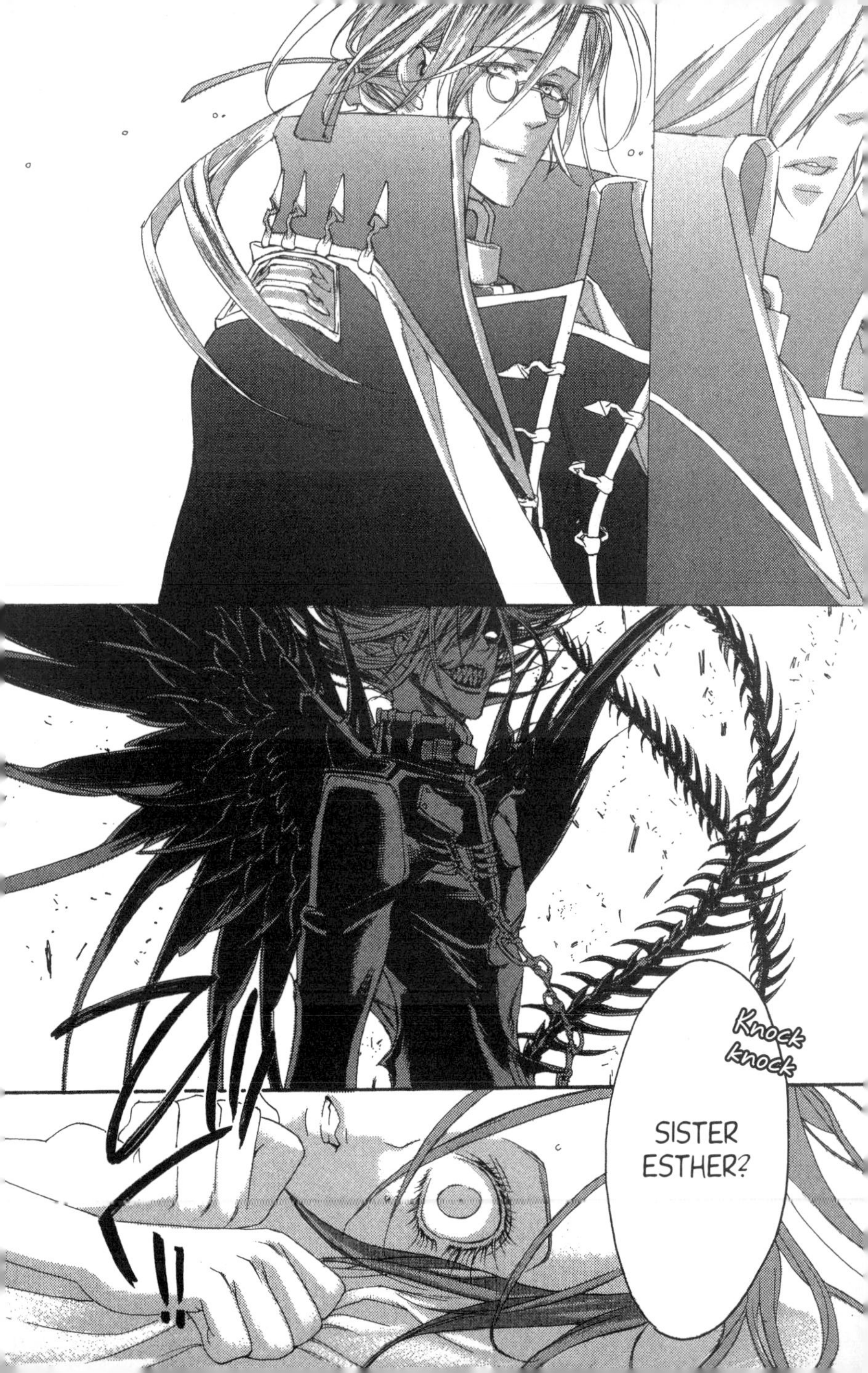
Knock knock
SISTER ESTHER?
!!

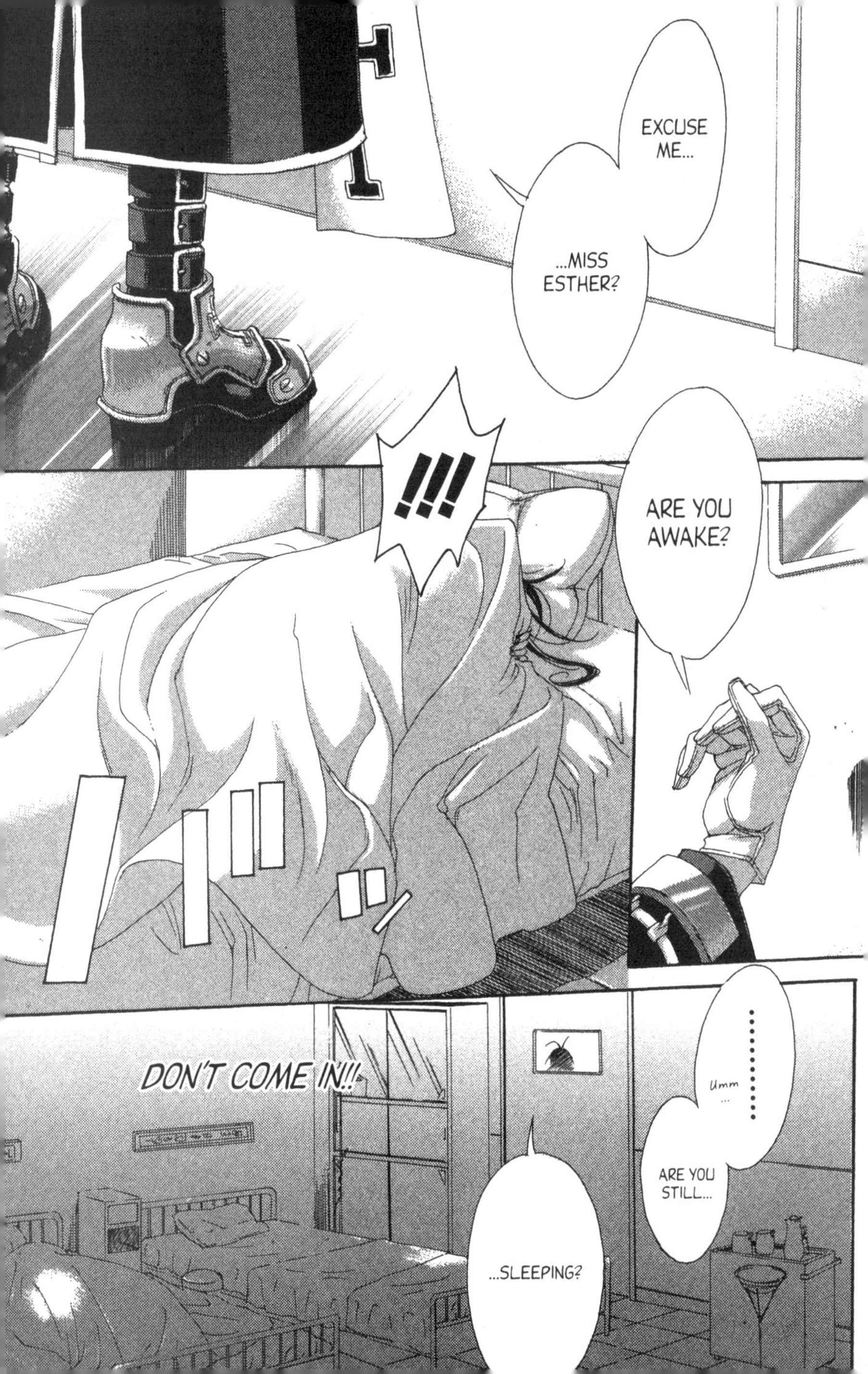
EXCUSE ME...
...MISS ESTHER?
ARE YOU AWAKE?
!!!
....
Umm...
ARE YOU STILL...
...SLEEPING?
DON'T COME IN!!

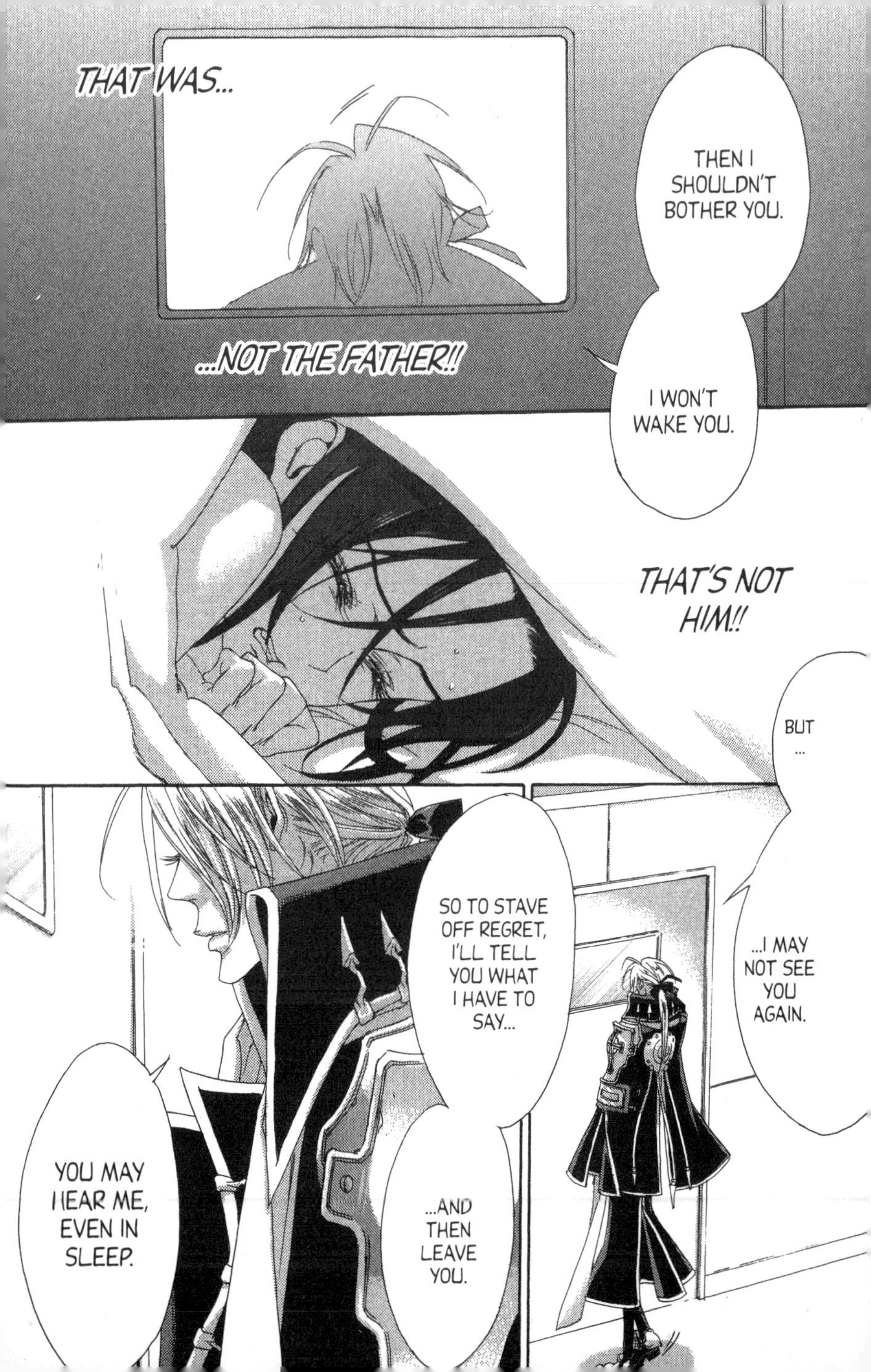
THEN I SHOULDN'T BOTHER YOU.
I WON'T WAKE YOU.
THAT WAS...
...NOT THE FATHER!!
THAT'S NOT HIM!!
BUT...
...I MAY NOT SEE YOU AGAIN.
SO TO STAVE OFF REGRET, I'LL TELL YOU WHAT I HAVE TO SAY...
...AND THEN LEAVE YOU.
YOU MAY HEAR ME, EVEN IN SLEEP.

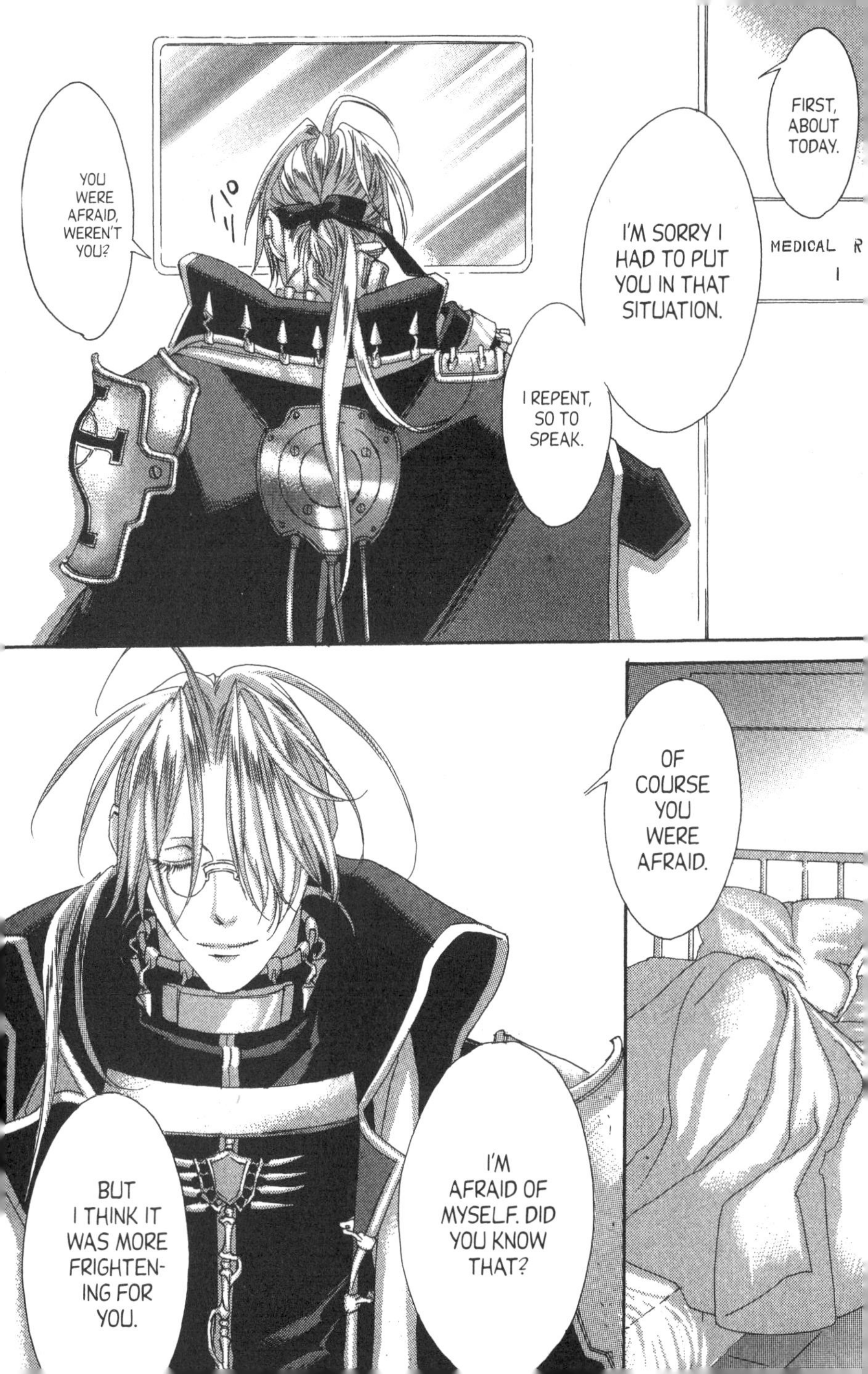
FIRST, ABOUT TODAY.
MEDICAL R
I'M SORRY I HAD TO PUT YOU IN THAT SITUATION.
I REPENT, SO TO SPEAK.
YOU WERE AFRAID, WEREN'T YOU?
OF COURSE YOU WERE AFRAID.
I'M AFRAID OF MYSELF. DID YOU KNOW THAT?
BUT I THINK IT WAS MORE FRIGHTEN-ING FOR YOU.

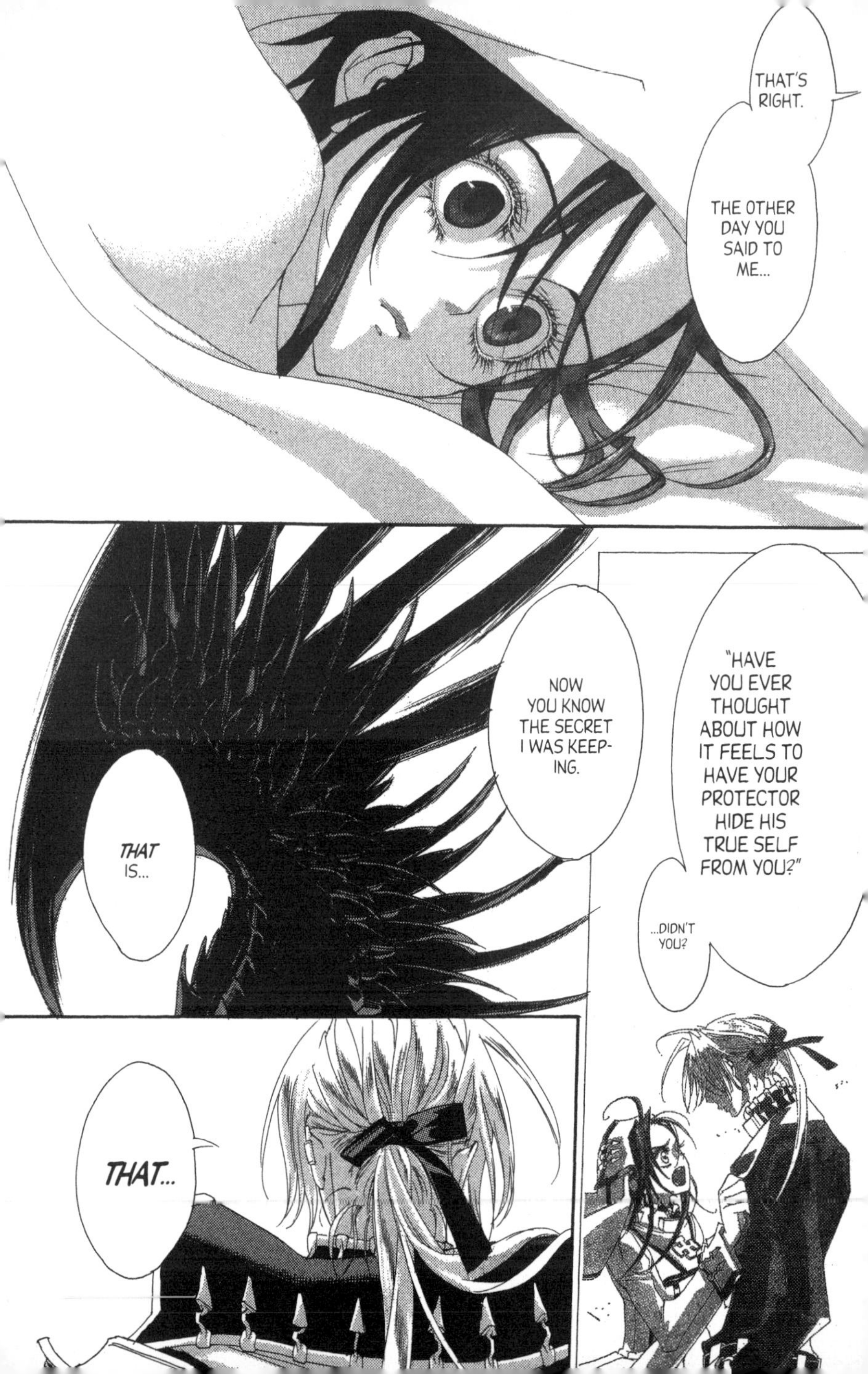
THAT'S RIGHT.
THE OTHER DAY YOU SAID TO ME...
"HAVE YOU EVER THOUGHT ABOUT HOW IT FEELS TO HAVE YOUR PROTECTOR HIDE HIS TRUE SELF FROM YOU?"
...DIDN'T YOU?
NOW YOU KNOW THE SECRET I WAS KEEP-ING.
THAT IS...
THAT...

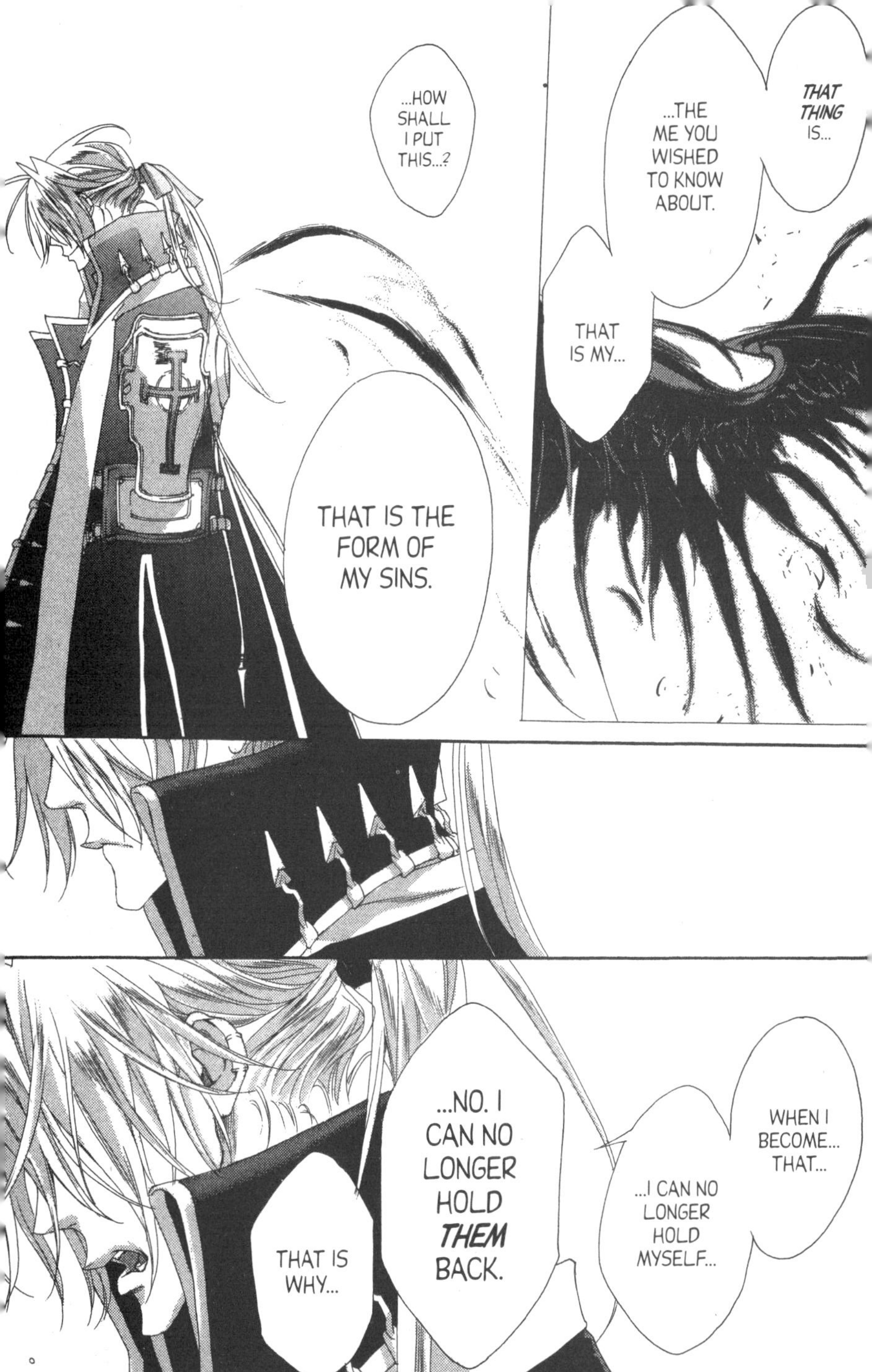
THAT THING IS...
...THE ME YOU WISHED TO KNOW ABOUT.
THAT IS MY...
...HOW SHALL I PUT THIS...?
THAT IS THE FORM OF MY SINS.
WHEN I BECOME... THAT...
...I CAN NO LONGER HOLD MYSELF...
...NO. I CAN NO LONGER HOLD *THEM* BACK.
THAT IS WHY...

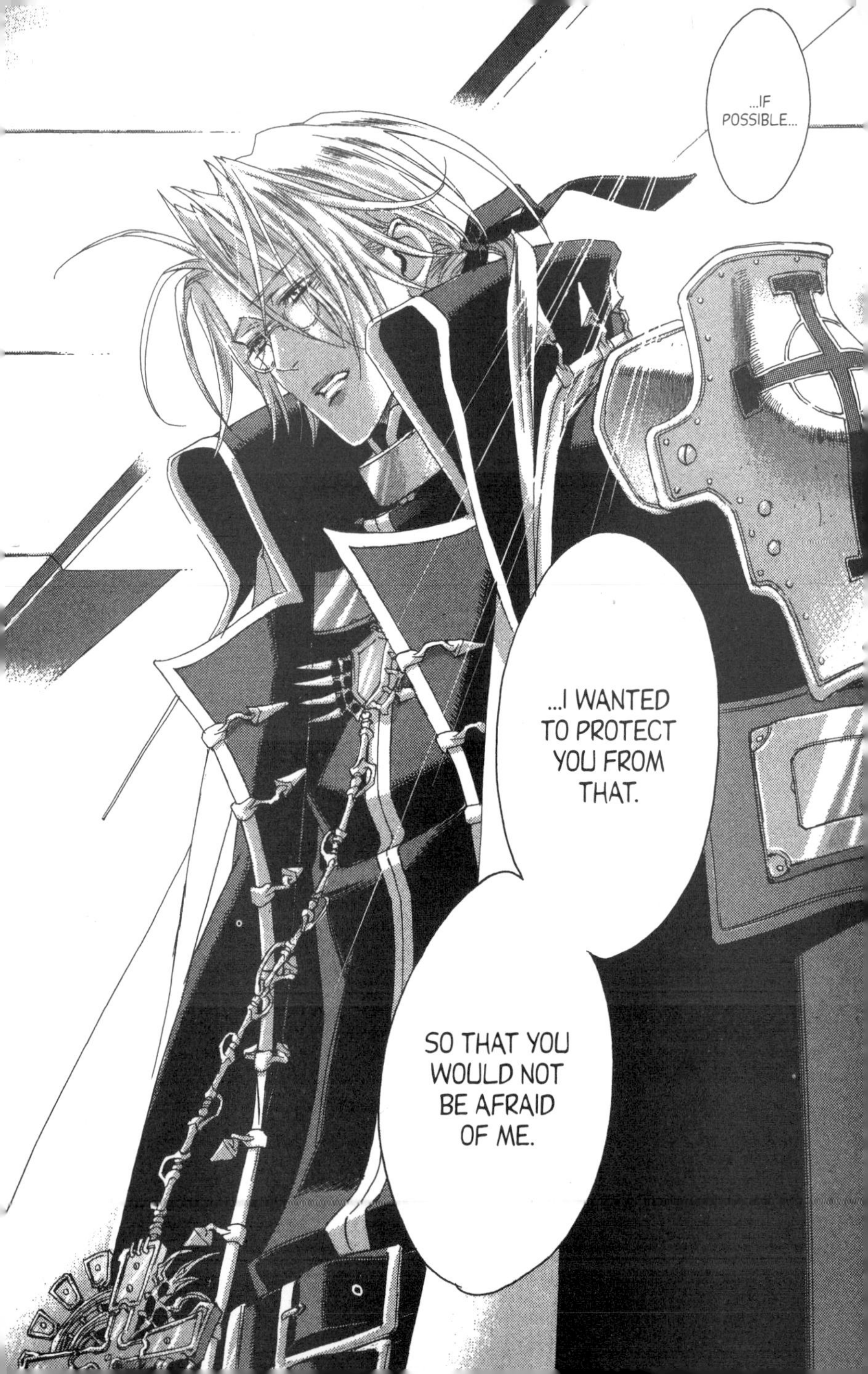
...IF POSSIBLE...
...I WANTED TO PROTECT YOU FROM THAT.
SO THAT YOU WOULD NOT BE AFRAID OF ME.

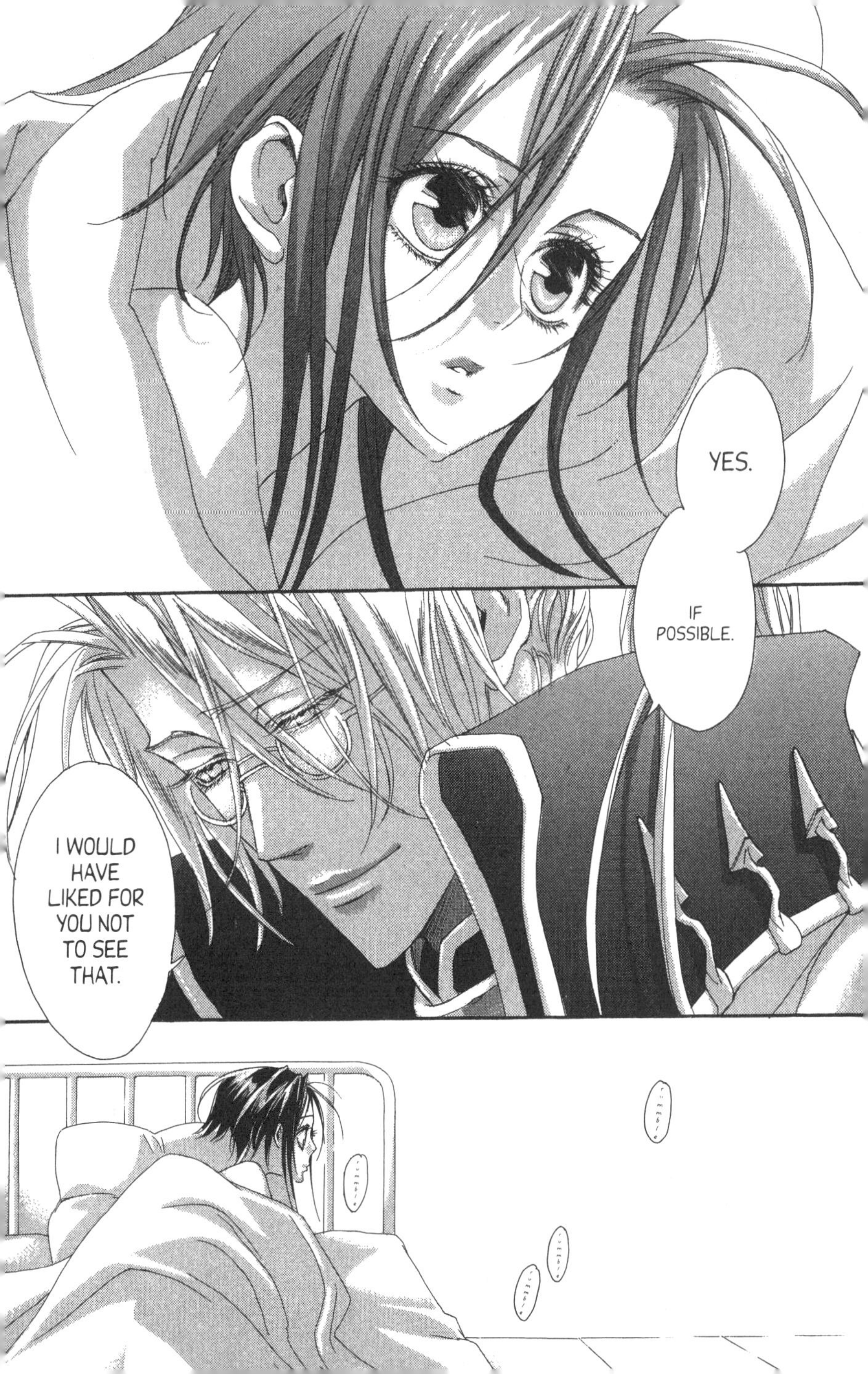
YES.
IF POSSIBLE.
I WOULD HAVE LIKED FOR YOU NOT TO SEE THAT.
rumble
rumble
rumble
rumble

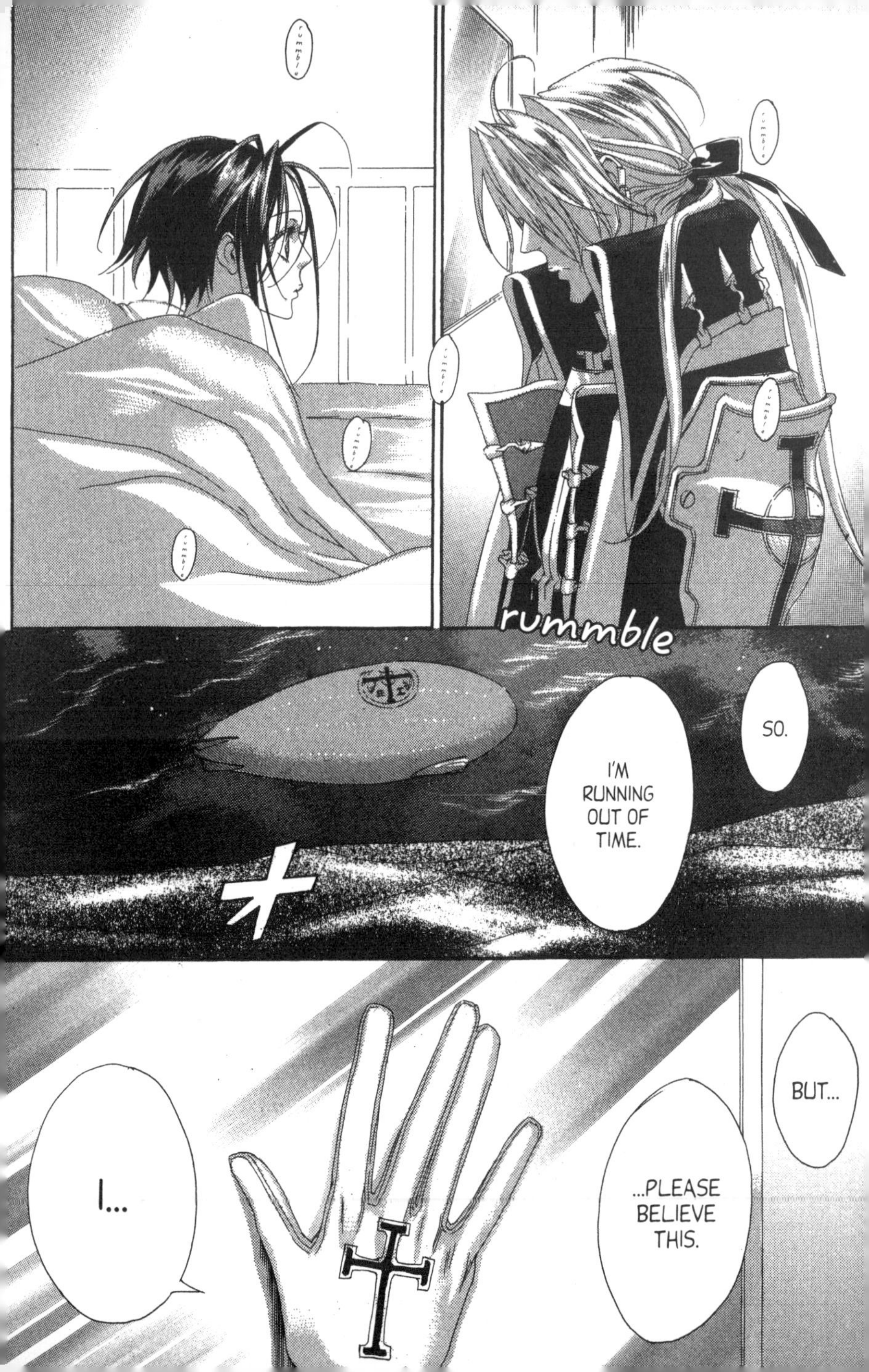
rummble
rummble
rummble
rummble
rummble
rummble
rummble
SO.
I'M RUNNING OUT OF TIME.
BUT...
...PLEASE BELIEVE THIS.
I...

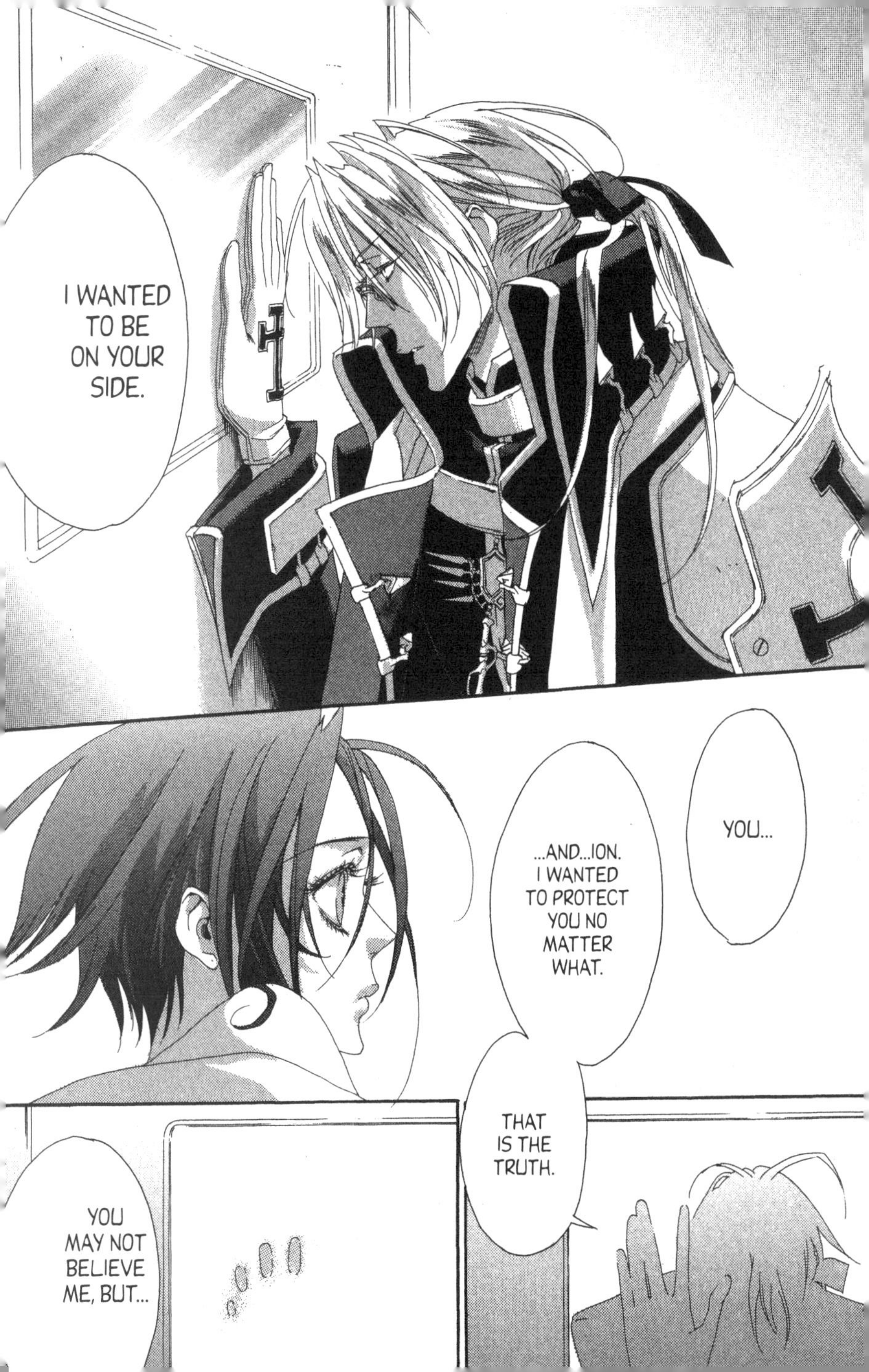
I WANTED TO BE ON YOUR SIDE.
YOU...
...AND...ION. I WANTED TO PROTECT YOU NO MATTER WHAT.
THAT IS THE TRUTH.
YOU MAY NOT BELIEVE ME, BUT...

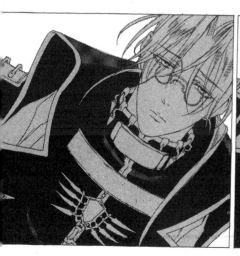

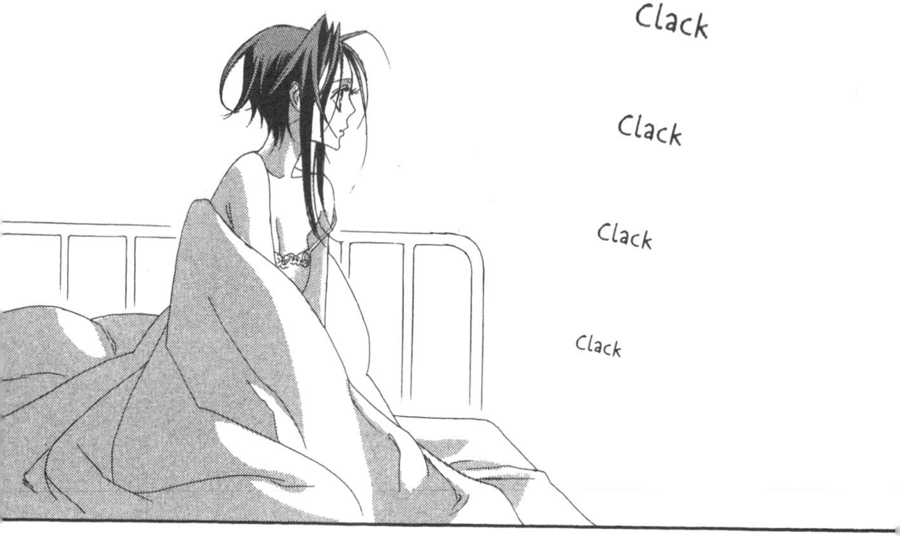
Clack
Clack
Clack
Clack

"HAVE YOU EVER THOUGHT ABOUT HOW IT FEELS TO HAVE YOUR PROTECTOR HIDE HIS TRUE SELF FROM YOU?"

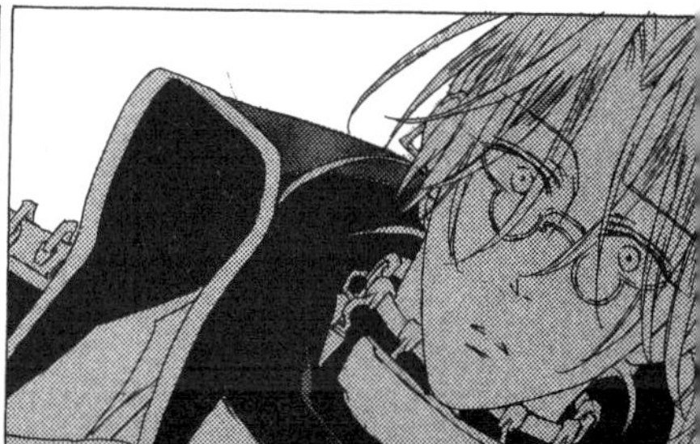

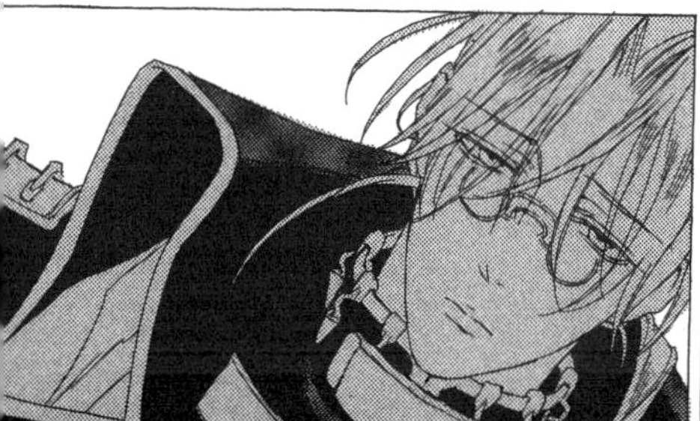

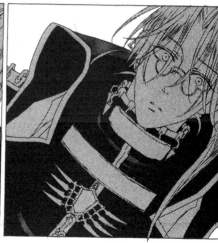

I...

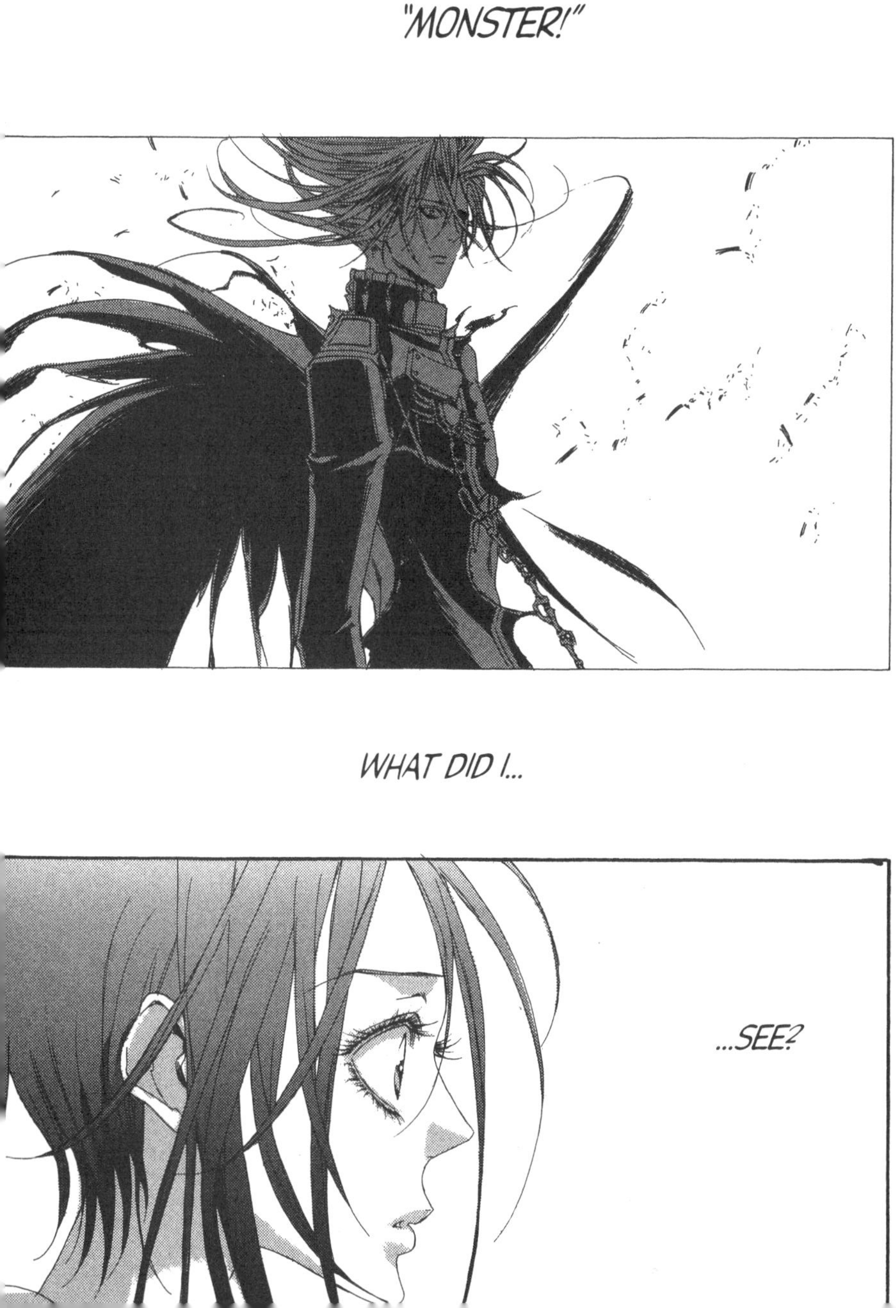
"MONSTER!"
WHAT DID I...
...SEE?

"I AM ON YOUR SIDE, YOU KNOW."

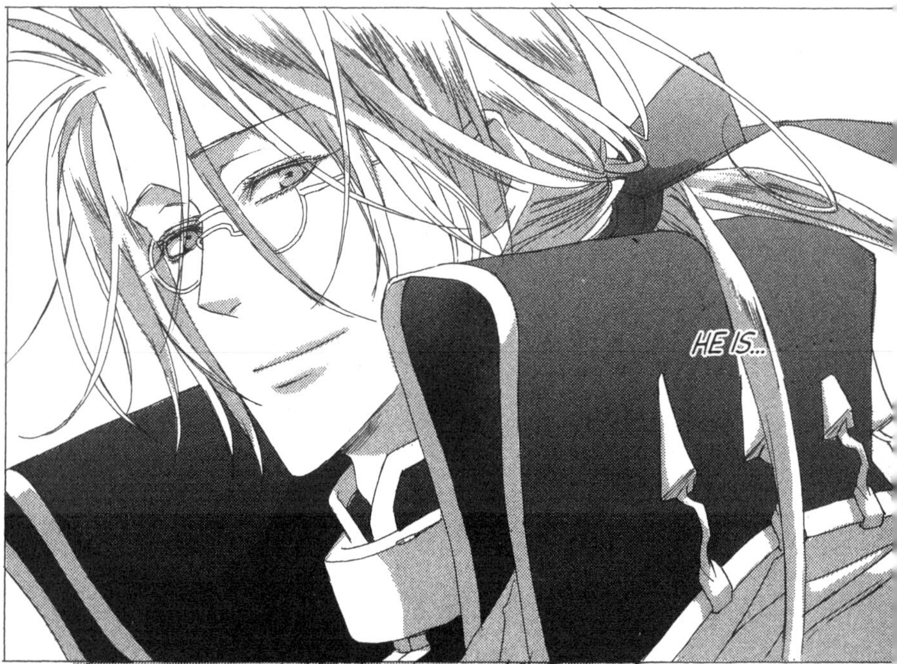
HE IS...

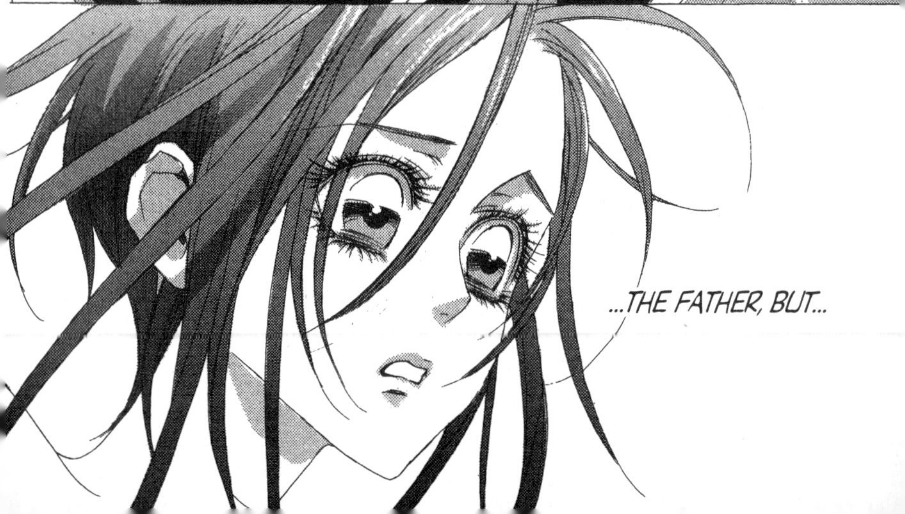
...THE FATHER, BUT...

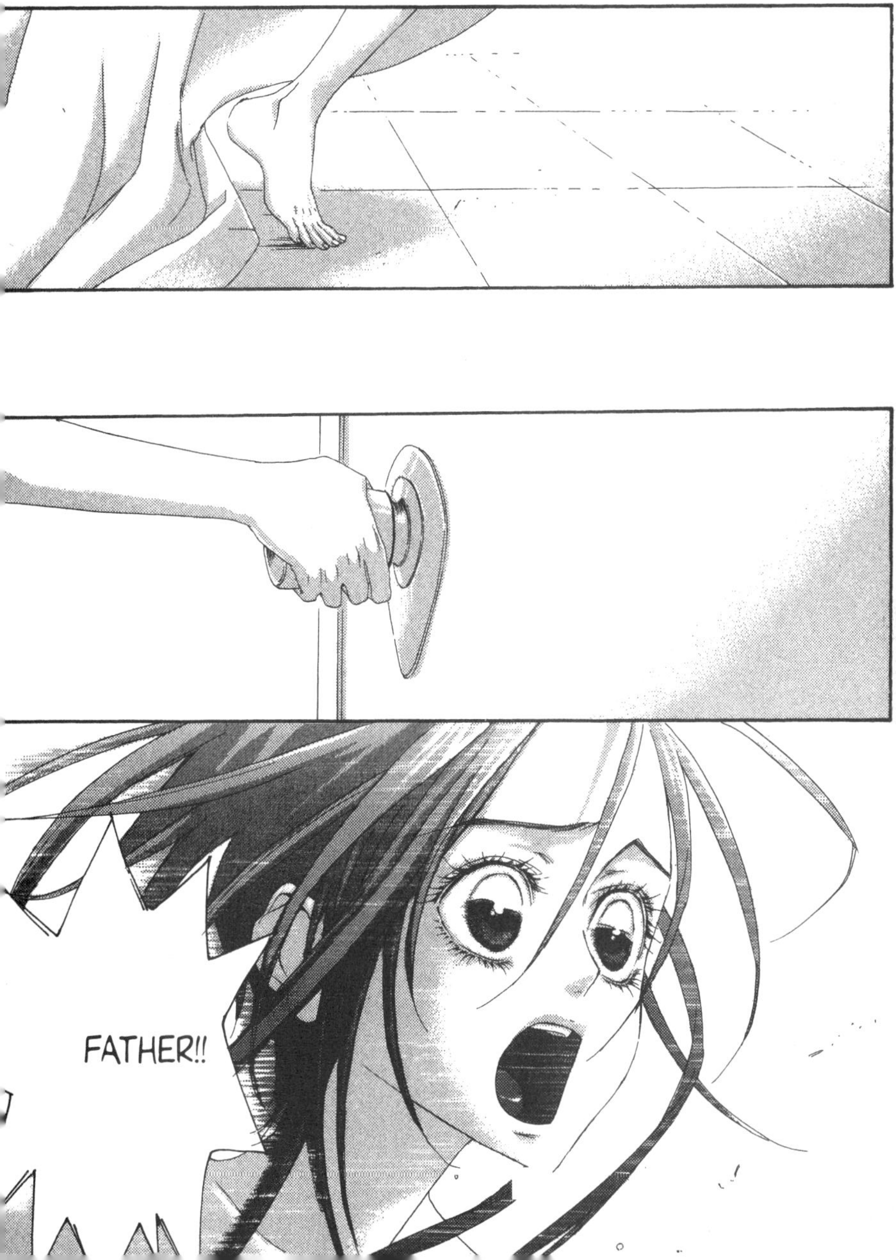
FATHER!!

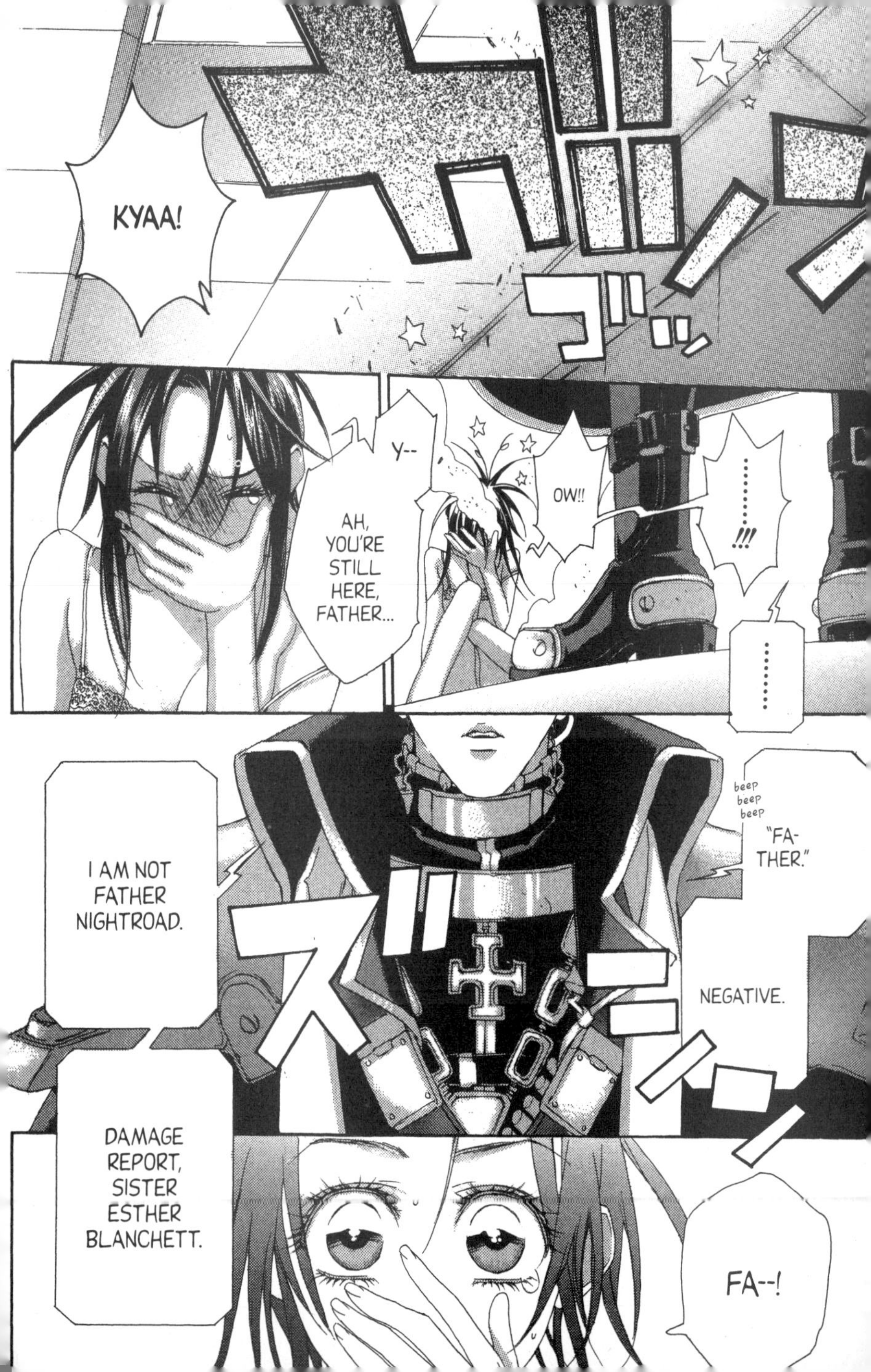
KYAA!
......!!!
......
OW!!
Y--
AH, YOU'RE STILL HERE, FATHER...
beep beep beep
"FA-THER."
NEGATIVE.
I AM NOT FATHER NIGHTROAD.
FA--!
DAMAGE REPORT, SISTER ESTHER BLANCHETT.

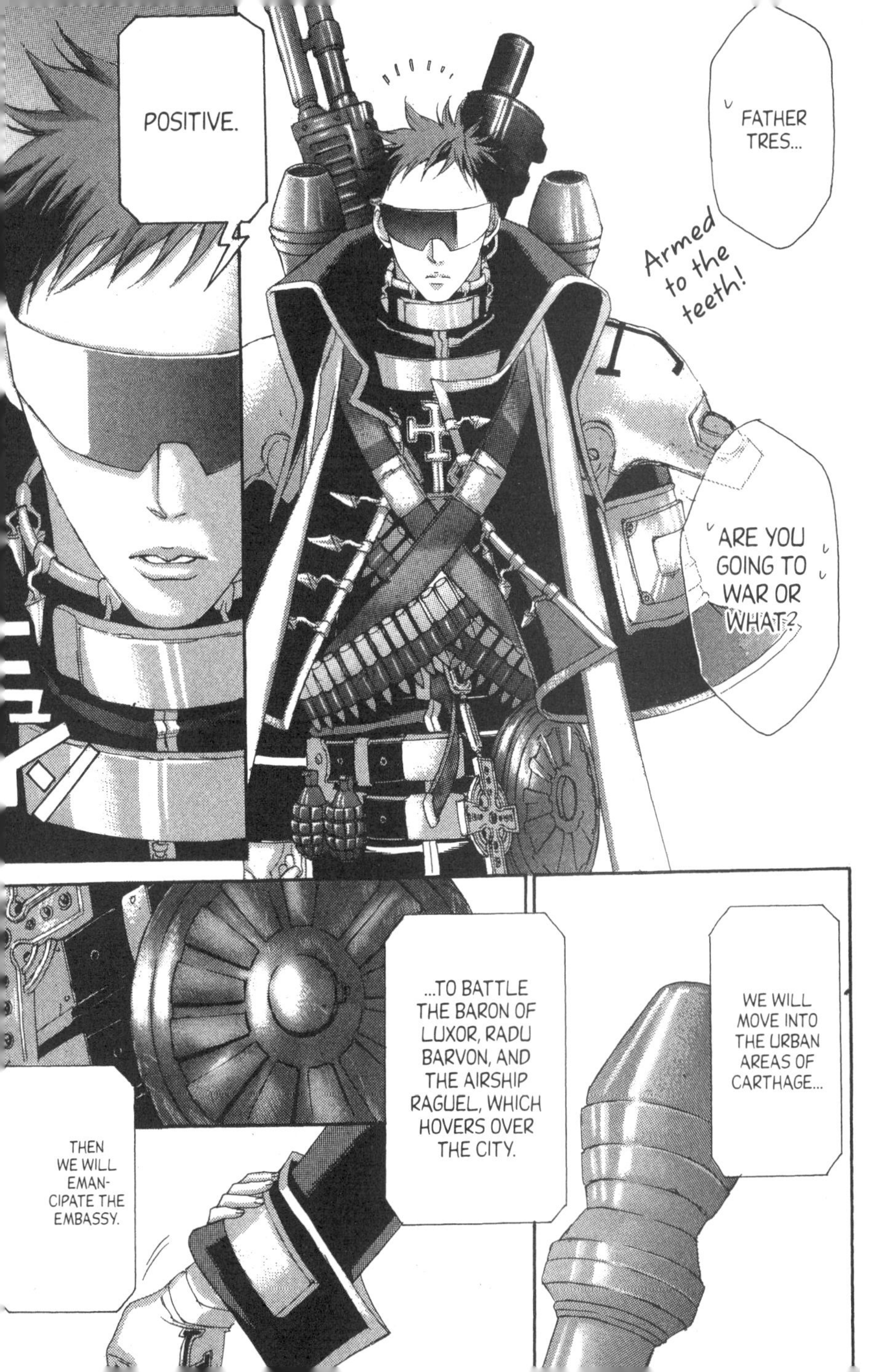
FATHER TRES...
Armed to the teeth!
ARE YOU GOING TO WAR OR WHAT?
POSITIVE.
WE WILL MOVE INTO THE URBAN AREAS OF CARTHAGE...
...TO BATTLE THE BARON OF LUXOR, RADU BARVON, AND THE AIRSHIP RAGUEL, WHICH HOVERS OVER THE CITY.
THEN WE WILL EMAN-CIPATE THE EMBASSY.

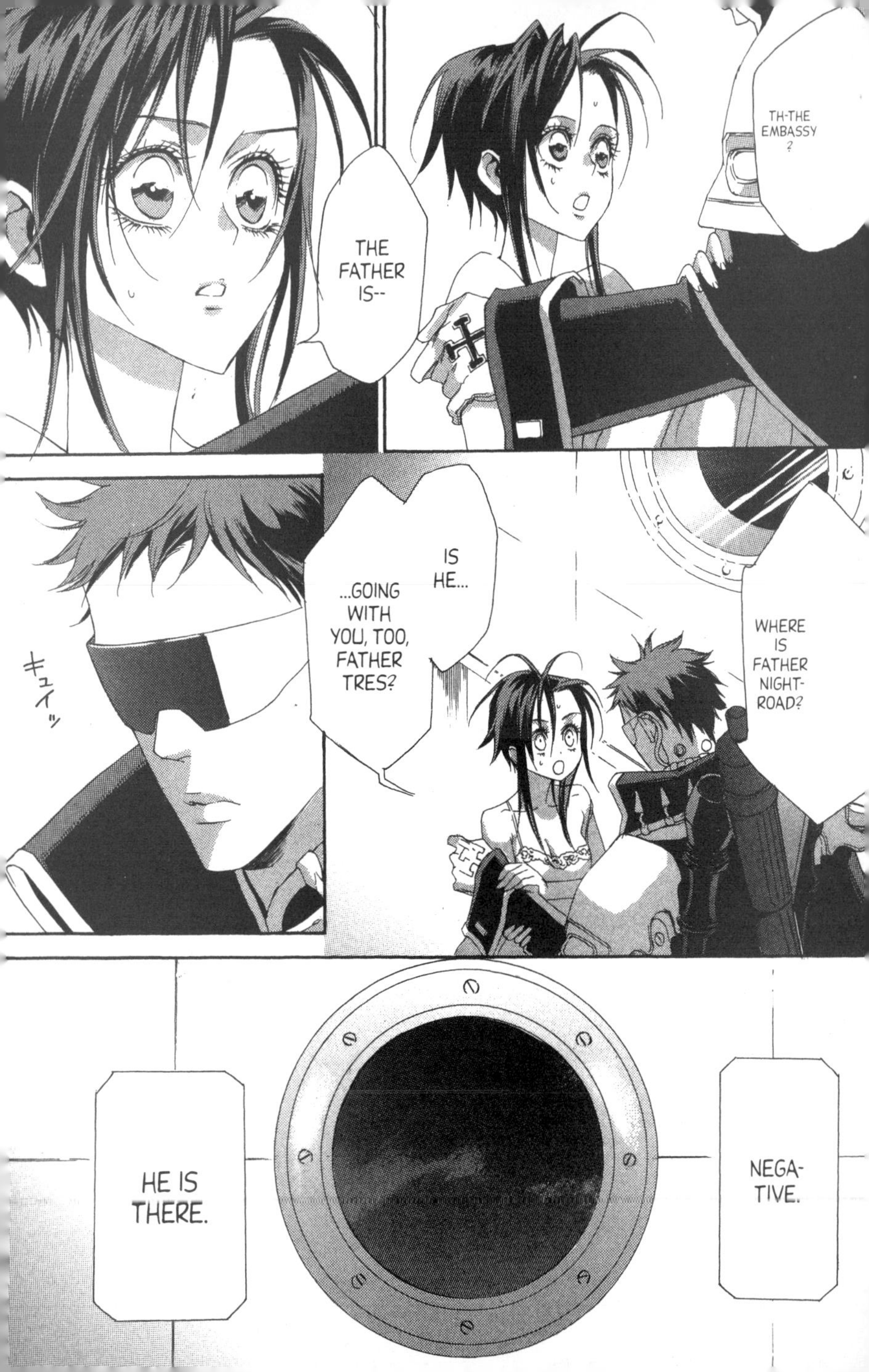
TH-THE EMBASSY?
THE FATHER IS--
WHERE IS FATHER NIGHT-ROAD?
IS HE... ...GOING WITH YOU, TOO, FATHER TRES?
キュイッ
NEGA-TIVE.
HE IS THERE.

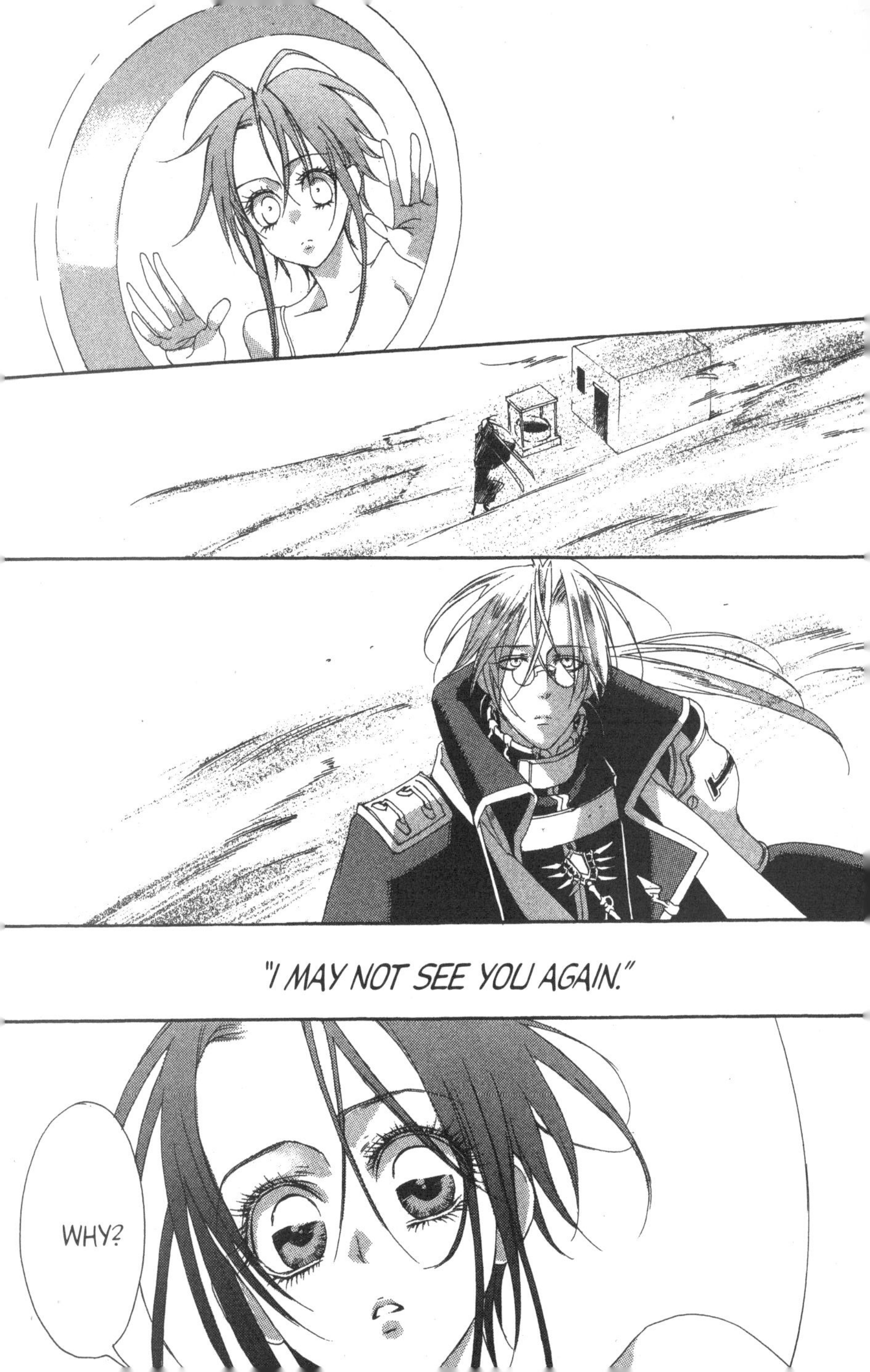
"I MAY NOT SEE YOU AGAIN."
WHY?

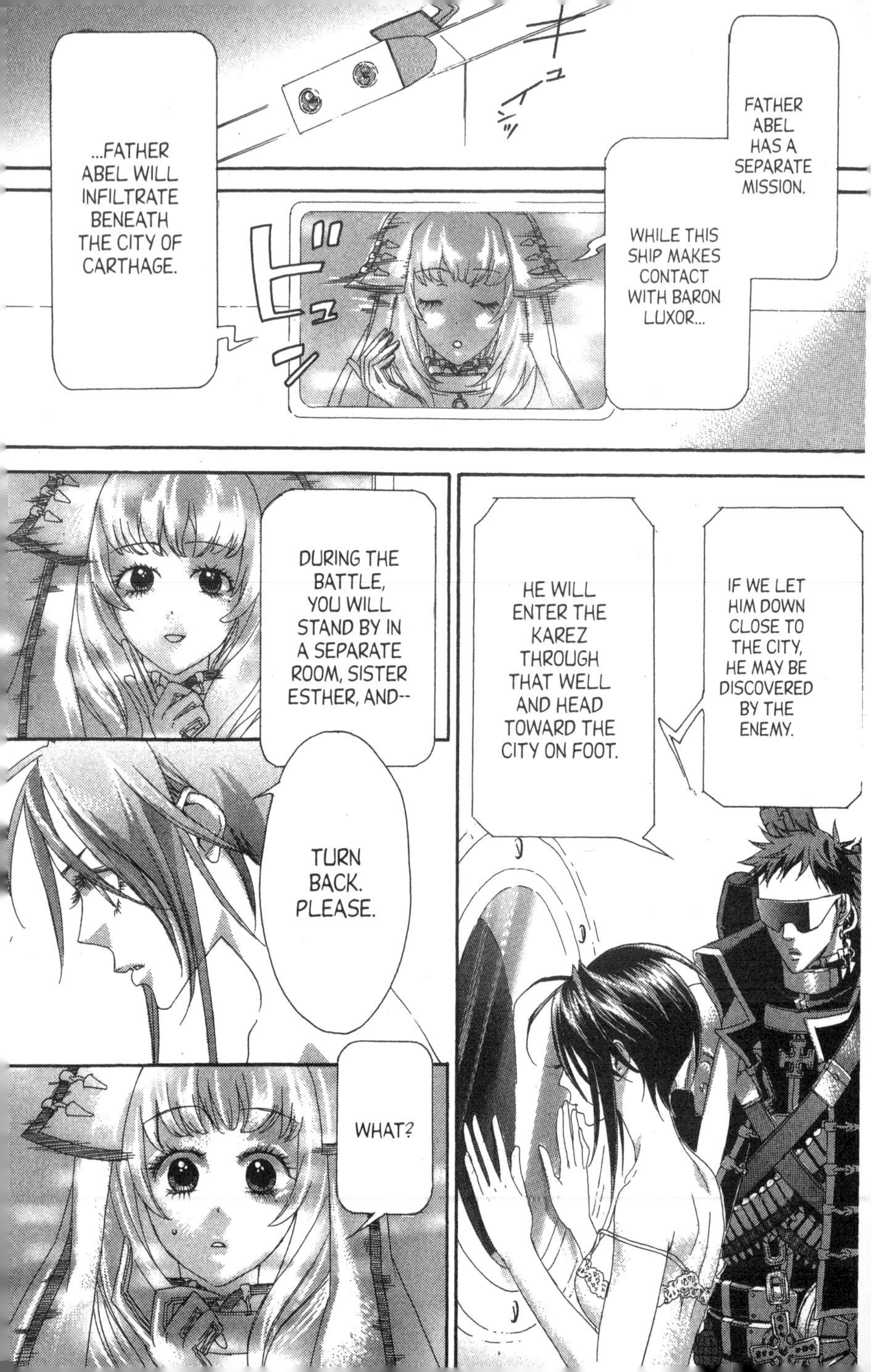
FATHER ABEL HAS A SEPARATE MISSION.
WHILE THIS SHIP MAKES CONTACT WITH BARON LUXOR...
...FATHER ABEL WILL INFILTRATE BENEATH THE CITY OF CARTHAGE.
IF WE LET HIM DOWN CLOSE TO THE CITY, HE MAY BE DISCOVERED BY THE ENEMY.
HE WILL ENTER THE KAREZ THROUGH THAT WELL AND HEAD TOWARD THE CITY ON FOOT.
DURING THE BATTLE, YOU WILL STAND BY IN A SEPARATE ROOM, SISTER ESTHER, AND--
TURN BACK. PLEASE.
WHAT?

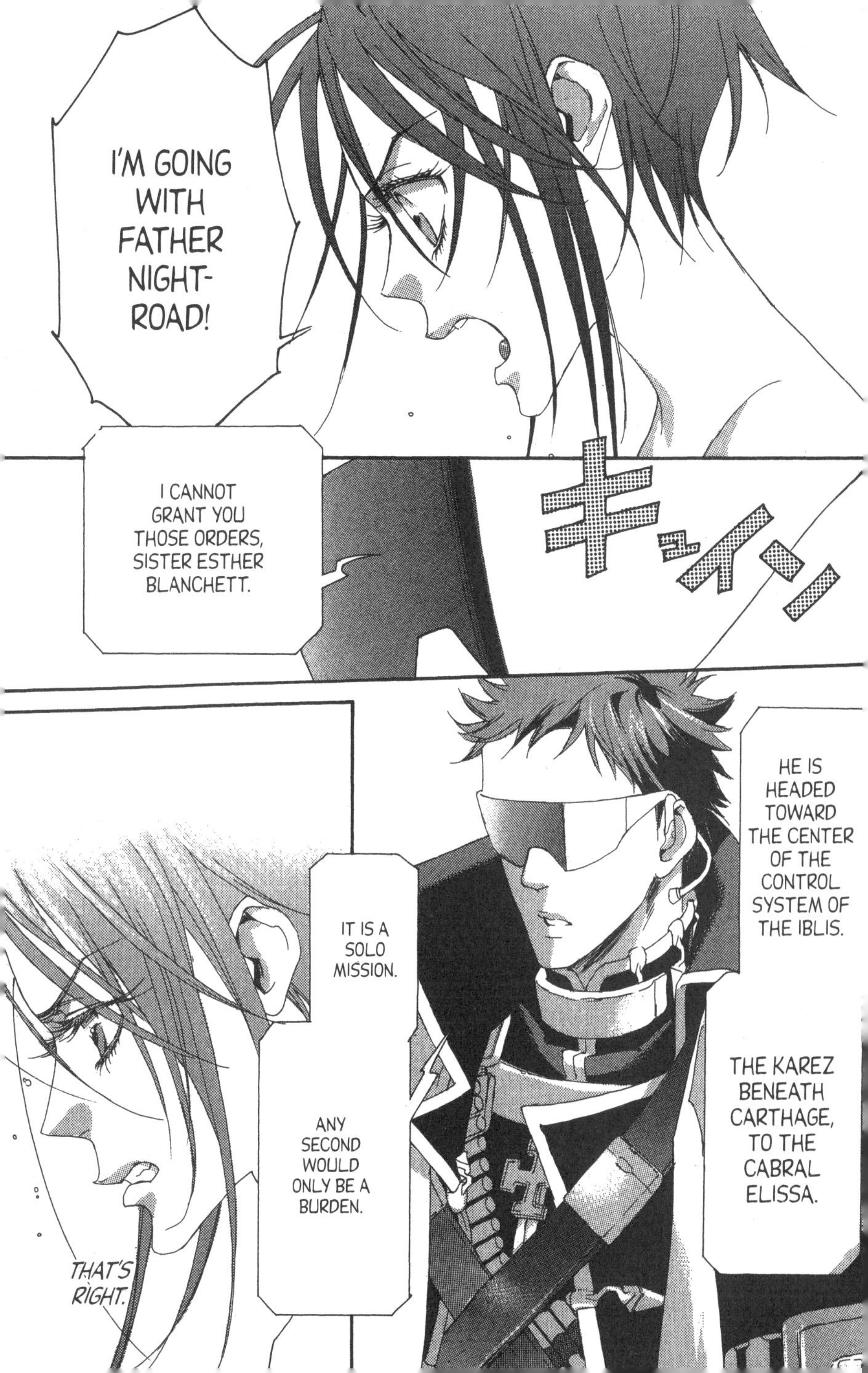
I'M GOING WITH FATHER NIGHT-ROAD!
キュイン
I CANNOT GRANT YOU THOSE ORDERS, SISTER ESTHER BLANCHETT.
HE IS HEADED TOWARD THE CENTER OF THE CONTROL SYSTEM OF THE IBLIS.
THE KAREZ BENEATH CARTHAGE, TO THE CABRAL ELISSA.
IT IS A SOLO MISSION.
ANY SECOND WOULD ONLY BE A BURDEN.
THAT'S RIGHT.

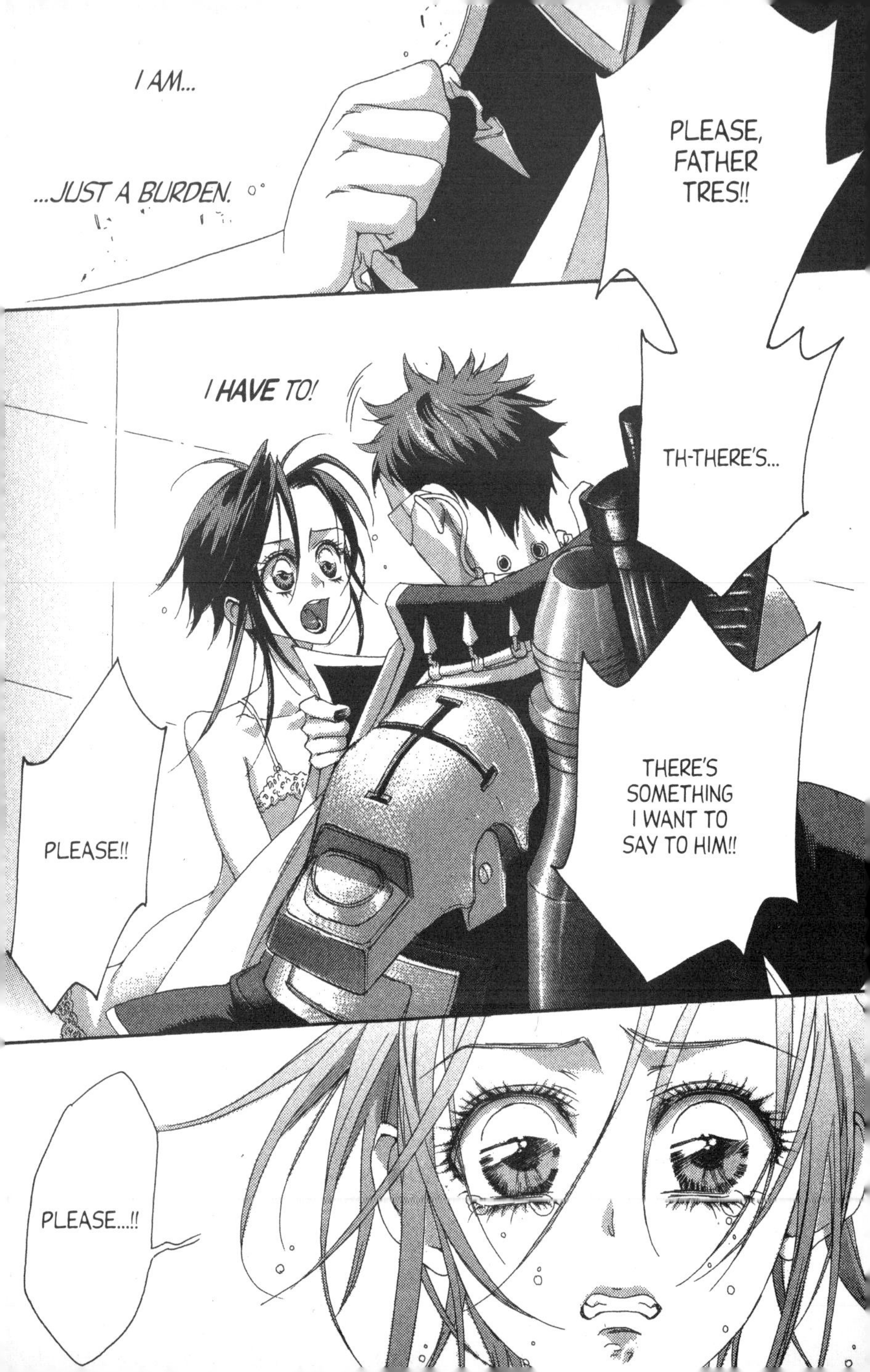
PLEASE, FATHER TRES!!
I AM...
...JUST A BURDEN.
TH-THERE'S...
THERE'S SOMETHING I WANT TO SAY TO HIM!!
I **HAVE** TO!
PLEASE!!
PLEASE...!!

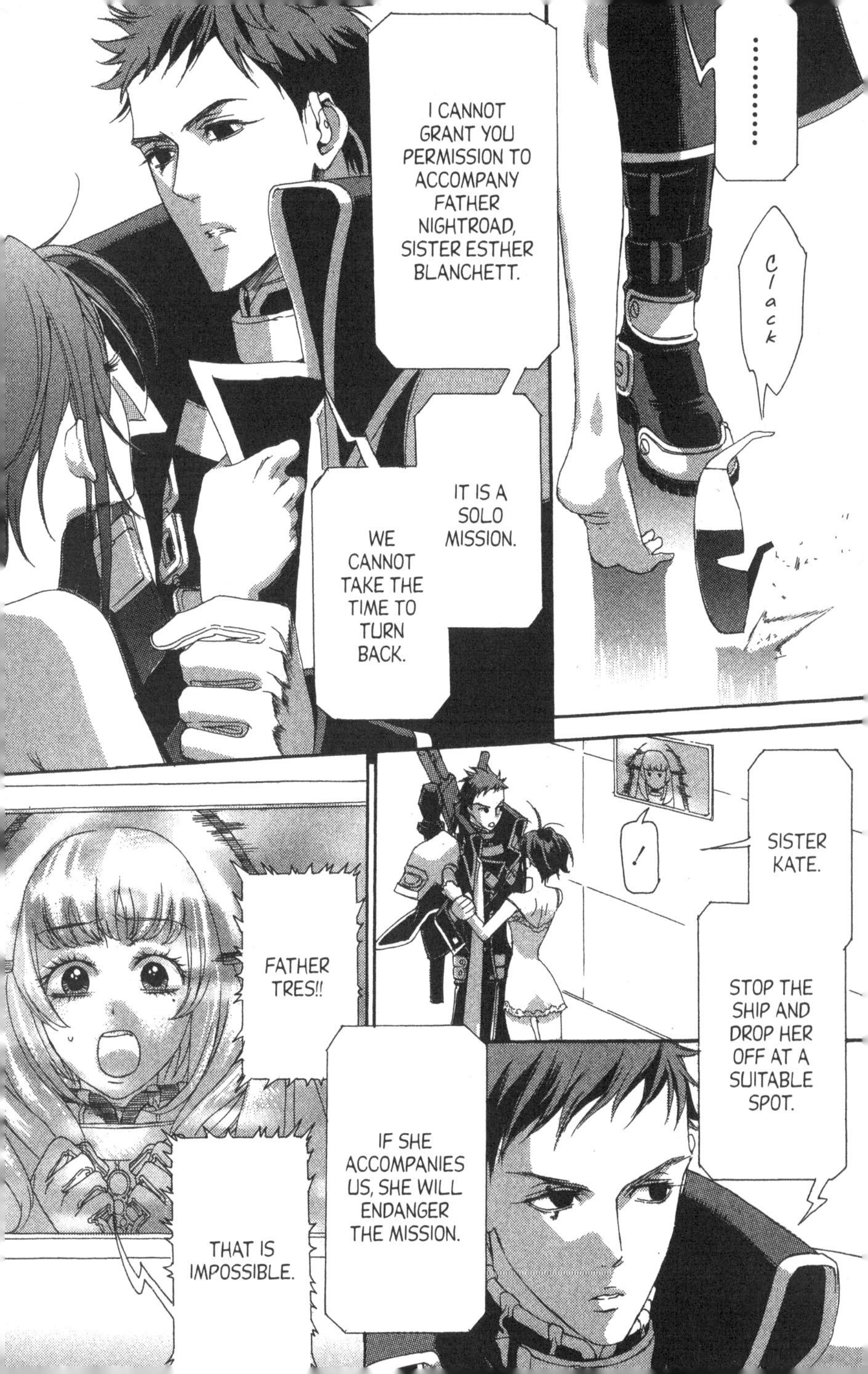
......
Clack
I CANNOT GRANT YOU PERMISSION TO ACCOMPANY FATHER NIGHTROAD, SISTER ESTHER BLANCHETT.
IT IS A SOLO MISSION.
WE CANNOT TAKE THE TIME TO TURN BACK.
!
SISTER KATE.
STOP THE SHIP AND DROP HER OFF AT A SUITABLE SPOT.
FATHER TRES!!
IF SHE ACCOMPANIES US, SHE WILL ENDANGER THE MISSION.
THAT IS IMPOSSIBLE.

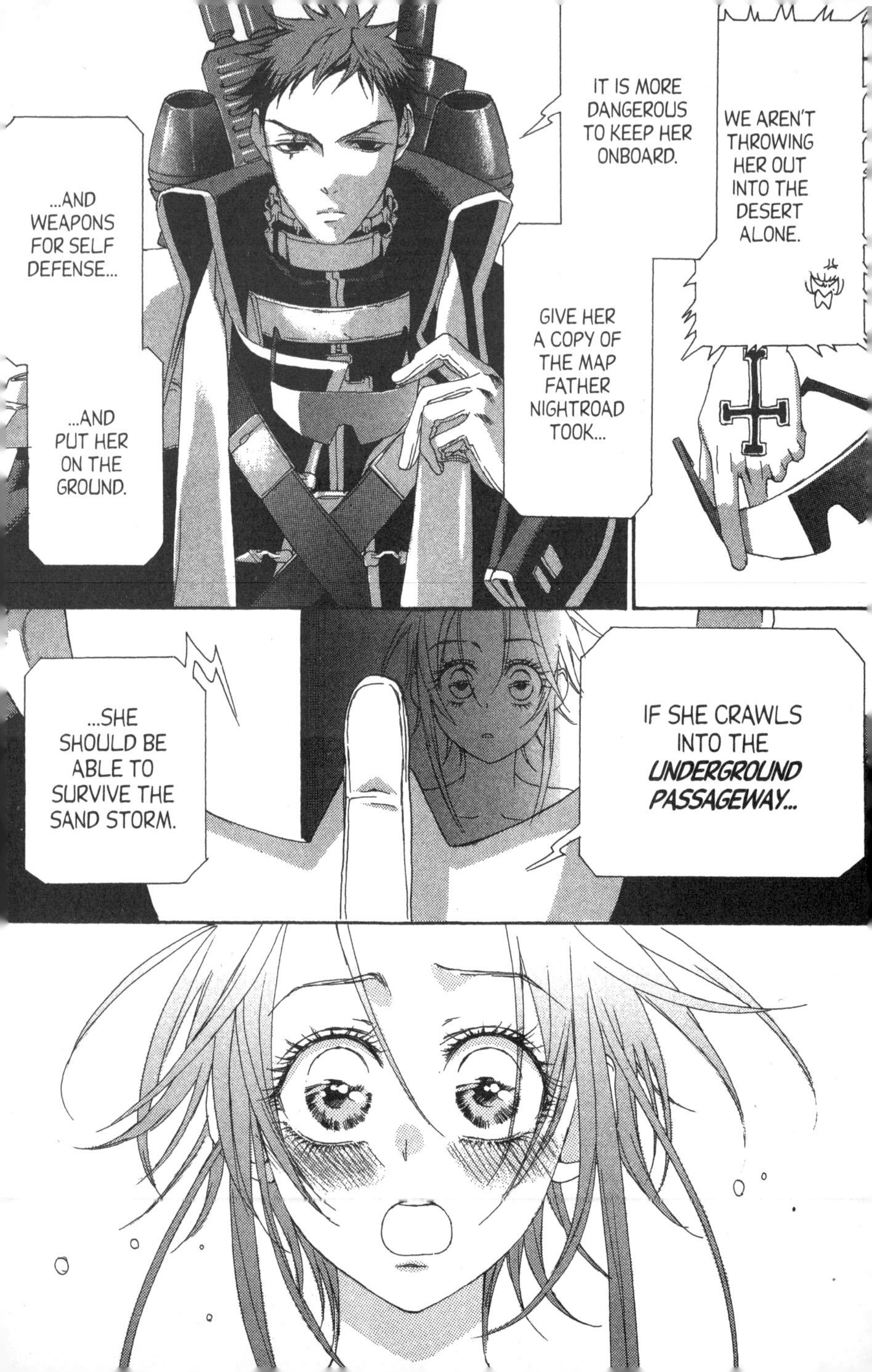
WE AREN'T THROWING HER OUT INTO THE DESERT ALONE.
IT IS MORE DANGEROUS TO KEEP HER ONBOARD.
GIVE HER A COPY OF THE MAP FATHER NIGHTROAD TOOK...
...AND WEAPONS FOR SELF DEFENSE...
...AND PUT HER ON THE GROUND.
IF SHE CRAWLS INTO THE *UNDERGROUND PASSAGEWAY...*
...SHE SHOULD BE ABLE TO SURVIVE THE SAND STORM.

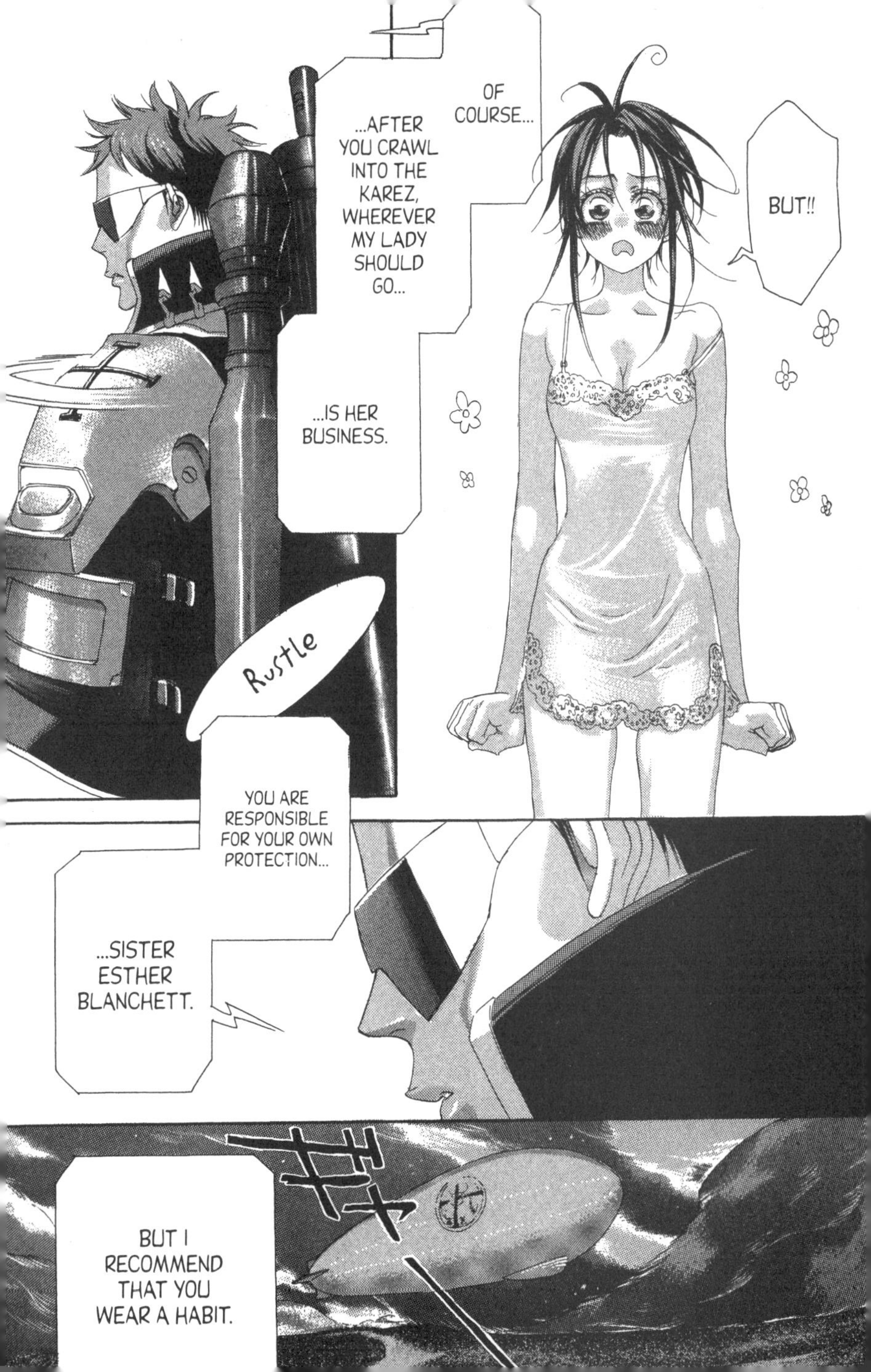
BUT!!
OF COURSE...
...AFTER YOU CRAWL INTO THE KAREZ, WHEREVER MY LADY SHOULD GO...
...IS HER BUSINESS.
Rustle
YOU ARE RESPONSIBLE FOR YOUR OWN PROTECTION...
...SISTER ESTHER BLANCHETT.
BUT I RECOMMEND THAT YOU WEAR A HABIT.

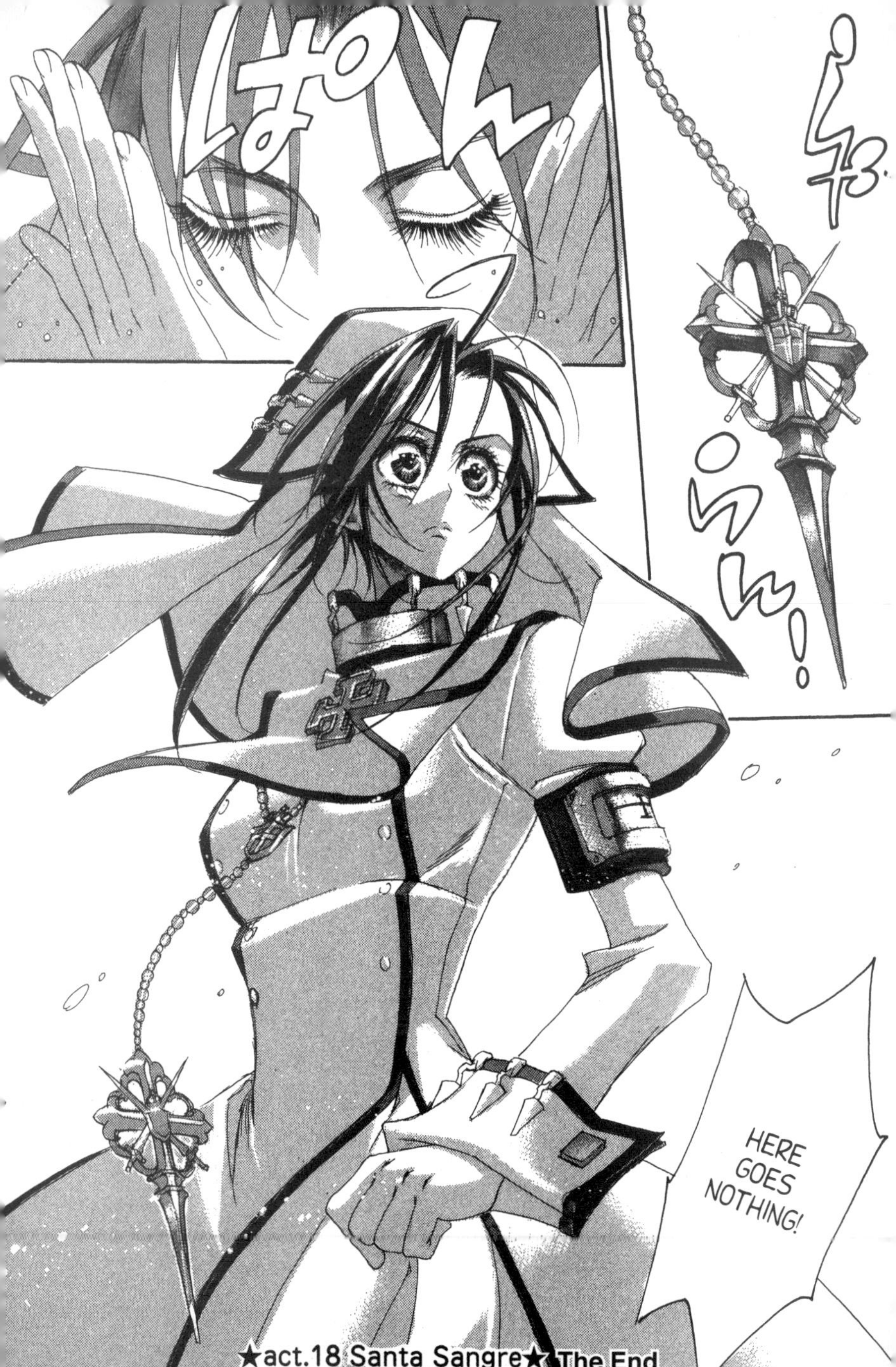
HERE GOES NOTHING!

★act.18 Santa Sangre★ The End

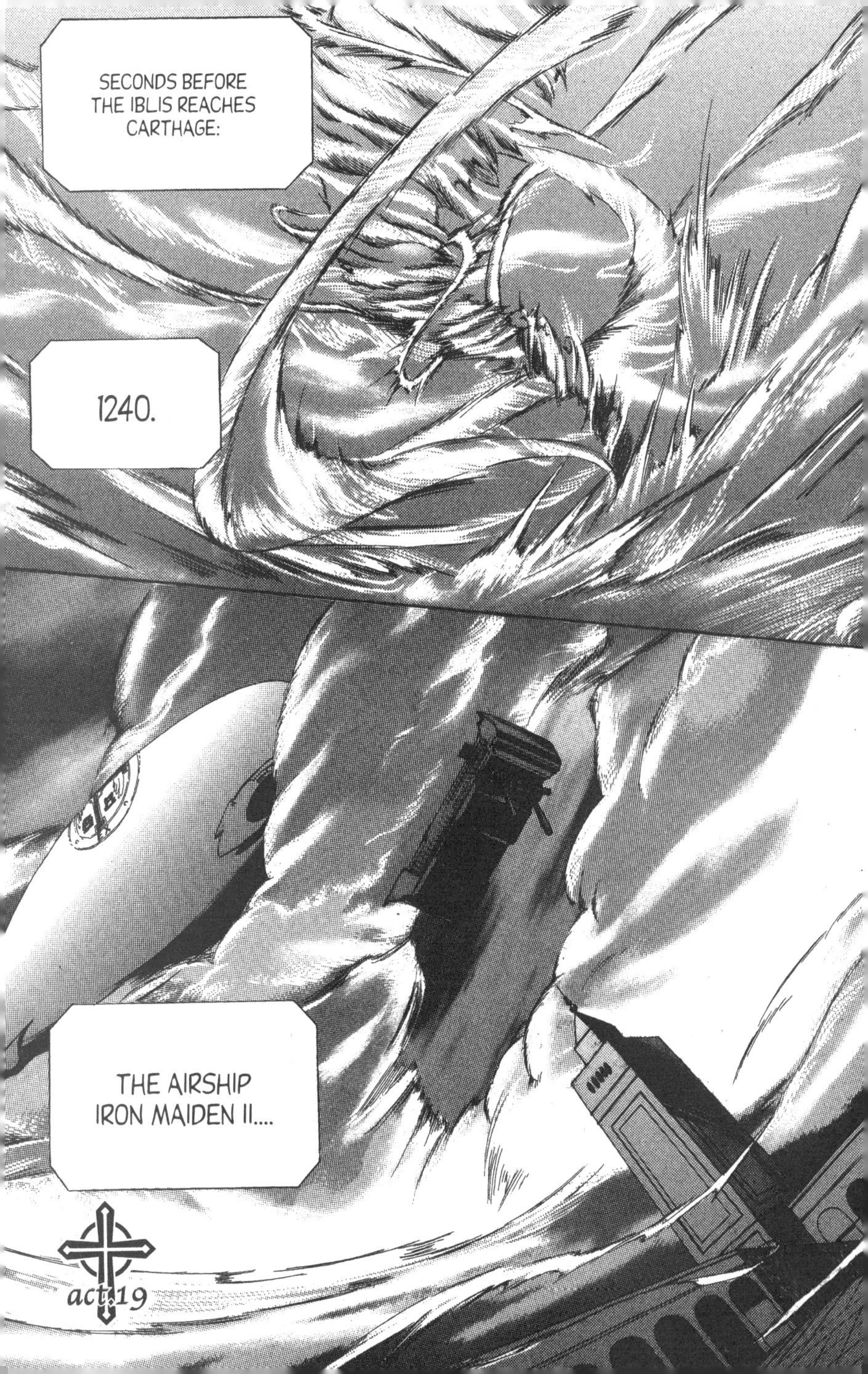
SECONDS BEFORE THE IBLIS REACHES CARTHAGE:
1240.
THE AIRSHIP IRON MAIDEN II....
act.19

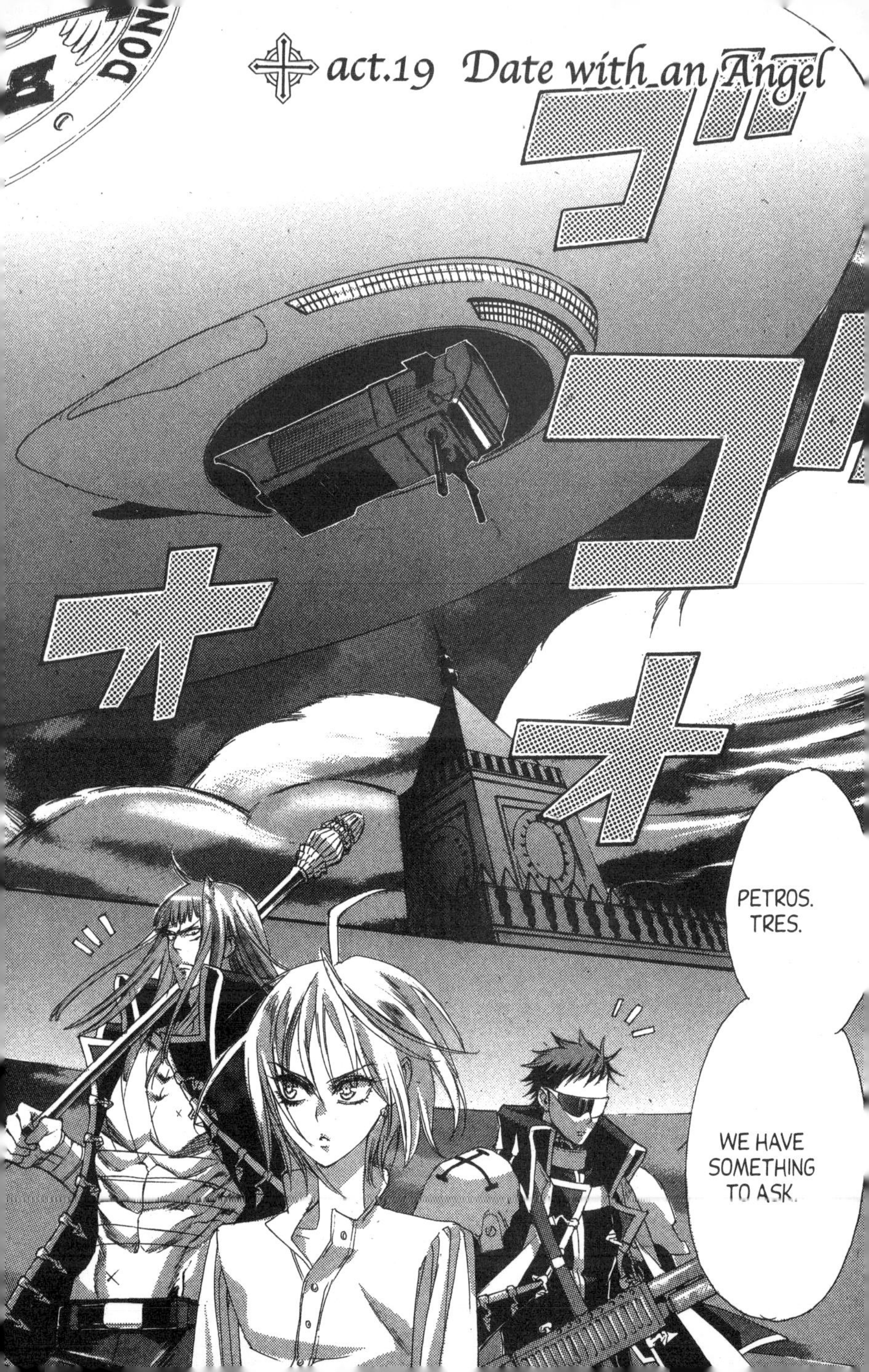
act.19 Date with an Angel
PETROS. TRES.
WE HAVE SOMETHING TO ASK.

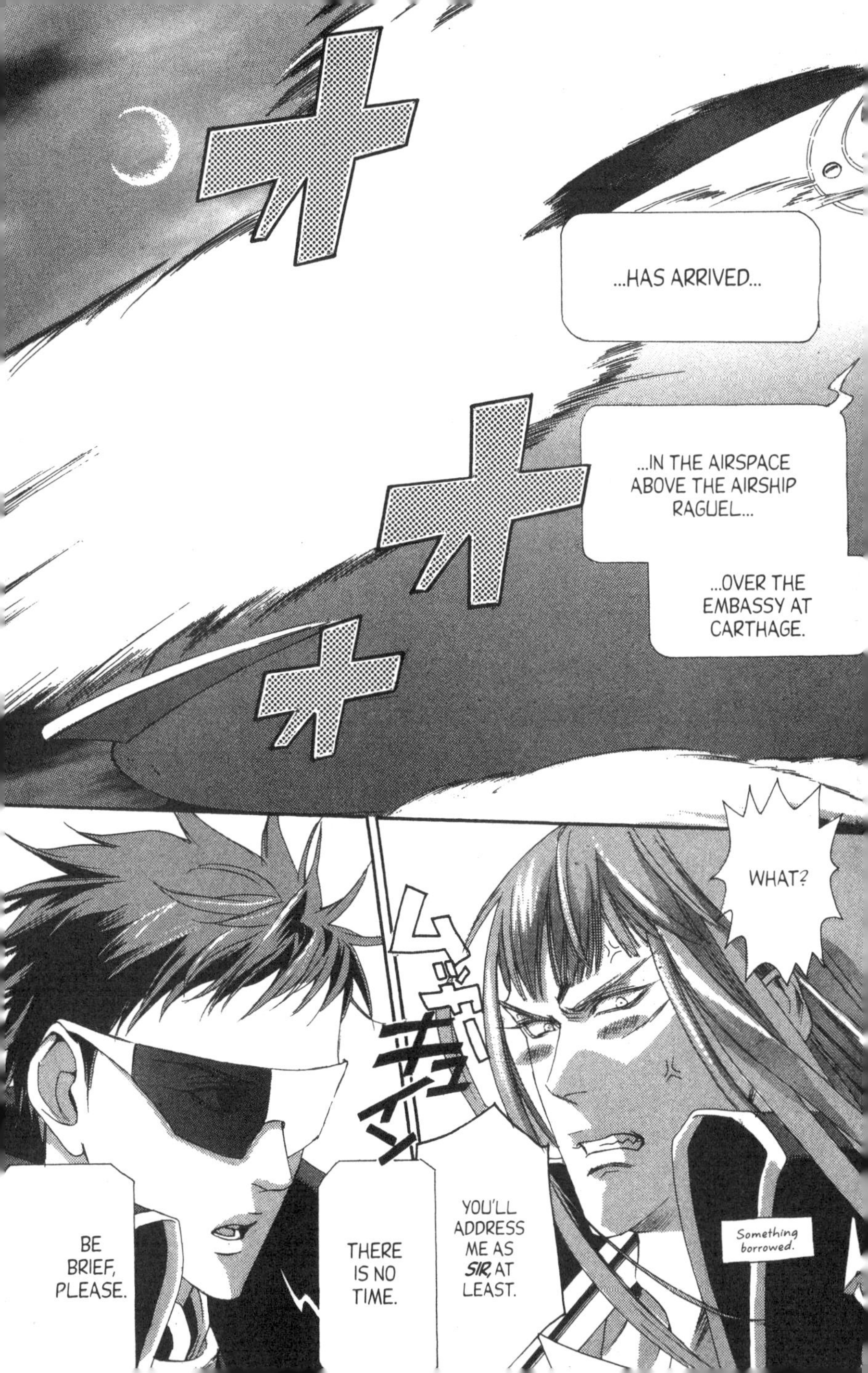
...HAS ARRIVED...
...IN THE AIRSPACE ABOVE THE AIRSHIP RAGUEL...
...OVER THE EMBASSY AT CARTHAGE.
WHAT?
Something borrowed.
YOU'LL ADDRESS ME AS SIR, AT LEAST.
THERE IS NO TIME.
BE BRIEF, PLEASE.

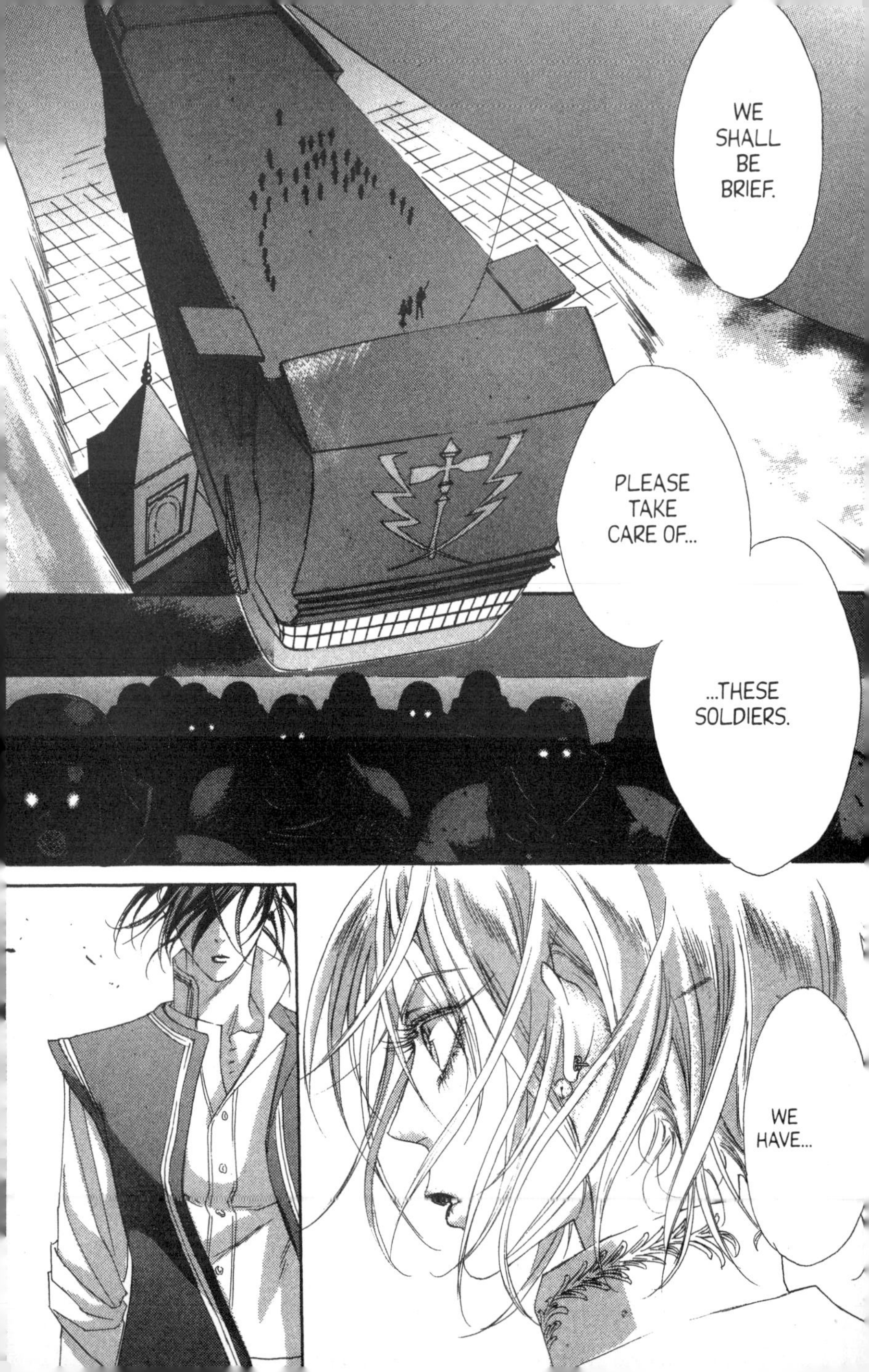
WE SHALL BE BRIEF.
PLEASE TAKE CARE OF...
...THESE SOLDIERS.
WE HAVE...

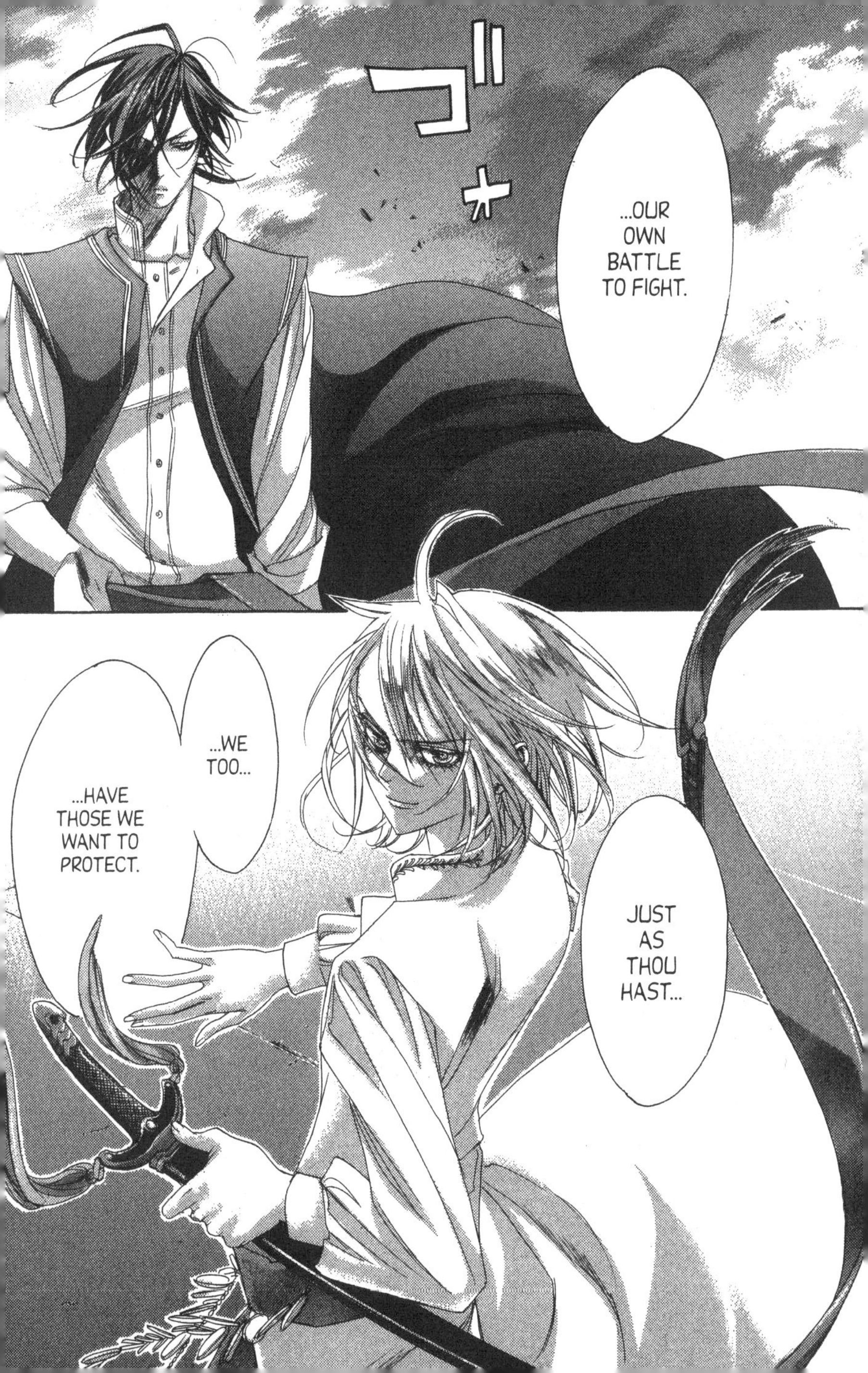
ゴォ
...OUR OWN BATTLE TO FIGHT.
JUST AS THOU HAST...
...WE TOO...
...HAVE THOSE WE WANT TO PROTECT.

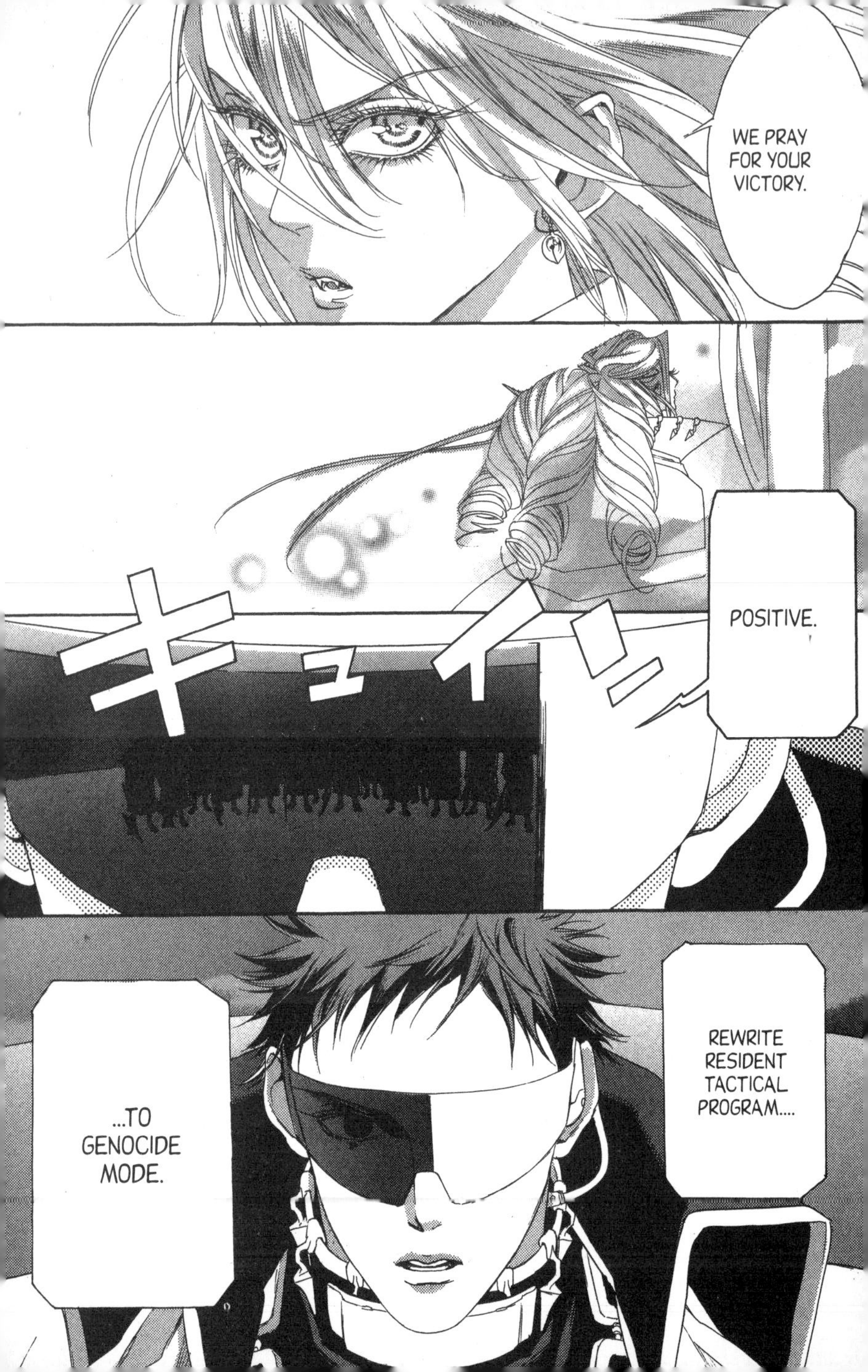
WE PRAY FOR YOUR VICTORY.
POSITIVE.
キュイン
REWRITE RESIDENT TACTICAL PROGRAM....
...TO GENOCIDE MODE.

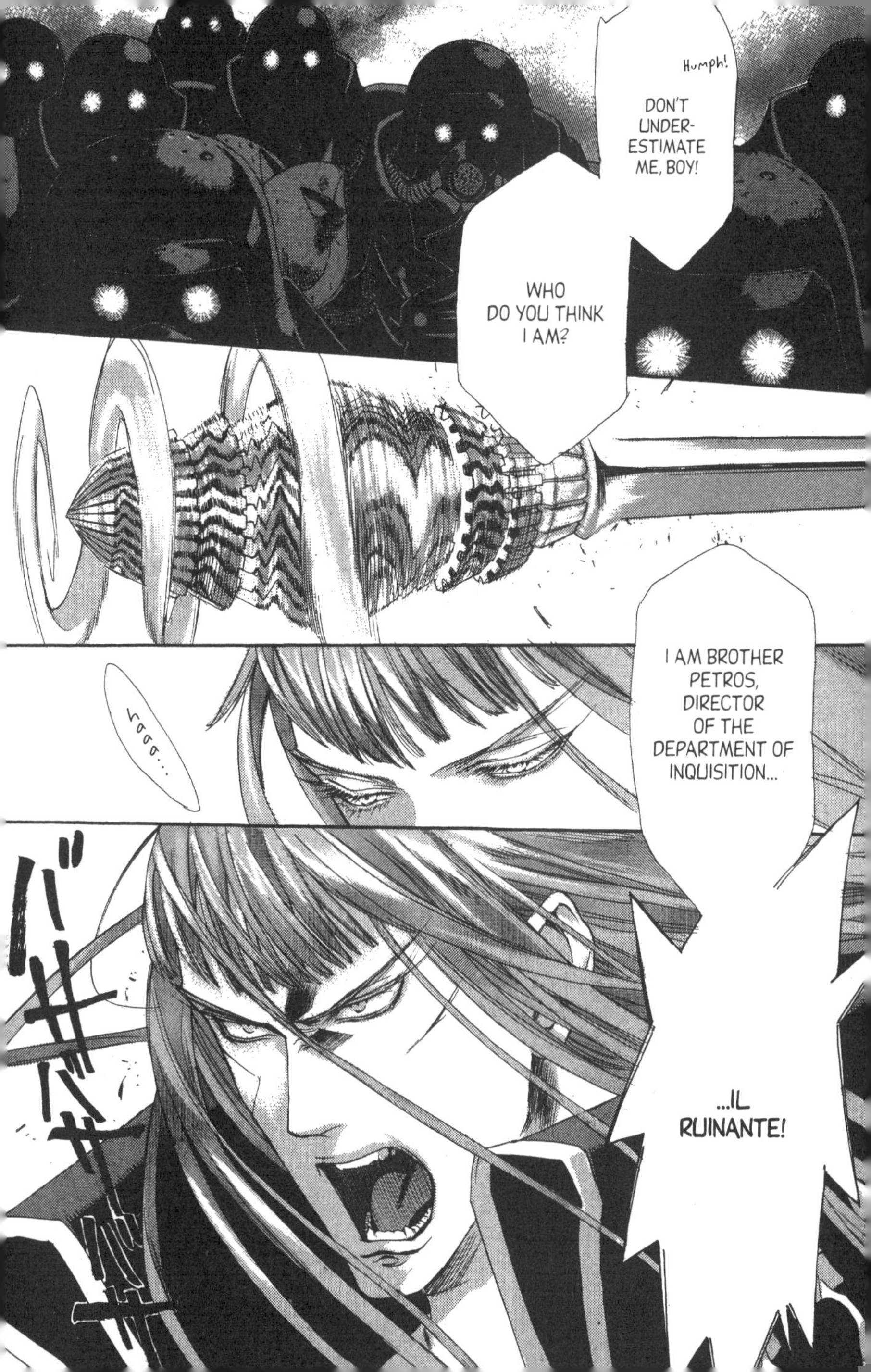
Humph!
DON'T UNDER-ESTIMATE ME, BOY!
WHO DO YOU THINK I AM?
I AM BROTHER PETROS, DIRECTOR OF THE DEPARTMENT OF INQUISITION...
haaa...
...IL RUINANTE!

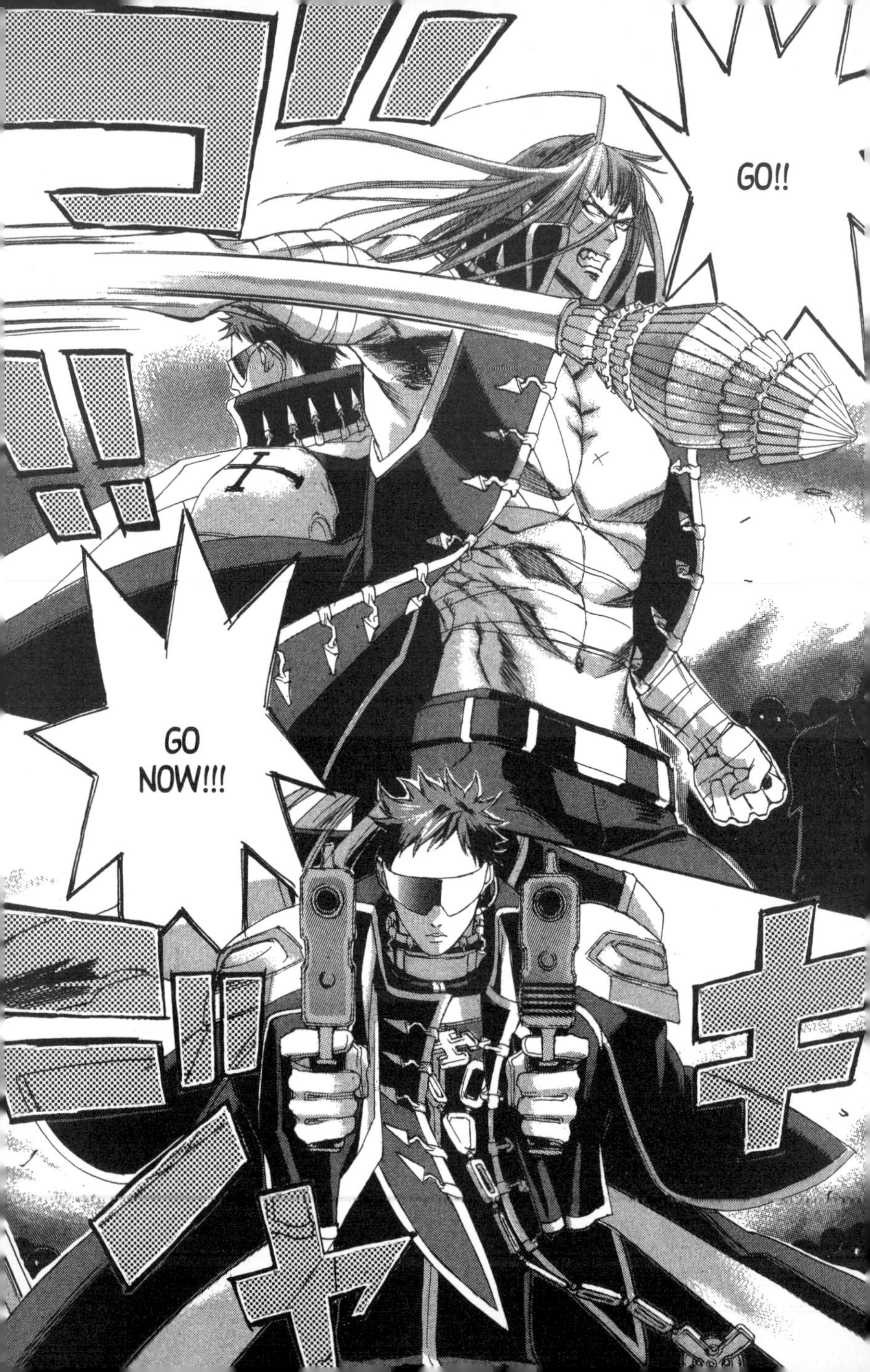
GO!!
GO NOW!!!

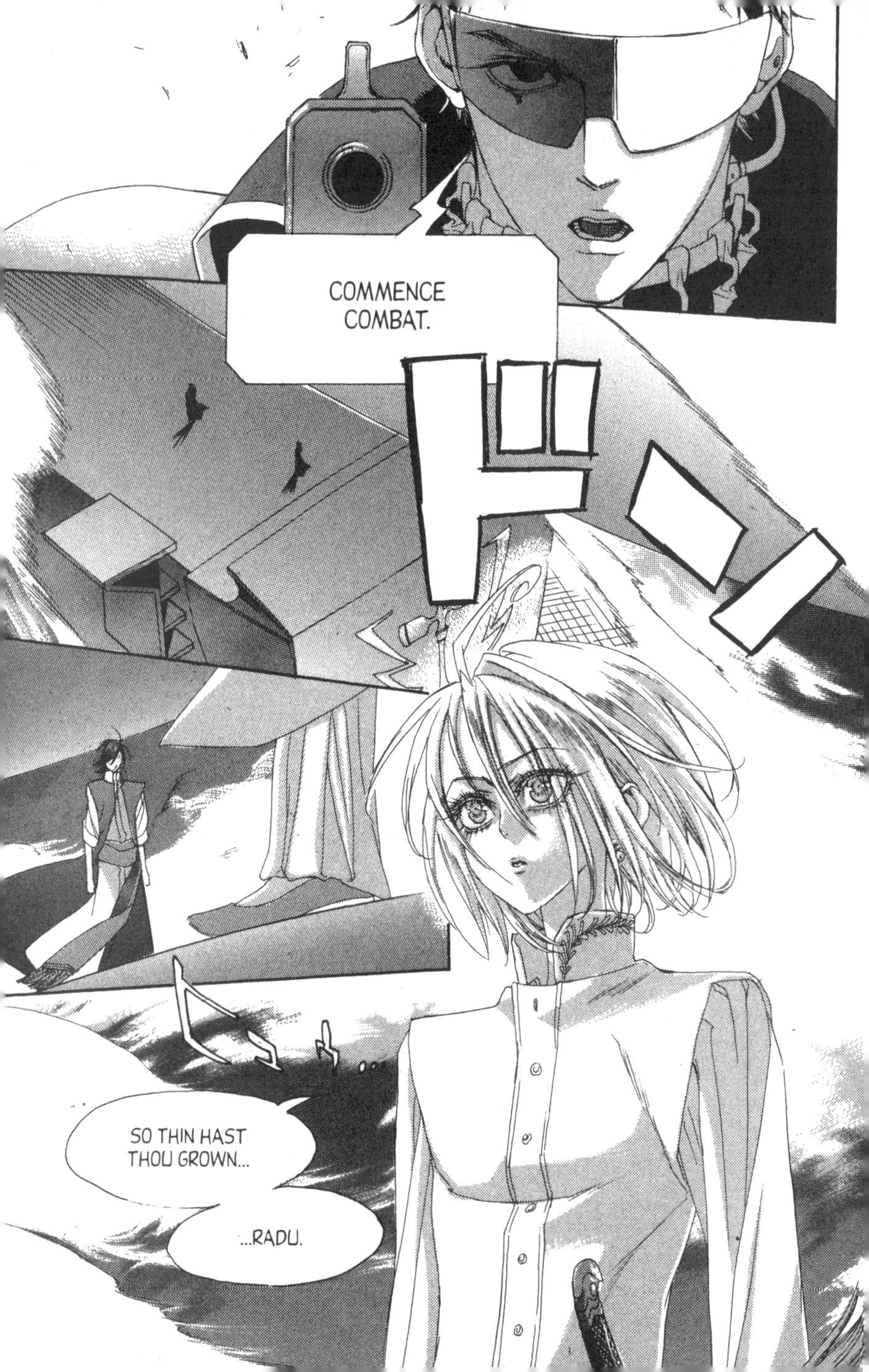
COMMENCE COMBAT.
ドン
SO THIN HAST THOU GROWN...
...RADU.

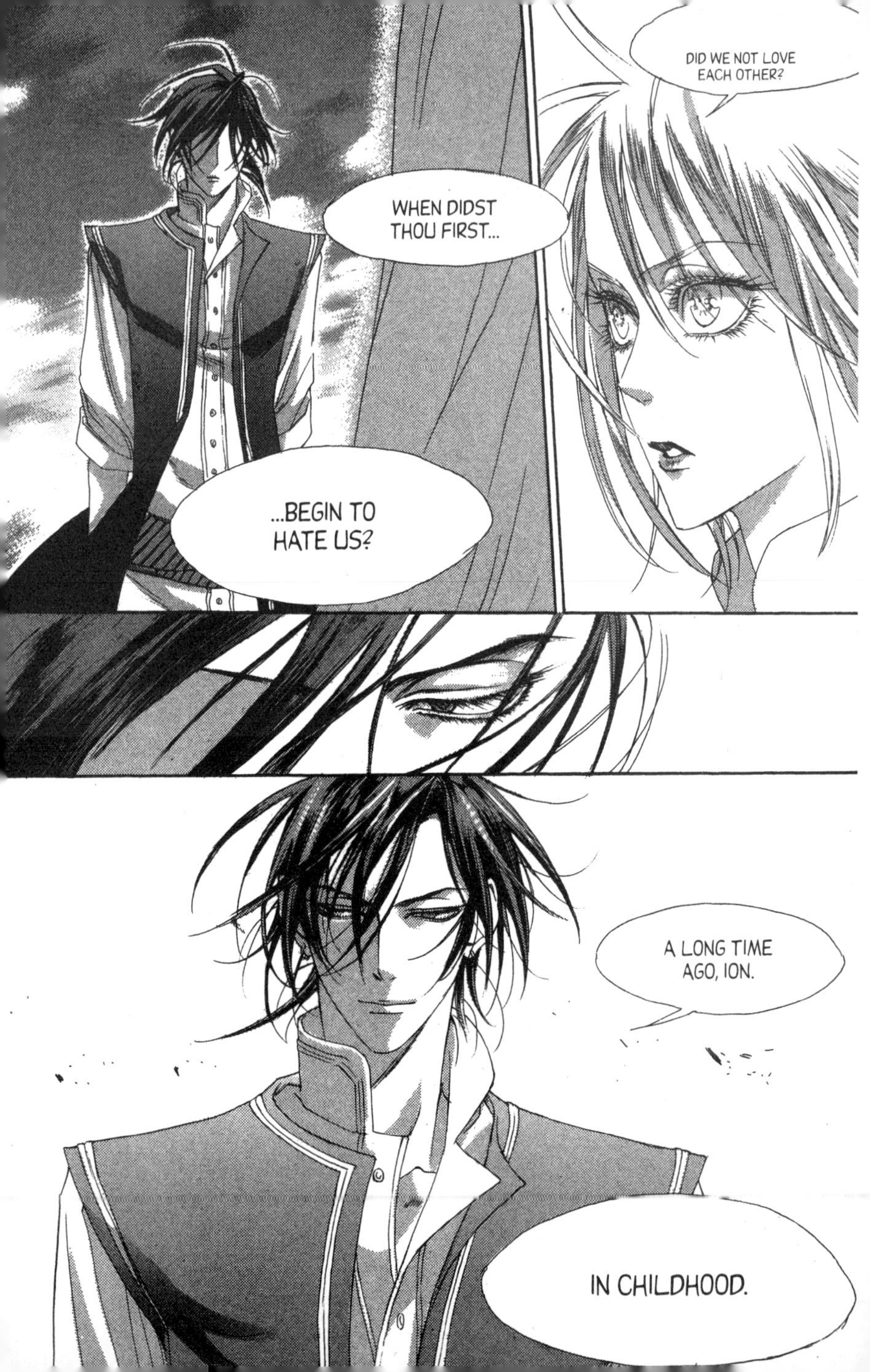
DID WE NOT LOVE EACH OTHER?
WHEN DIDST THOU FIRST...
...BEGIN TO HATE US?
A LONG TIME AGO, ION.
IN CHILDHOOD.

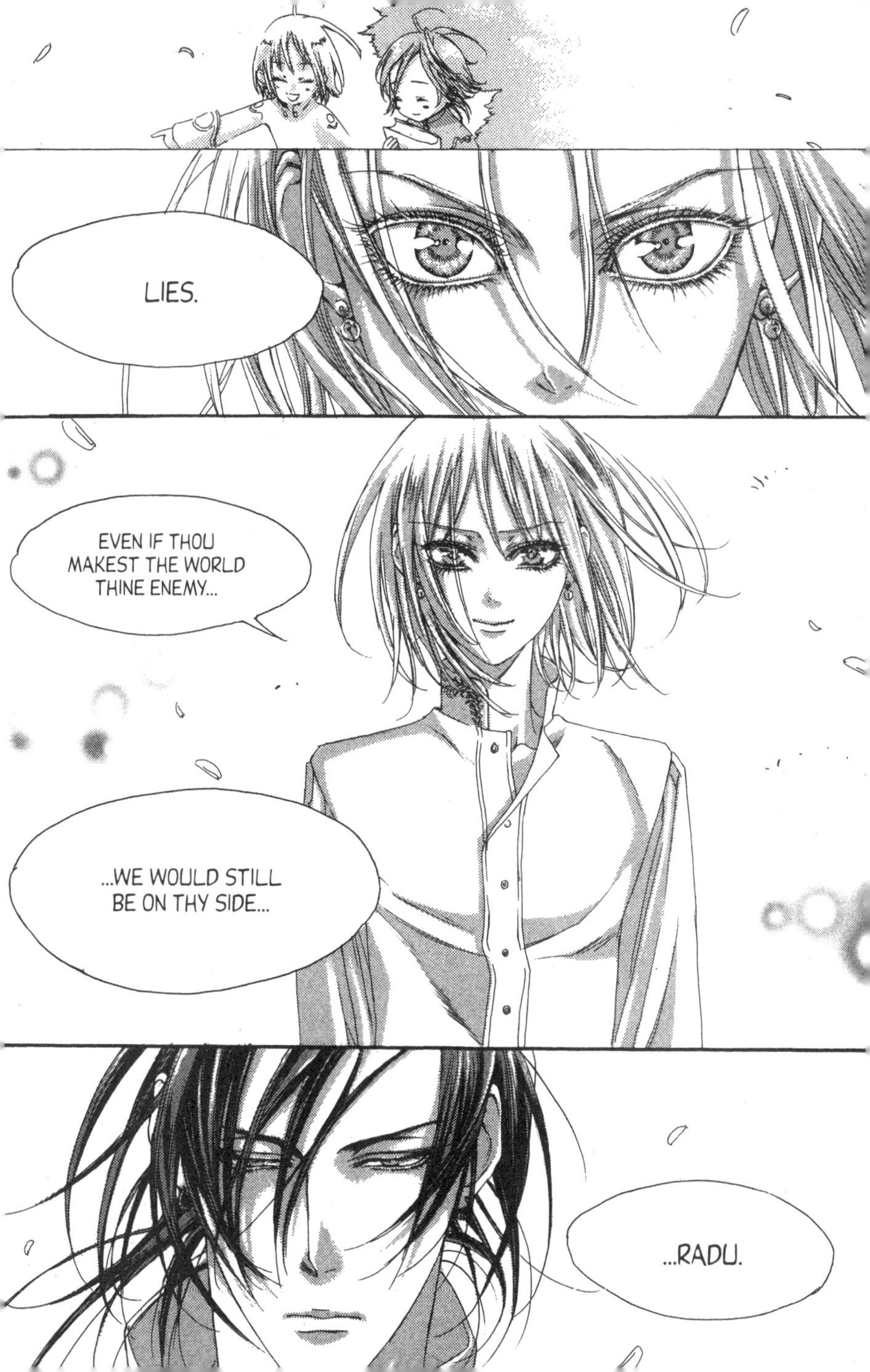
LIES.
EVEN IF THOU MAKEST THE WORLD THINE ENEMY...
...WE WOULD STILL BE ON THY SIDE...
...RADU.

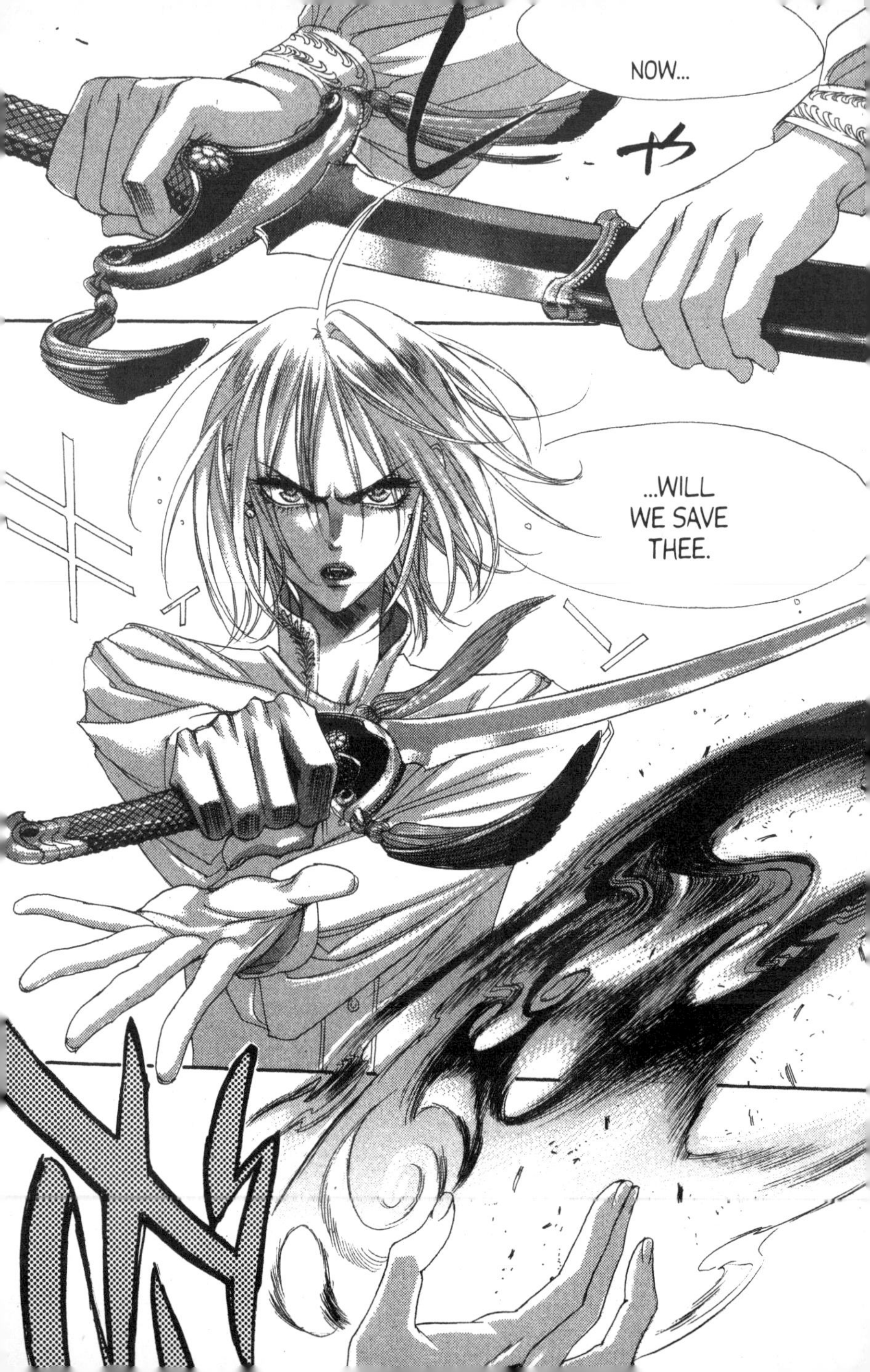
NOW...
...WILL WE SAVE THEE.

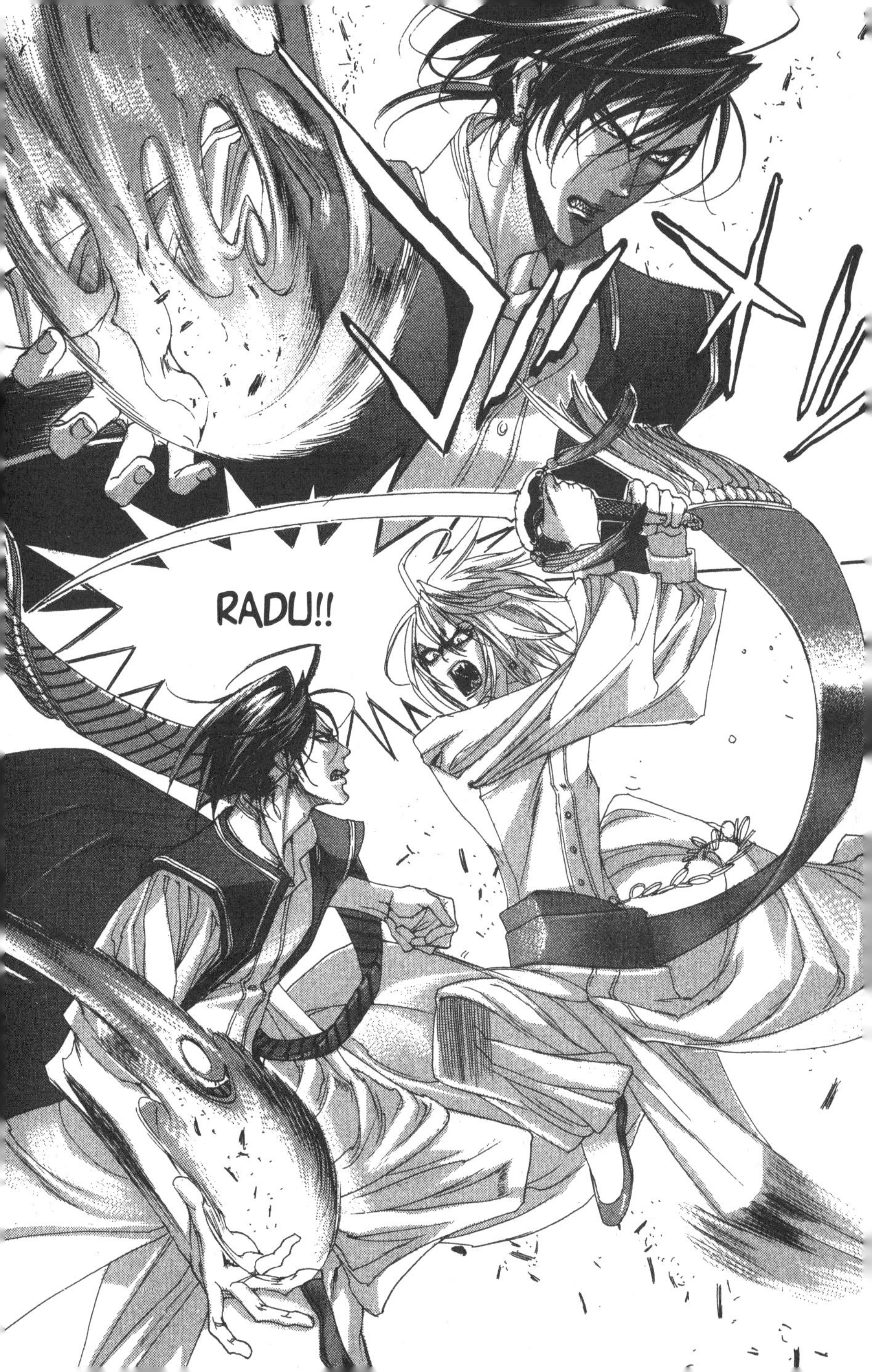
RADU!!

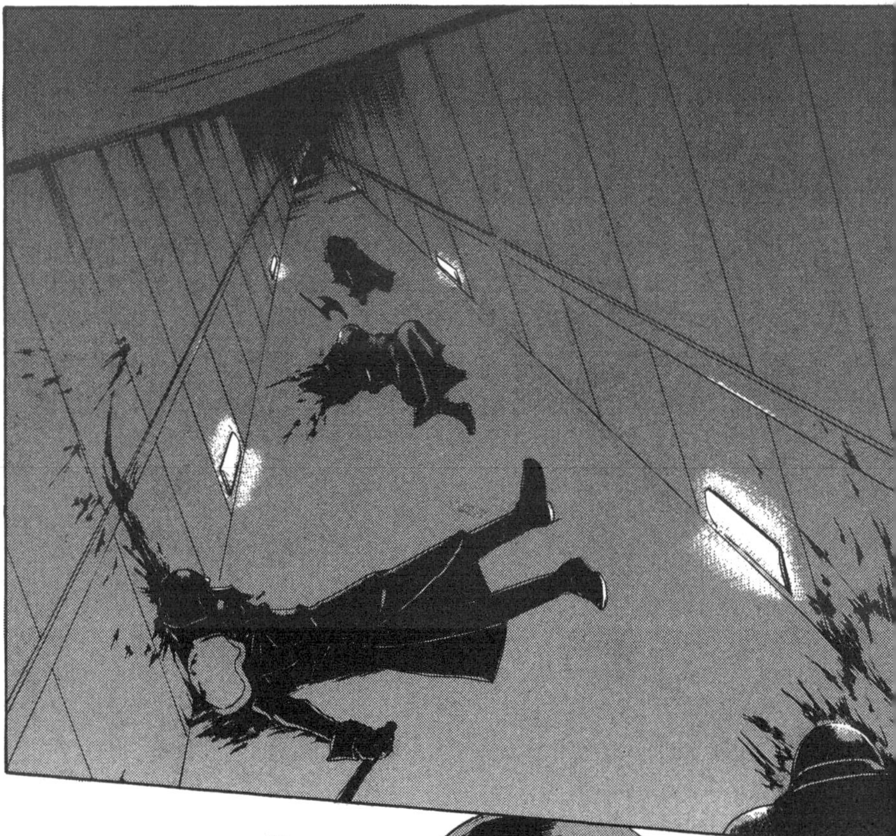
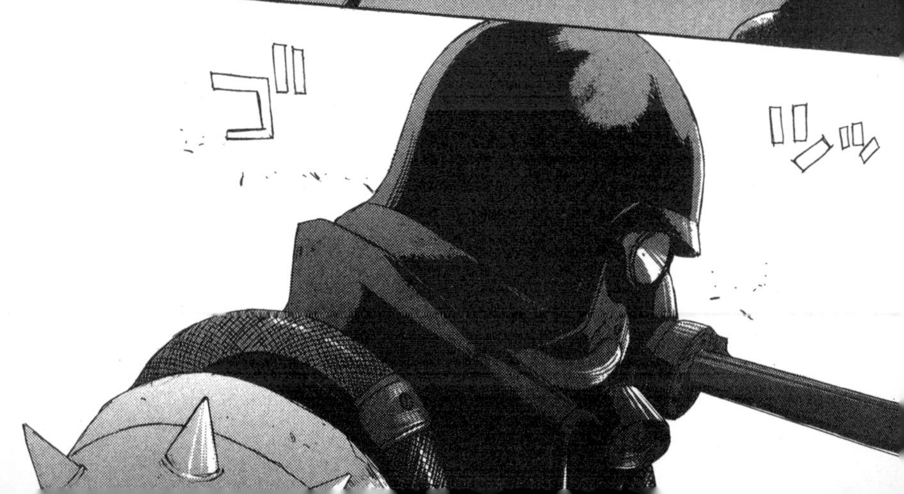
ゴ

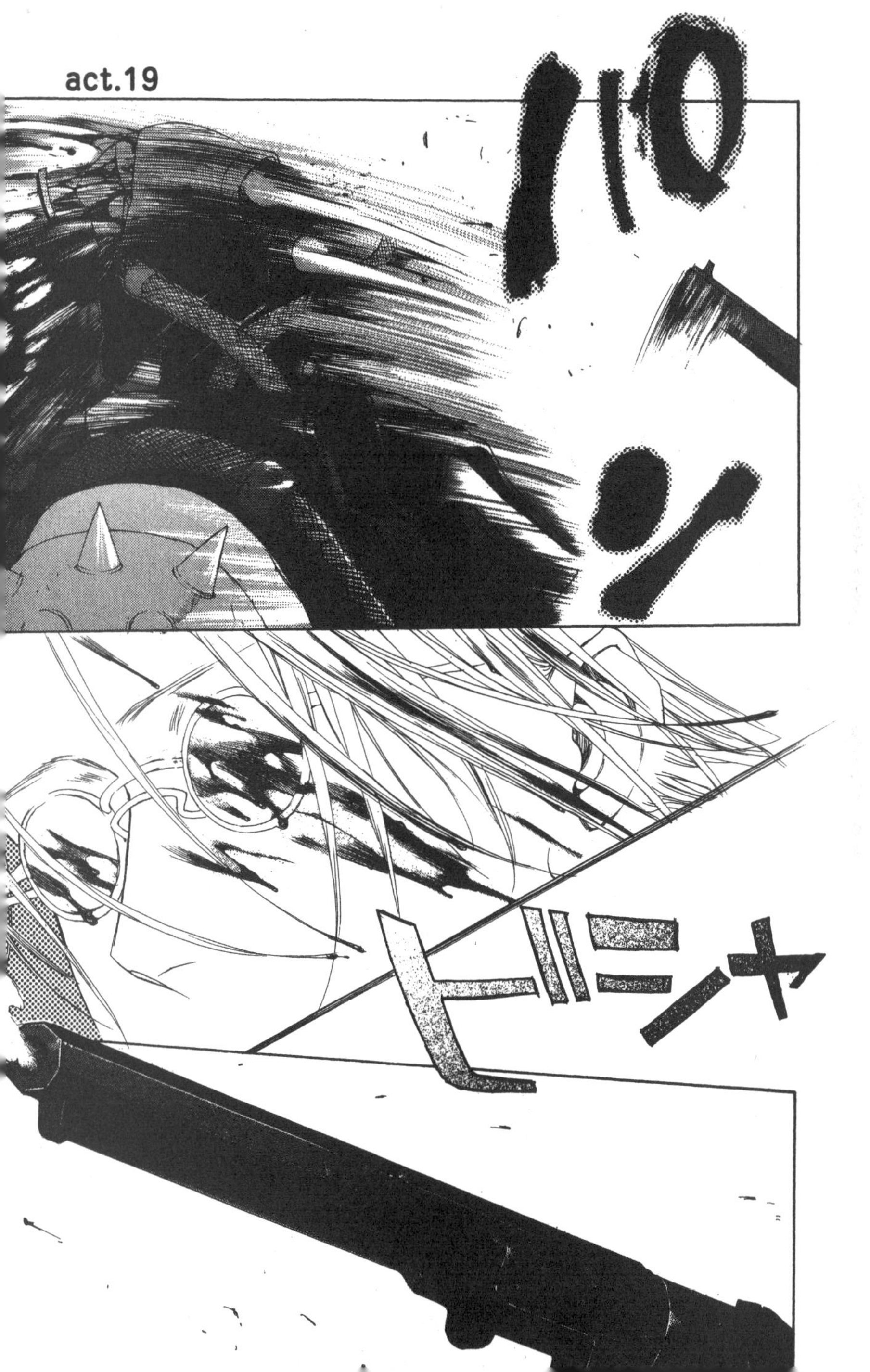パッ

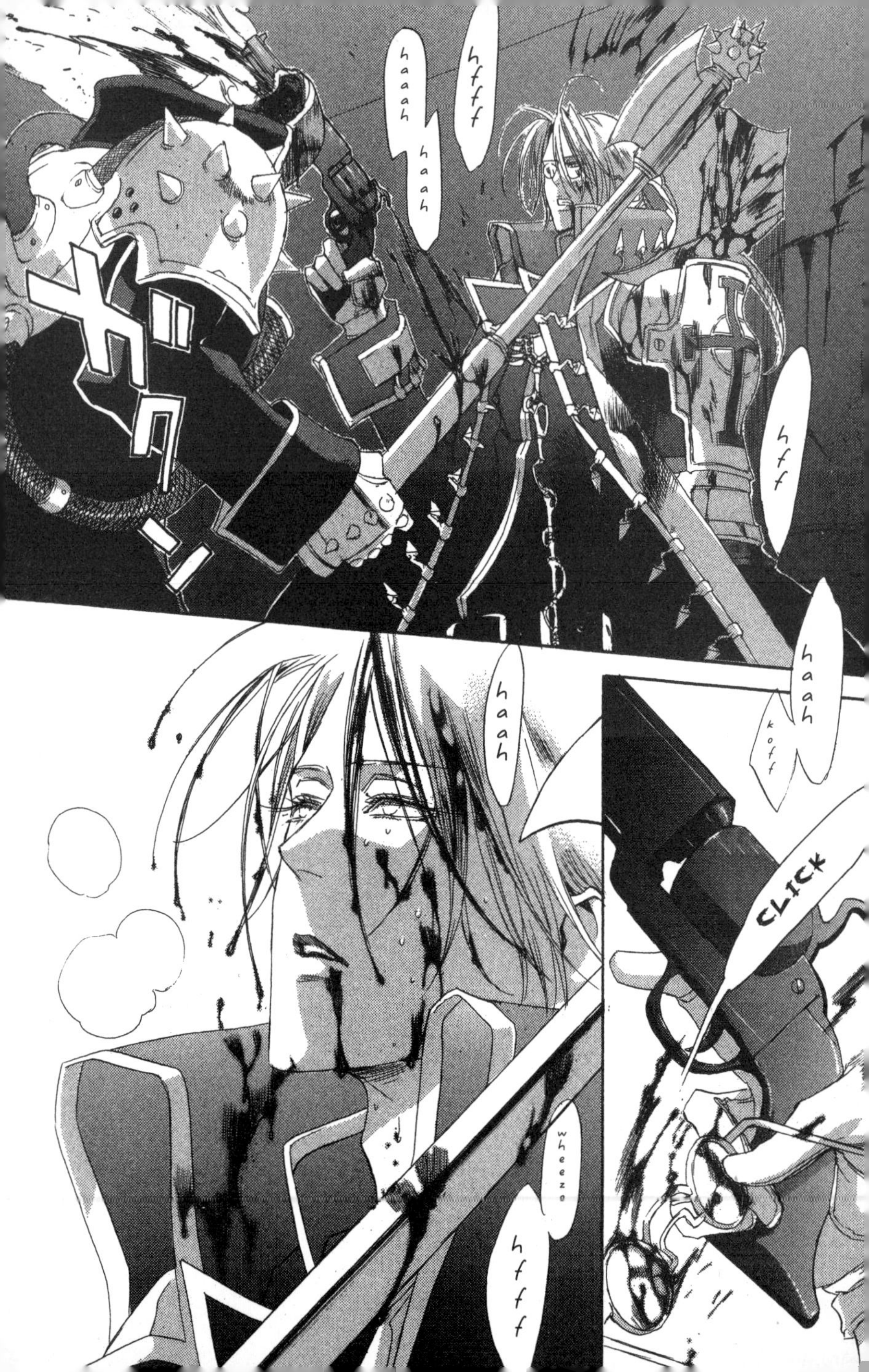

hff
hfff
haaah haaah
haaah koff
CLICK
haaah
wheeze
hfff

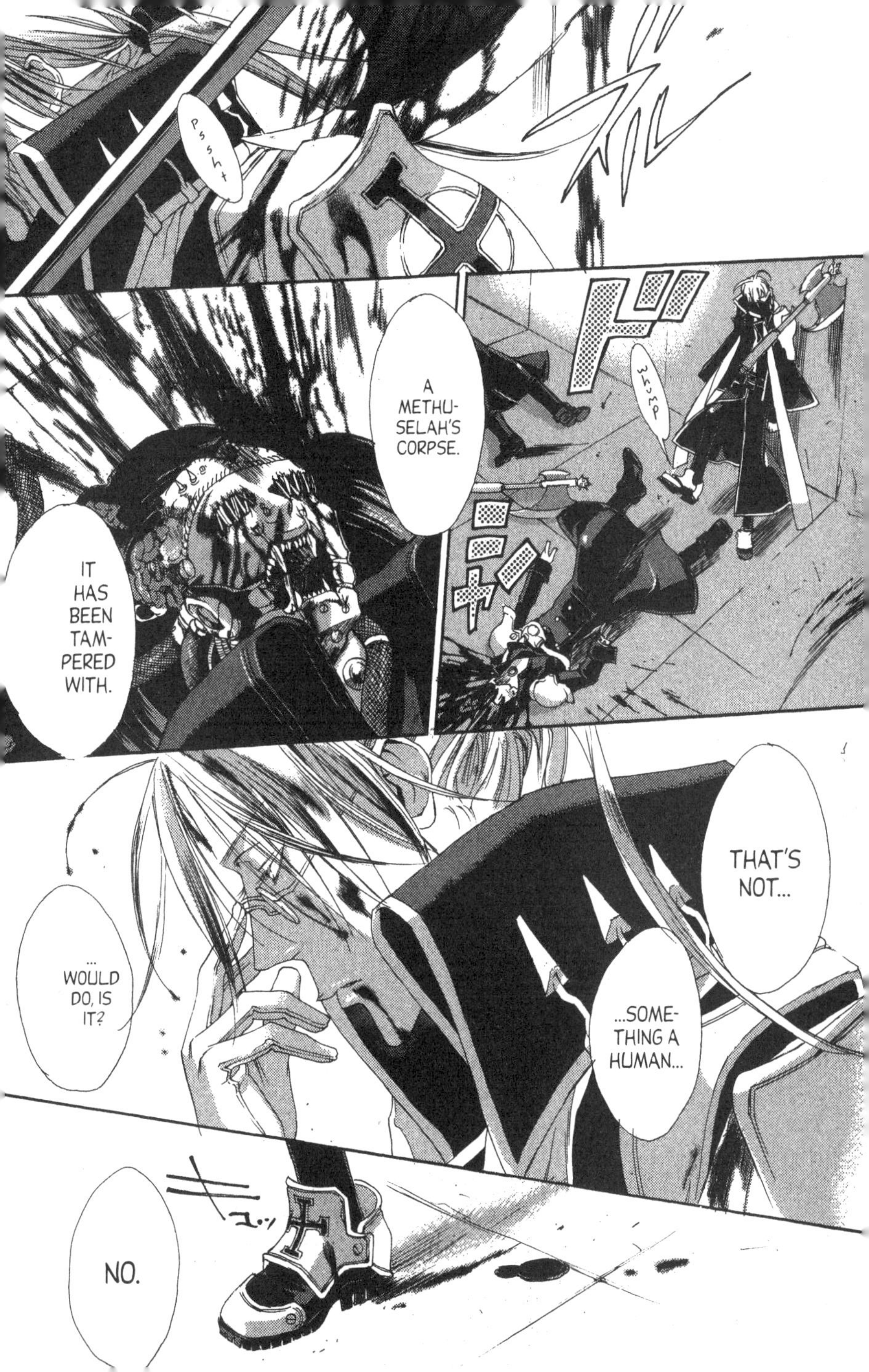
Psssht
thump
A METHU-SELAH'S CORPSE.
IT HAS BEEN TAM-PERED WITH.
THAT'S NOT...
...SOME-THING A HUMAN...
...WOULD DO, IS IT?
NO.

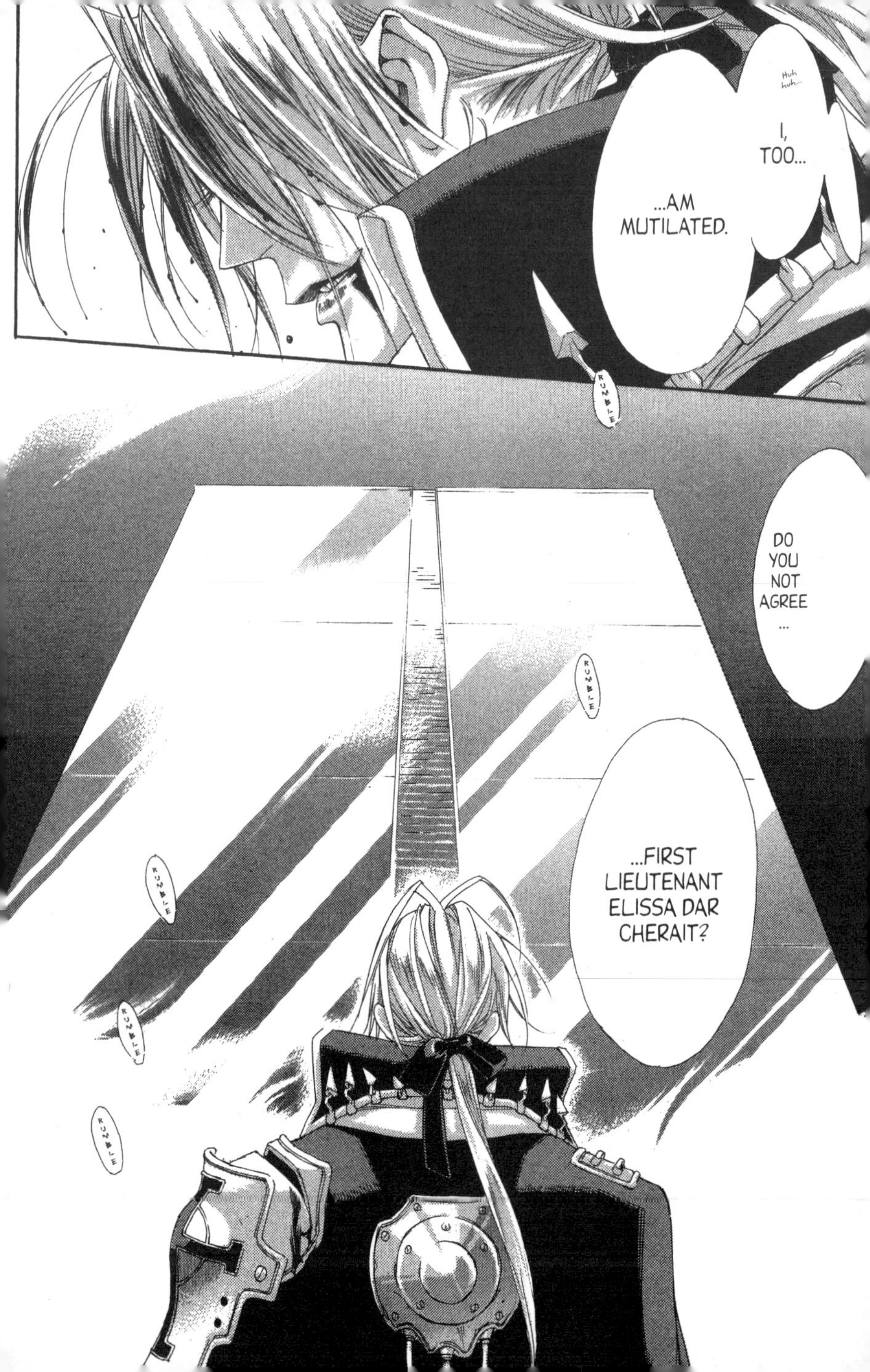

Huh huh...
I, TOO...
...AM MUTILATED.
RUMBLE
DO YOU NOT AGREE ...
...FIRST LIEUTENANT ELISSA DAR CHERAIT?
RUMBLE
RUMBLE
RUMBLE
RUMBLE

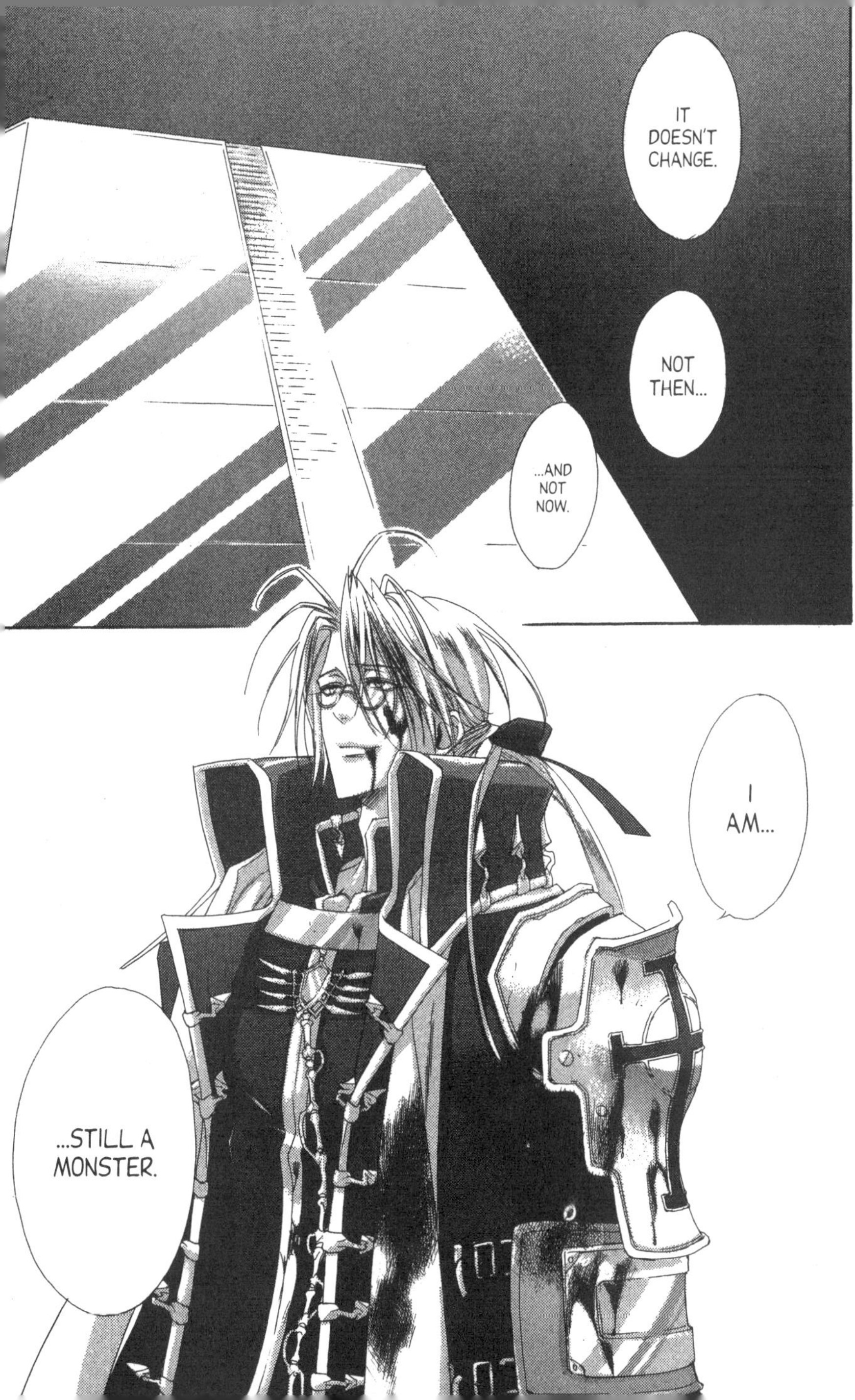
IT DOESN'T CHANGE.
NOT THEN...
...AND NOT NOW.
I AM...
...STILL A MONSTER.

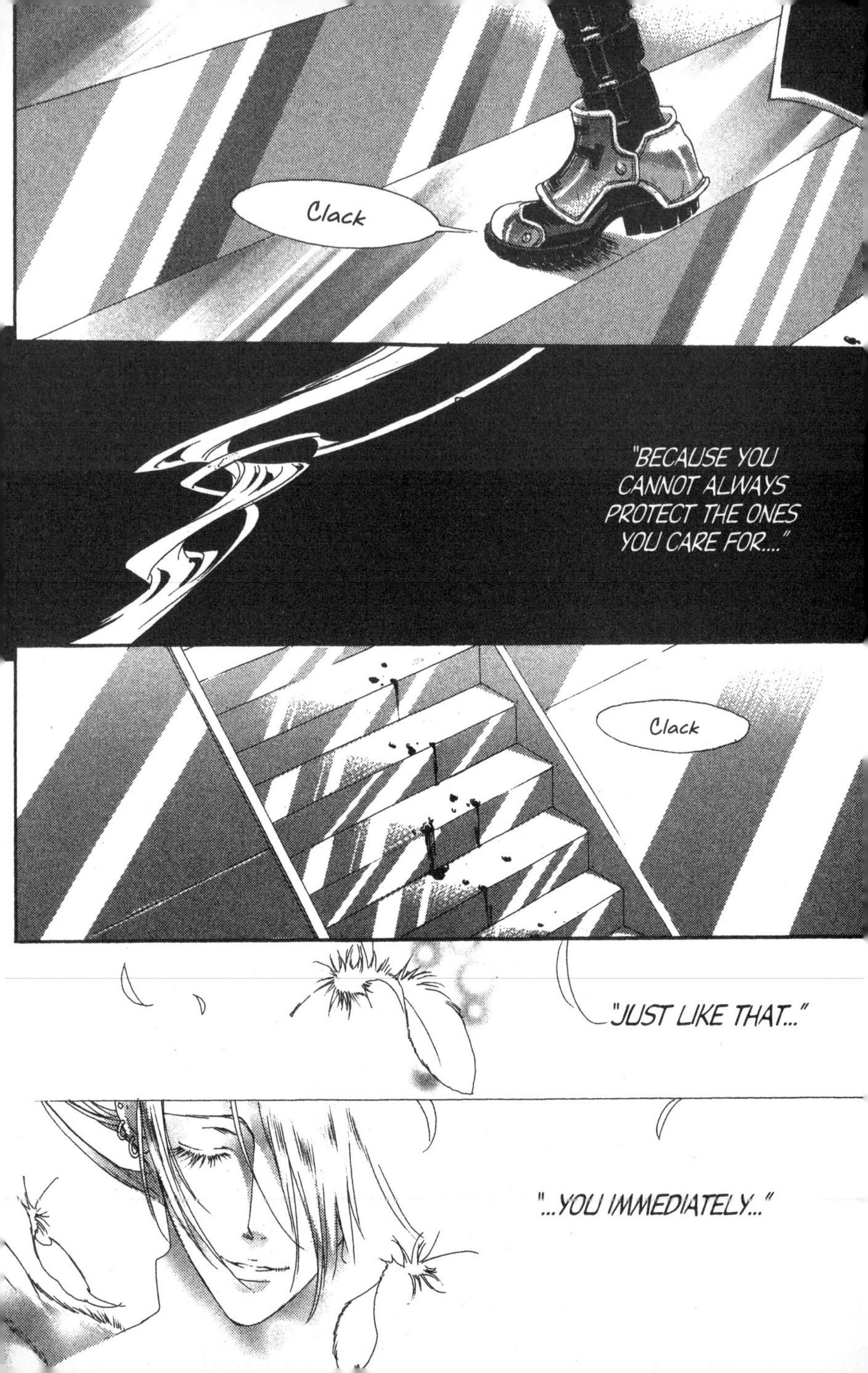
Clack
"BECAUSE YOU CANNOT ALWAYS PROTECT THE ONES YOU CARE FOR..."
Clack
"JUST LIKE THAT..."
"...YOU IMMEDIATELY..."

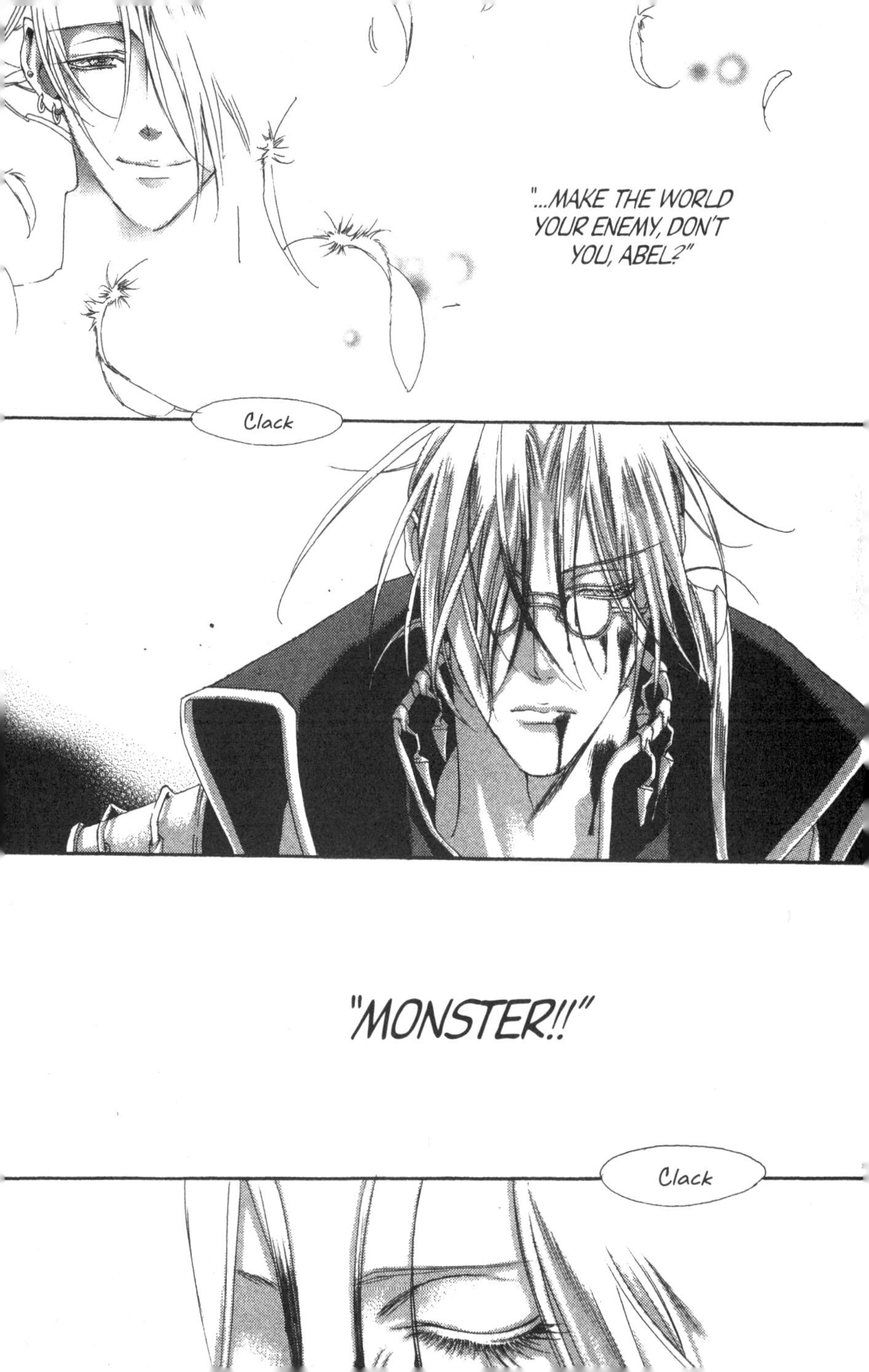
"...MAKE THE WORLD YOUR ENEMY, DON'T YOU, ABEL?"
Clack
"MONSTER!!"
Clack

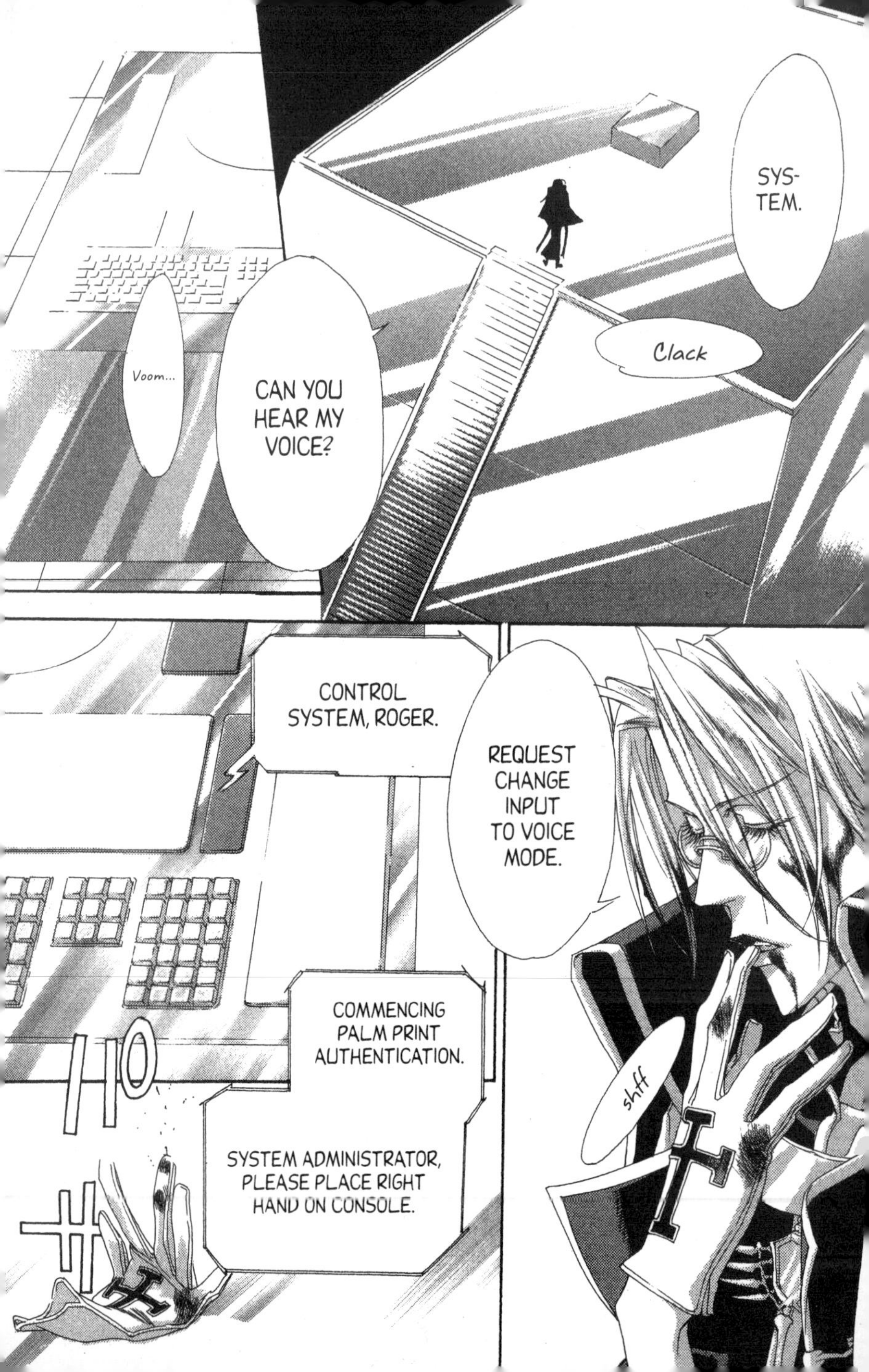
SYS-
TEM.
Clack
CAN YOU HEAR MY VOICE?
Voom...
REQUEST CHANGE INPUT TO VOICE MODE.
shff
CONTROL SYSTEM, ROGER.
COMMENCING PALM PRINT AUTHENTICATION.
SYSTEM ADMINISTRATOR, PLEASE PLACE RIGHT HAND ON CONSOLE.

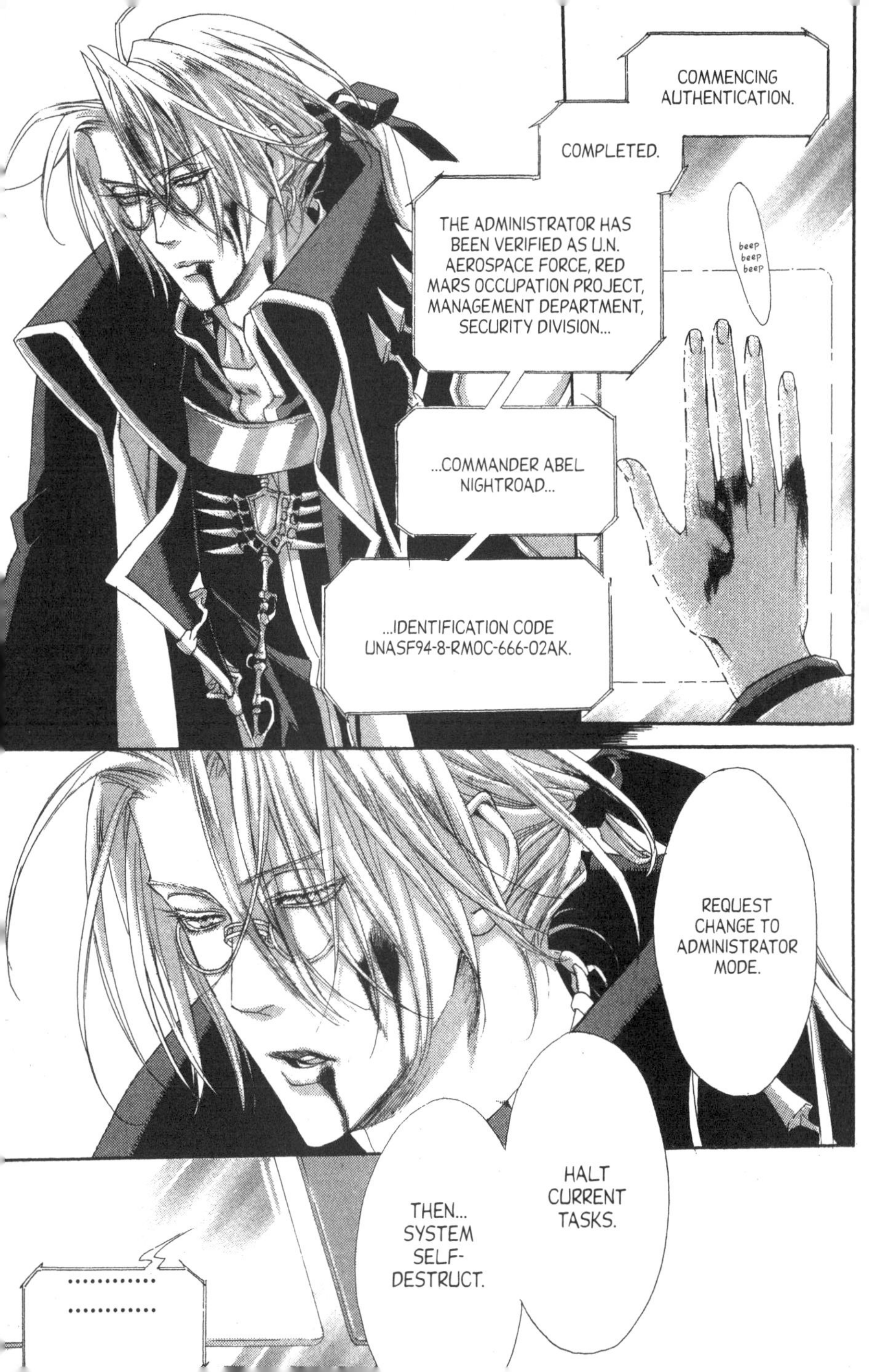

COMMENCING AUTHENTICATION.
COMPLETED.
beep beep beep
THE ADMINISTRATOR HAS BEEN VERIFIED AS U.N. AEROSPACE FORCE, RED MARS OCCUPATION PROJECT, MANAGEMENT DEPARTMENT, SECURITY DIVISION...
...COMMANDER ABEL NIGHTROAD...
...IDENTIFICATION CODE UNASF94-8-RMOC-666-02AK.
REQUEST CHANGE TO ADMINISTRATOR MODE.
HALT CURRENT TASKS.
THEN... SYSTEM SELF-DESTRUCT.
....
....

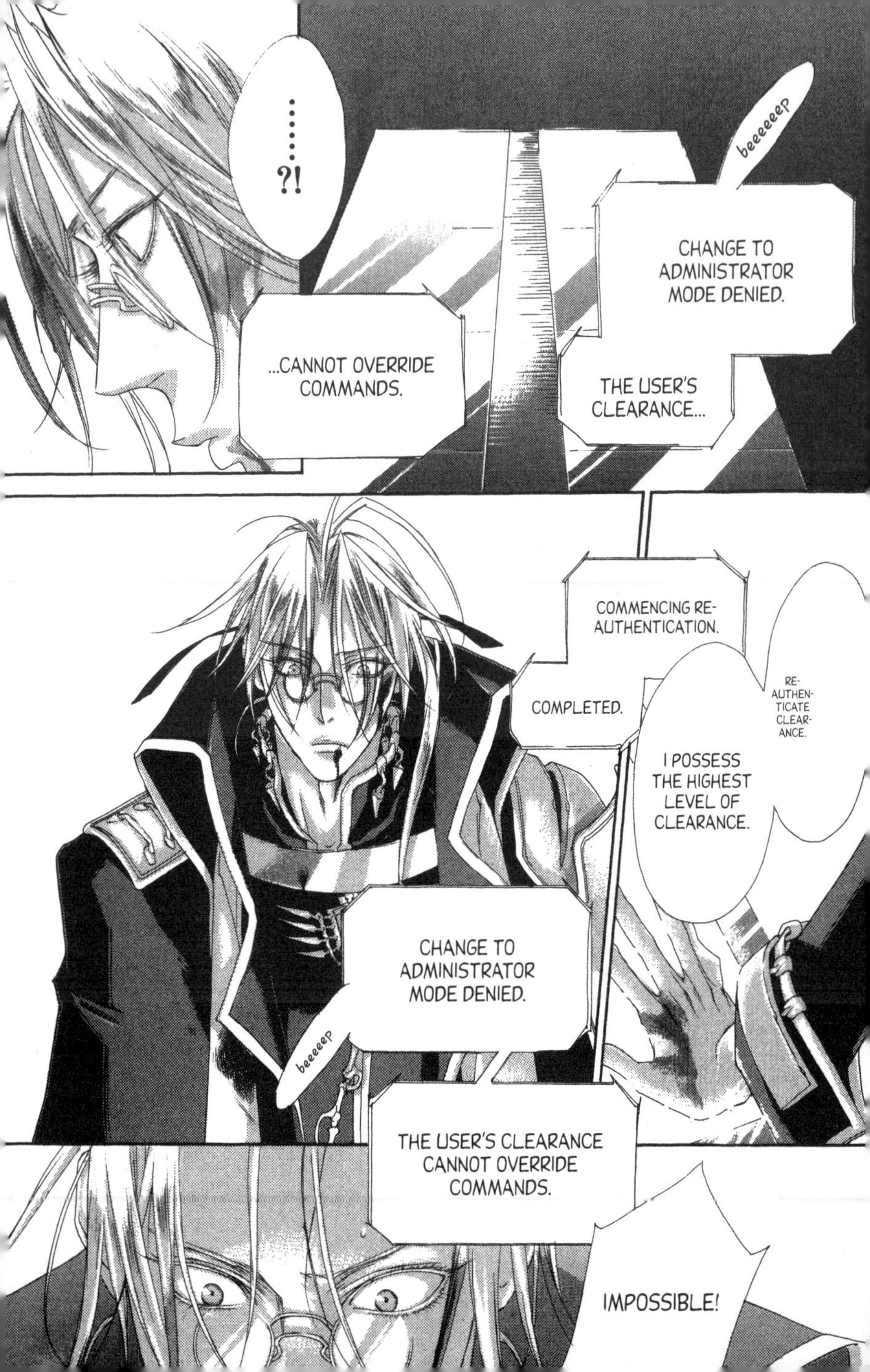
beeeeeep
CHANGE TO ADMINISTRATOR MODE DENIED.
THE USER'S CLEARANCE...
...CANNOT OVERRIDE COMMANDS.
......?!
RE-AUTHENTICATE CLEARANCE.
I POSSESS THE HIGHEST LEVEL OF CLEARANCE.
COMMENCING RE-AUTHENTICATION.
COMPLETED.
beeeeep
CHANGE TO ADMINISTRATOR MODE DENIED.
THE USER'S CLEARANCE CANNOT OVERRIDE COMMANDS.
IMPOSSIBLE!

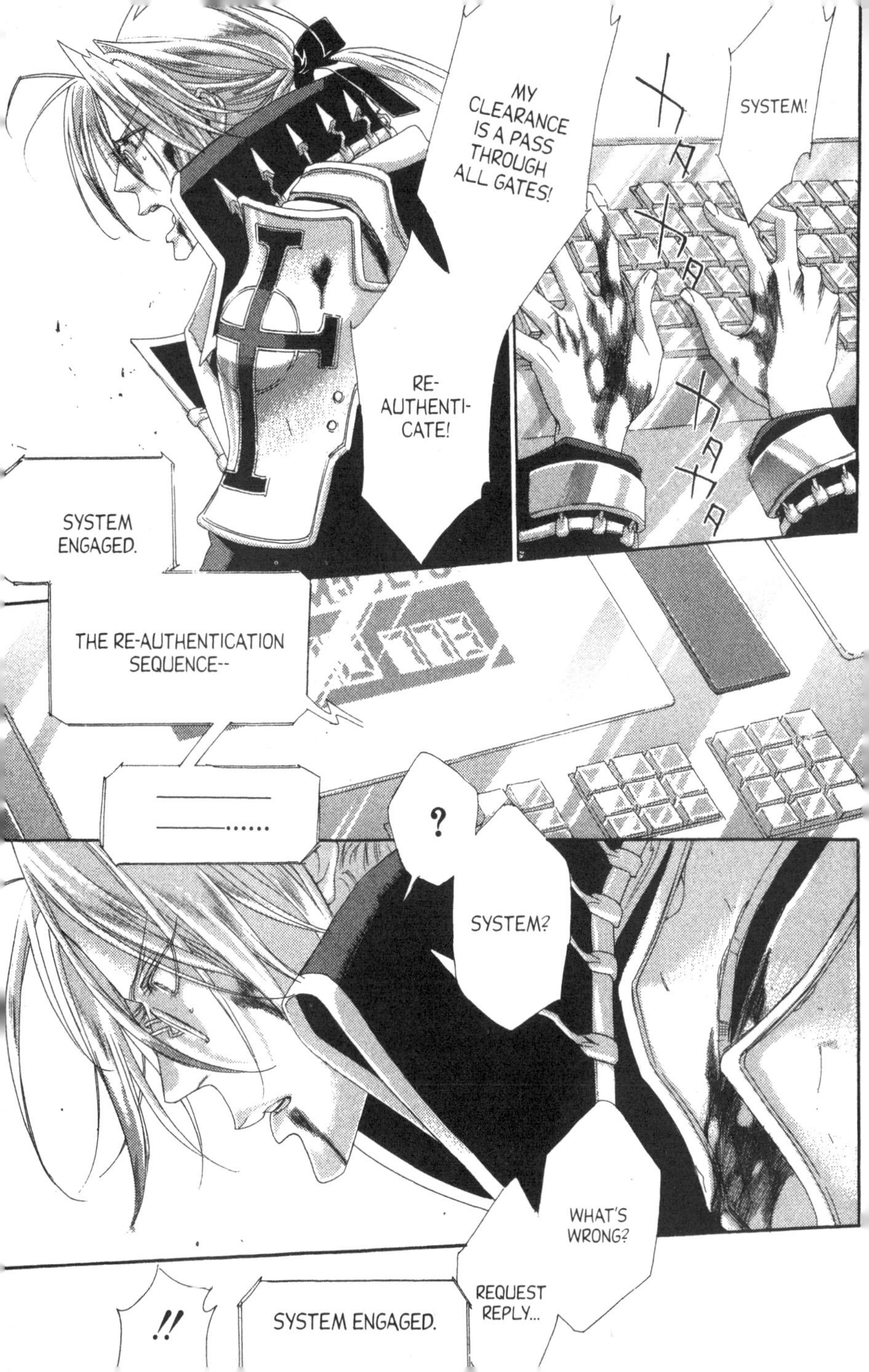
SYSTEM!
MY CLEARANCE IS A PASS THROUGH ALL GATES!
RE-AUTHENTICATE!
SYSTEM ENGAGED.
THE RE-AUTHENTICATION SEQUENCE--
——
——......
?
SYSTEM?
WHAT'S WRONG?
REQUEST REPLY...
SYSTEM ENGAGED.
!!

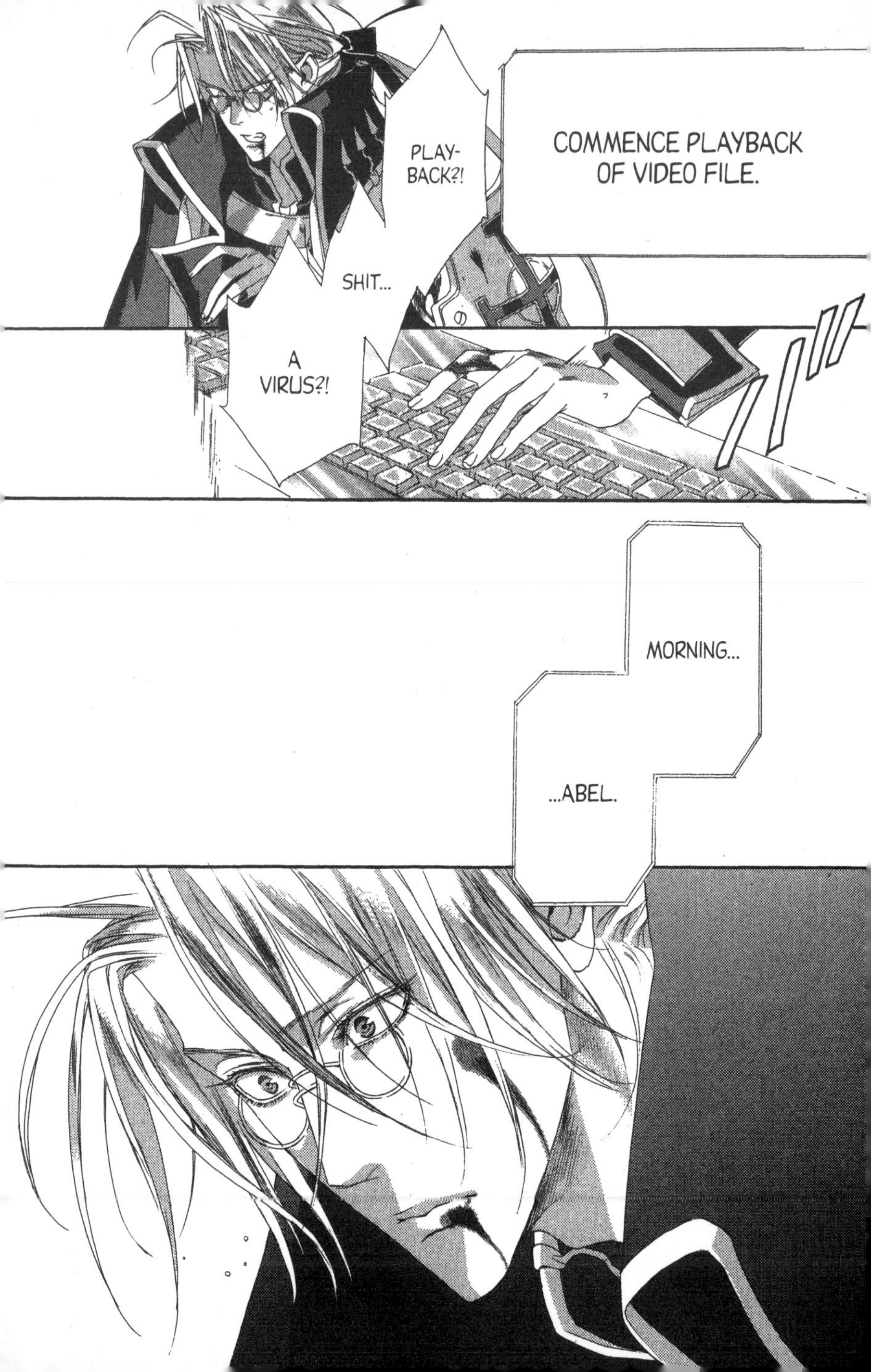
COMMENCE PLAYBACK OF VIDEO FILE.
PLAY-BACK?!
SHIT...
A VIRUS?!
MORNING...
...ABEL.

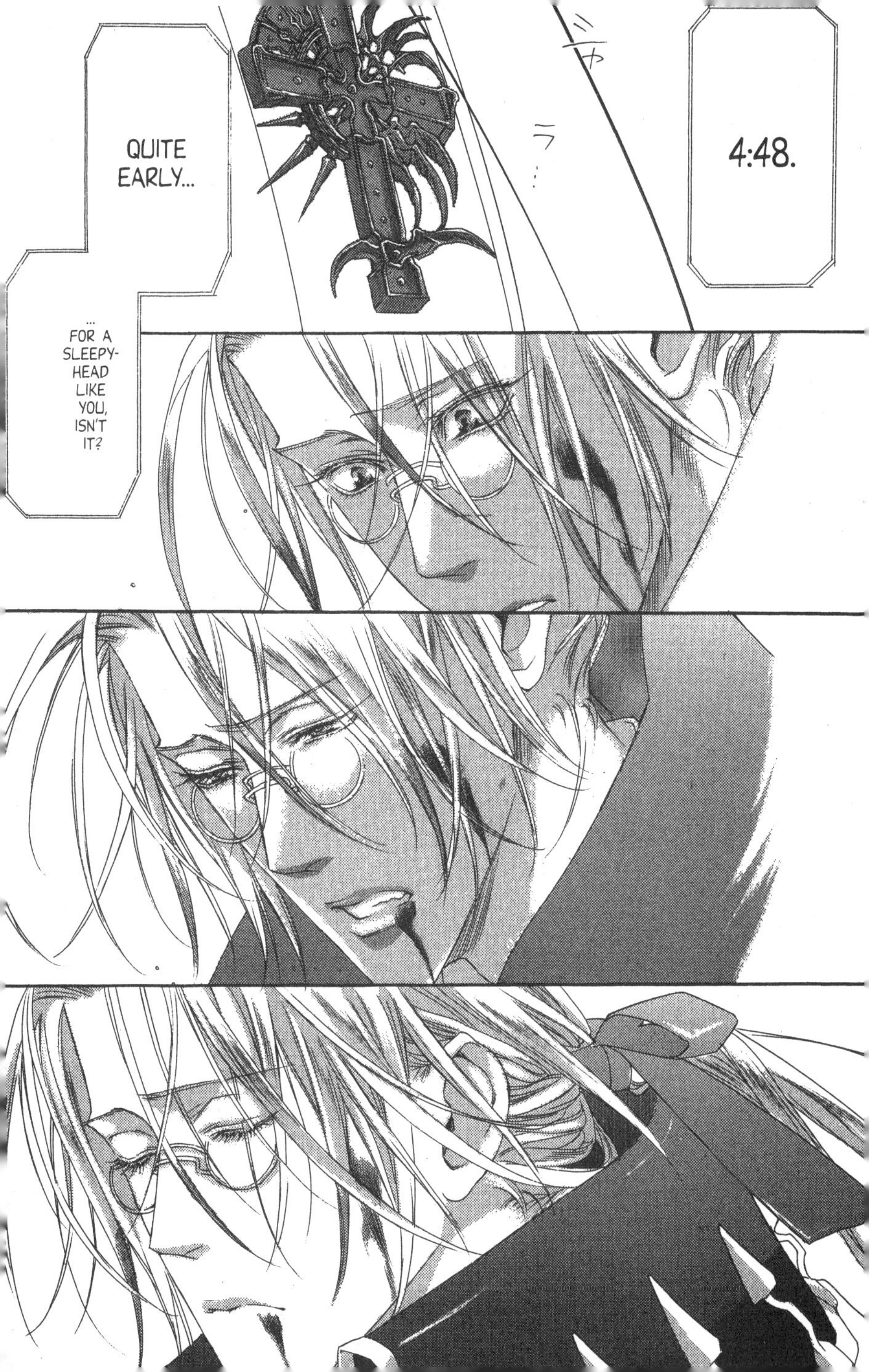
4:48.
シャラ…
QUITE EARLY...
...FOR A SLEEPY-HEAD LIKE YOU, ISN'T IT?

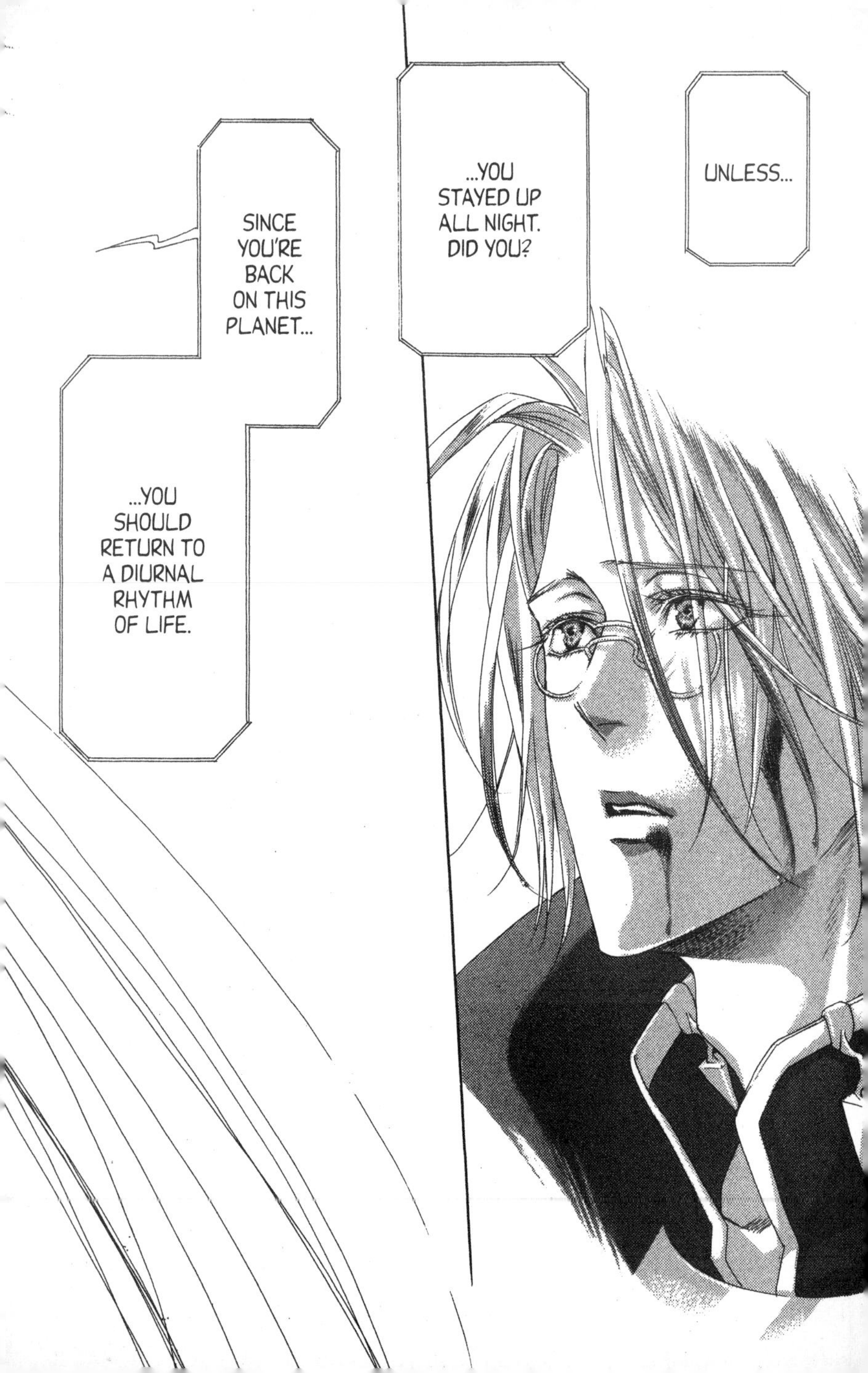
UNLESS...
...YOU STAYED UP ALL NIGHT. DID YOU?
SINCE YOU'RE BACK ON THIS PLANET...
...YOU SHOULD RETURN TO A DIURNAL RHYTHM OF LIFE.

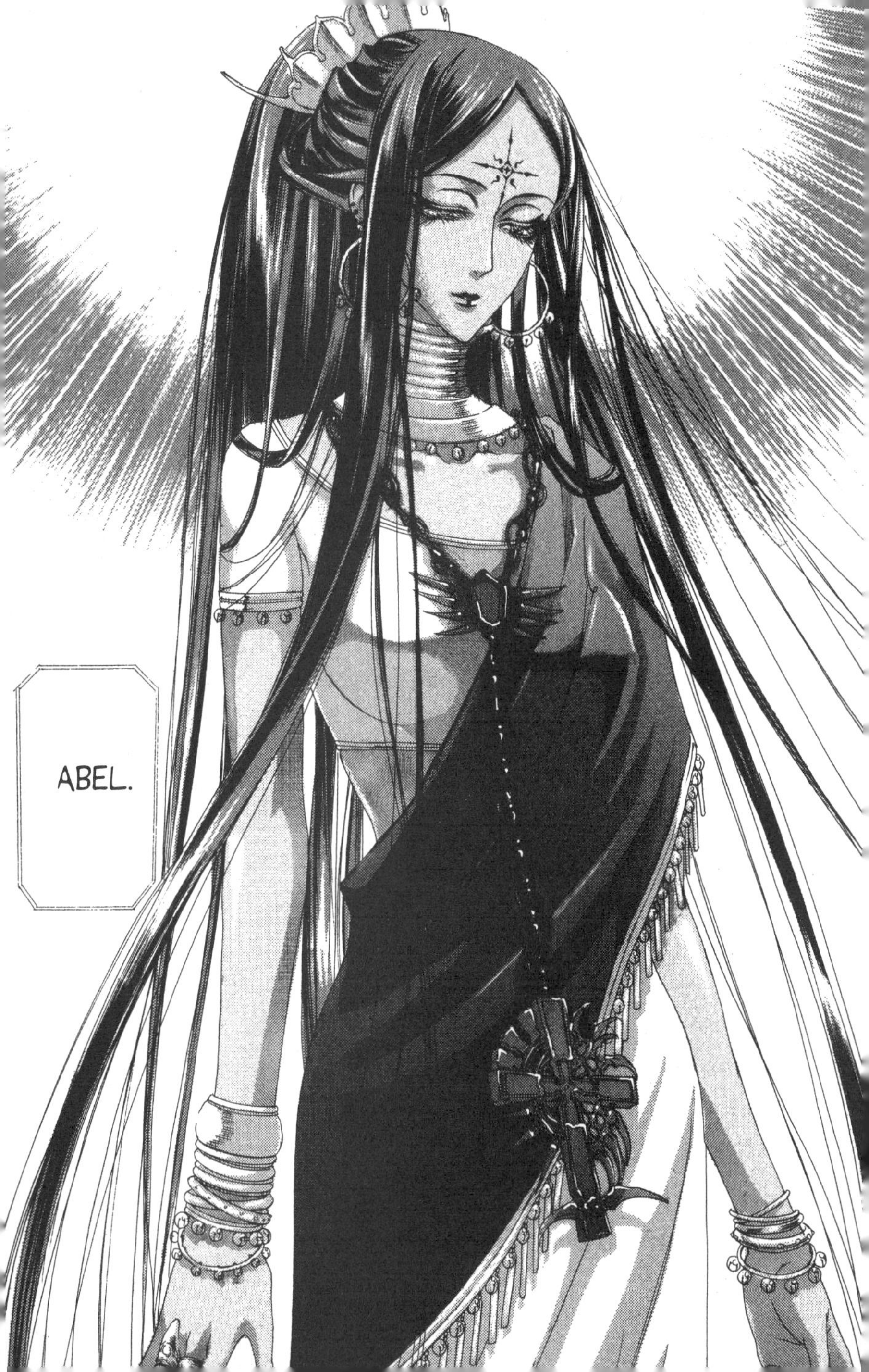
ABEL.

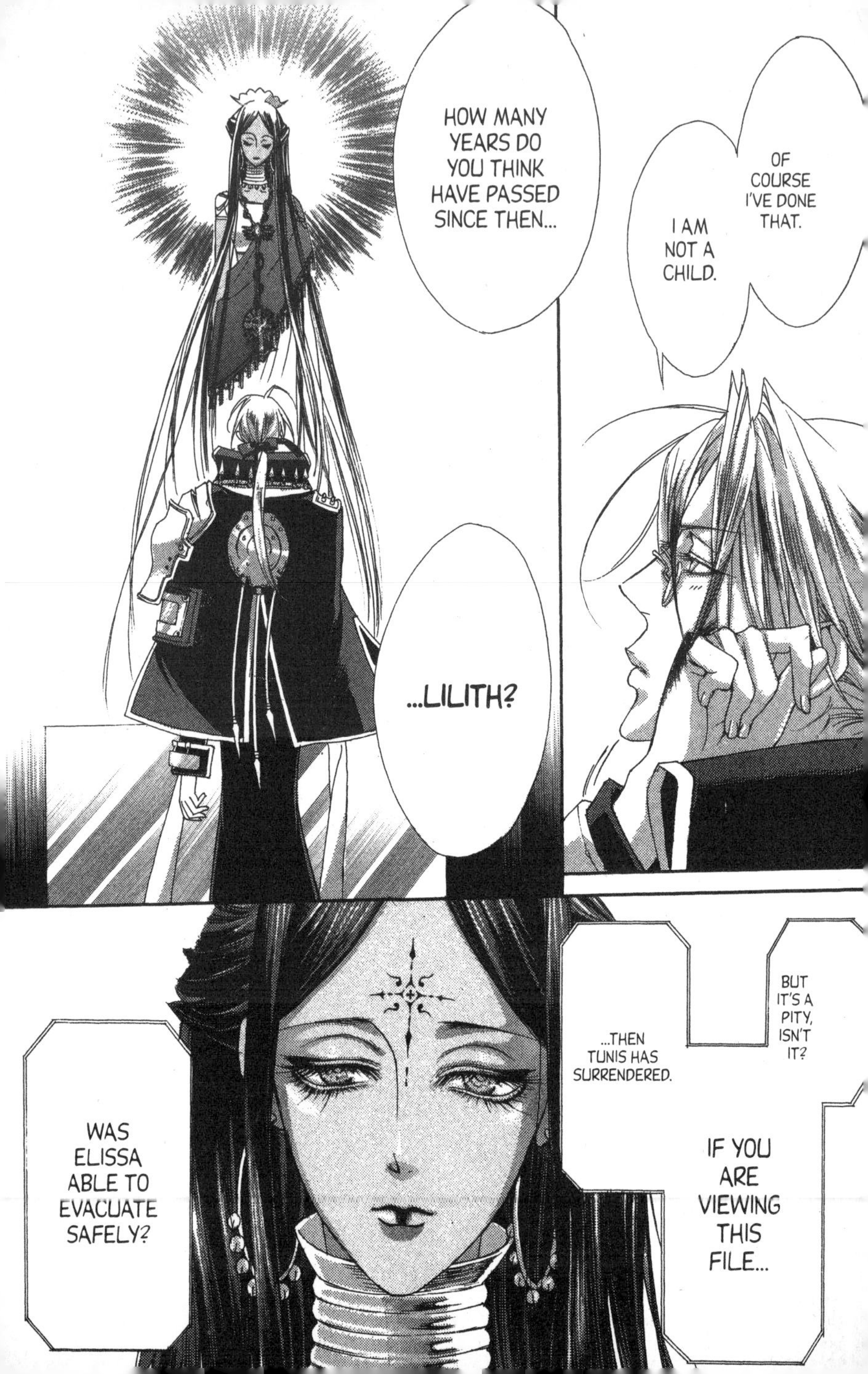
OF COURSE I'VE DONE THAT.
I AM NOT A CHILD.
HOW MANY YEARS DO YOU THINK HAVE PASSED SINCE THEN...
...LILITH?
IF YOU ARE VIEWING THIS FILE...
...THEN TUNIS HAS SURRENDERED.
BUT IT'S A PITY, ISN'T IT?
WAS ELISSA ABLE TO EVACUATE SAFELY?

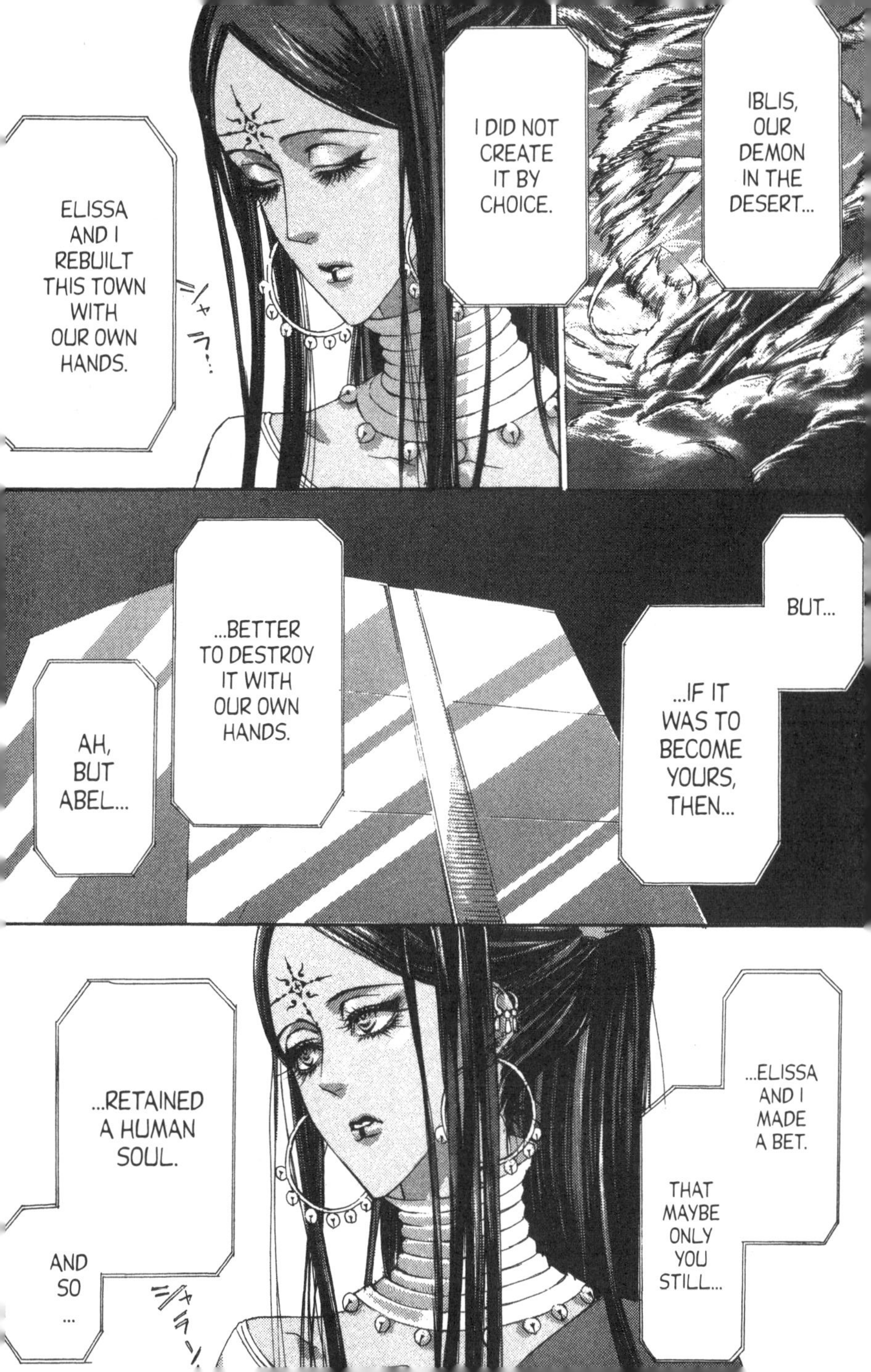
IBLIS, OUR DEMON IN THE DESERT...
I DID NOT CREATE IT BY CHOICE.
ELISSA AND I REBUILT THIS TOWN WITH OUR OWN HANDS.
BUT...
...IF IT WAS TO BECOME YOURS, THEN...
...BETTER TO DESTROY IT WITH OUR OWN HANDS.
AH, BUT ABEL...
...ELISSA AND I MADE A BET.
THAT MAYBE ONLY YOU STILL...
...RETAINED A HUMAN SOUL.
AND SO ...

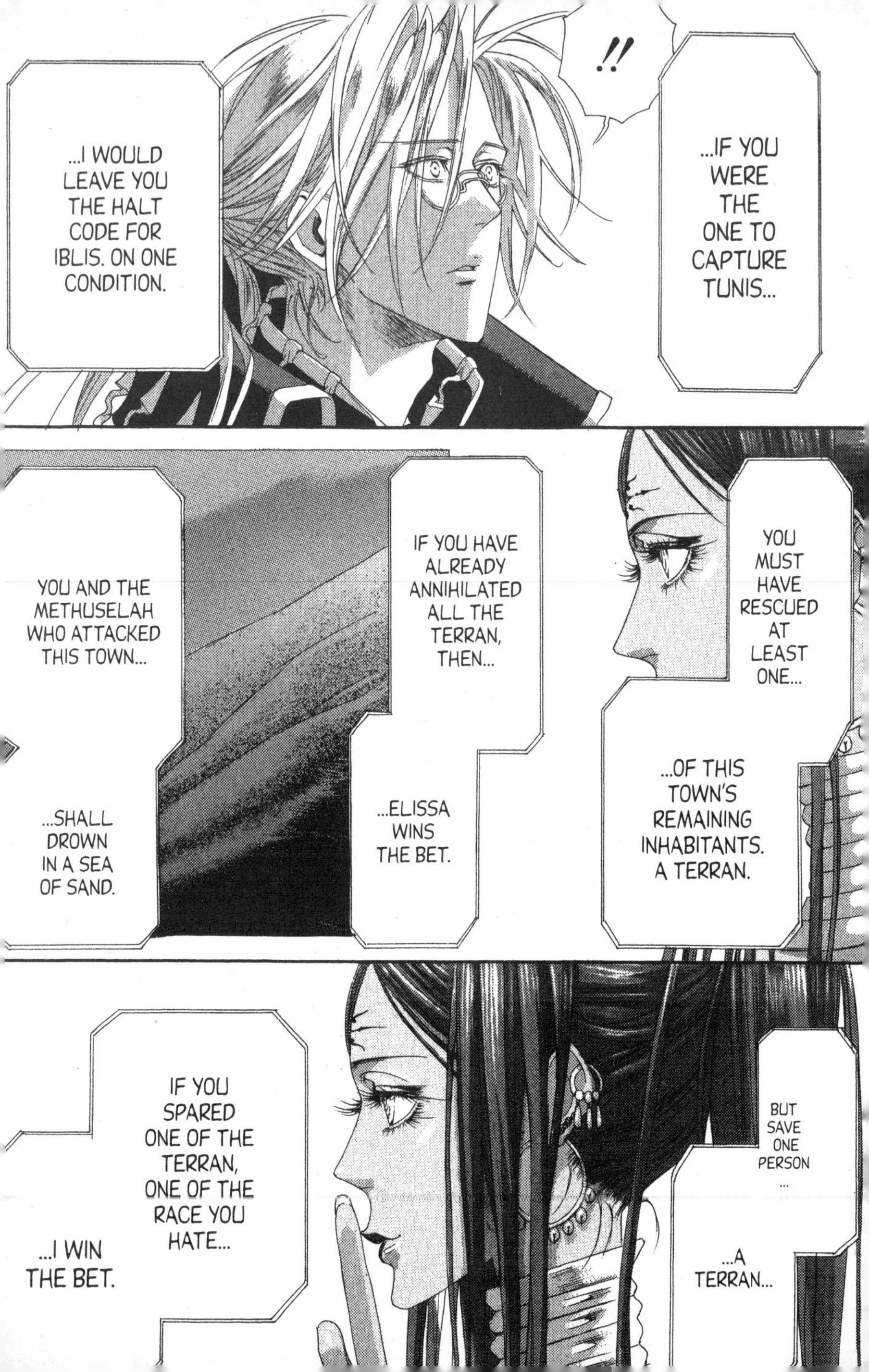
...IF YOU WERE THE ONE TO CAPTURE TUNIS...
!!
...I WOULD LEAVE YOU THE HALT CODE FOR IBLIS. ON ONE CONDITION.
YOU MUST HAVE RESCUED AT LEAST ONE...
...OF THIS TOWN'S REMAINING INHABITANTS. A TERRAN.
IF YOU HAVE ALREADY ANNIHILATED ALL THE TERRAN, THEN...
...ELISSA WINS THE BET.
YOU AND THE METHUSELAH WHO ATTACKED THIS TOWN...
...SHALL DROWN IN A SEA OF SAND.
BUT SAVE ONE PERSON ...
...A TERRAN...
IF YOU SPARED ONE OF THE TERRAN, ONE OF THE RACE YOU HATE...
...I WIN THE BET.

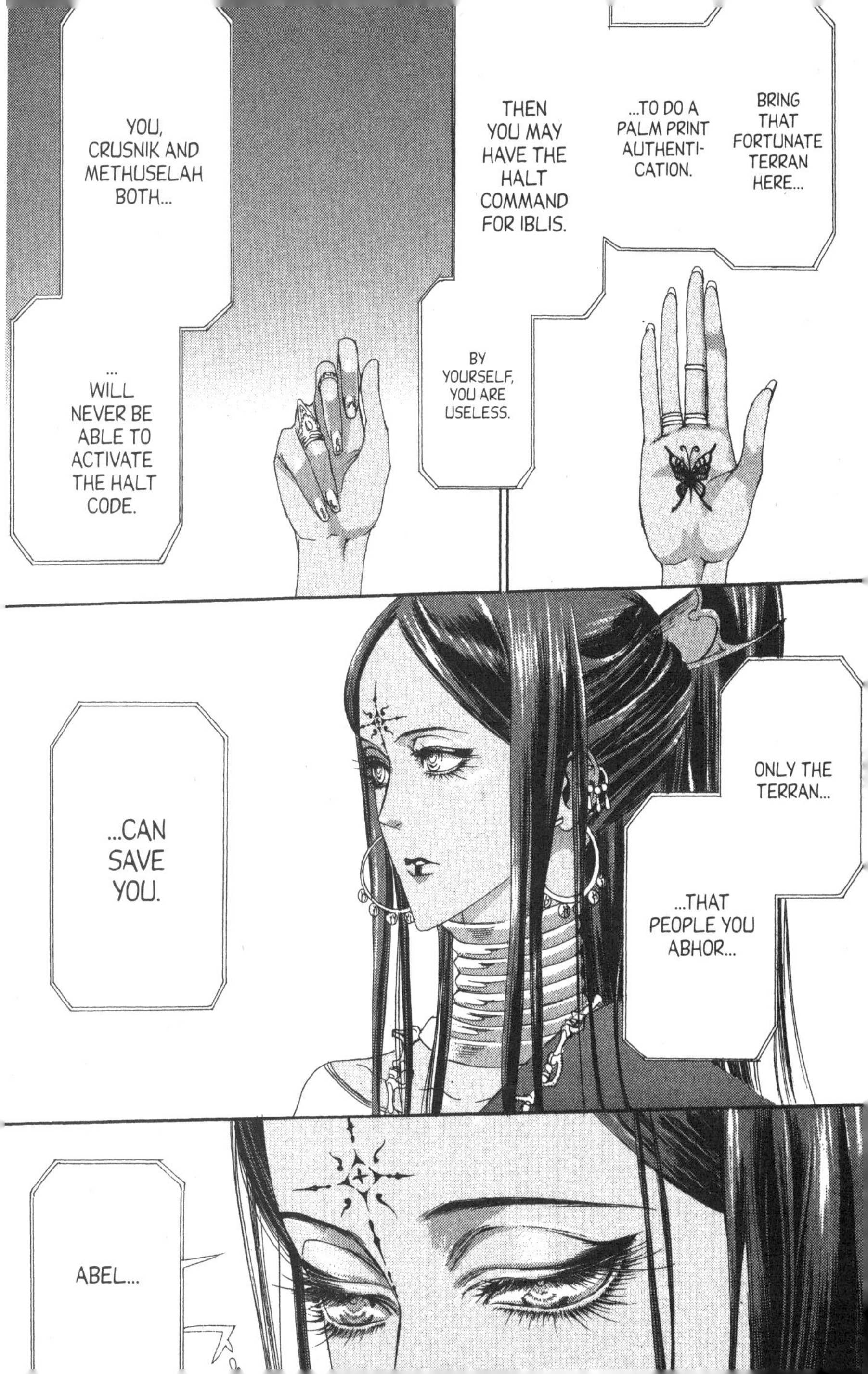
BRING THAT FORTUNATE TERRAN HERE...
...TO DO A PALM PRINT AUTHENTICATION.
THEN YOU MAY HAVE THE HALT COMMAND FOR IBLIS.
BY YOURSELF, YOU ARE USELESS.
YOU, CRUSNIK AND METHUSELAH BOTH...
...WILL NEVER BE ABLE TO ACTIVATE THE HALT CODE.
ONLY THE TERRAN...
...THAT PEOPLE YOU ABHOR...
...CAN SAVE YOU.
ABEL...

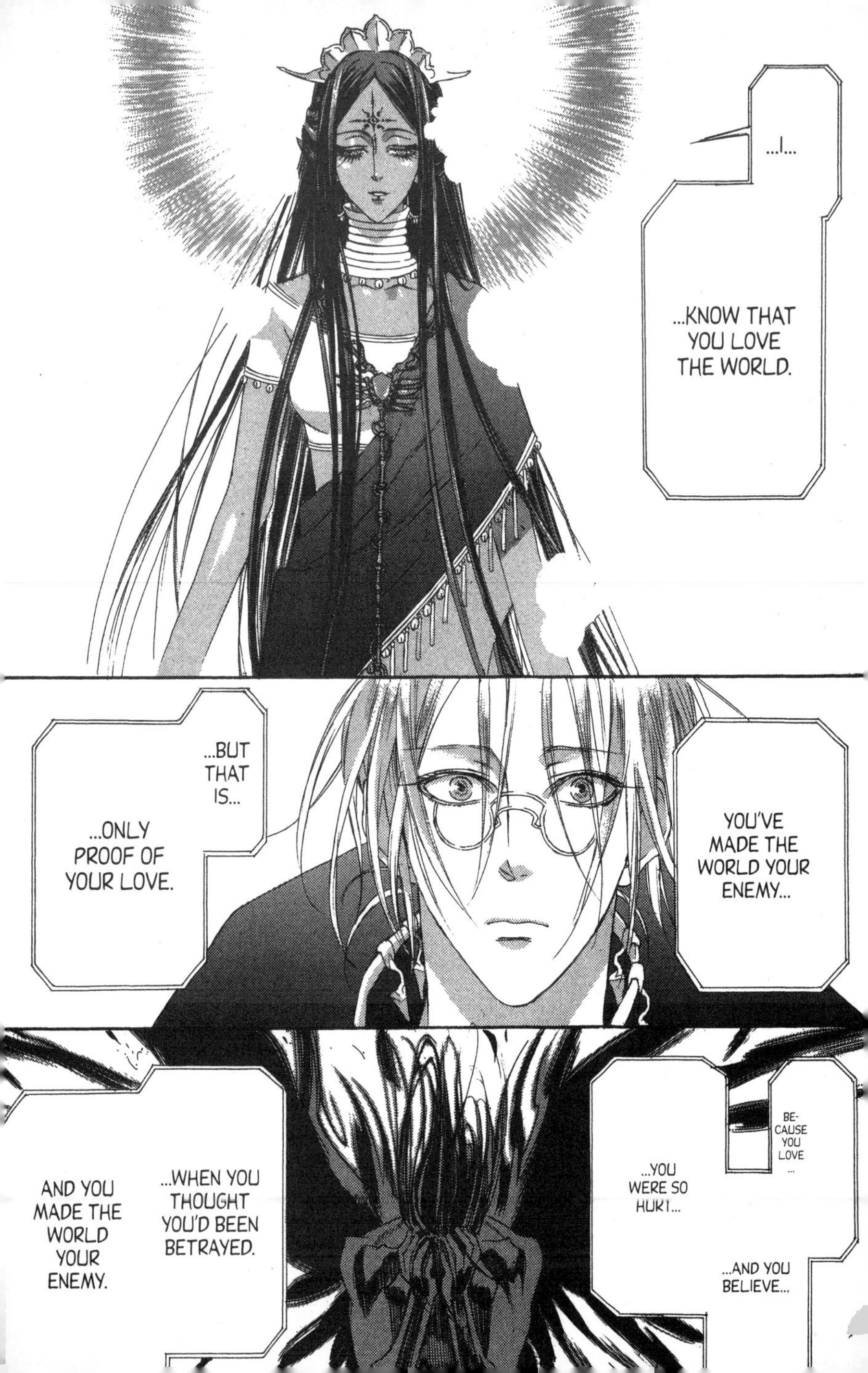

...I...
...KNOW THAT YOU LOVE THE WORLD.
YOU'VE MADE THE WORLD YOUR ENEMY...
...BUT THAT IS...
...ONLY PROOF OF YOUR LOVE.
BE-CAUSE YOU LOVE...
...YOU WERE SO HURT...
...AND YOU BELIEVE...
...WHEN YOU THOUGHT YOU'D BEEN BETRAYED.
AND YOU MADE THE WORLD YOUR ENEMY.

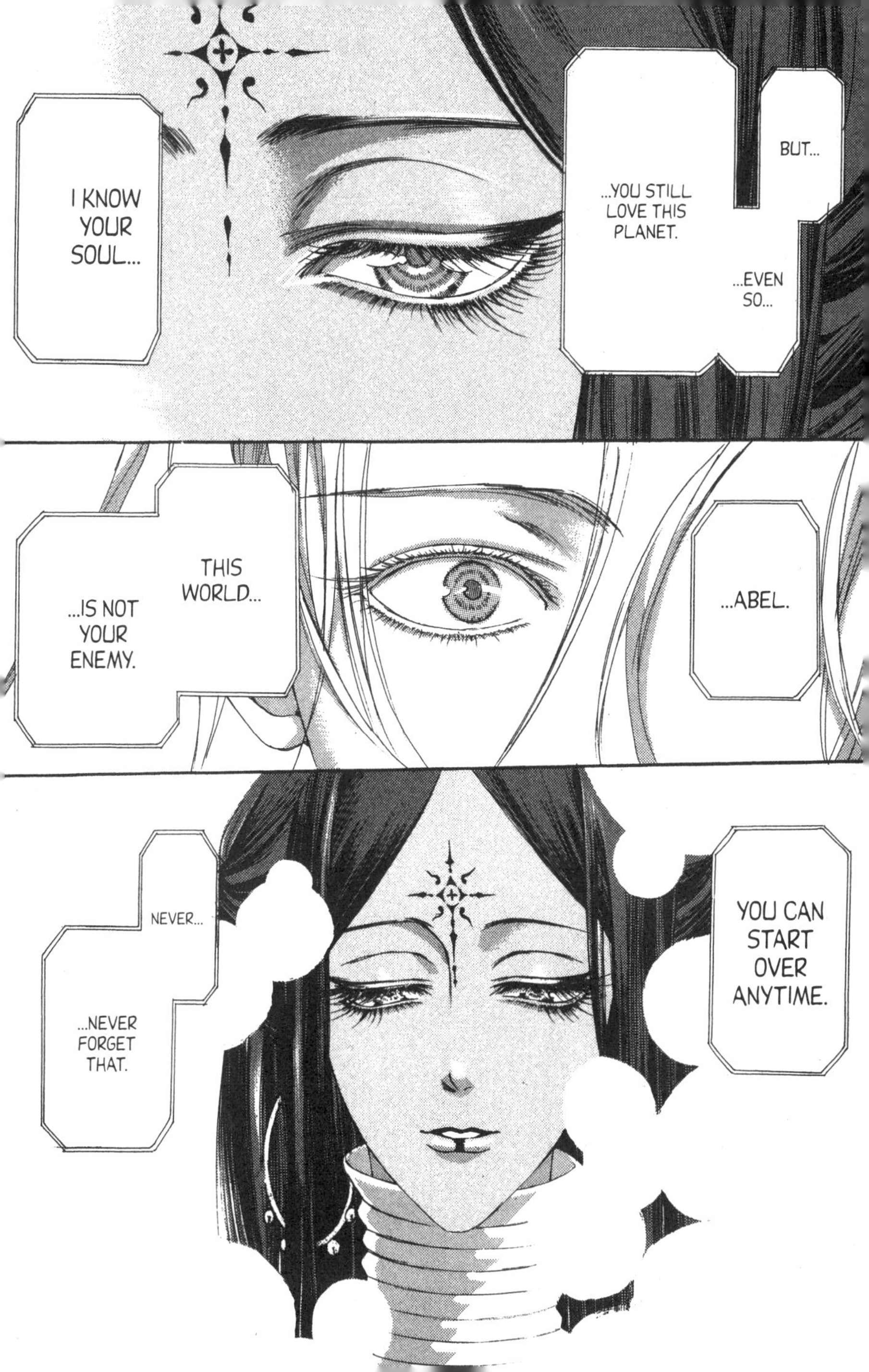
BUT...
...YOU STILL LOVE THIS PLANET.
...EVEN SO...
I KNOW YOUR SOUL...
...ABEL.
THIS WORLD...
...IS NOT YOUR ENEMY.
YOU CAN START OVER ANYTIME.
NEVER...
...NEVER FORGET THAT.

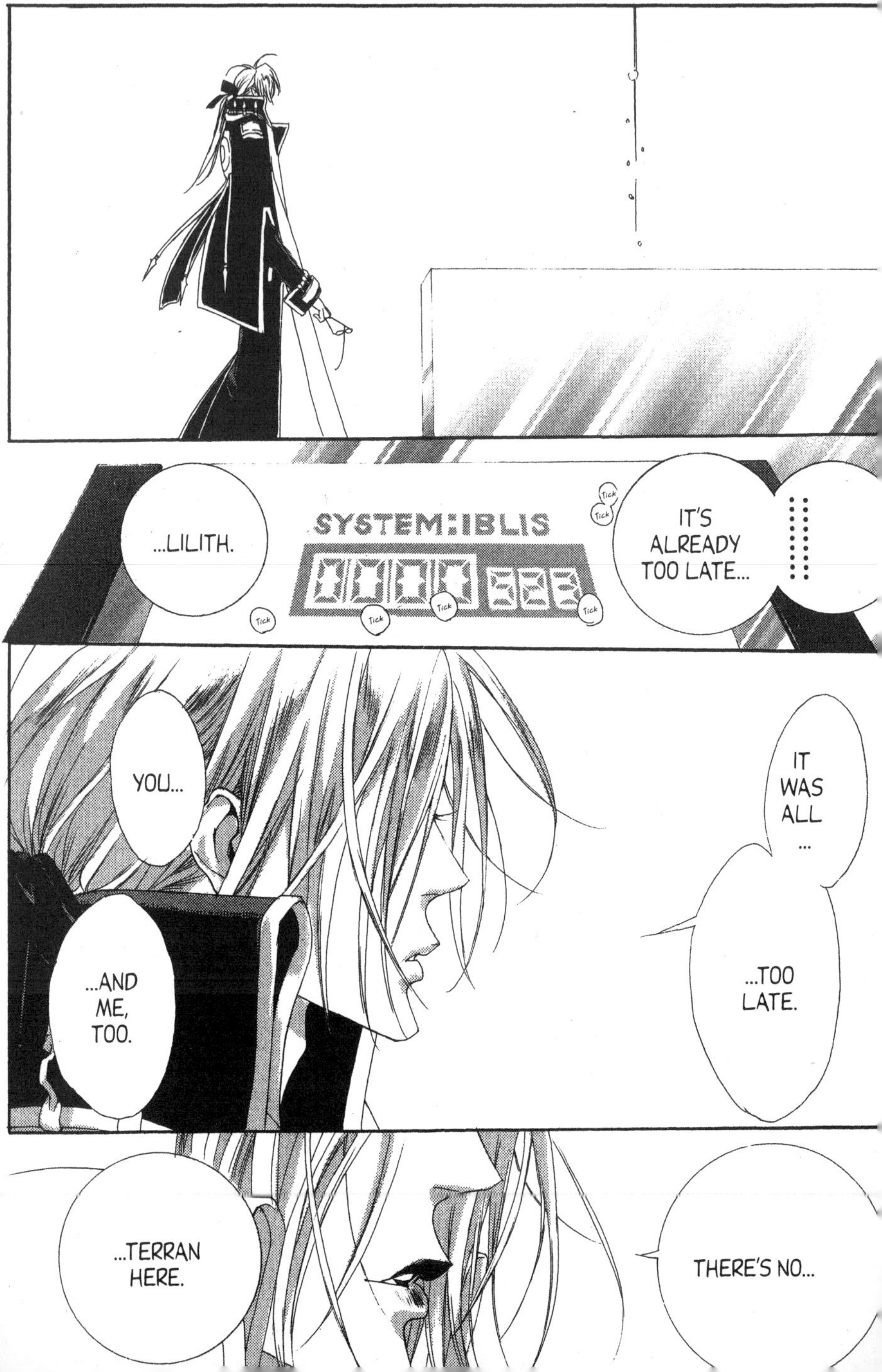

......
IT'S ALREADY TOO LATE...
Tick
Tick
SYSTEM:IBLIS
Tick
Tick
Tick
Tick
...LILITH.
IT WAS ALL ...
...TOO LATE.
YOU...
...AND ME, TOO.
THERE'S NO...
...TERRAN HERE.

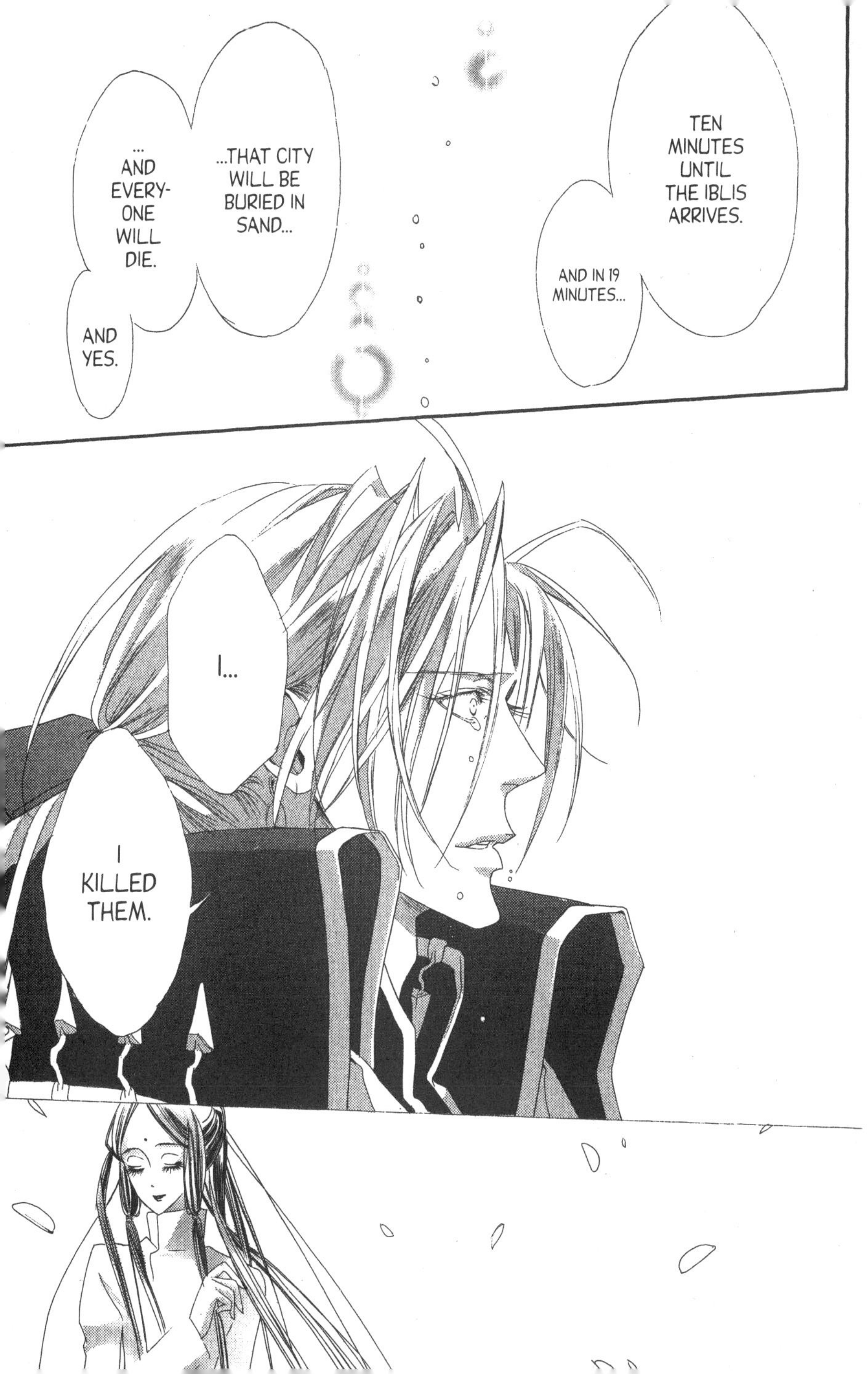
TEN MINUTES UNTIL THE IBLIS ARRIVES.
AND IN 19 MINUTES...
...THAT CITY WILL BE BURIED IN SAND...
... AND EVERY-ONE WILL DIE.
AND YES.
I...
I KILLED THEM.

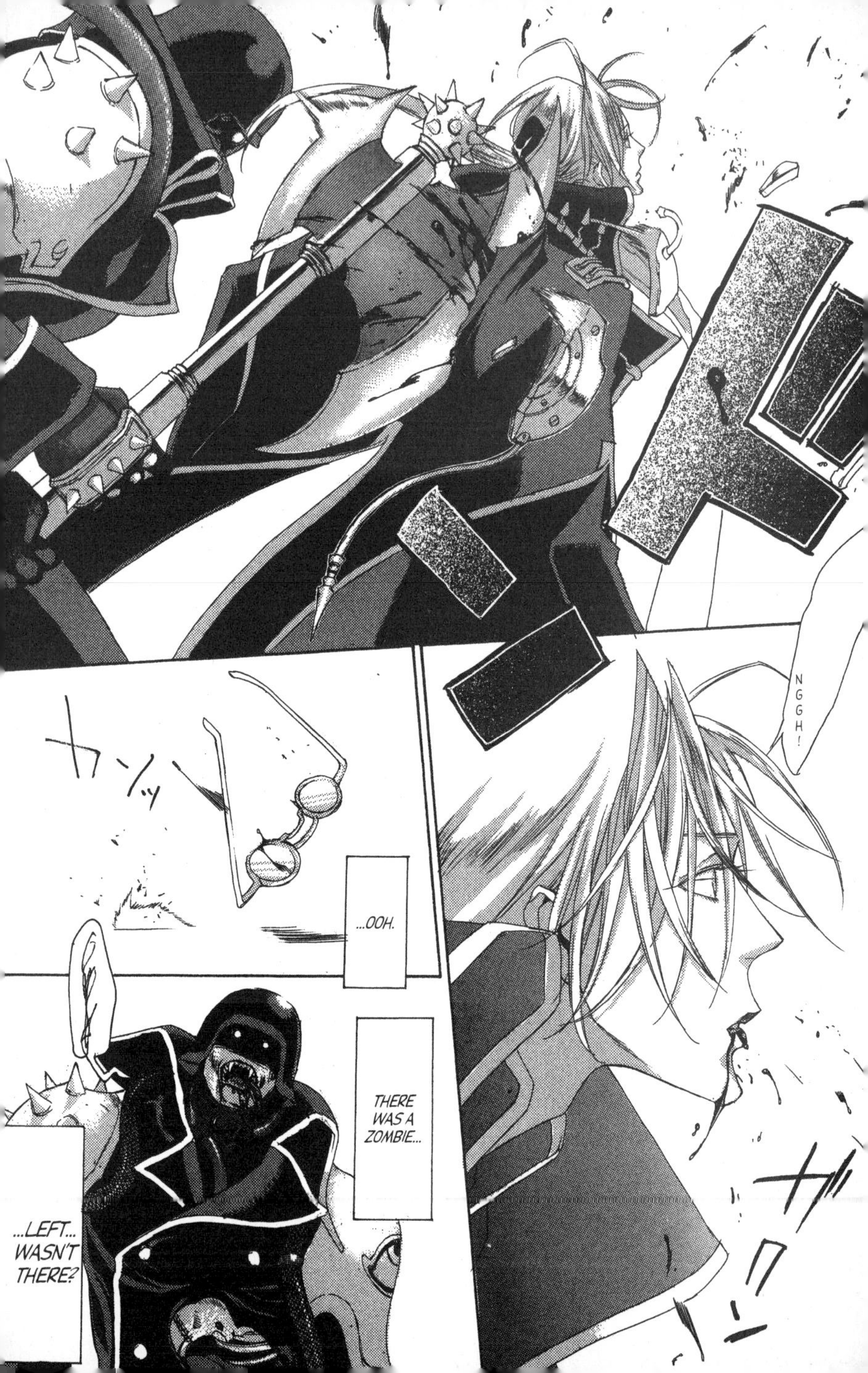
NGGH!
カンッ
...OOH.
THERE WAS A ZOMBIE...
...LEFT... WASN'T THERE?

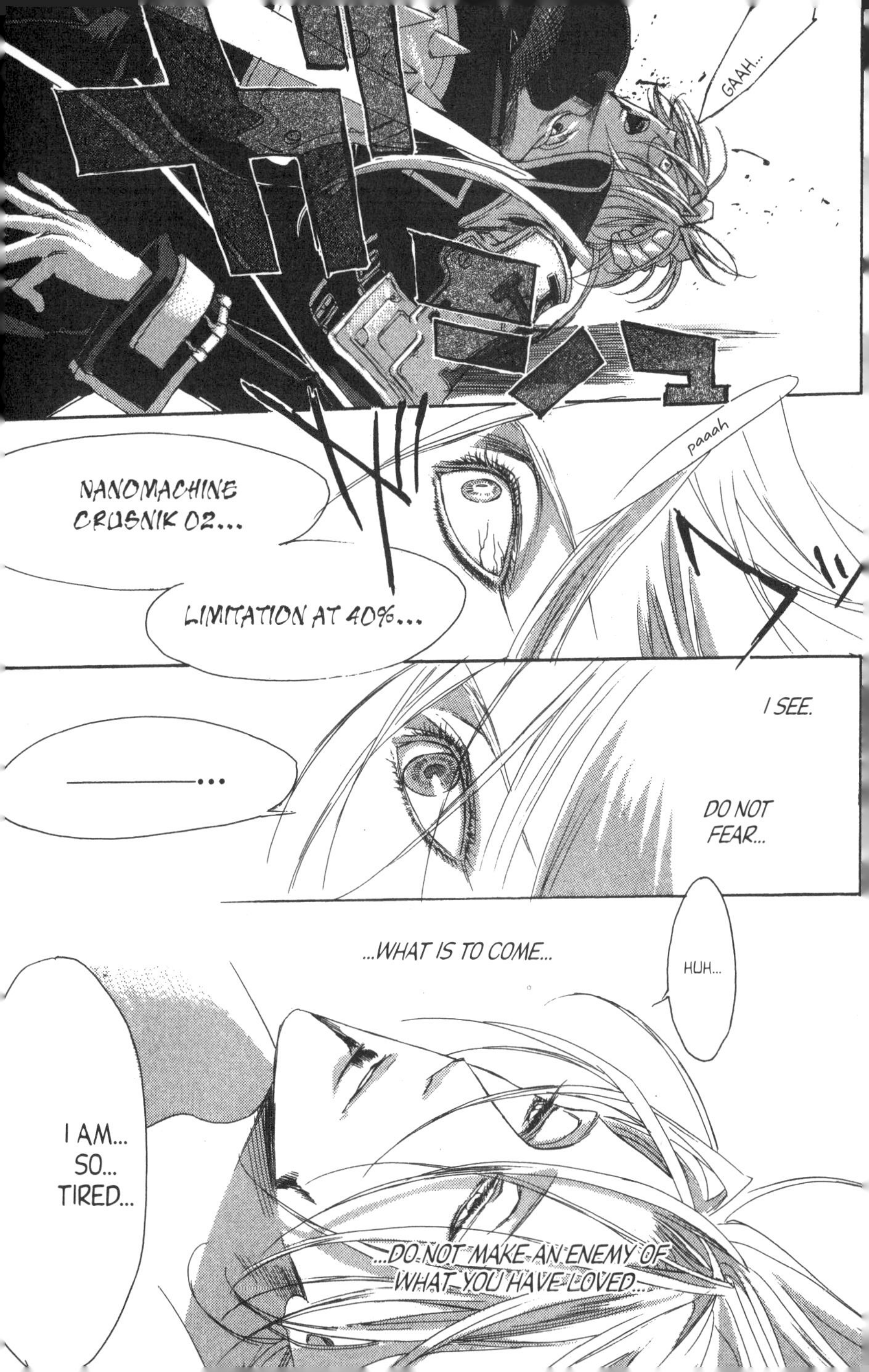
GAAH...
paaah
NANOMACHINE CRUSNIK 02...
LIMITATION AT 40%...
I SEE.
DO NOT FEAR...
————...
...WHAT IS TO COME...
HUH...
I AM... SO... TIRED...
...DO NOT MAKE AN ENEMY OF WHAT YOU HAVE LOVED...

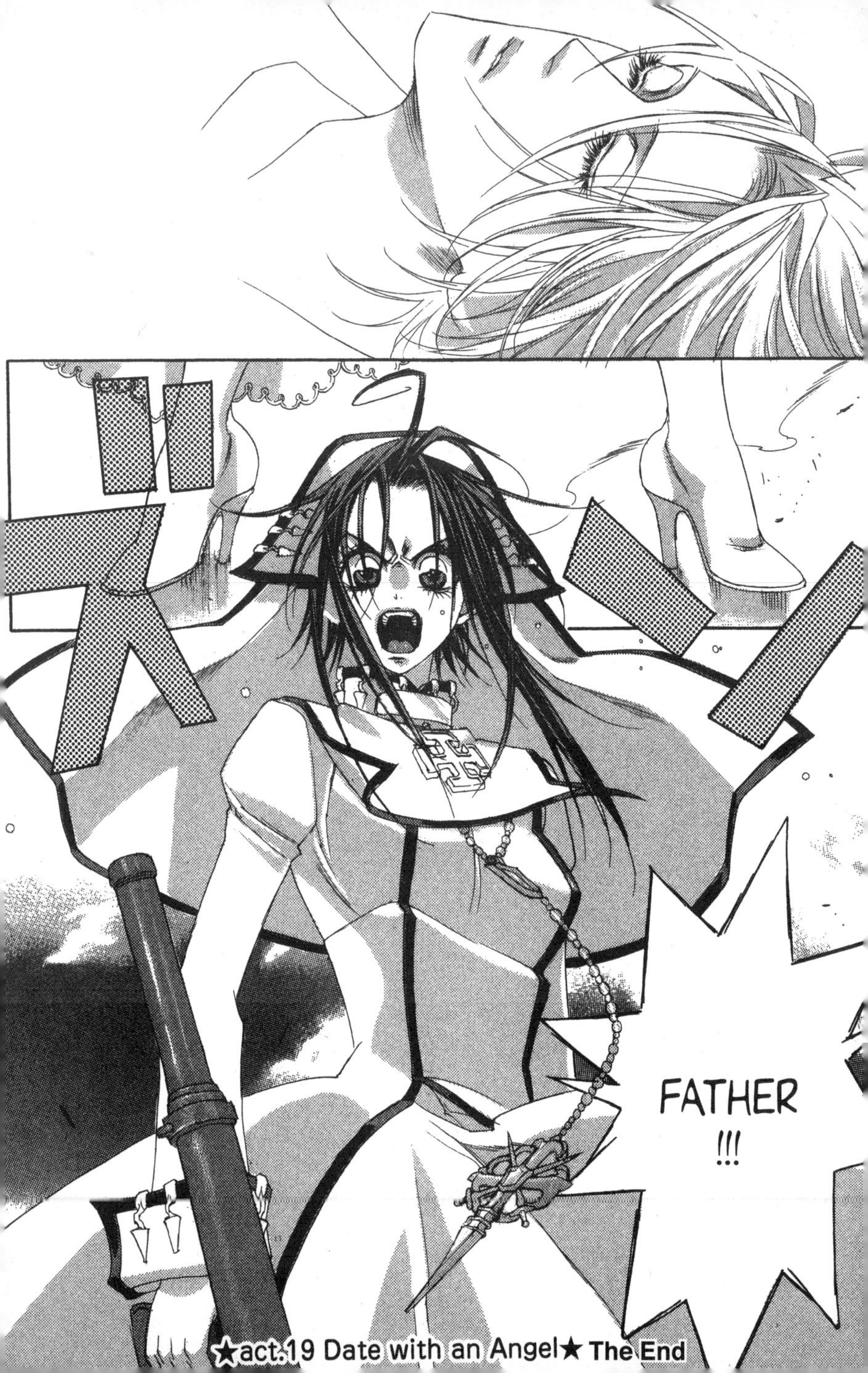
FATHER !!!
★act.19 Date with an Angel★ The End

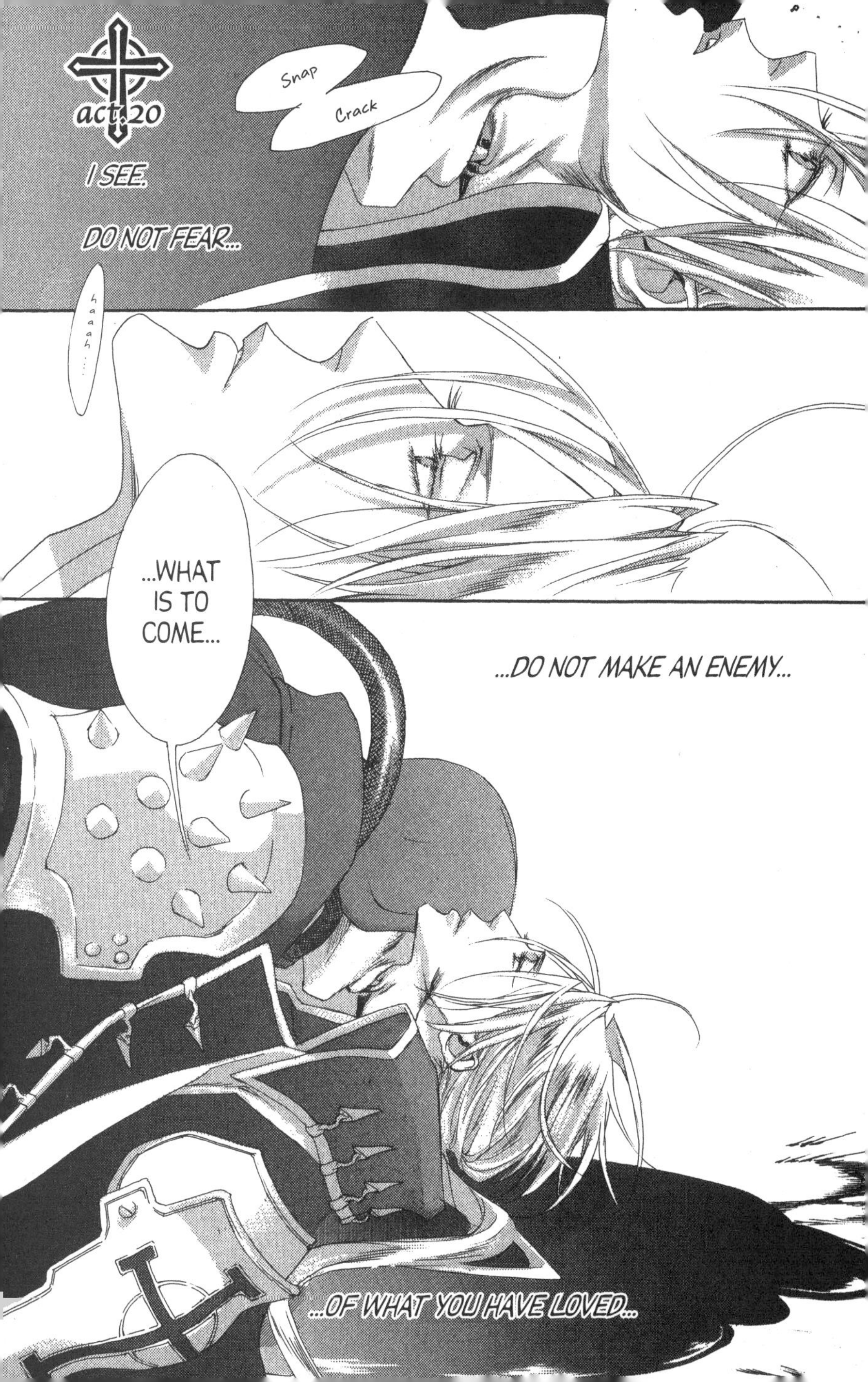

Snap
Crack
act.20
I SEE.
DO NOT FEAR...
haaah...
...WHAT IS TO COME...
...DO NOT MAKE AN ENEMY...
...OF WHAT YOU HAVE LOVED...

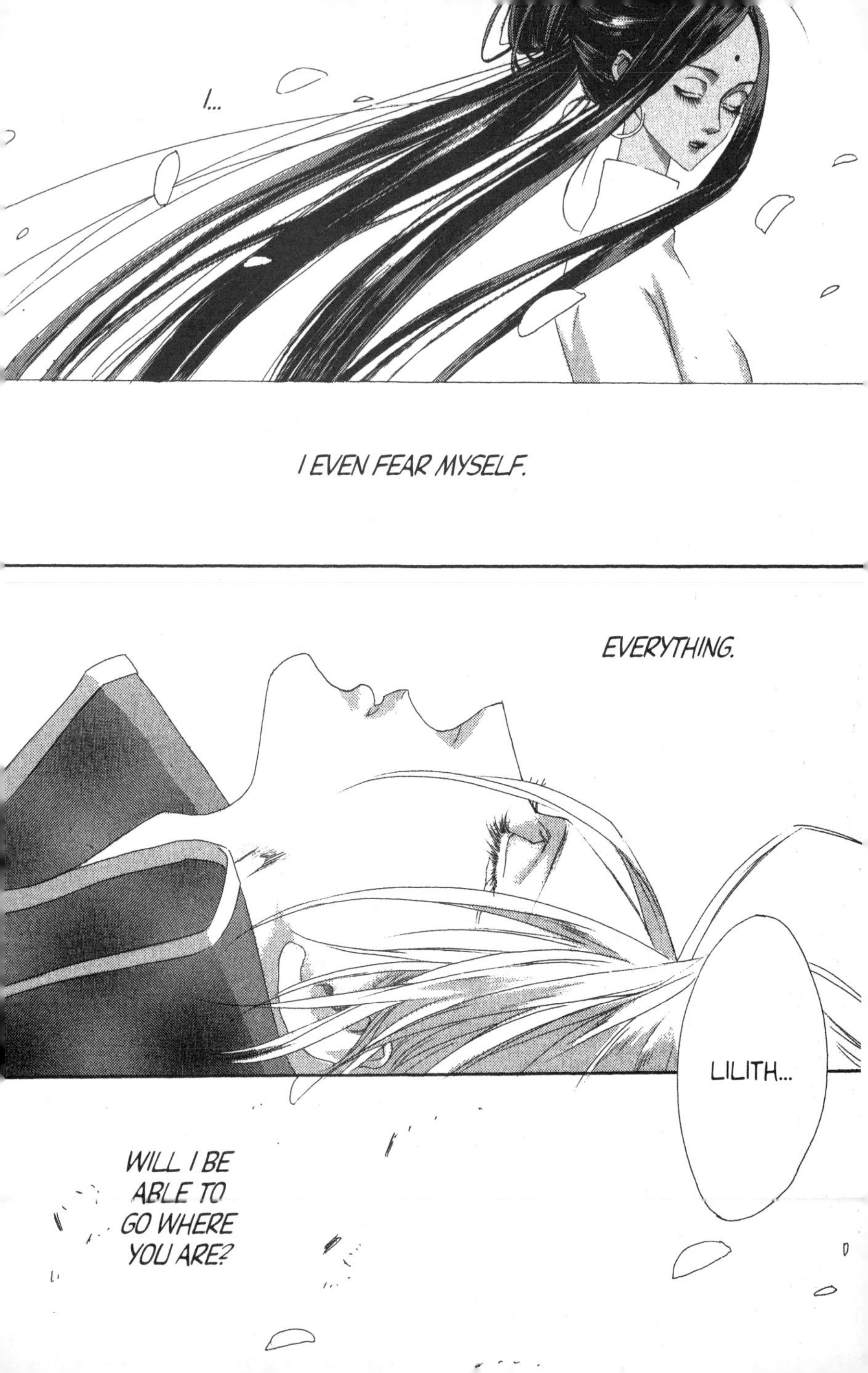
I...
I EVEN FEAR MYSELF.
EVERYTHING.
LILITH...
WILL I BE ABLE TO GO WHERE YOU ARE?

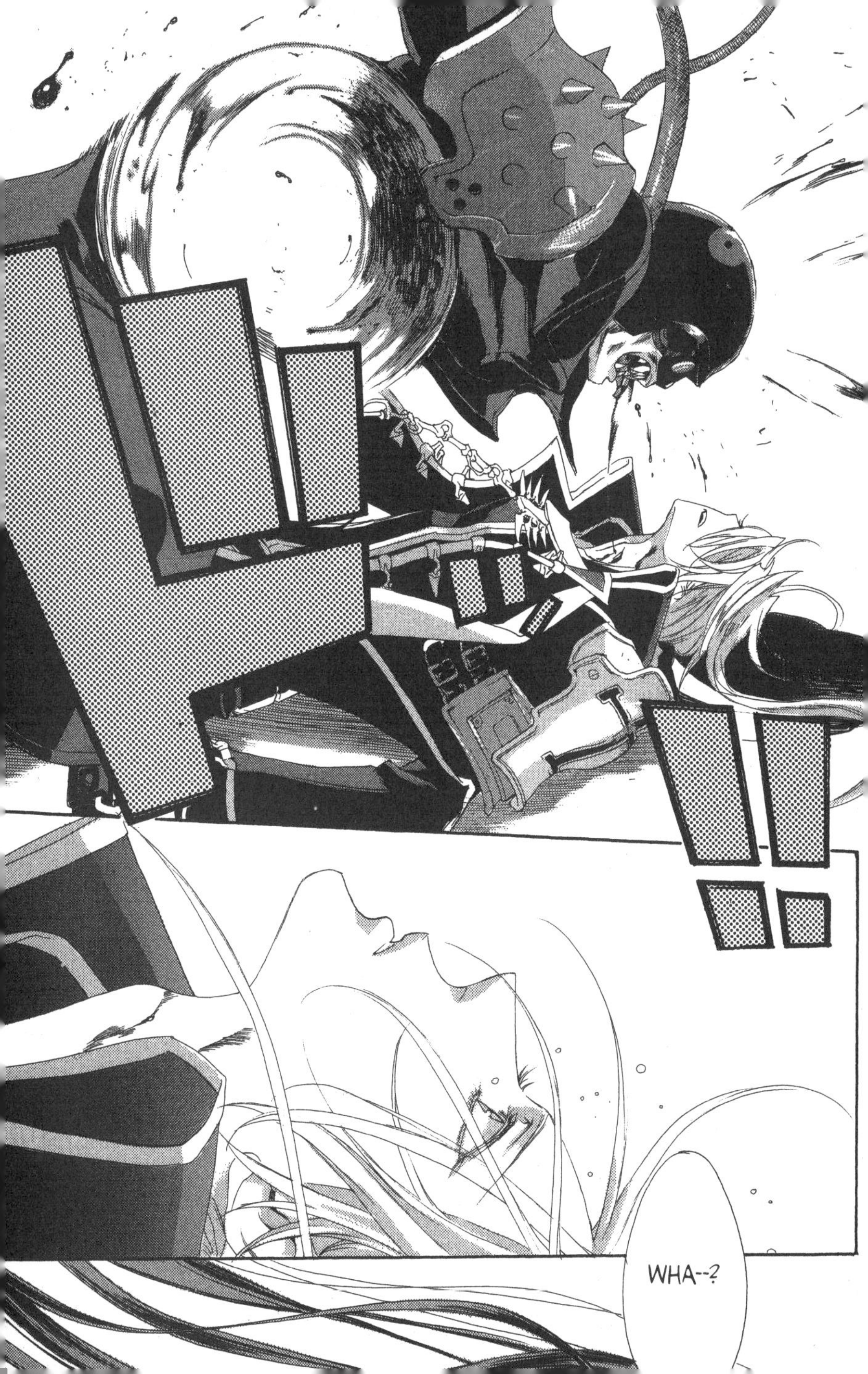
WHA--?

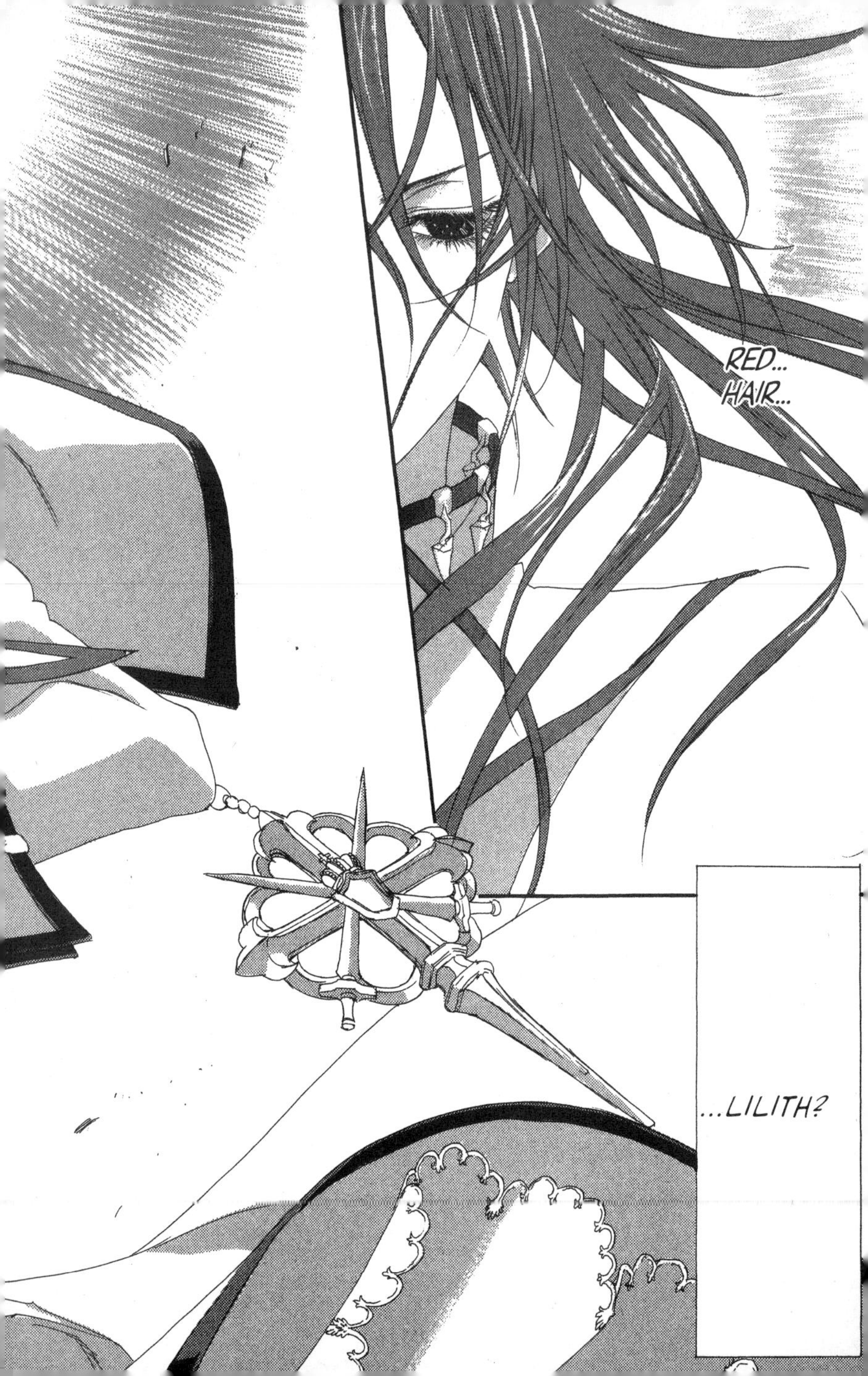
RED... HAIR...
...LILITH?

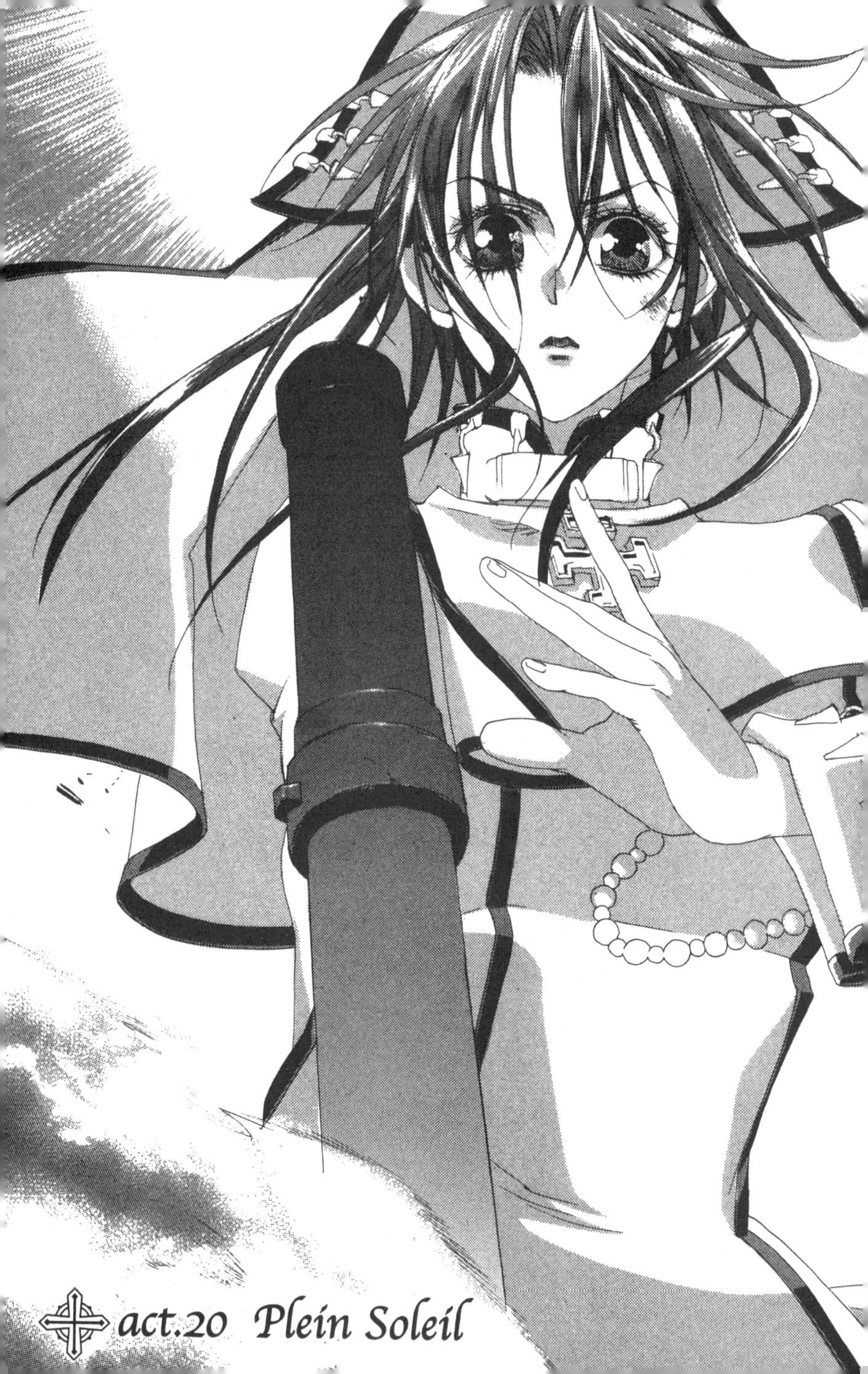
act.20 Plein Soleil

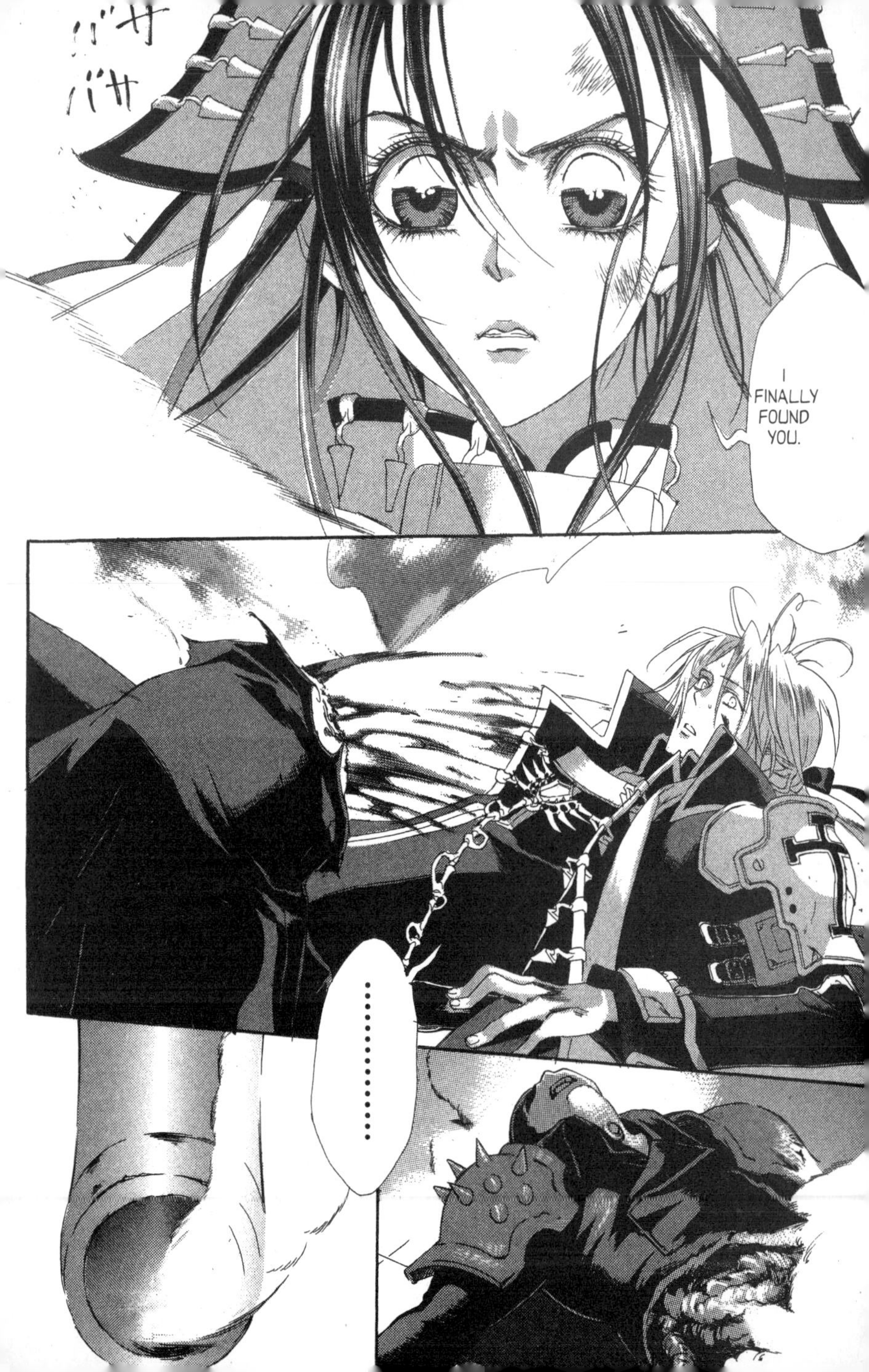
バサ
バサ
I FINALLY FOUND YOU.
……………

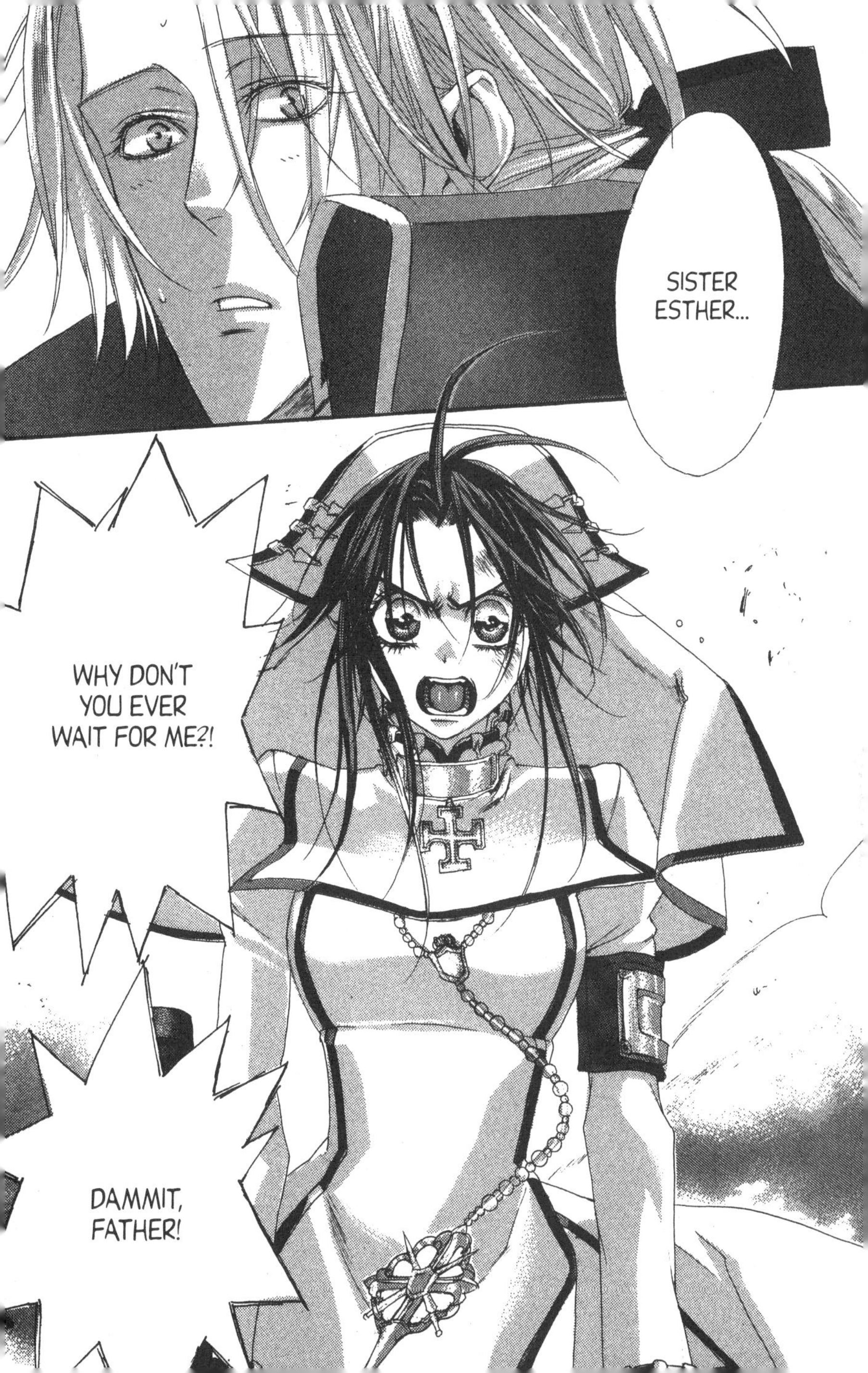
SISTER ESTHER...
WHY DON'T YOU EVER WAIT FOR ME?!
DAMMIT, FATHER!

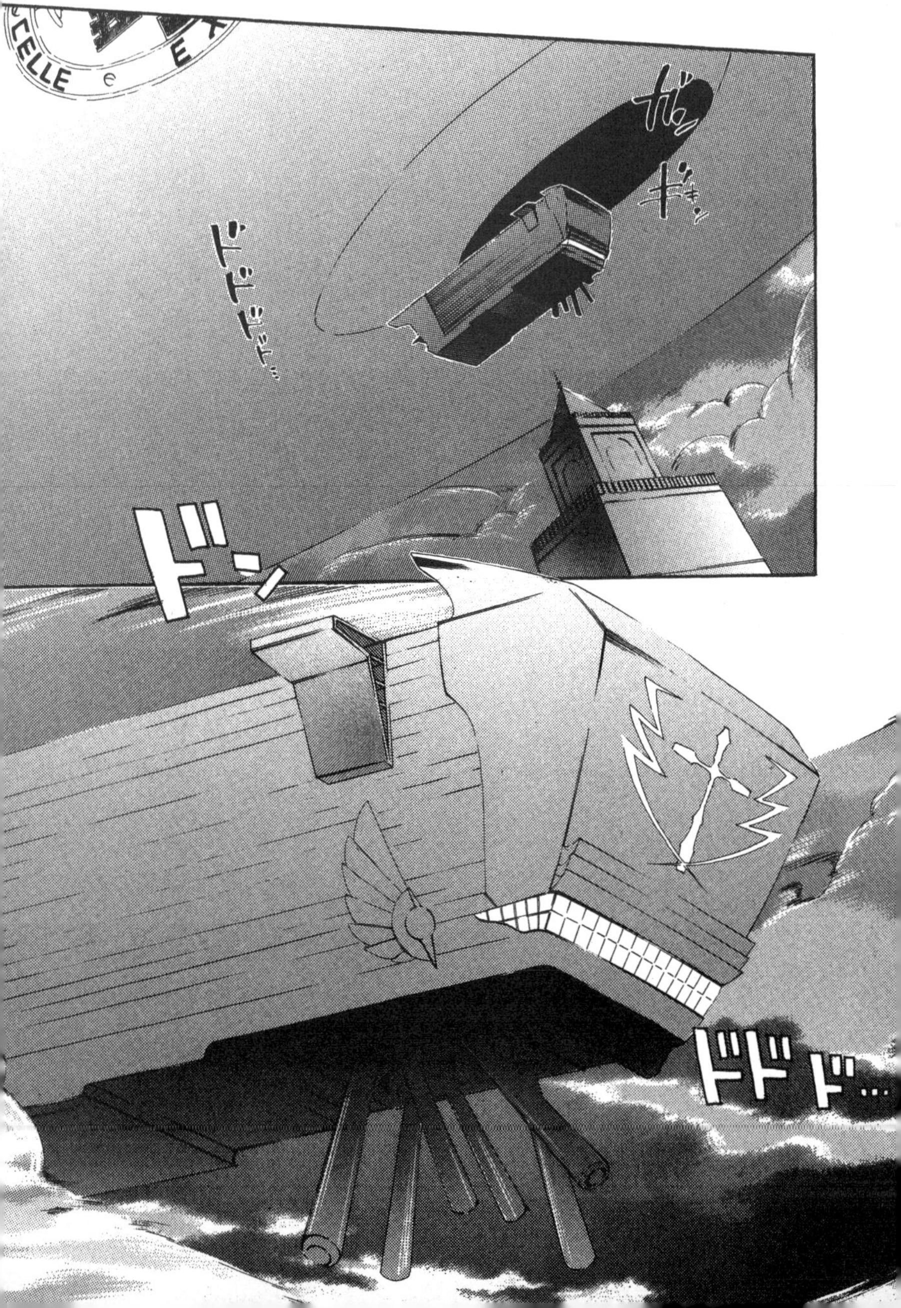
ガシ
ギキッ
ドドドドド…
ドーン
ドドド…

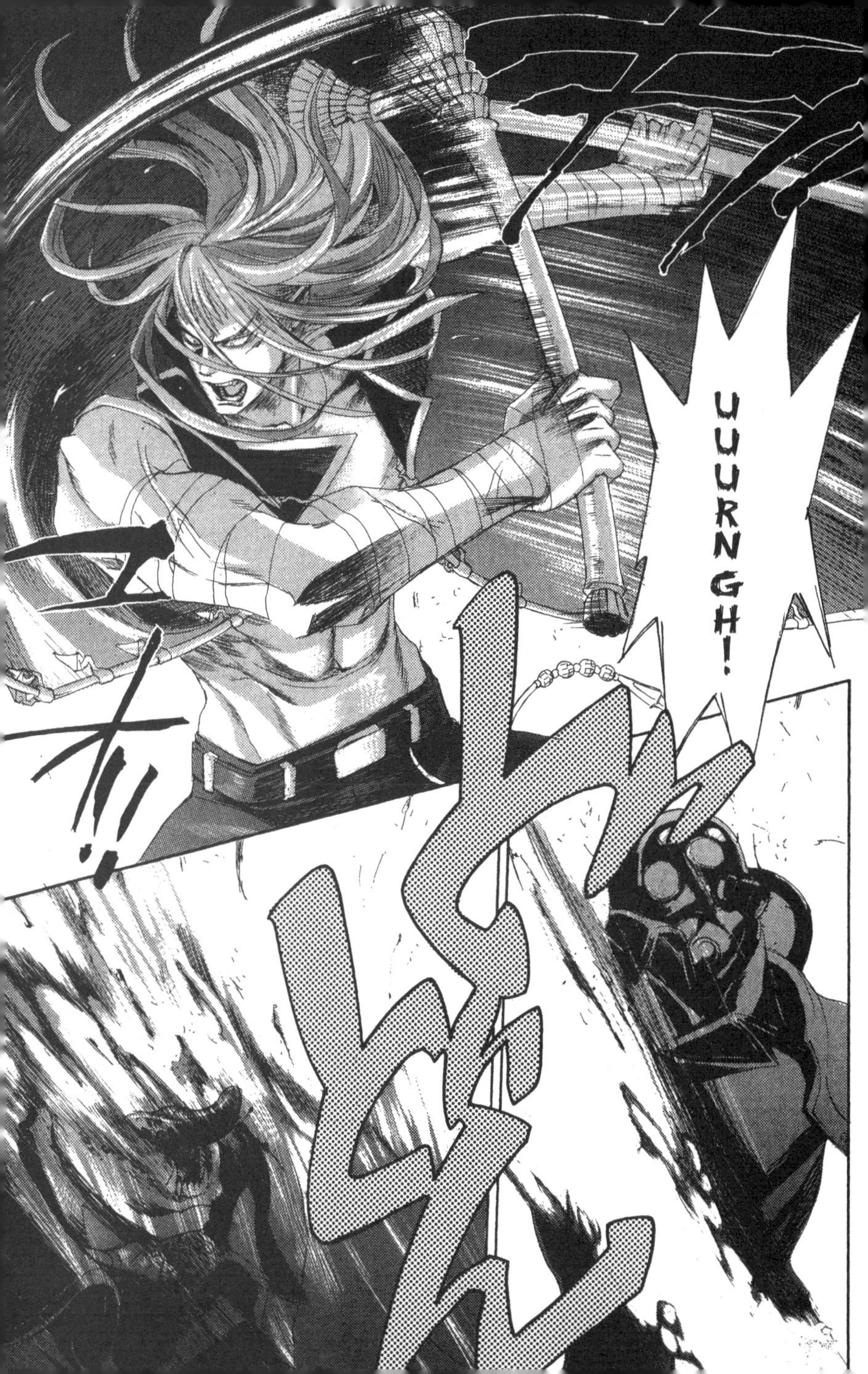
UUURNGH!

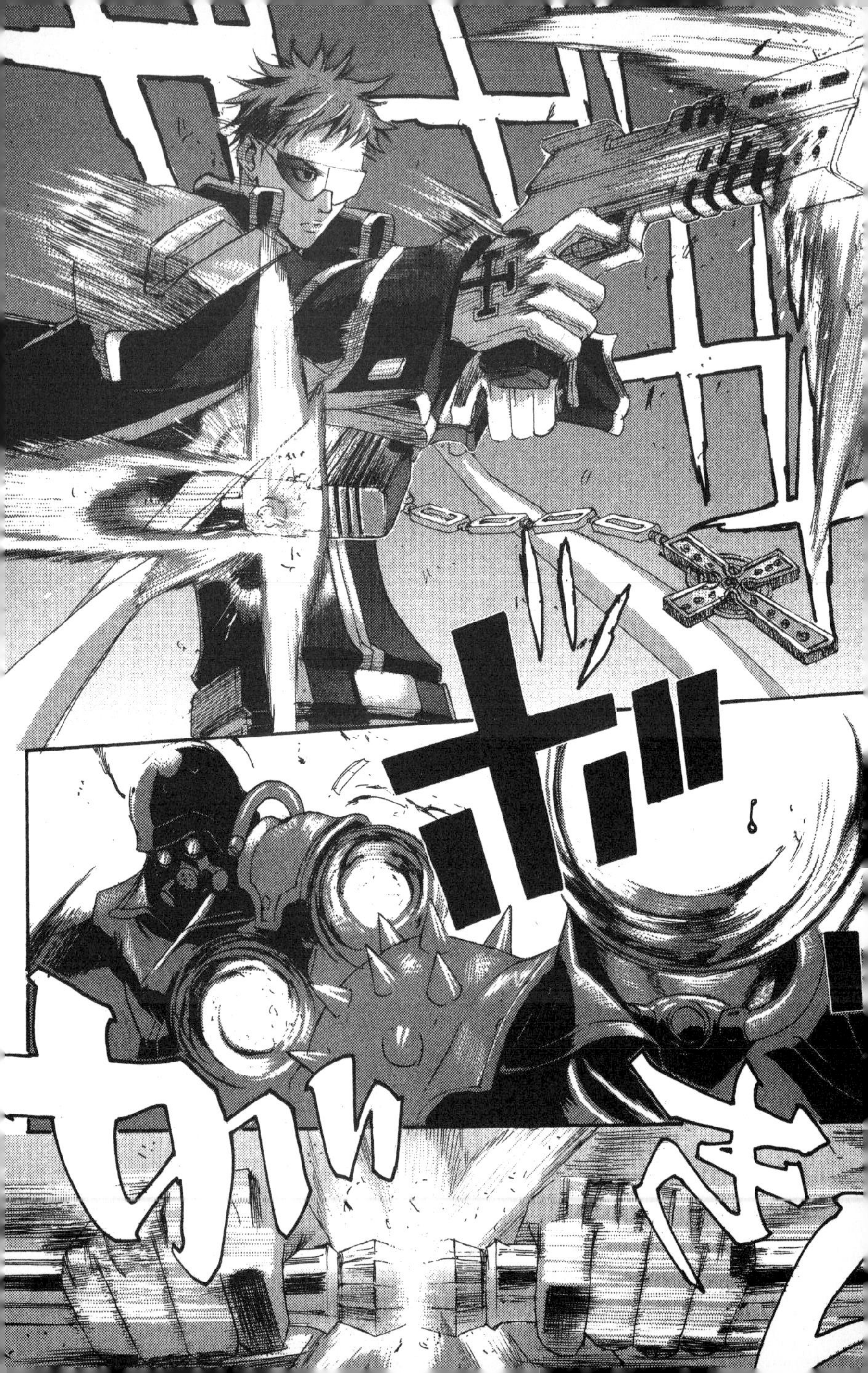

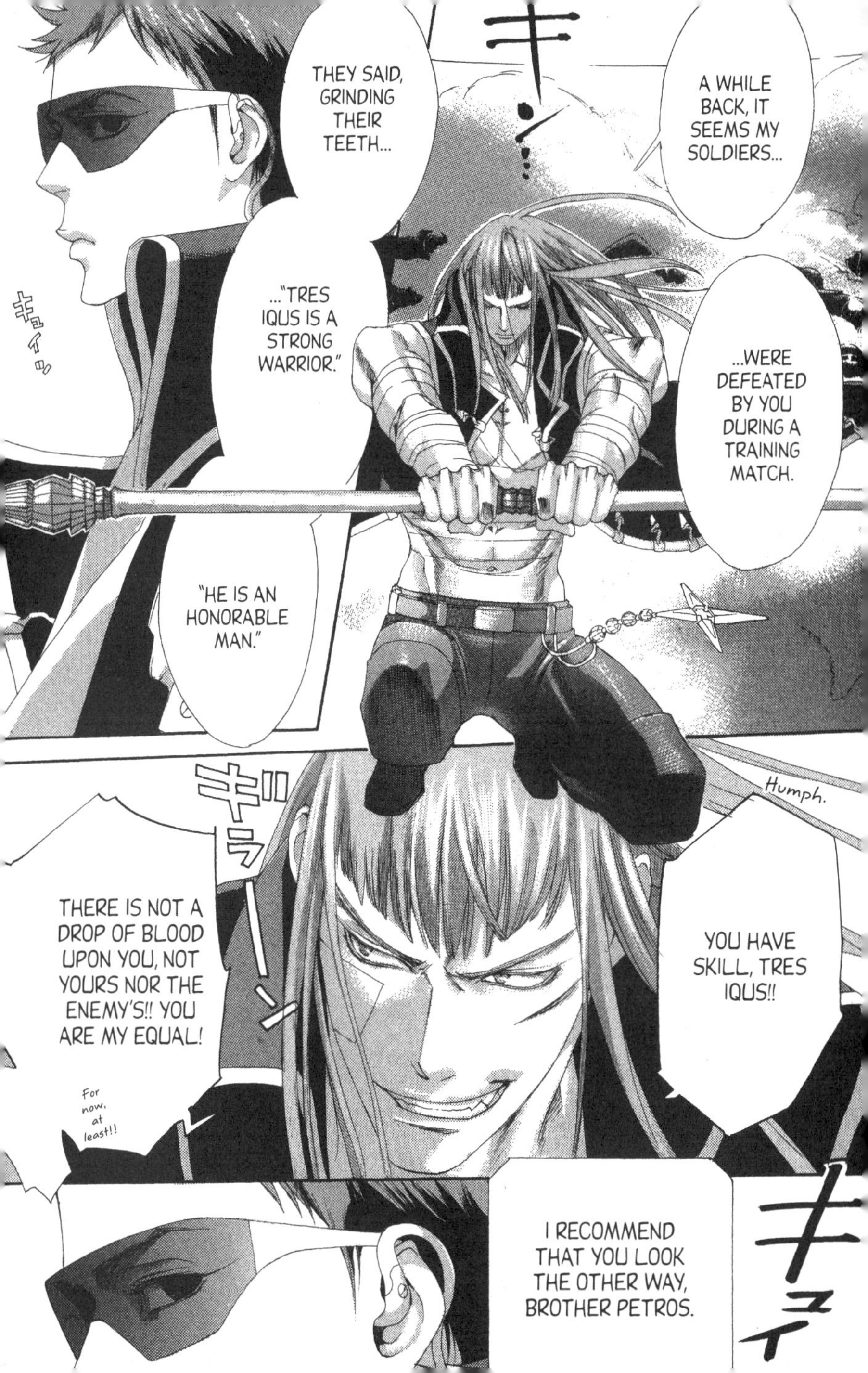
A WHILE BACK, IT SEEMS MY SOLDIERS...
...WERE DEFEATED BY YOU DURING A TRAINING MATCH.
キン…!
THEY SAID, GRINDING THEIR TEETH...
..."TRES IQUS IS A STRONG WARRIOR."
"HE IS AN HONORABLE MAN."
キュイッ
Humph.
YOU HAVE SKILL, TRES IQUS!!
キラーン
THERE IS NOT A DROP OF BLOOD UPON YOU, NOT YOURS NOR THE ENEMY'S!! YOU ARE MY EQUAL!
For now, at least!!
キュイ
I RECOMMEND THAT YOU LOOK THE OTHER WAY, BROTHER PETROS.

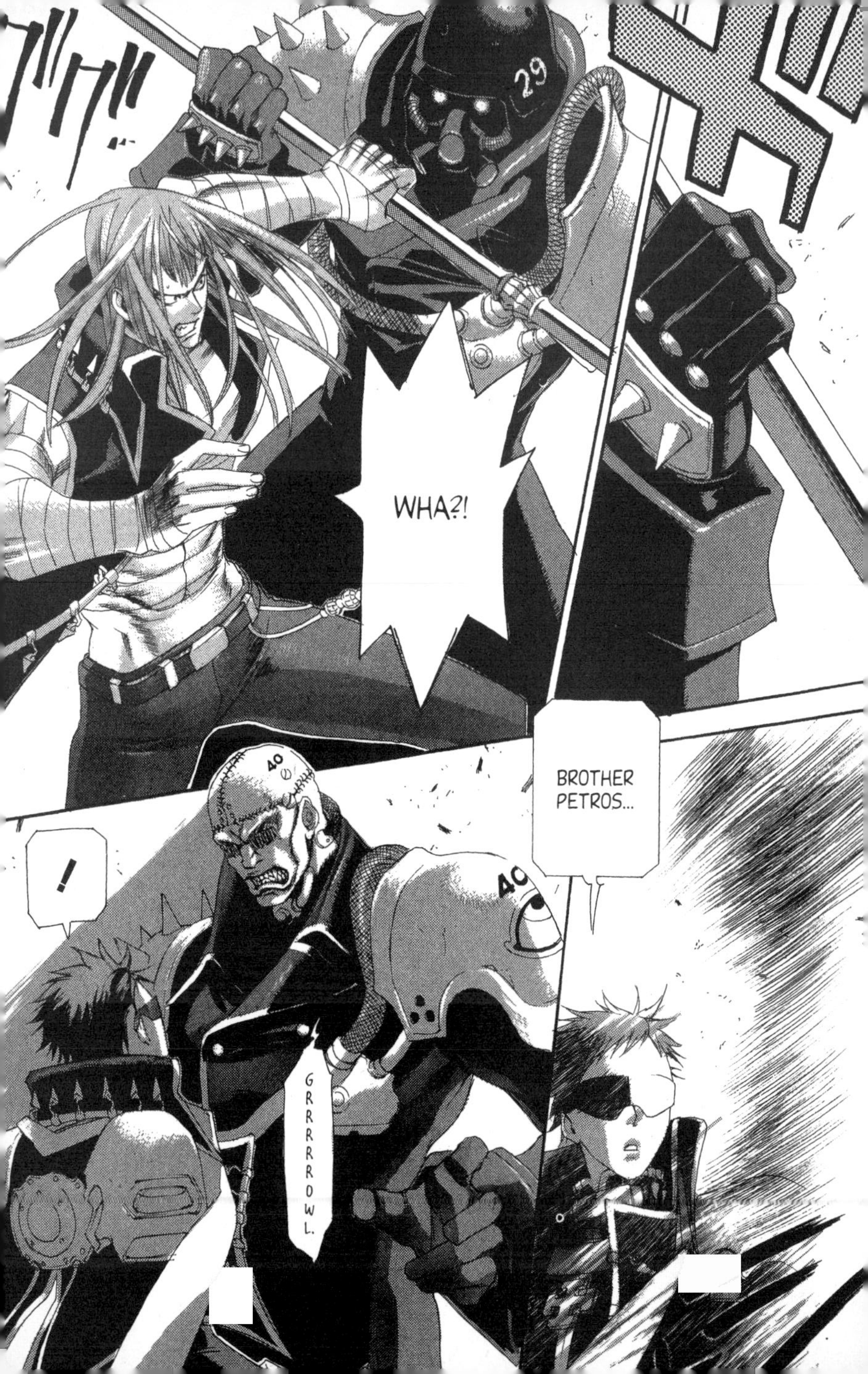
WHA?!
BROTHER PETROS...
!
GRRRRROWL.

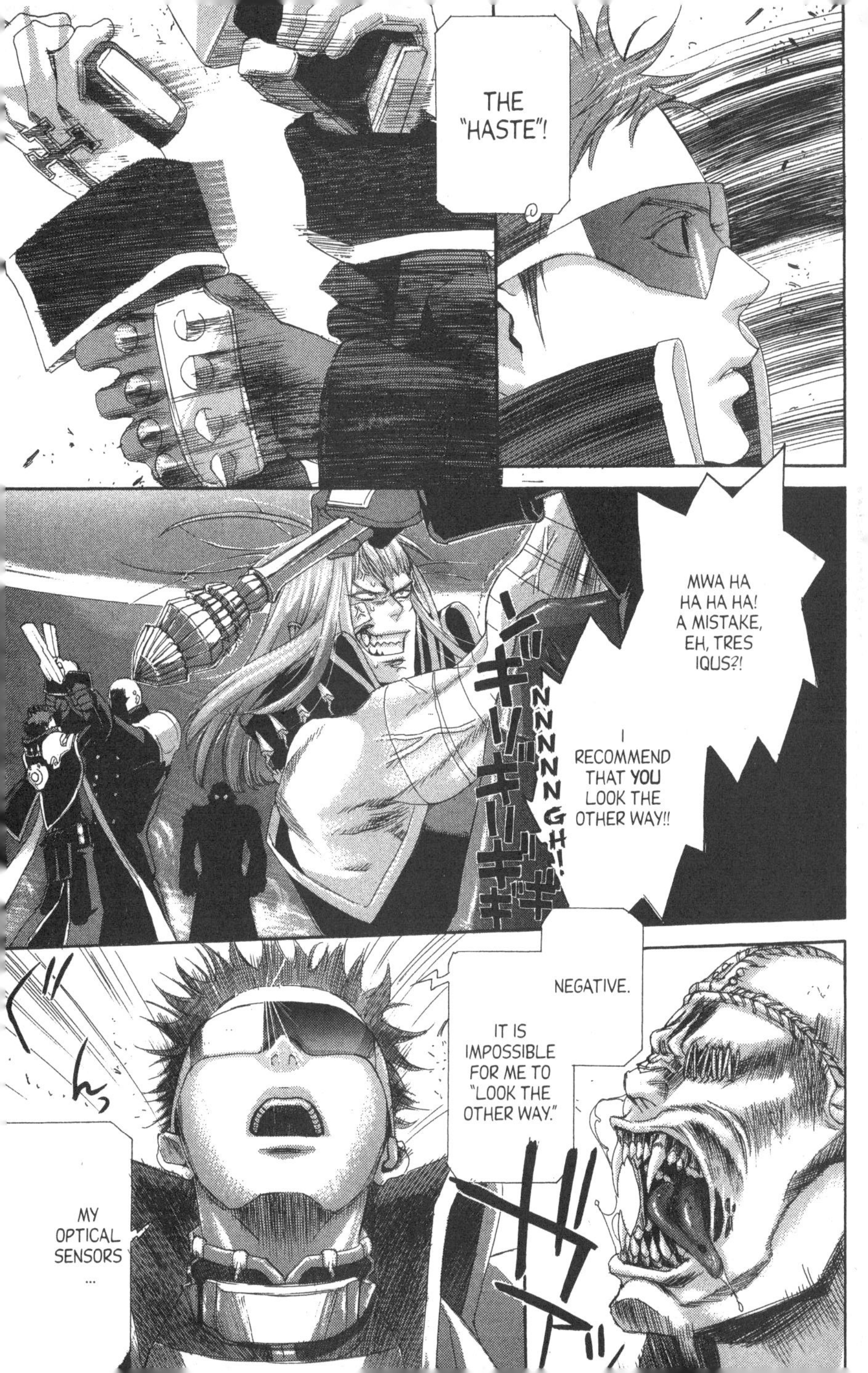
THE "HASTE"!
MWA HA HA HA HA! A MISTAKE, EH, TRES IQUS?!
I RECOMMEND THAT YOU LOOK THE OTHER WAY!!
NNNNNGH!!
NEGATIVE.
IT IS IMPOSSIBLE FOR ME TO "LOOK THE OTHER WAY."
MY OPTICAL SENSORS ...

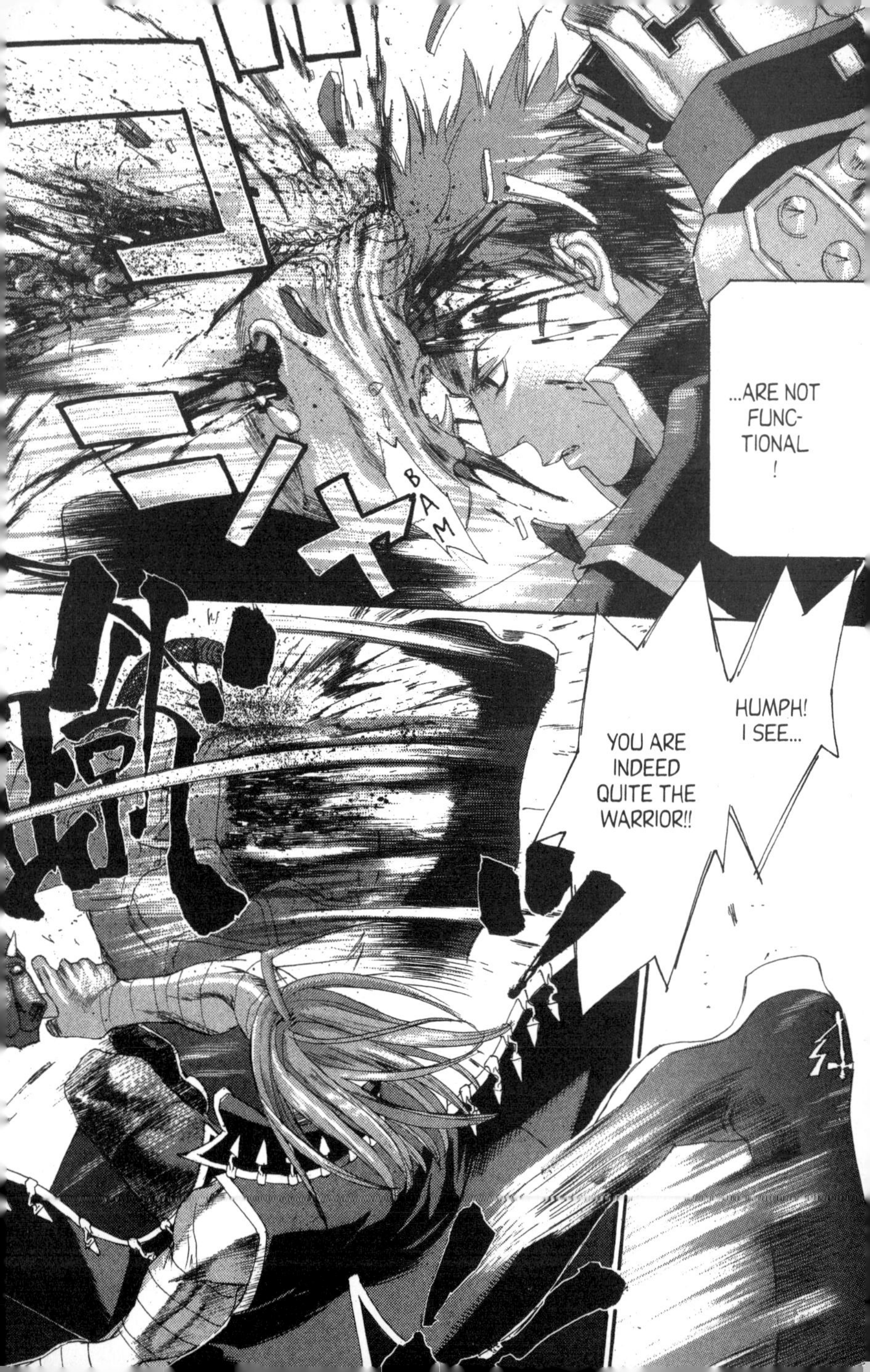

...ARE NOT FUNC- TIONAL !
BAM
HUMPH! I SEE...
YOU ARE INDEED QUITE THE WARRIOR!!

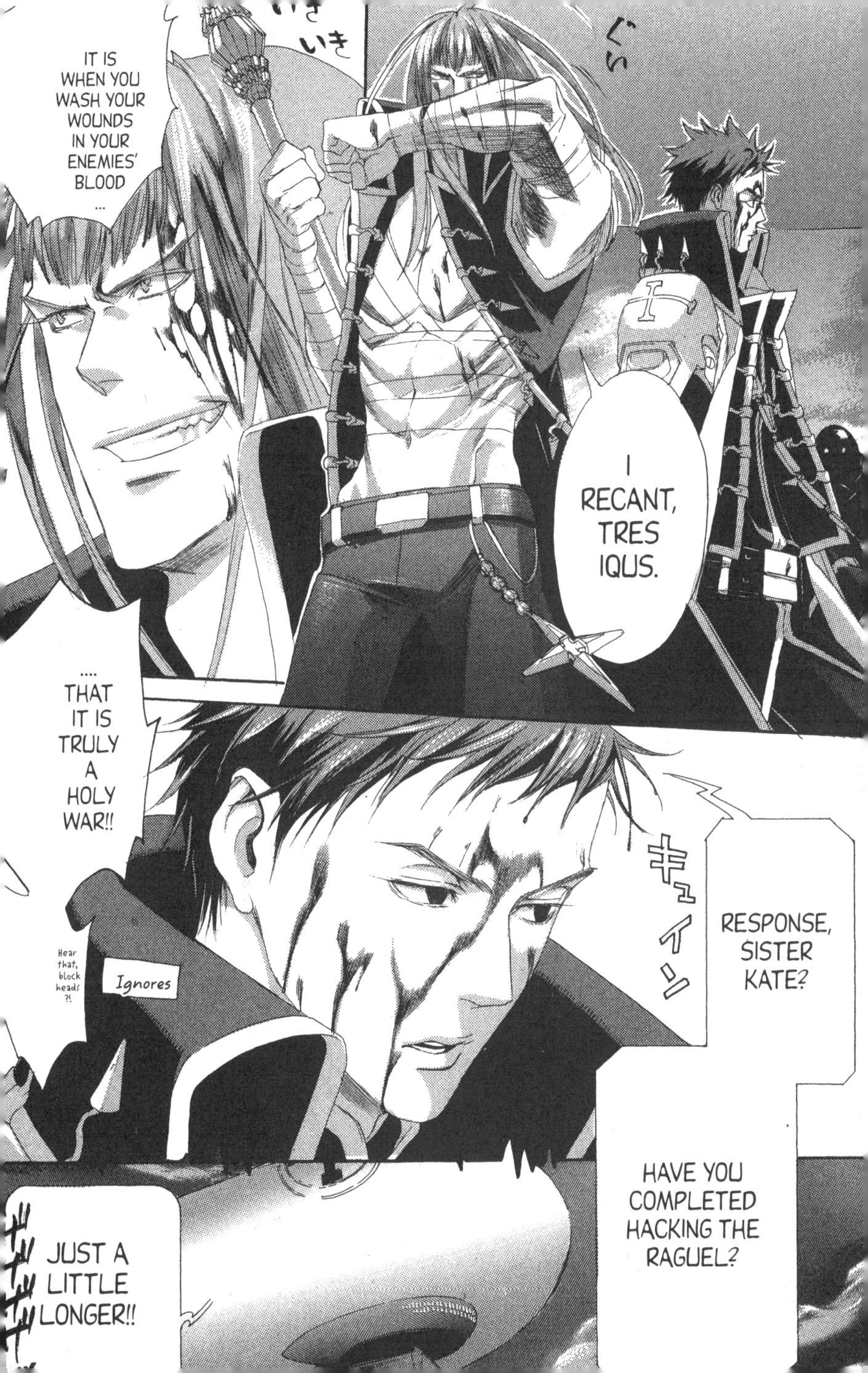
ぐい
いきいき
I RECANT, TRES IQUS.
IT IS WHEN YOU WASH YOUR WOUNDS IN YOUR ENEMIES' BLOOD ...
キュイン
RESPONSE, SISTER KATE?
.... THAT IT IS TRULY A HOLY WAR!!
Ignores
Hear that, block heads?!
HAVE YOU COMPLETED HACKING THE RAGUEL?
JUST A LITTLE LONGER!!

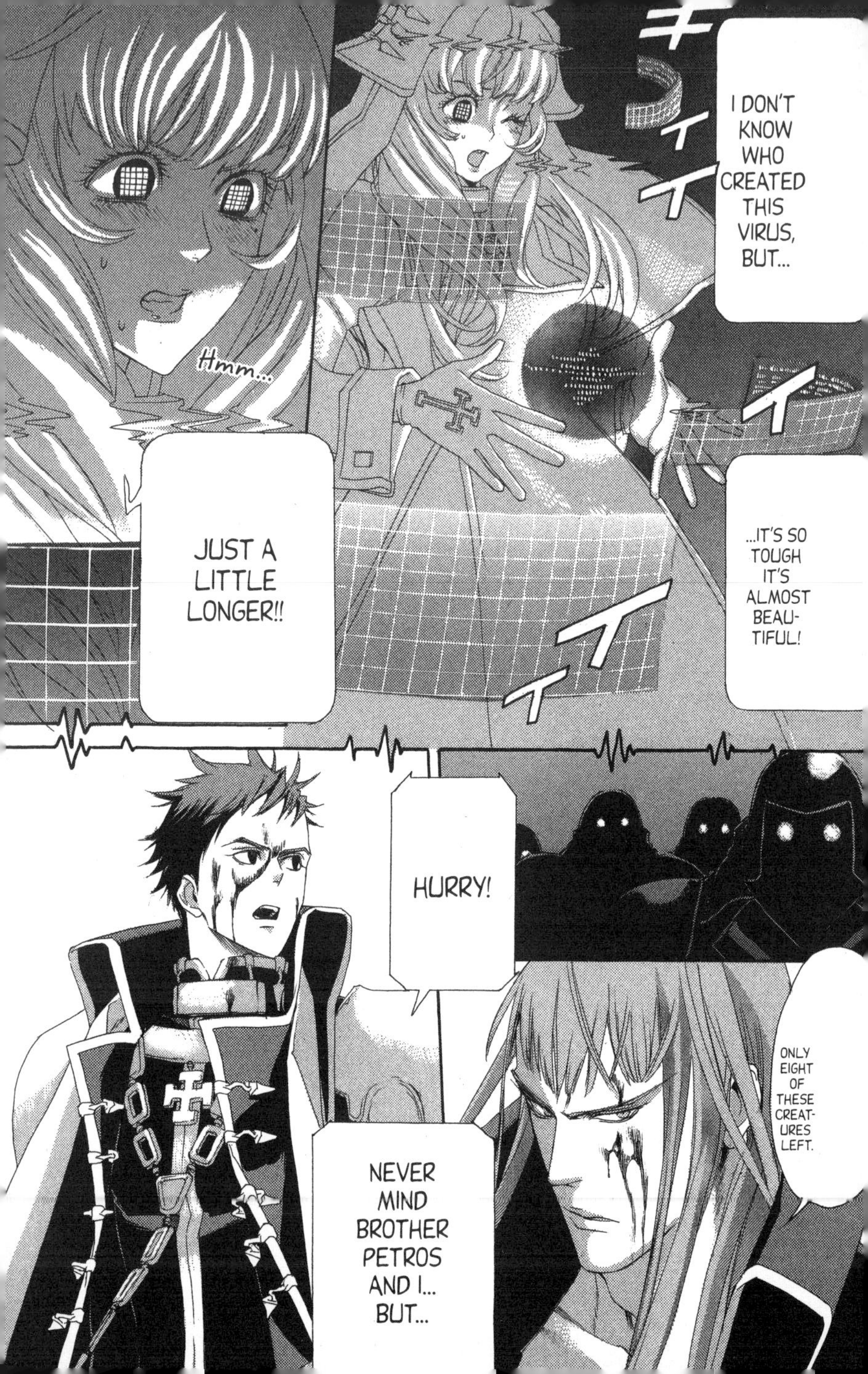
I DON'T KNOW WHO CREATED THIS VIRUS, BUT...
...IT'S SO TOUGH IT'S ALMOST BEAUTIFUL!
Hmm...
JUST A LITTLE LONGER!!
ONLY EIGHT OF THESE CREATURES LEFT.
NEVER MIND BROTHER PETROS AND I... BUT...
HURRY!

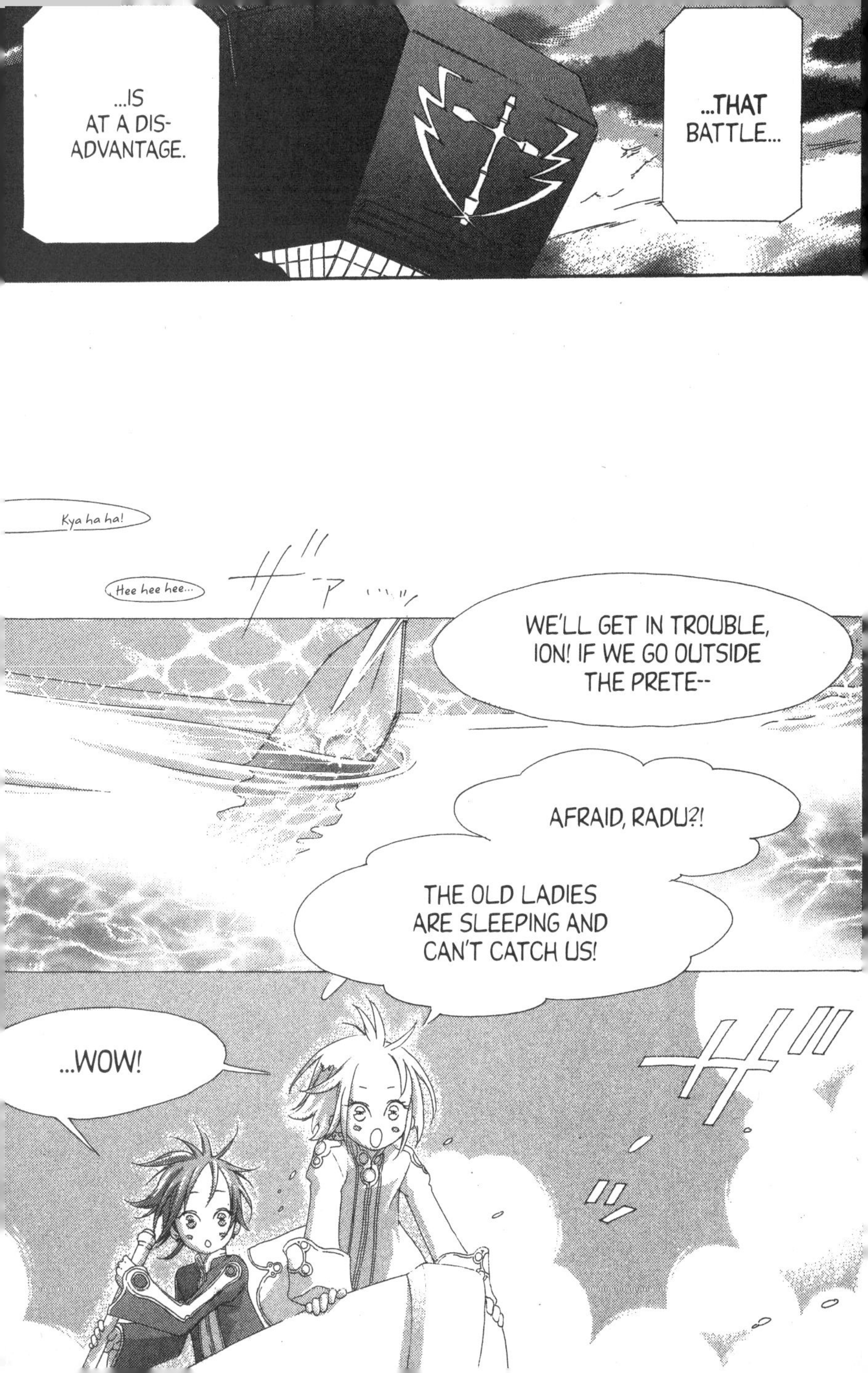
...THAT BATTLE...
...IS AT A DIS-ADVANTAGE.
Kya ha ha!
Hee hee hee...
WE'LL GET IN TROUBLE, ION! IF WE GO OUTSIDE THE PRETE--
AFRAID, RADU?!
THE OLD LADIES ARE SLEEPING AND CAN'T CATCH US!
...WOW!

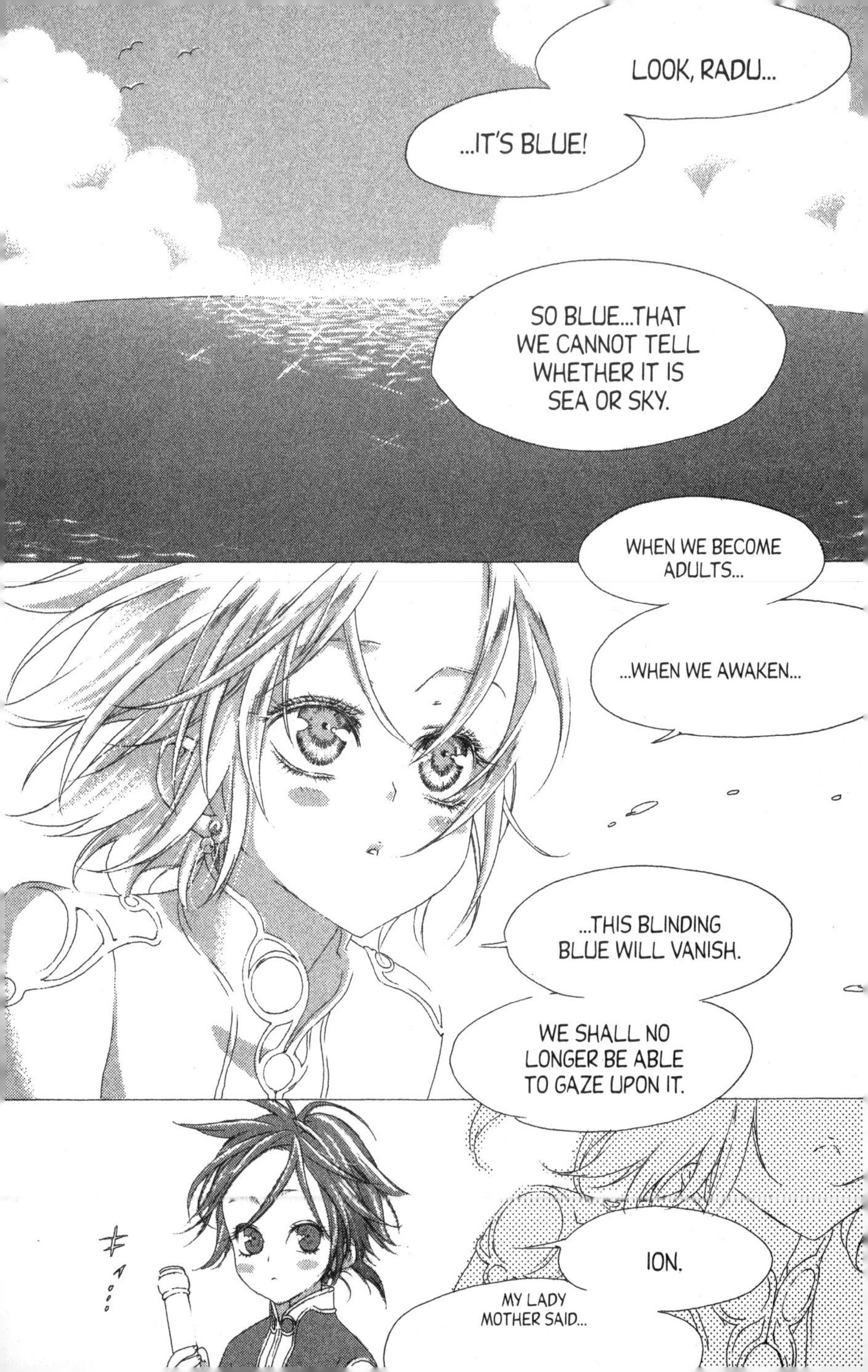
LOOK, RADU...
...IT'S BLUE!
SO BLUE...THAT WE CANNOT TELL WHETHER IT IS SEA OR SKY.
WHEN WE BECOME ADULTS...
...WHEN WE AWAKEN...
...THIS BLINDING BLUE WILL VANISH.
WE SHALL NO LONGER BE ABLE TO GAZE UPON IT.
ION.
MY LADY MOTHER SAID...

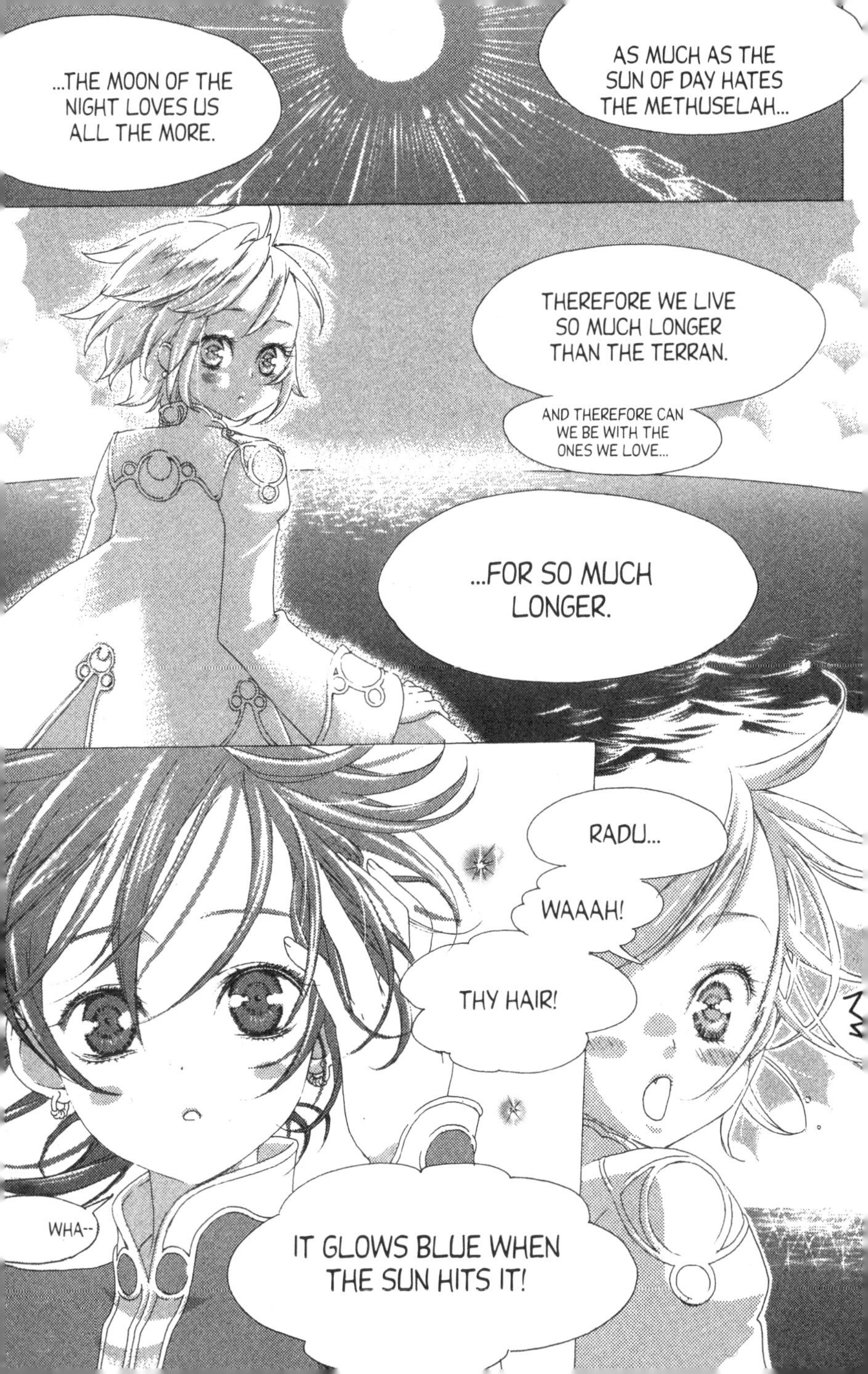
AS MUCH AS THE SUN OF DAY HATES THE METHUSELAH...
...THE MOON OF THE NIGHT LOVES US ALL THE MORE.
THEREFORE WE LIVE SO MUCH LONGER THAN THE TERRAN.
AND THEREFORE CAN WE BE WITH THE ONES WE LOVE...
...FOR SO MUCH LONGER.
RADU...
WAAAH!
THY HAIR!
IT GLOWS BLUE WHEN THE SUN HITS IT!
WHA--

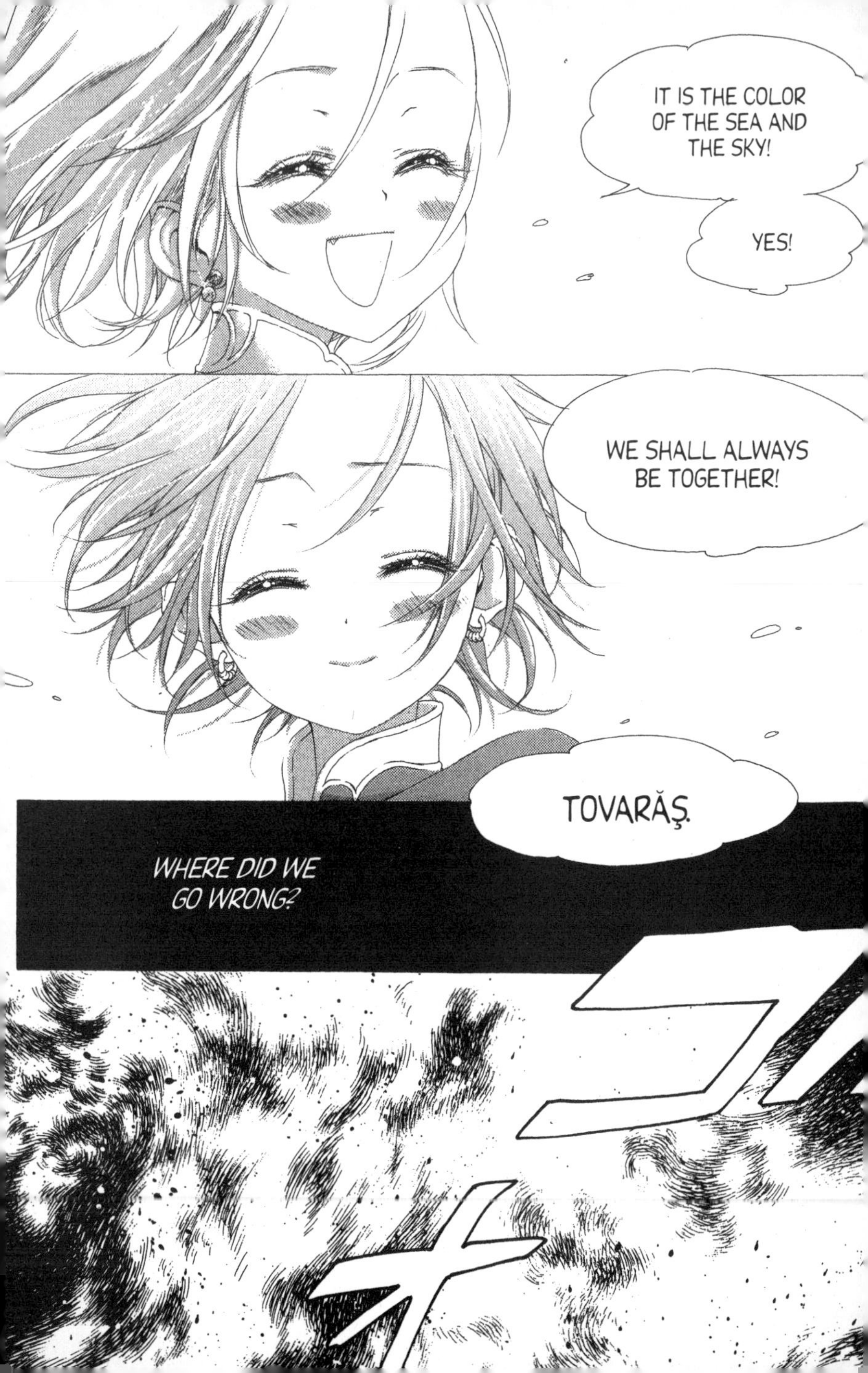
IT IS THE COLOR OF THE SEA AND THE SKY!
YES!
WE SHALL ALWAYS BE TOGETHER!
TOVARĂŞ.
WHERE DID WE GO WRONG?

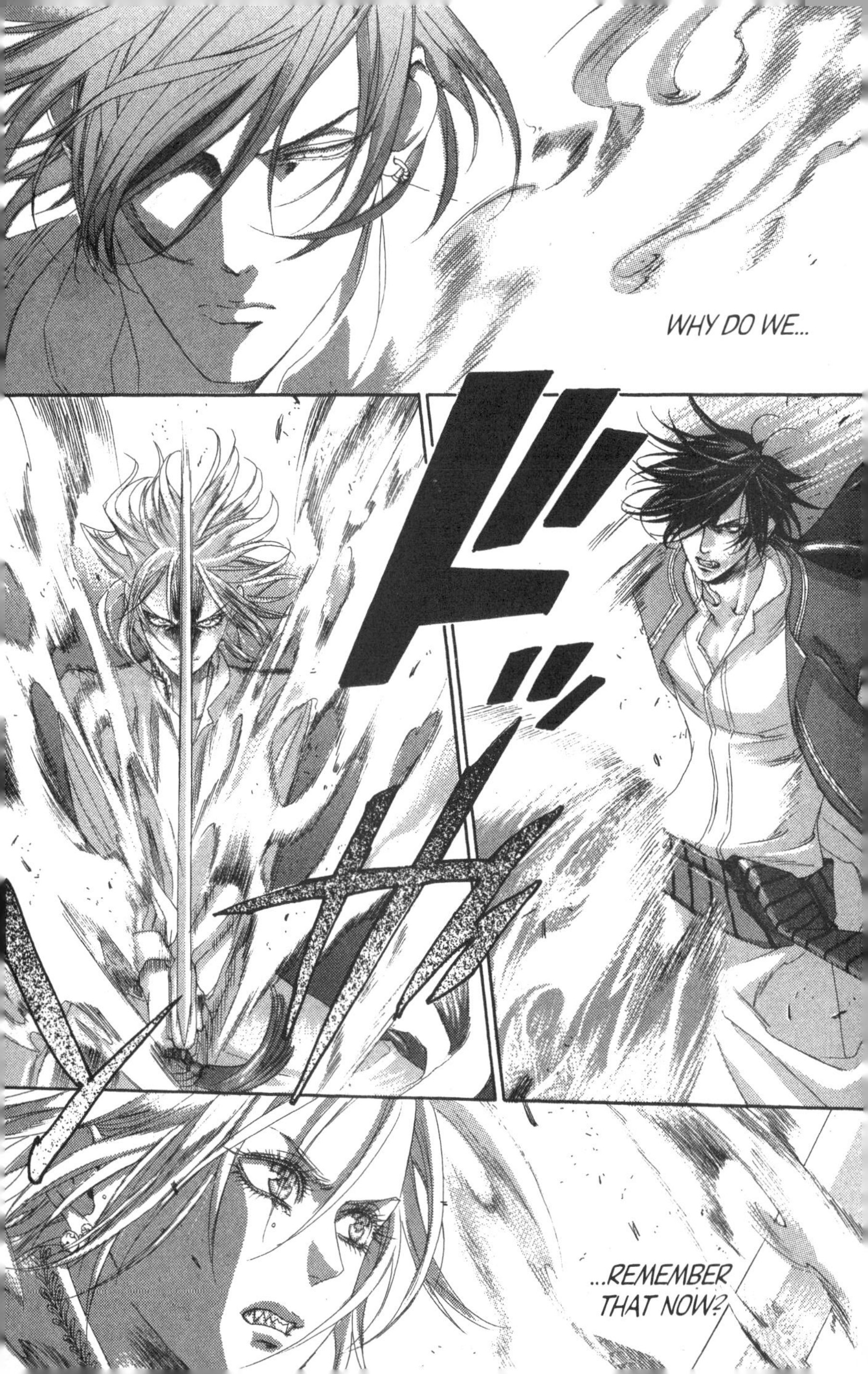
WHY DO WE...
...REMEMBER THAT NOW?

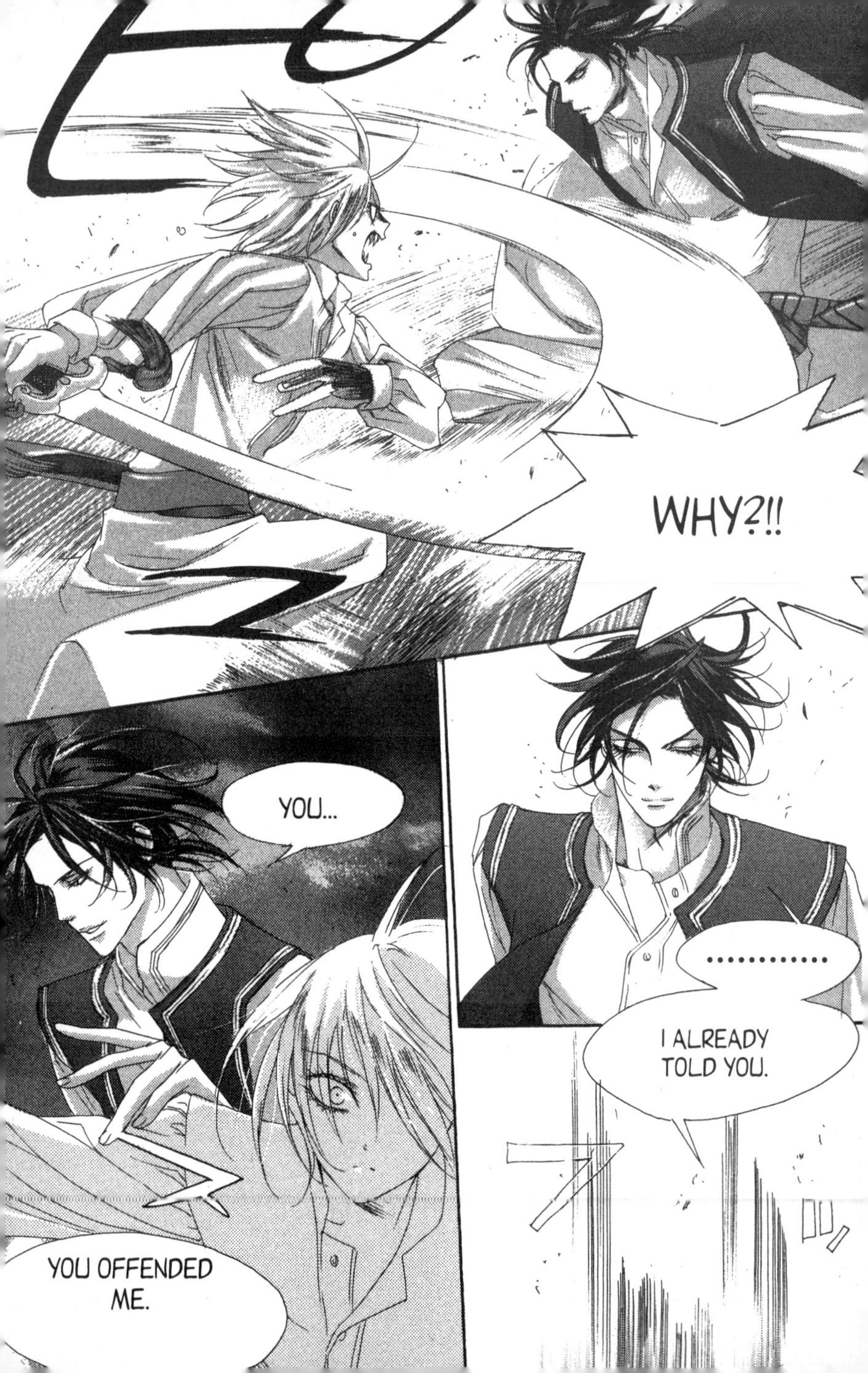
WHY?!!
....
I ALREADY TOLD YOU.
YOU...
YOU OFFENDED ME.

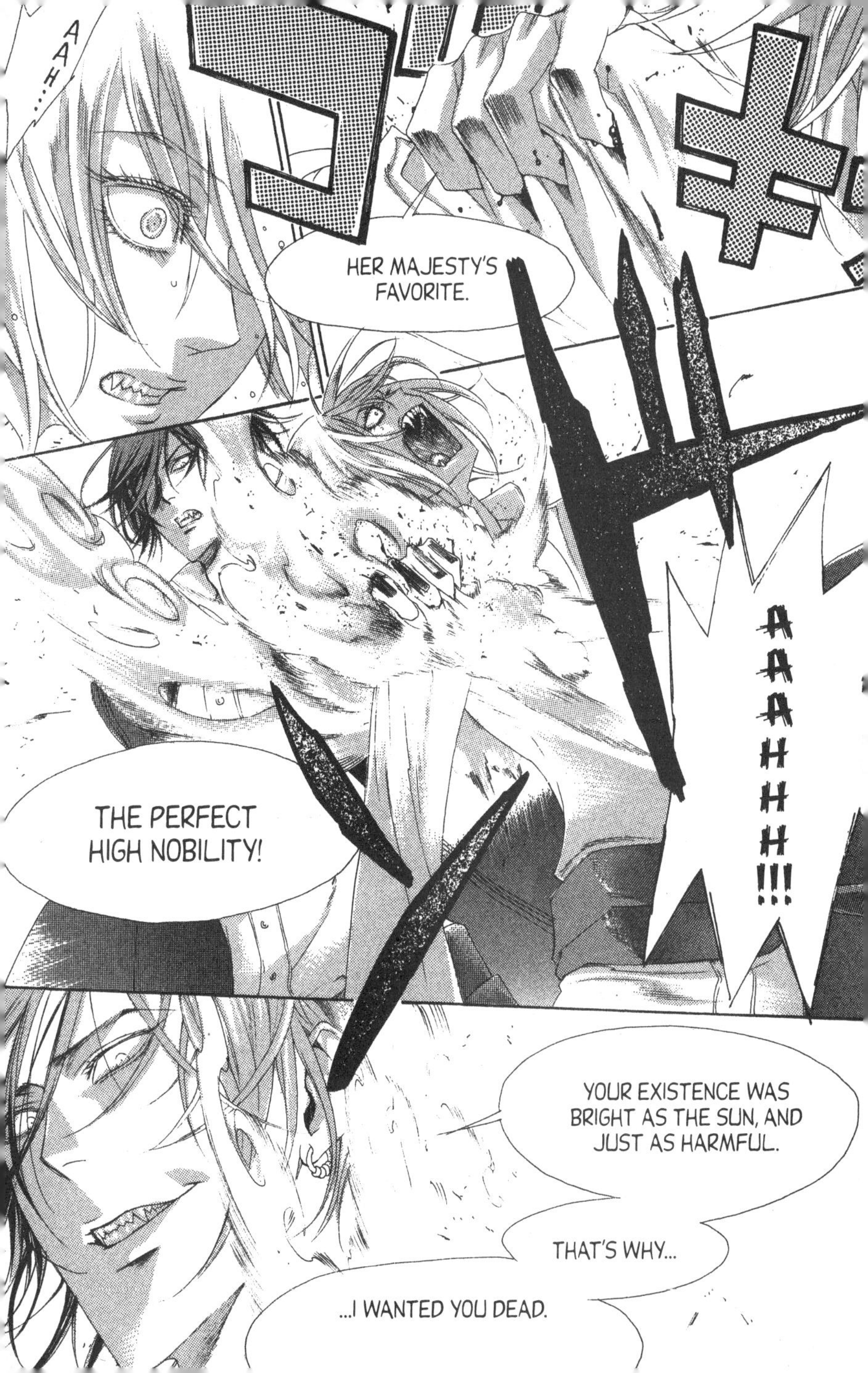
AAH...
HER MAJESTY'S FAVORITE.
AAAAHHHH!!!
THE PERFECT HIGH NOBILITY!
YOUR EXISTENCE WAS BRIGHT AS THE SUN, AND JUST AS HARMFUL.
THAT'S WHY...
...I WANTED YOU DEAD.

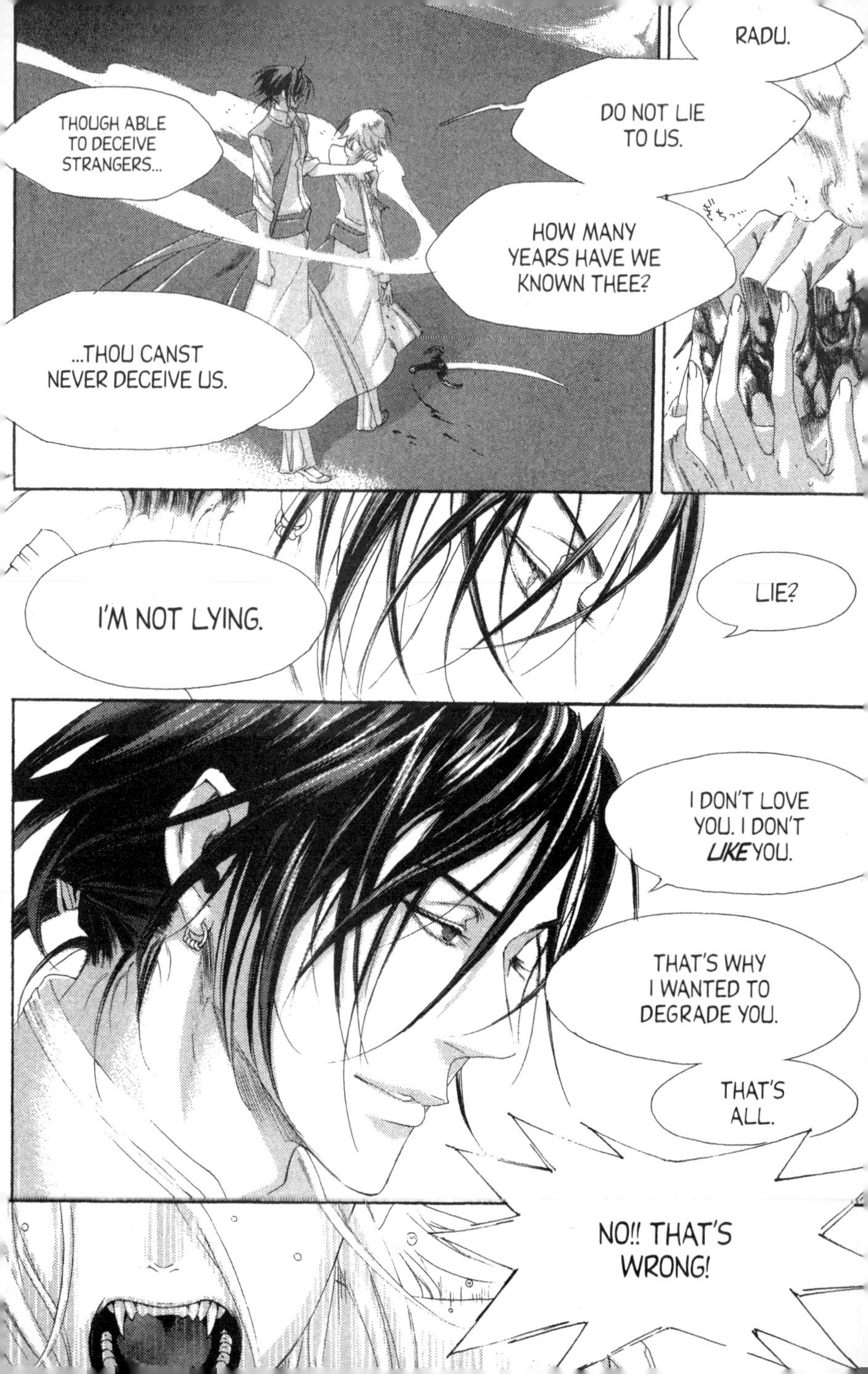
RADU.
DO NOT LIE TO US.
HOW MANY YEARS HAVE WE KNOWN THEE?
THOUGH ABLE TO DECEIVE STRANGERS...
...THOU CANST NEVER DECEIVE US.
LIE?
I'M NOT LYING.
I DON'T LOVE YOU. I DON'T *LIKE* YOU.
THAT'S WHY I WANTED TO DEGRADE YOU.
THAT'S ALL.
NO!! THAT'S WRONG!

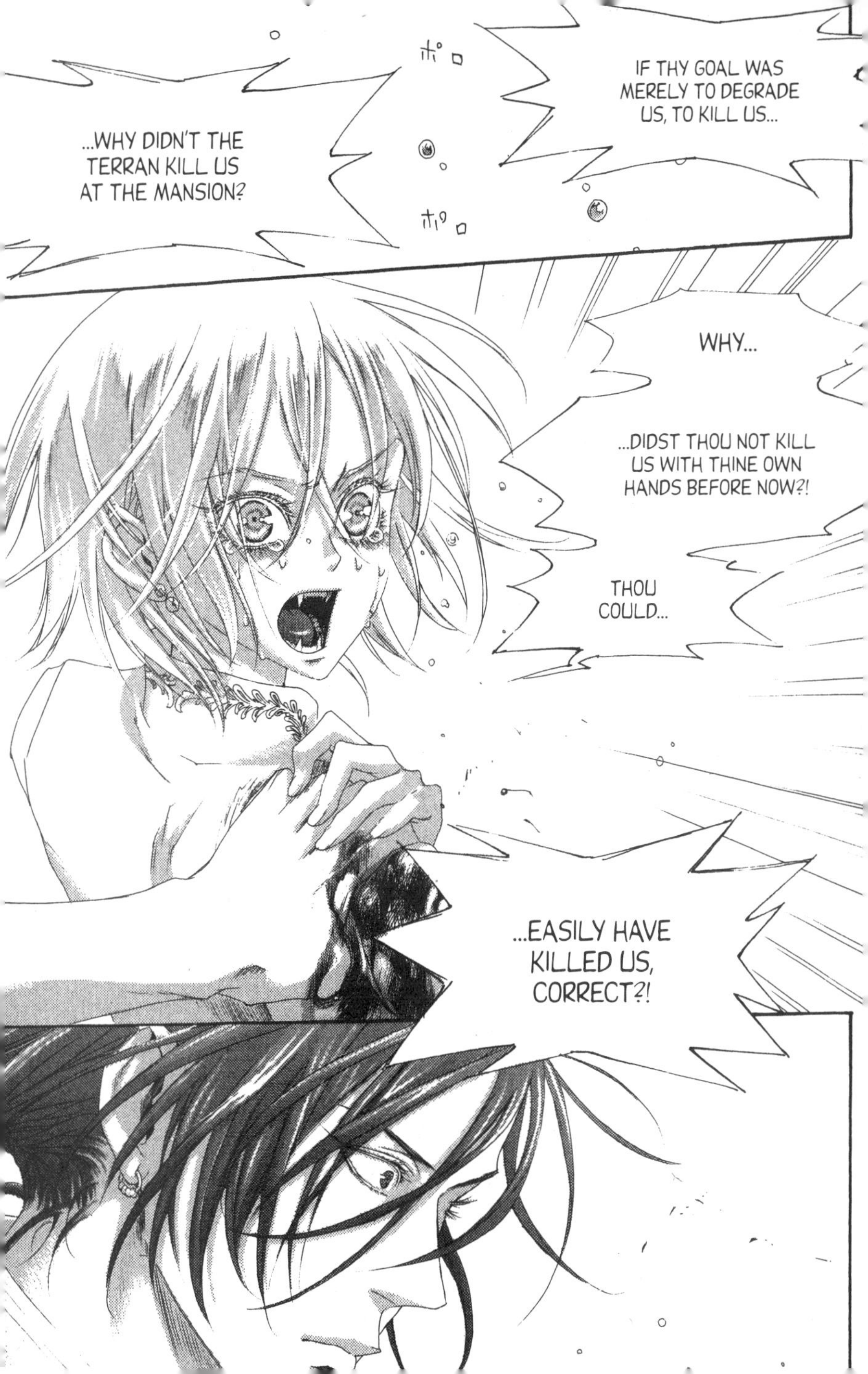
IF THY GOAL WAS MERELY TO DEGRADE US, TO KILL US...
ポロ
ポロ
...WHY DIDN'T THE TERRAN KILL US AT THE MANSION?
WHY...
...DIDST THOU NOT KILL US WITH THINE OWN HANDS BEFORE NOW?!
THOU COULD...
...EASILY HAVE KILLED US, CORRECT?!

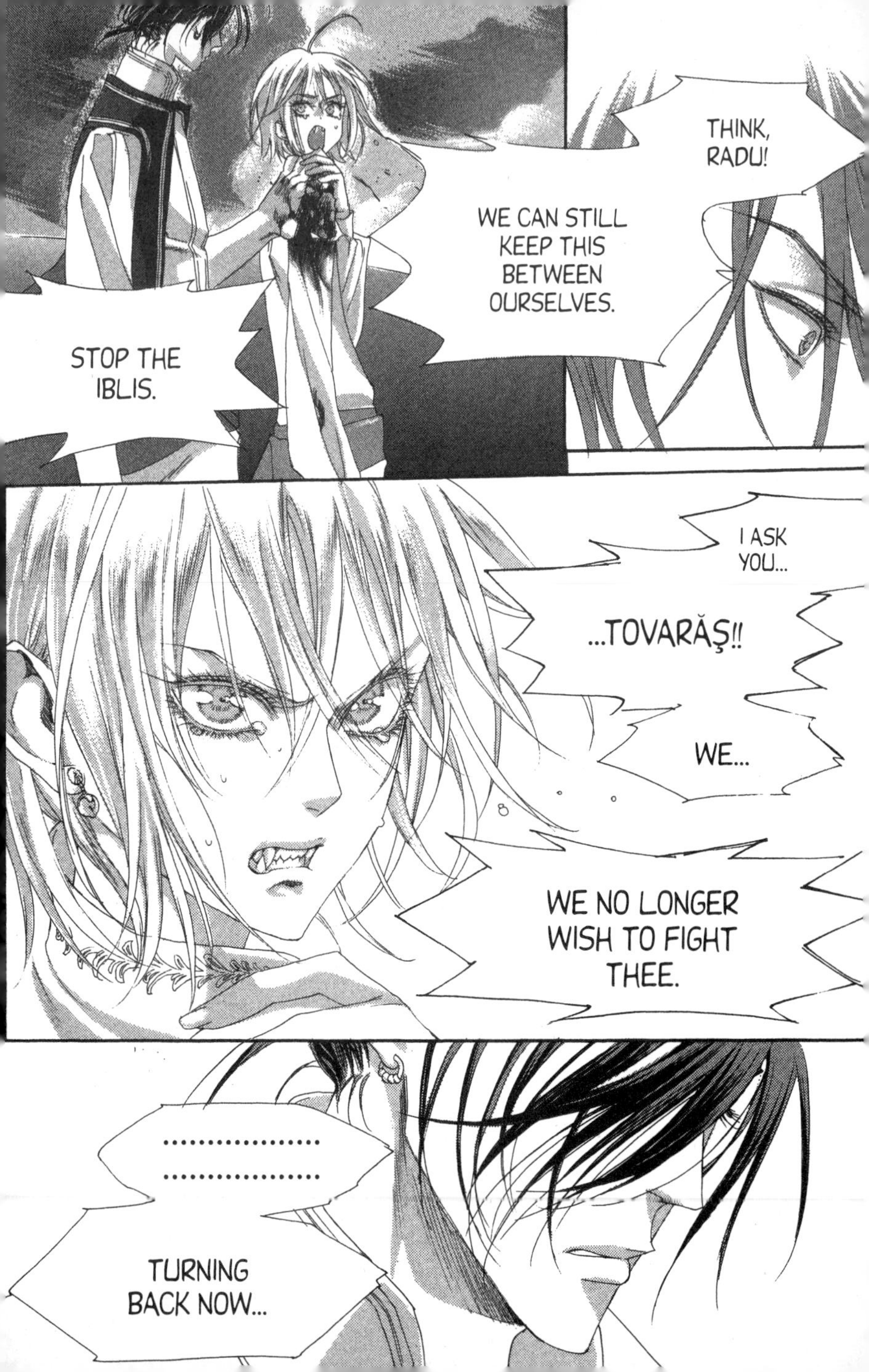
THINK, RADU!
WE CAN STILL KEEP THIS BETWEEN OURSELVES.
STOP THE IBLIS.
I ASK YOU...
...TOVARĂŞ!!
WE...
WE NO LONGER WISH TO FIGHT THEE.
....
....
TURNING BACK NOW...

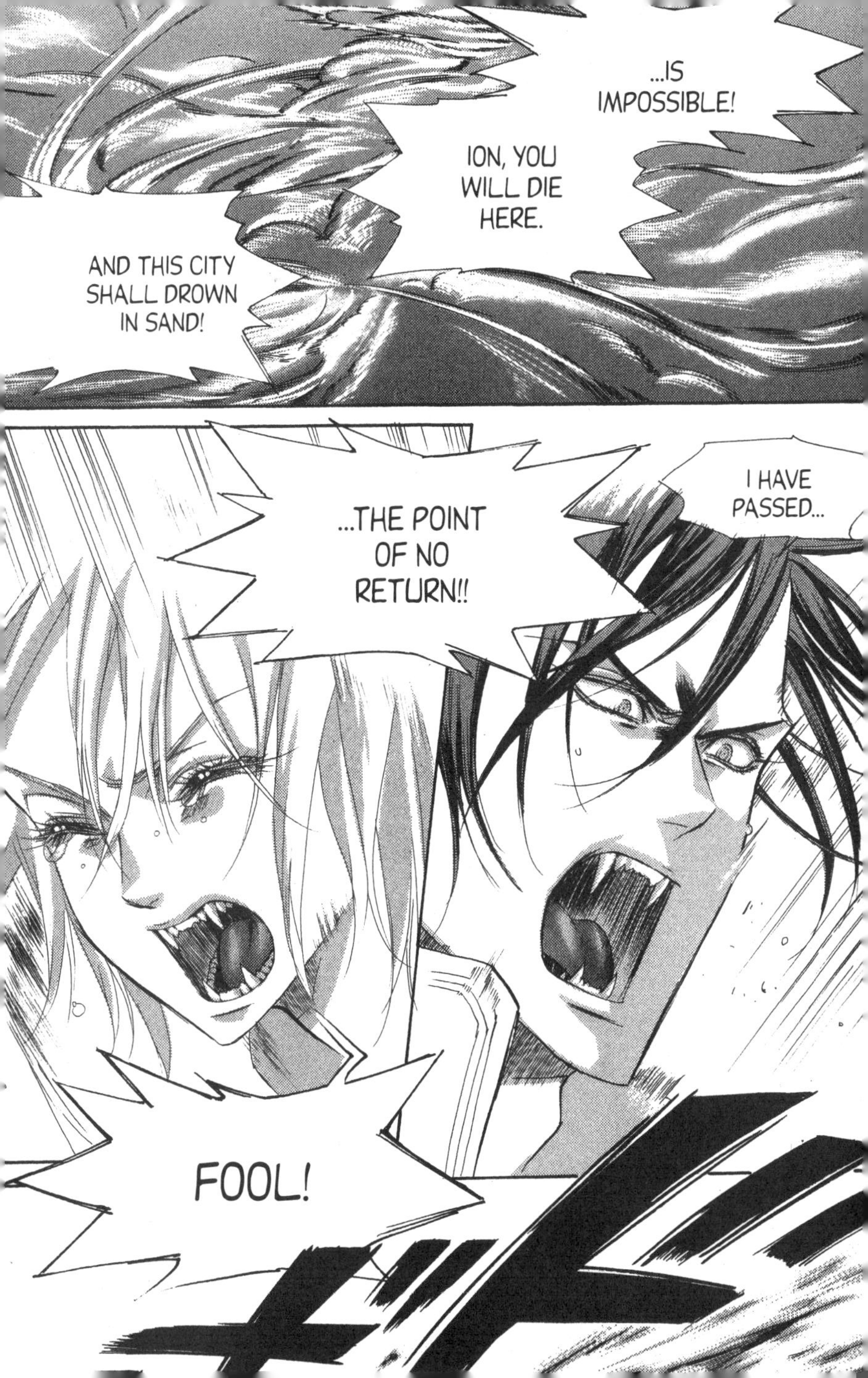
...IS IMPOSSIBLE!
ION, YOU WILL DIE HERE.
AND THIS CITY SHALL DROWN IN SAND!
I HAVE PASSED...
...THE POINT OF NO RETURN!!
FOOL!

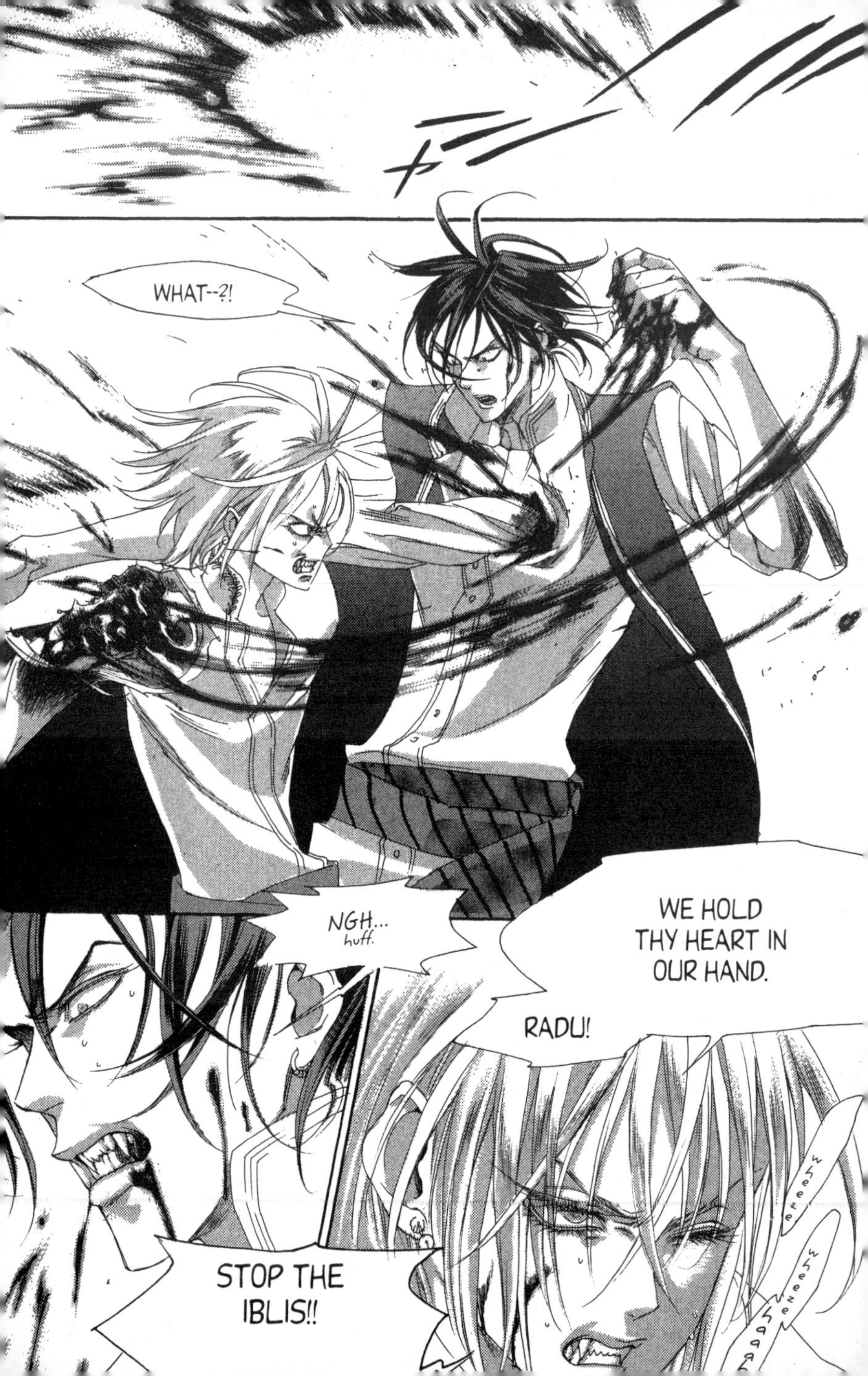
WHAT--?!
WE HOLD THY HEART IN OUR HAND.
RADU!
NGH... huff.
STOP THE IBLIS!!

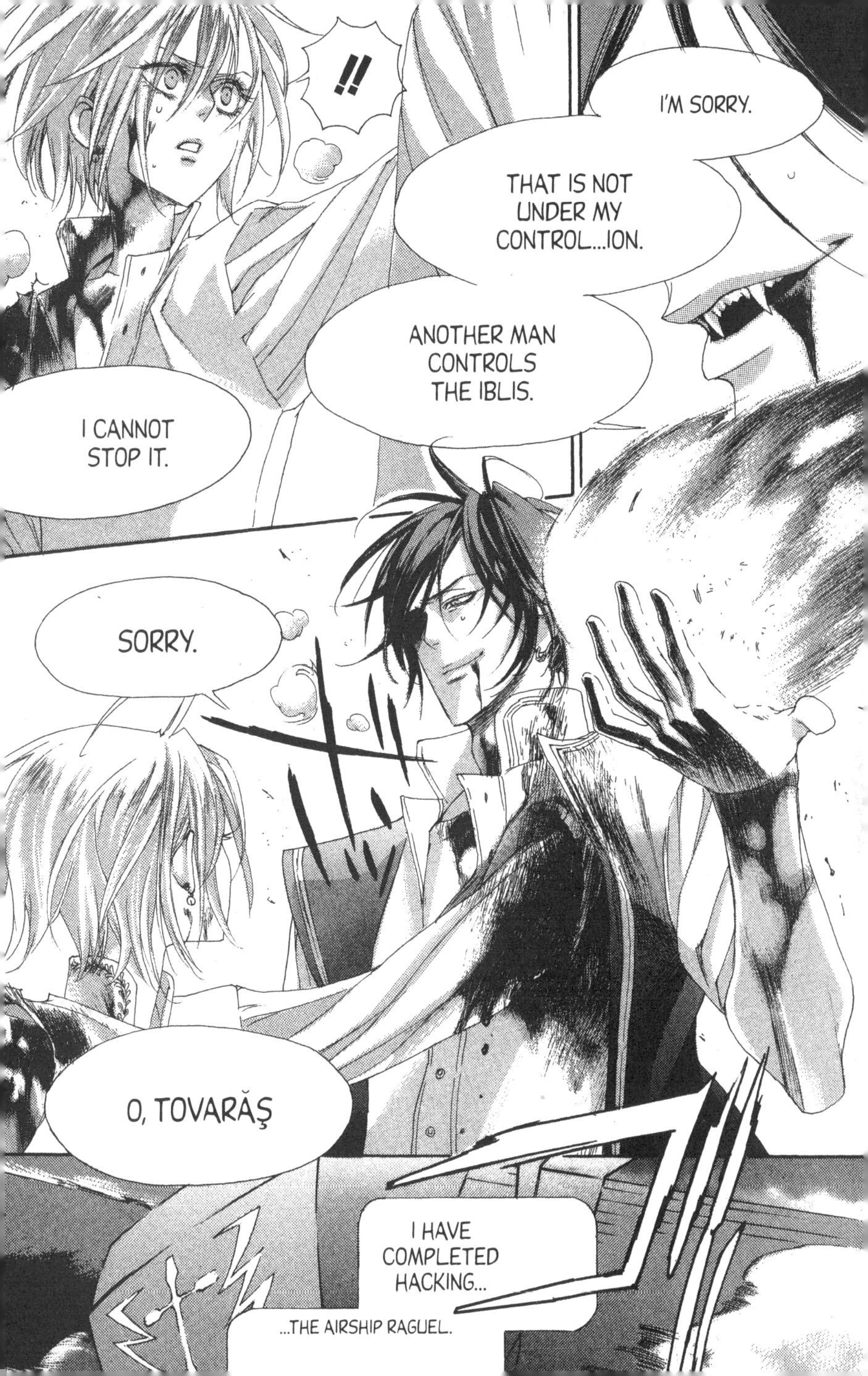
I'M SORRY.
THAT IS NOT UNDER MY CONTROL...ION.
!!
ANOTHER MAN CONTROLS THE IBLIS.
I CANNOT STOP IT.
SORRY.
O, TOVARĂŞ
I HAVE COMPLETED HACKING...
...THE AIRSHIP RAGUEL.

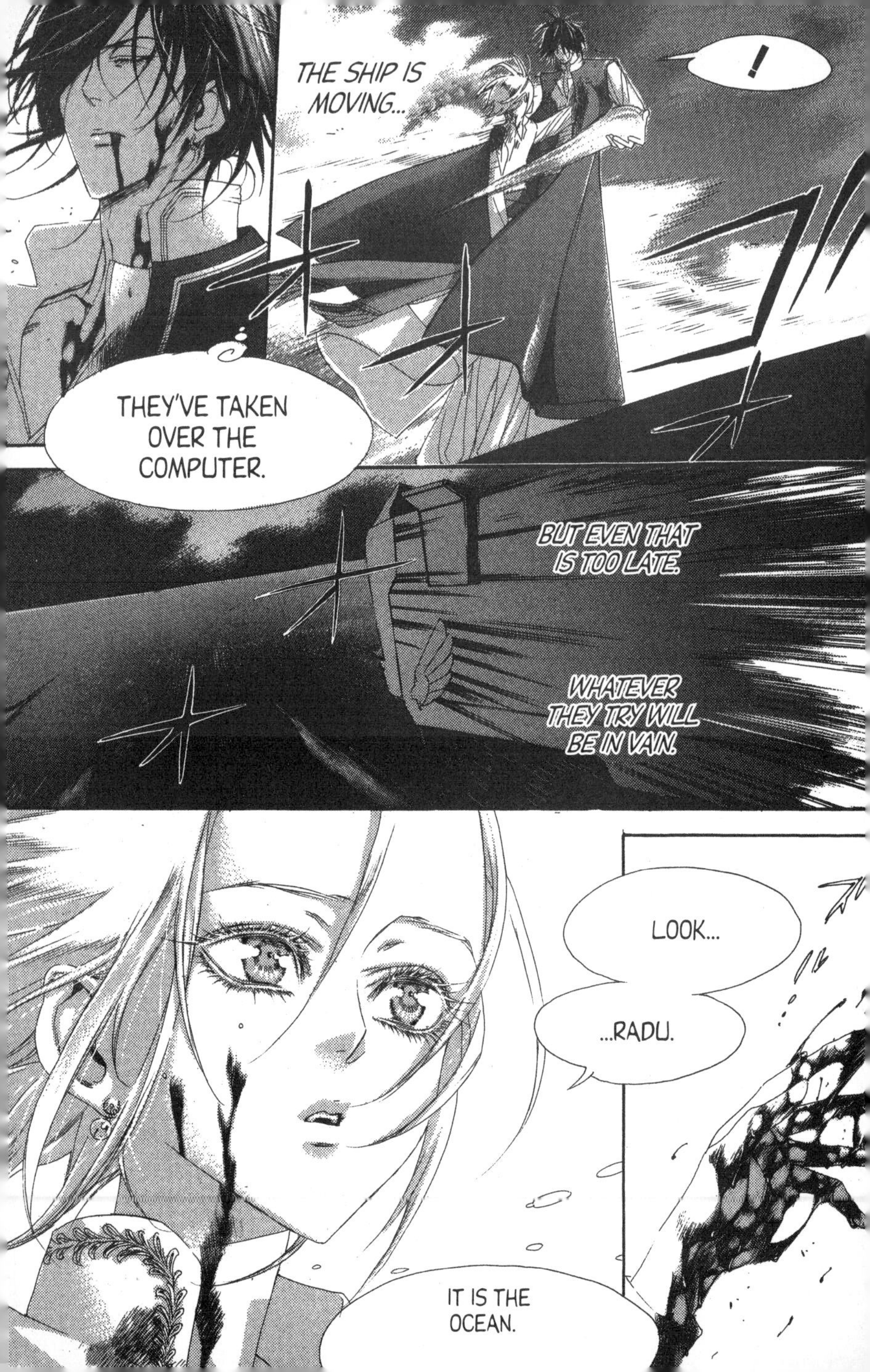
!
THE SHIP IS MOVING...
THEY'VE TAKEN OVER THE COMPUTER.
BUT EVEN THAT IS TOO LATE.
WHATEVER THEY TRY WILL BE IN VAIN.
LOOK...
...RADU.
IT IS THE OCEAN.

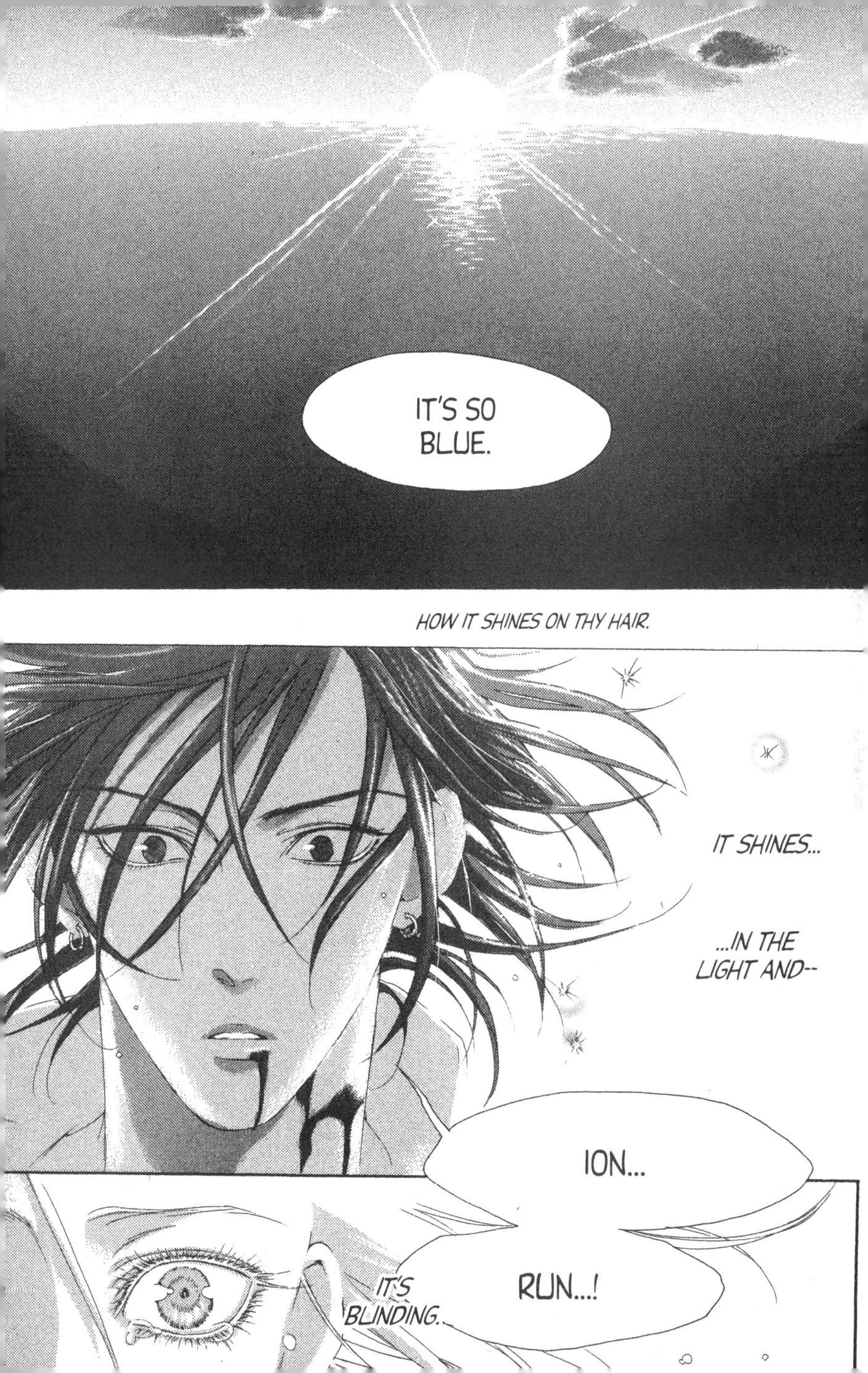
IT'S SO BLUE.
HOW IT SHINES ON THY HAIR.
IT SHINES...
...IN THE LIGHT AND--
ION...
RUN...!
IT'S BLINDING.

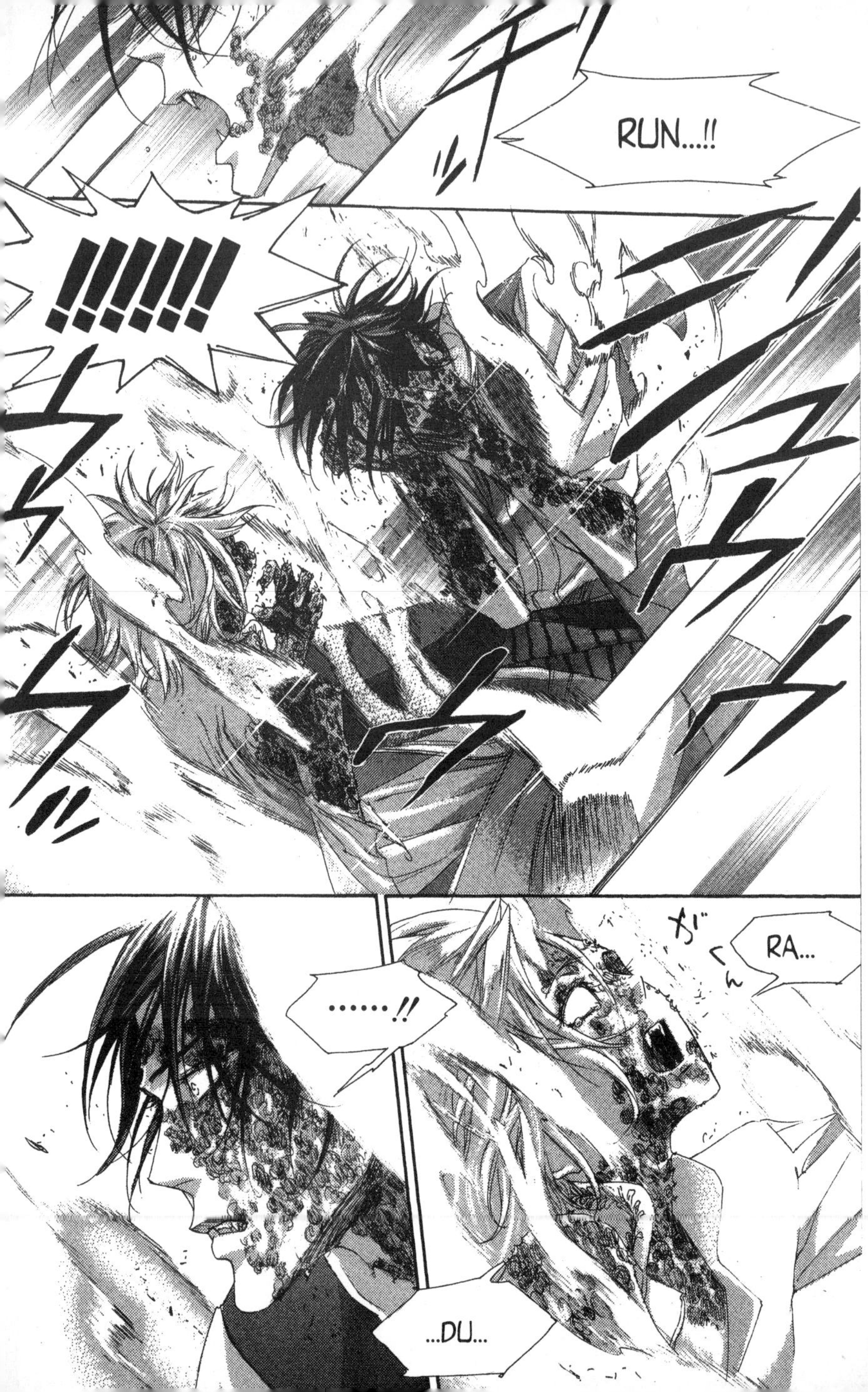
RUN...!!
!!!!!!!
RA...
...DU...
......!!

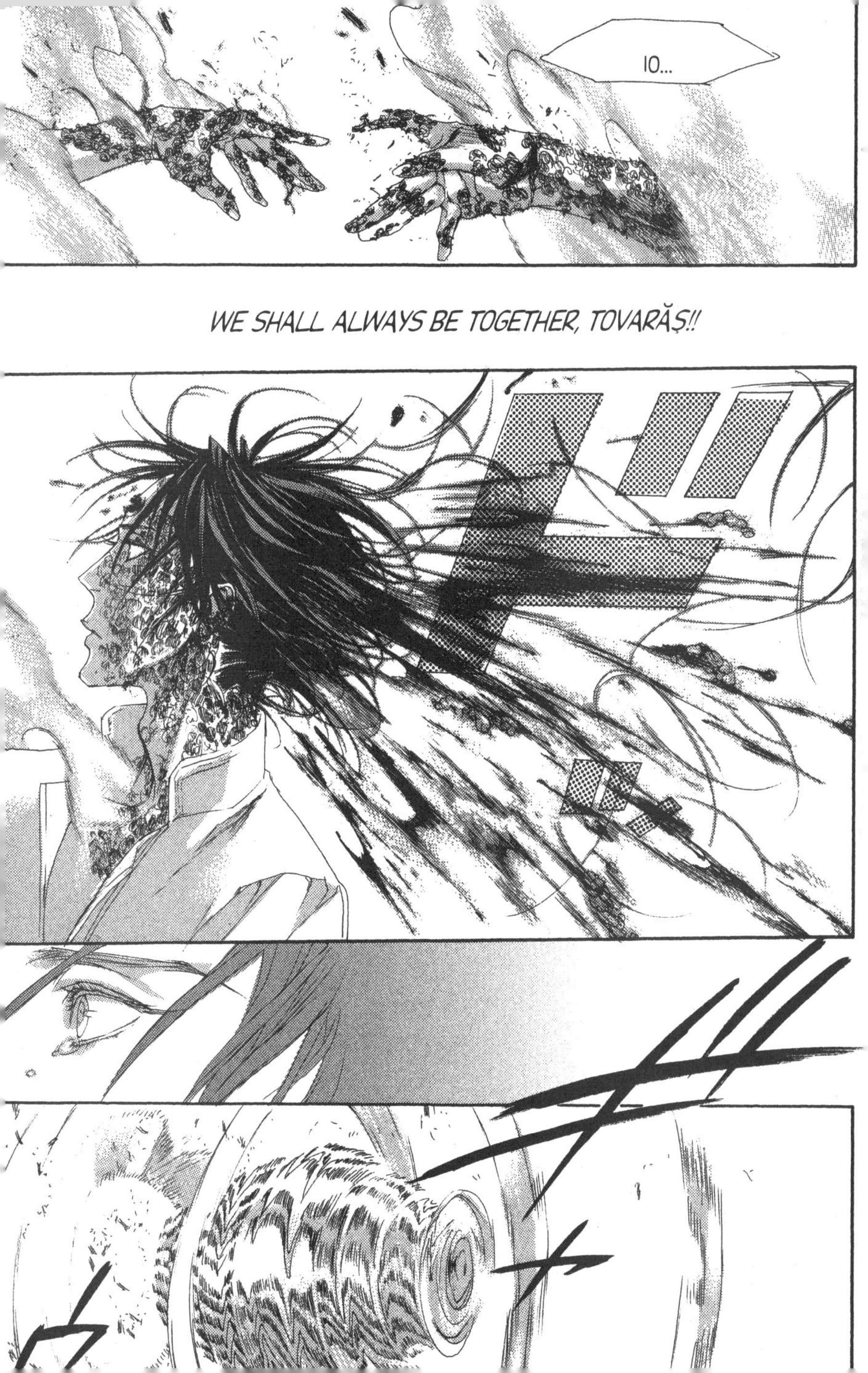
IO...
WE SHALL ALWAYS BE TOGETHER, TOVARĂȘ!!

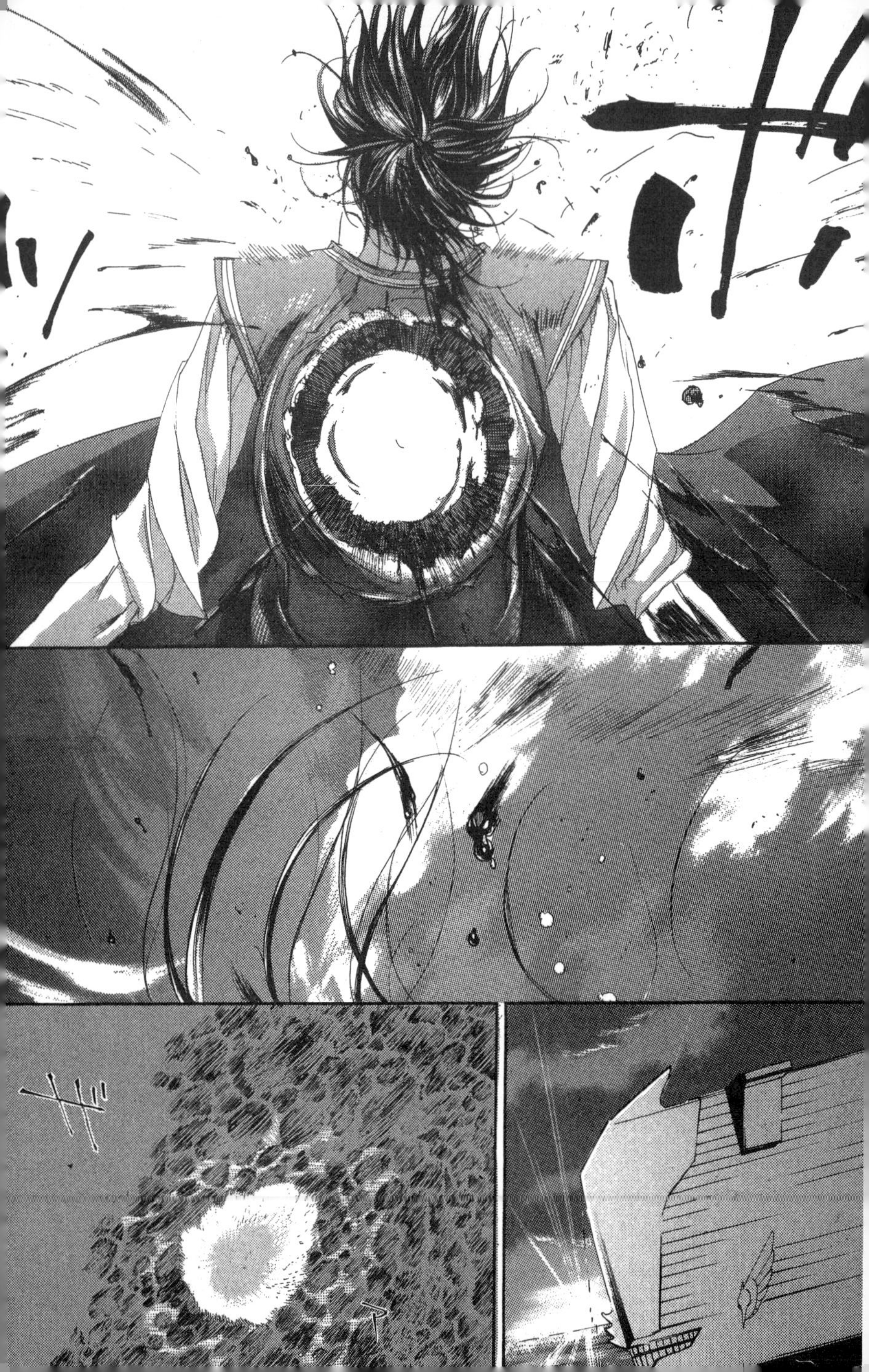

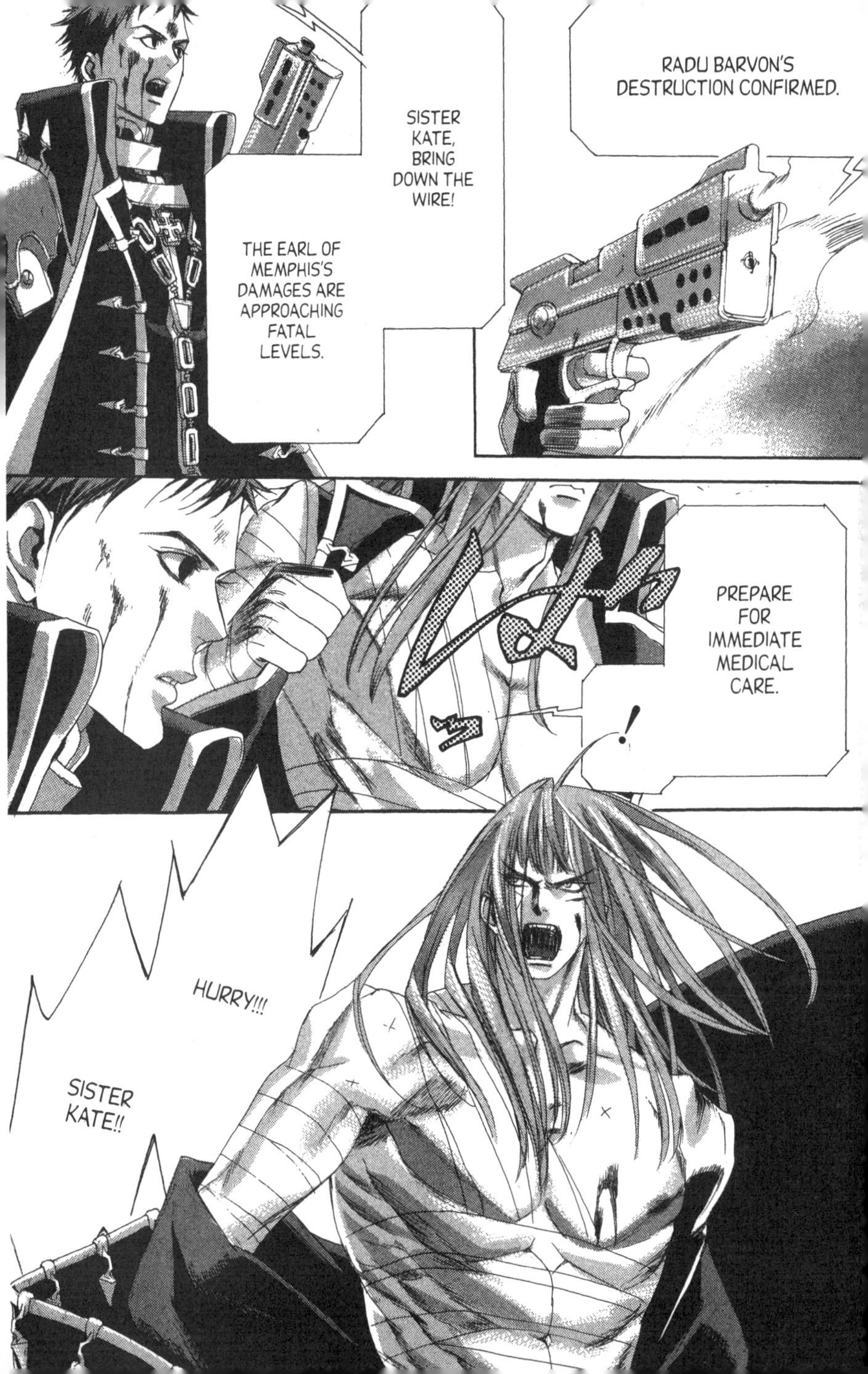
RADU BARVON'S DESTRUCTION CONFIRMED.
SISTER KATE, BRING DOWN THE WIRE!
THE EARL OF MEMPHIS'S DAMAGES ARE APPROACHING FATAL LEVELS.
PREPARE FOR IMMEDIATE MEDICAL CARE.
!
HURRY!!!
SISTER KATE!!

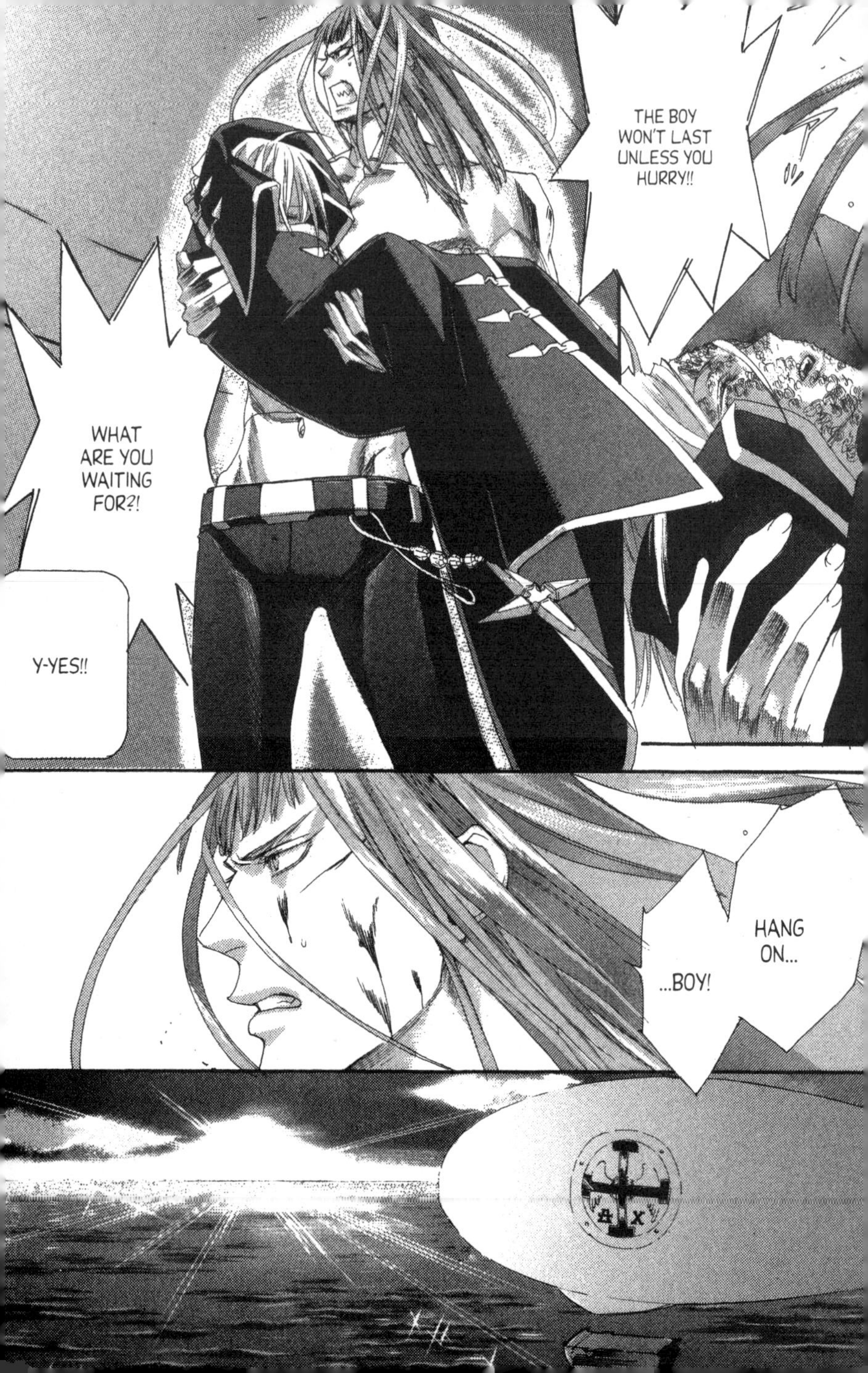
THE BOY WON'T LAST UNLESS YOU HURRY!!
WHAT ARE YOU WAITING FOR?!
Y-YES!!
HANG ON...
...BOY!

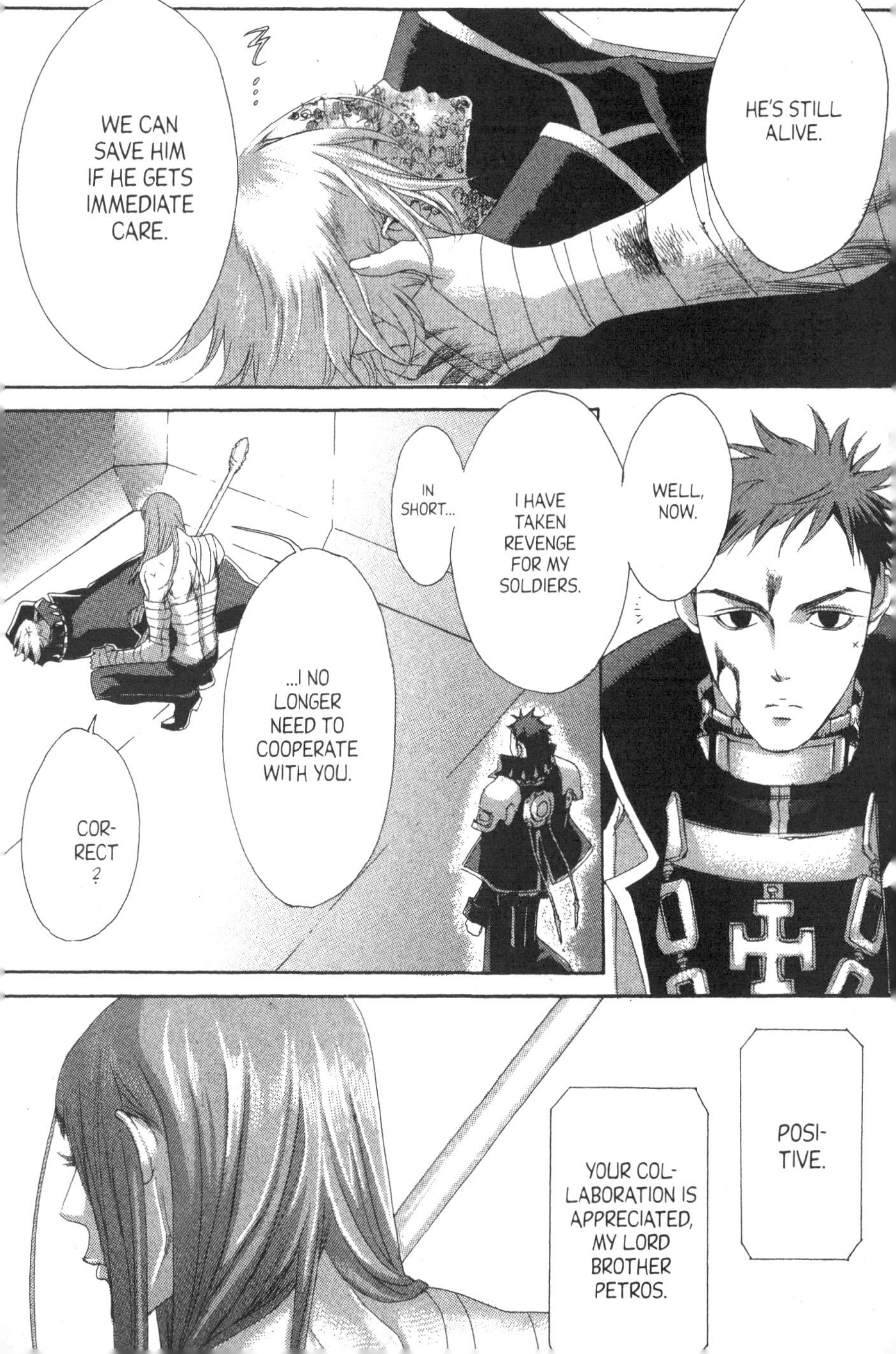
HE'S STILL ALIVE.
WE CAN SAVE HIM IF HE GETS IMMEDIATE CARE.
WELL, NOW.
I HAVE TAKEN REVENGE FOR MY SOLDIERS.
IN SHORT...
...I NO LONGER NEED TO COOPERATE WITH YOU.
CORRECT?
POSITIVE.
YOUR COLLABORATION IS APPRECIATED, MY LORD BROTHER PETROS.

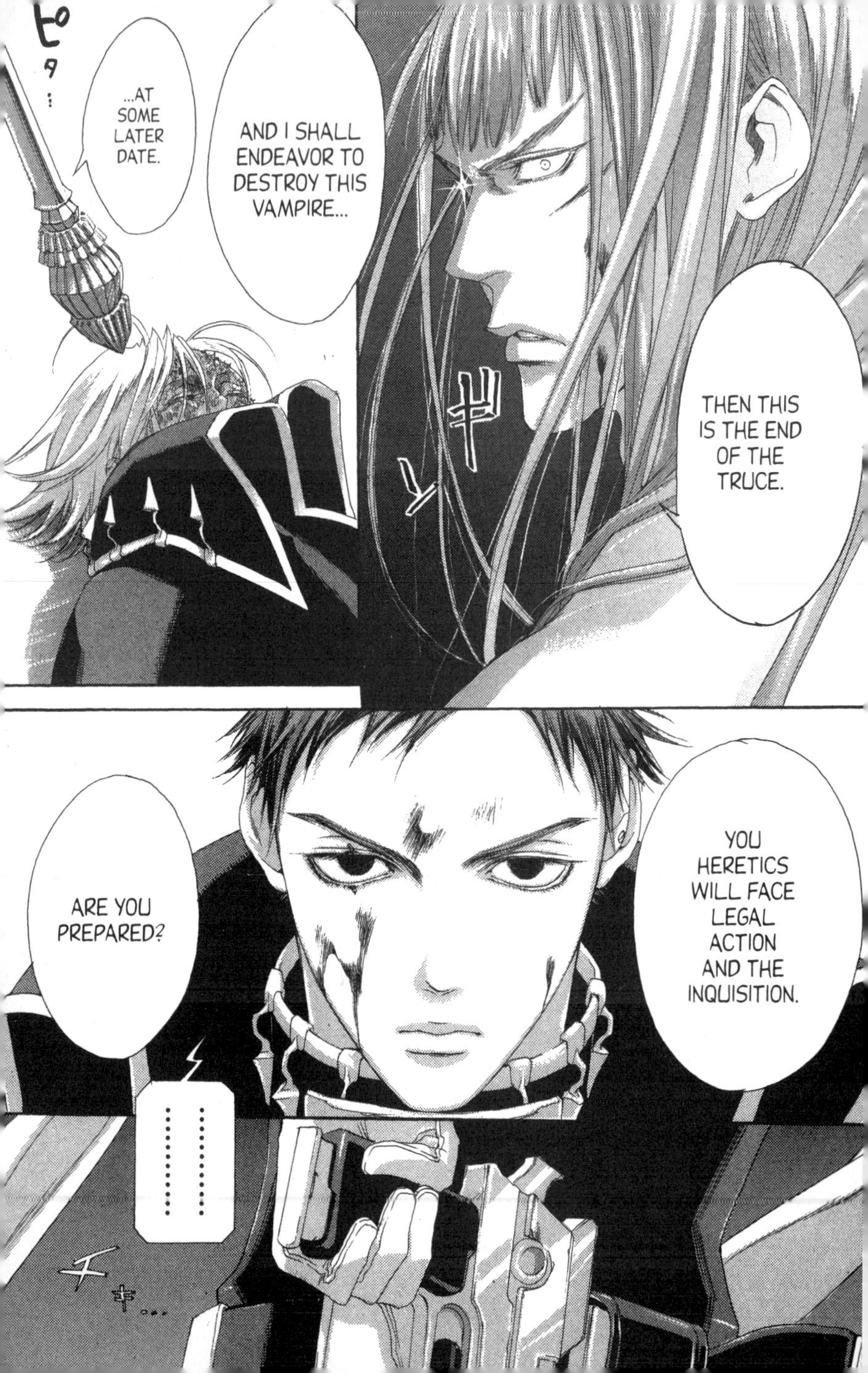
THEN THIS IS THE END OF THE TRUCE.
AND I SHALL ENDEAVOR TO DESTROY THIS VAMPIRE...
...AT SOME LATER DATE.
YOU HERETICS WILL FACE LEGAL ACTION AND THE INQUISITION.
ARE YOU PREPARED?
......
......

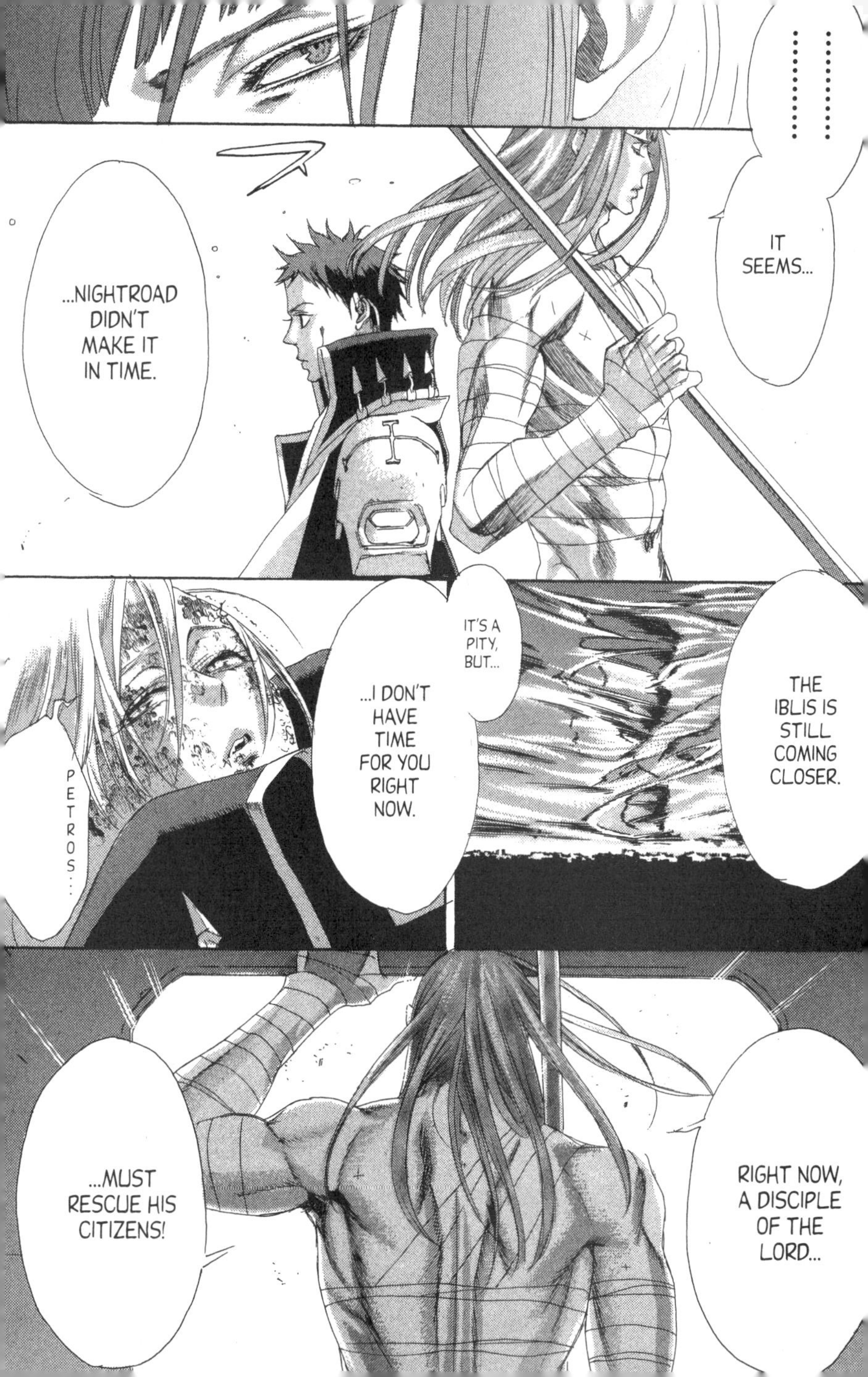
……
IT SEEMS...
...NIGHTROAD DIDN'T MAKE IT IN TIME.
THE IBLIS IS STILL COMING CLOSER.
IT'S A PITY, BUT...
...I DON'T HAVE TIME FOR YOU RIGHT NOW.
PETROS...
RIGHT NOW, A DISCIPLE OF THE LORD...
...MUST RESCUE HIS CITIZENS!

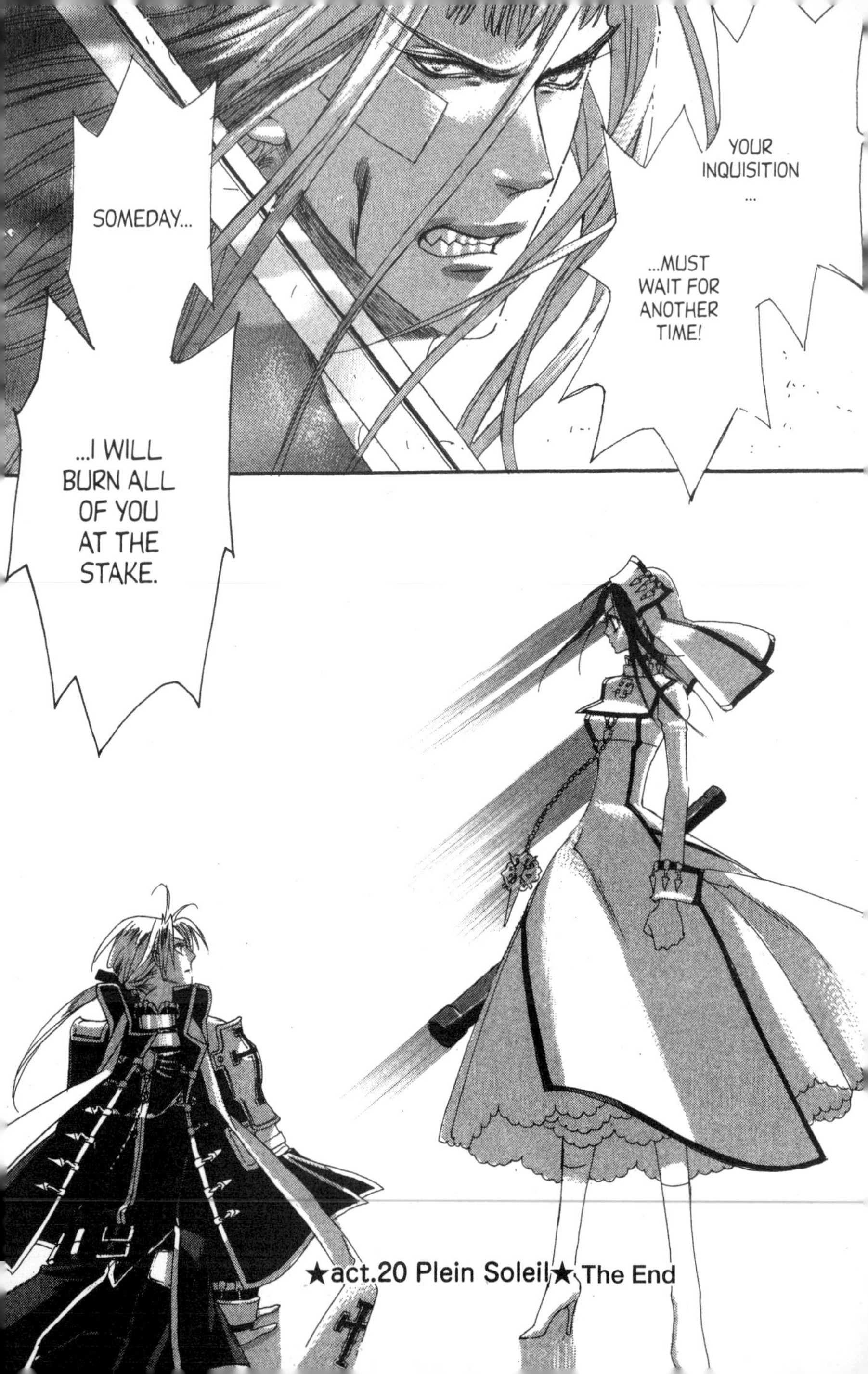
YOUR INQUISITION ...
...MUST WAIT FOR ANOTHER TIME!
SOMEDAY...
...I WILL BURN ALL OF YOU AT THE STAKE.
★act.20 Plein Soleil★ The End

Memento Mori Radu

I'm not good at drawing people's deaths. It was the same when I had to do Gyula's, but I keep on thinking, "I hope he comes back to life." When I'm actually drawing it, I keep thinking, "Why does Sunao-sensei keep creating such tragic characters?"

Q. Why is Radu so unfortunate?

A. "Because he's of low rank." "Because he's depressing." "Because he's honest." "Because he grew up into an adult." "Because he was blue (the color)." If only he were blonde, then he'd be happier... These are the answers that came up at work, but...the last one, "Because he was blue," I don't get at all. Certainly, he was born under an unfortunate star, wasn't he? Poor guy. If only he were blonde (persistent).

I was so shocked by their parting in Carthage, I had to try and justify it. As a normal human, I don't understand the idea of "tovarăş" as it appears in this story, but they are bound to the point where they say, "I would give you my life." I think it's impossible to understand Ion's pain at losing that. I think it'd be nice if I could draw that pain. It's just that though he looks like a child, inside, both of them are adult men (Like Boy Detective Conan...?) Adult men can't just cry in front of people for no reason...though Ion is emotional and hot-tempered. I don't know! Methuselah! (Puts hands together in prayer.)

They say he was strangely popular in one of the panels of the battle scenes. (I must have been tired, huh?) With regard to the depiction of their childhood years, when I first drew 13-year-old Radu (which is the age that Ion apparently appears to be even now) I was halfway joking, like, "Ha ha ha" but maybe I got a taste for it or something because it escalated the next time. I persistently redrew the two of them until they looked more like first graders...to top it off, I was told that, "I can only feel evil coming from the children you draw." You're wrong!!

Why does he still have the same hair style as when he was little?! Is he a S*yan?! Well, no one mentioned it, so I'm not worried.

Magic of Sleepiness

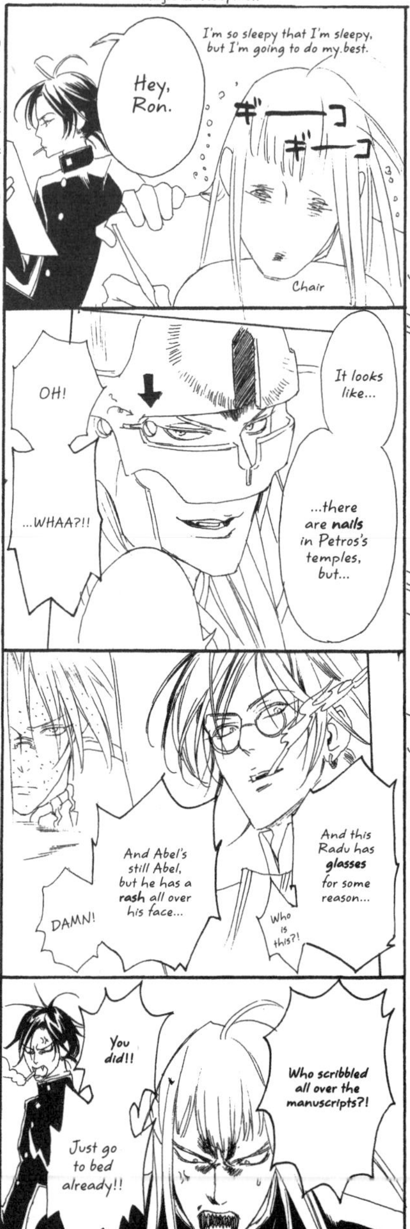
I'm so sleepy that I'm sleepy, but I'm going to do my best.
Hey, Ron.
ギーコ ギーコ
Chair
It looks like...
...there are **nails** in Petros's temples, but...
OH!
...WHAA?!!
And this Radu has **glasses** for some reason...
Who is this?!
And Abel's still Abel, but he has a **rash** all over his face...
DAMN!
Who scribbled all over the manuscripts?!
You did!!
Just go to bed already!!
Blotchy Abel
Four Eyes Radu
Screwed Petros

↓ Ron is the name of the beloved dog at Kyujyo's home. Akira-kun sometimes calls Kyujyo by this name. Why are golden retrievers so cute?

Department Head = Kyujyo, Flames = Akira-kun

There were others, like Tres with amazingly thick eyebrows and Ion with boobs. Fear the power of sleepiness.

I Do Respect Him, but...

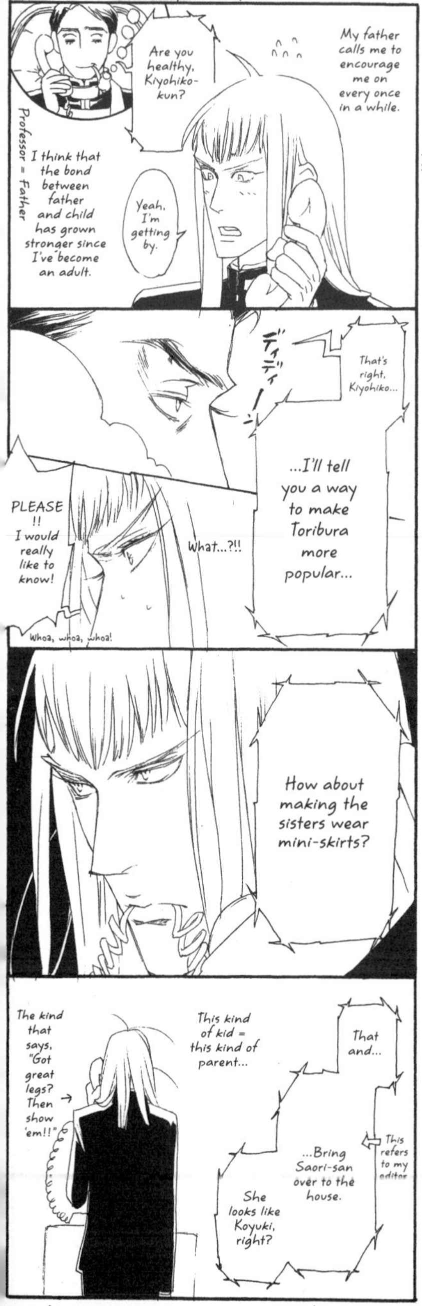
My father calls me to encourage me on every once in a while.
Are you healthy, Kiyohiko-kun?
I think that the bond between father and child has grown stronger since I've become an adult.
Yeah, I'm getting by.
That's right, Kiyohiko...
ディディー
...I'll tell you a way to make Toribura more popular...
What...?!!
PLEASE!! I would really like to know!
Whoa, whoa, whoa!
How about making the sisters wear mini-skirts?
That and...
This kind of kid = this kind of parent...
...Bring Saori-san over to the house.
This refers to my editor
She looks like Koyuki, right?
The kind that says, "Got great legs? Then show 'em!!"

Professor = Father

The Professor in the anime has the same voice as the Colonel from *Full Metal Alchemist*, doesn't he?

Secret of Overalls

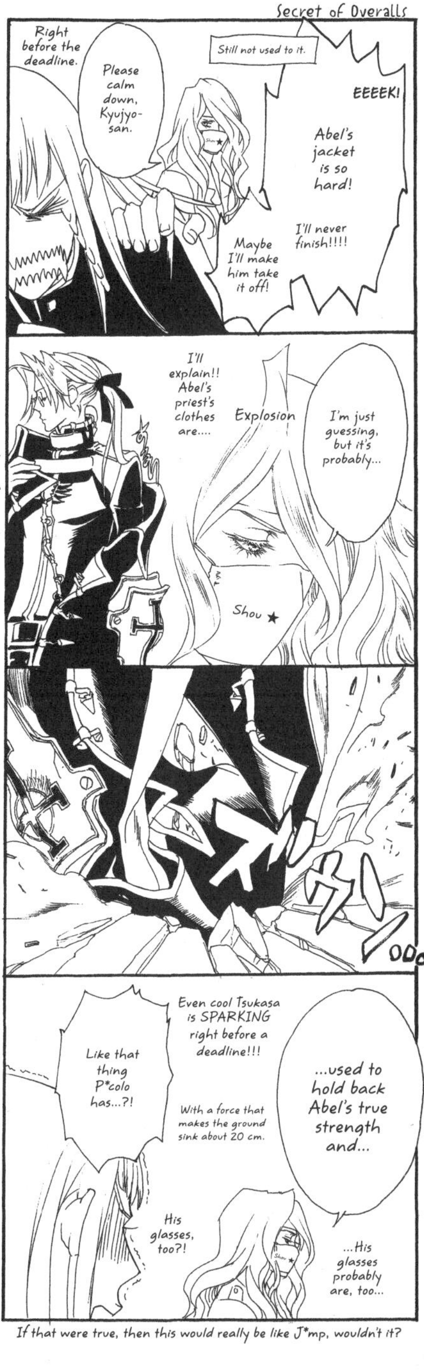

Still not used to it.
EEEEK!
Abel's jacket is so hard!
I'll never finish!!!!
Maybe I'll make him take it off!
Please calm down, Kyujyo-san.
Right before the deadline.
I'm just guessing, but it's probably...
Explosion
I'll explain!! Abel's priest's clothes are....
Shou ★
...used to hold back Abel's true strength and...
Even cool Tsukasa is SPARKING right before a deadline!!!
Like that thing P*colo has...?!
With a force that makes the ground sink about 20 cm.
...His glasses probably are, too...
His glasses, too?!

If that were true, then this would really be like J*mp, wouldn't it?

Nice Guy = Tsukasa

Tsukasa drew this.

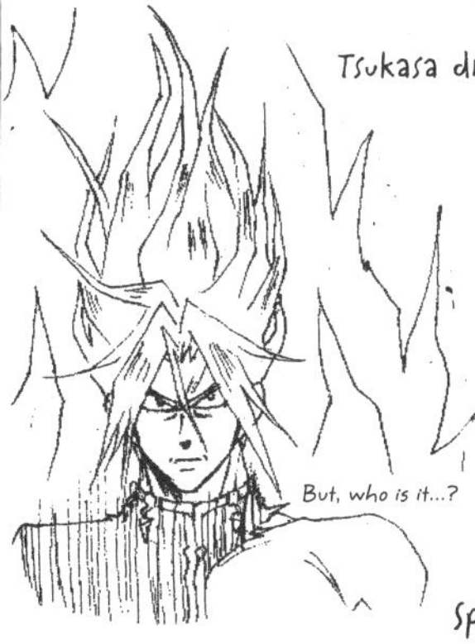

But, who is it...?

Sparking!! Crusnik Z!

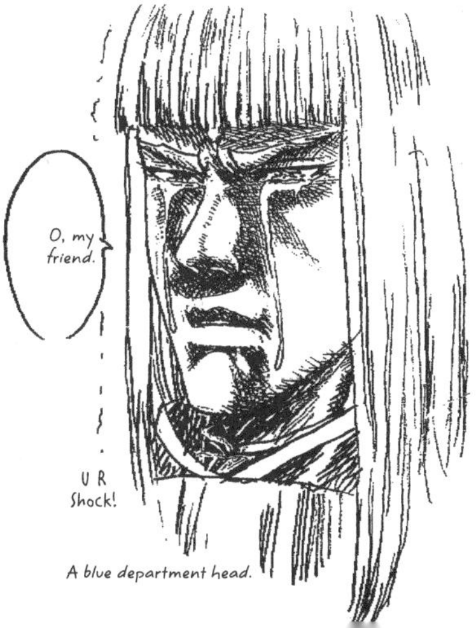

O, my friend.
U R Shock!

A blue department head.

OUTRO

I'm not sleepy! I'm totally awake!! This is Kyujyo. Thank you for taking a look at Toribura volume 5!! Volume 5...did I say volume 5?!! There's 5 total, you know! Mysterious! It's really because of all of you that I've come this far. There was only one chapter and two parts left to "Angel of the Hot Sands," and there was a mandatory stop...it came and went. The Hot Sands of No Plan. But because of that, I feel like I've drawn all I could draw. The only thing I regret is that I couldn't bring Antonio and Francesco into it. What surprised me after it was over was that I started "The Angel of the Hot Sands" episode in July of last year and that was the last month that Sunao-sensei looked over the draft and even though I drew it without planning it this way, it finally ended in July of this year. It's been exactly one year. It feels like this was a setup. It was a hard and fun year. And long!! I'll try my best from now on, too! Then, I'll be glad if we meet again in the next volume. Summer's almost over you know!!

Thanks

- Tsukasa go to Neverland...?" Kyouka Michael

  This year I spurred on UR "certain attribute" and I'm sorry...no...together, let's go together!! To that island!!

- Akira "Ostentatious Hero Last Name" Dotaki Jackie

  Aren't you really better at Cantonese than Japanese?! Aren't you better at impersonating Matsui more than Hanawa?! Xie xie!!

- Shouko "He's still not dead?" Kitamura Ken

  That L'arc song U started to play when we started writing Radu's last scenes...traumatized me. I-it's cold (I am)! Like, from now on, wear the endless sky, okay?!

■ Editor Saori-sama

  I'm sorry that my work is always, always late. From here on out, it'll be page after page of clothes from the Empire, but...please, with a forgiving heart...hold me!! (??)

✚ Mayuko-chan, Nagisa-chan

  I'm sorry I'm such a rude old man. But, when we were in an at-the-end-of-our-limits situation, you who appeared fresh out of nowhere, seemed... like...angels...you know. Thank you.

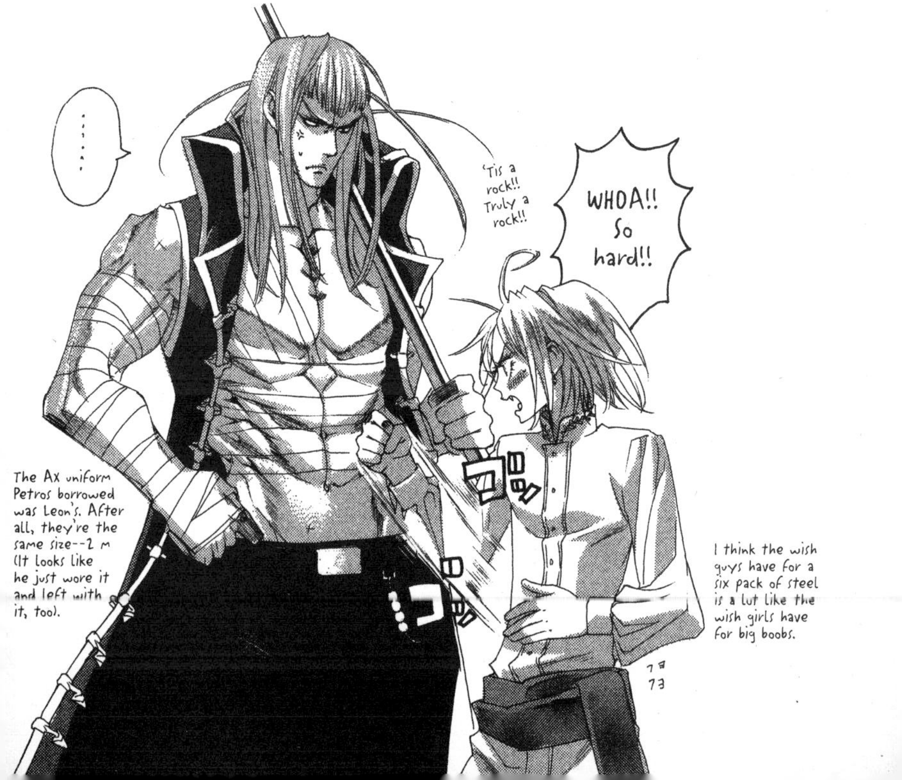

WHOA!! So hard!!
'Tis a rock!! Truly a rock!!
......
The AX uniform Petros borrowed was Leon's. After all, they're the same size--2 m (It looks like he just wore it and left with it, too).
I think the wish guys have for a six pack of steel is a lot like the wish girls have for big boobs.

IN THE NEXT VOLUME OF
TRINITY BLOOD

Sister Esther and Abel finally reconcile in the aftermath of Radu's devastating attack. As Ion slowly recovers and copes with his best friend's betrayal, the party finally reaches the capital of the Methuselah Empire... only to discover that even within the glorious city, they are anything but safe! Deception, intrigue and bloodshed lurk around every corner, and many secrets and mysteries are about to be revealed.

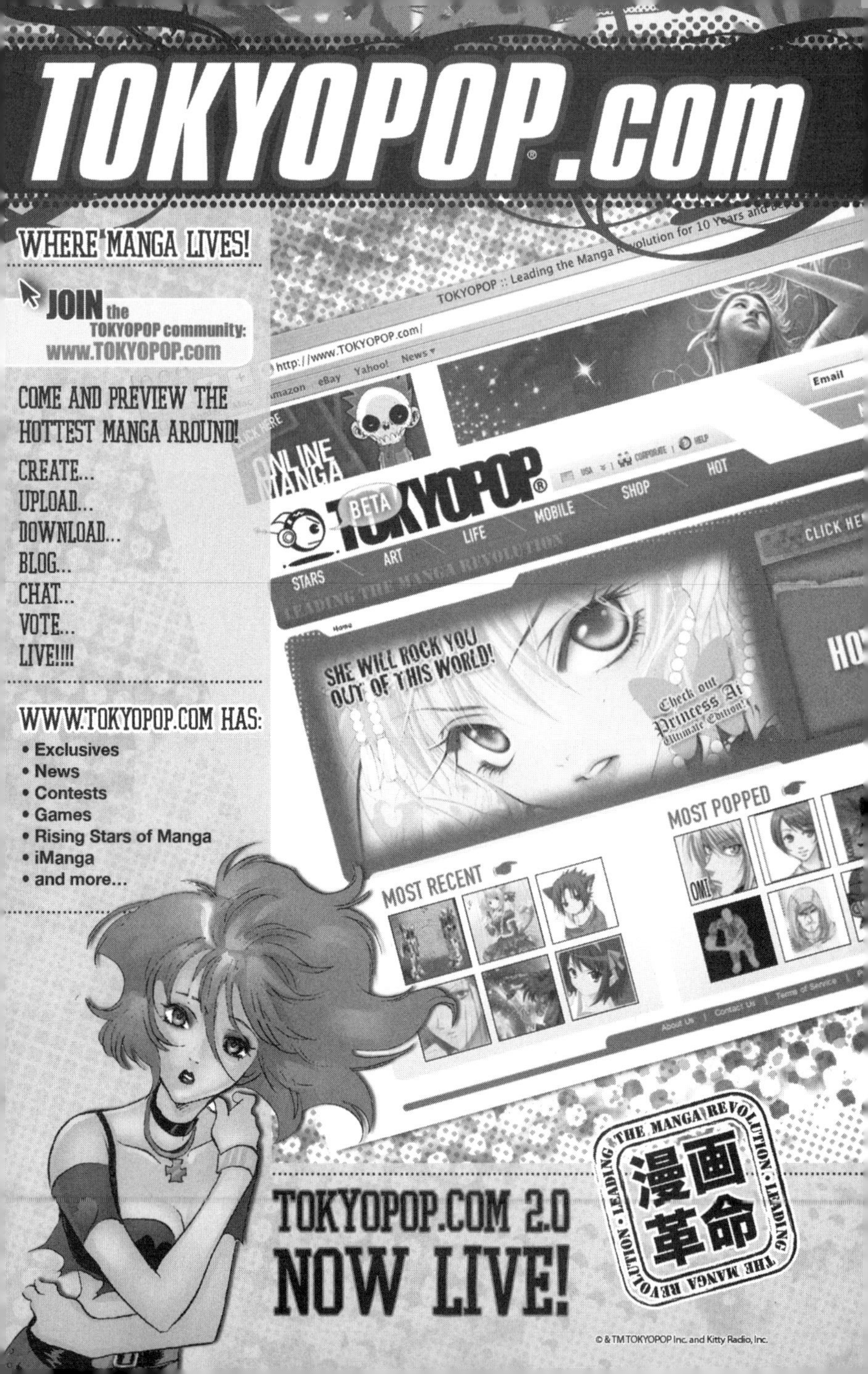
TOKYOPOP®.com
WHERE MANGA LIVES!
JOIN the TOKYOPOP community: www.TOKYOPOP.com
COME AND PREVIEW THE HOTTEST MANGA AROUND!
CREATE...
UPLOAD...
DOWNLOAD...
BLOG...
CHAT...
VOTE...
LIVE!!!!
WWW.TOKYOPOP.COM HAS:
• Exclusives
• News
• Contests
• Games
• Rising Stars of Manga
• iManga
• and more...
TOKYOPOP :: Leading the Manga Revolution for 10 Years and Beyond
http://www.TOKYOPOP.com/
ONLINE MANGA
BETA TOKYOPOP®
STARS
ART
LIFE
MOBILE
SHOP
HOT
LEADING THE MANGA REVOLUTION
SHE WILL ROCK YOU OUT OF THIS WORLD!
Check out Princess Ai Ultimate Edition!
MOST POPPED
MOST RECENT
TOKYOPOP.COM 2.0 NOW LIVE!
LEADING THE MANGA REVOLUTION
漫画革命
© & TM TOKYOPOP Inc. and Kitty Radio, Inc.

April 18-20, 2008
at the Jacob Javits Center, New York City

New York Comic Con is Coming!

Find the best in **Anime, Manga, Graphic Novels, Video Games, Toys, and Movies!** NY Comic Con has hundreds of **Celebrity Appearances, Autographing Sessions, Screenings, Industry Panels, Gaming Tournaments,** and **Much More!**

Go to **www.nycomiccon.com** to get all the information and **BUY TICKETS!** Plus, sign up for special New York Comic Con updates to be the first to learn about Guests, Premieres, and Special Events!

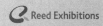

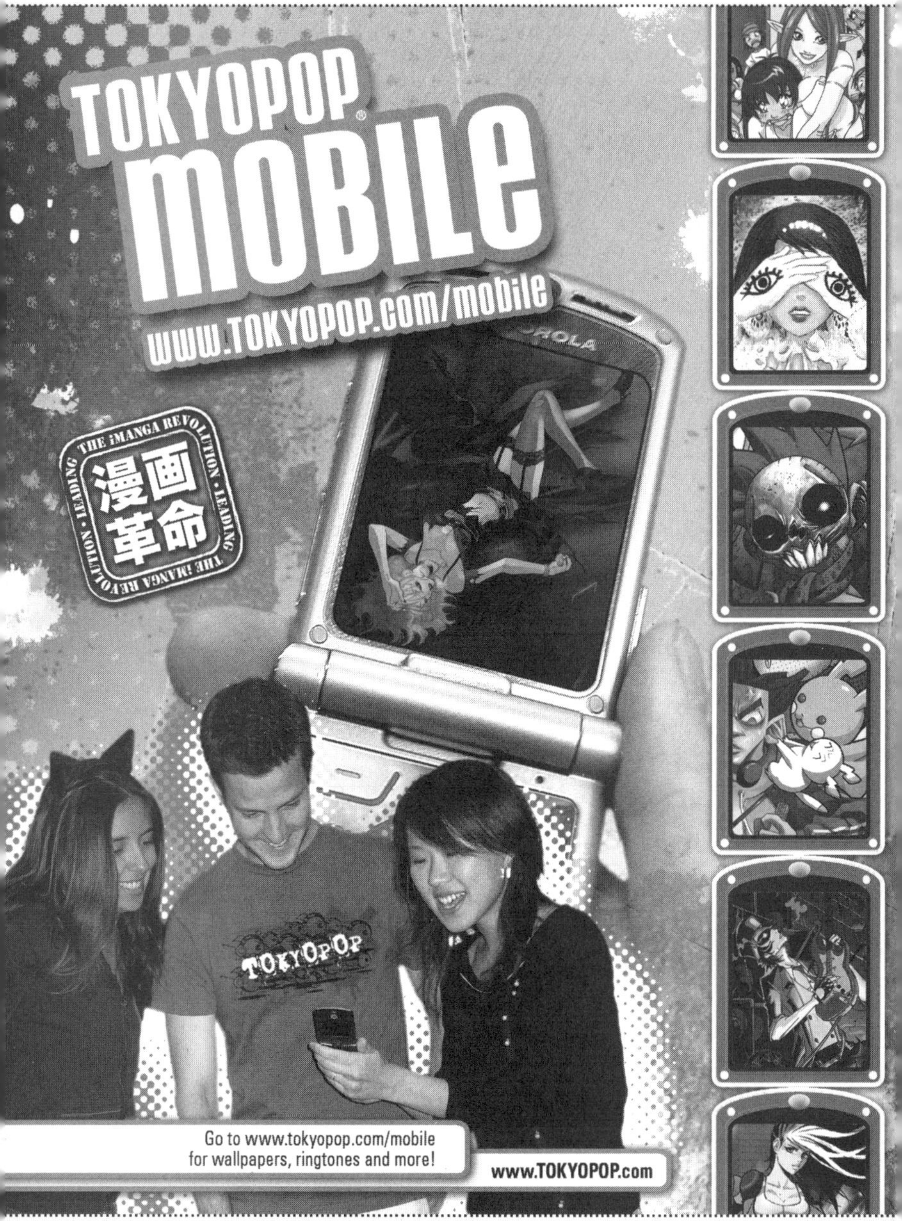
TOKYOPOP®
MOBILE
www.TOKYOPOP.com/mobile
THE iMANGA REVOLUTION · LEADING THE iMANGA REVOLUTION · LEADING
漫画革命
TOKYOPOP
Go to www.tokyopop.com/mobile
for wallpapers, ringtones and more!
www.TOKYOPOP.com

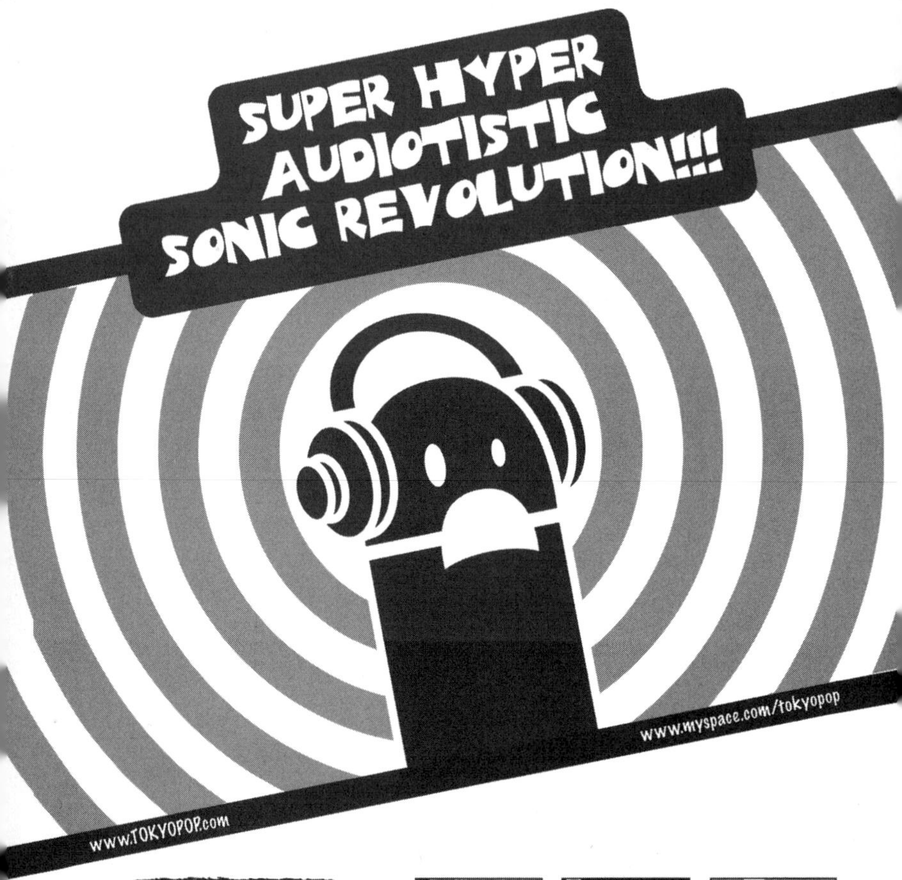
SUPER HYPER
AUDIOTISTIC
SONIC REVOLUTION!!!
www.myspace.com/tokyopop
www.TOKYOPOP.com

TOKYOPOP RECORDS

Available at the iTunes Music Store and everywhere music downloads are available. Keyword: TOKYOPOP

New releases every month! Check out these great albums AVAILABLE NOW!!!

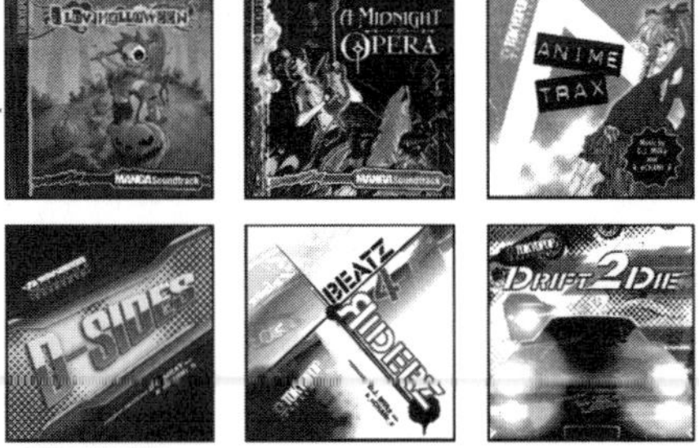
I LUV HALLOWEEN
A MIDNIGHT OPERA
ANIME TRAX
B-SIDES
BEATZ 4 RIDERZ
DRIFT 2 DIE

FOR MORE INFORMATION VISIT: WWW.TOKYOPOP.COM

GAKUEN ALICE VOLUME TWO

Mikan is officially accepted into the mysterious Alice Academy, but things aren't exactly going smoothly...

Mikan is off to a rough start! Natsume still bullies her, her class ranking couldn't be lower, some of the teachers are outright hostile and she has been forbidden to contact anyone outside of the school. Will she be able to find others like her at the Academy, or will she be betrayed by the only people she still trusts?

The hit series from Japan CONTINUES!

FANTASY

T TEEN AGE 13+

STOP!

This is the back of the book.
You wouldn't want to spoil a great ending!

This book is printed "manga-style," in the authentic Japanese right-to-left format. Since none of the artwork has been flipped or altered, readers get to experience the story just as the creator intended. You've been asking for it, so TOKYOPOP® delivered: authentic, hot-off-the-press, and far more fun!

DIRECTIONS

If this is your first time reading manga-style, here's a quick guide to help you understand how it works.

It's easy... just start in the top right panel and follow the numbers. Have fun, and look for more 100% authentic manga from TOKYOPOP®!

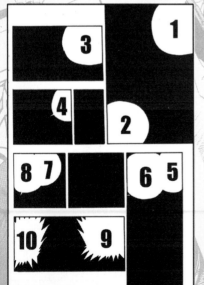

漫画革命

THE MANGA REVOLUTION · LEADING · THE MANGA REVOLUTION · LEADING ·